D0450080

A Young Man Without Magic

Tor Books by Lawrence Watt-Evans

THE OBSIDIAN CHRONICLES

Dragon Weather

The Dragon Society

Dragon Venom

LEGENDS OF ETHSHAR

Night of Madness

Ithanalin's Restoration

Touched by the Gods

Split Heirs (with Esther Friesner)

THE ANNALS OF THE CHOSEN

The Wizard Lord

The Ninth Talisman

The Summer Palace

LAWRENCE WATT-EVANS

A Young Man Without Magic

A TOM DOHERTY ASSOCIATES BOOK
NEW YORK

This is a work of fiction. All of the characters, organizations, and events portrayed in this novel are either products of the author's imagination or are used fictitiously.

A YOUNG MAN WITHOUT MAGIC

Map by Rhys Davies

A Tor Book
Published by Tom Doherty Associates, LLC
175 Fifth Avenue
New York, NY 10010

www.tor-forge.com

Library of Congress Cataloging-in-Publication Data

Watt-Evans, Lawrence, 1954–
A young man without magic / Lawrence Watt-Evans. — 1st ed.
p. cm.
"A Tom Doherty Associates book."
ISBN 978-0-7653-2279-1
I. Title.
PS3573.A859Y68 2009
813'.54—dc22

2009031654

First Edition: November 2009

Printed in the United States of America

0 9 8 7 6 5 4 3 2 1

Dedicated to the memory of Rafael Sabatini

N
BUIGAR
KERDERY
REIDENS
Raish River
Alzur
Naith
Galdin River
Beynos
Lume
AULIX
DEMERREN
AVIDEN
MELLINISE
The Quandish Archipelago
Quand
The Dragonlands
Lume
Limit of the Bound Lands
The Walasian Empire
The Cousins
NORODA
Ermetia
The Mystery Lands
Rhys Davies 2009

A Young Man Without Magic

1

In Which Anrel Murau Returns Home to an Uncertain Reception

The rain had finally stopped, and the public coach's sole occupant was able to roll up the blinds and look out the unglazed windows without getting soaked. The countryside was still green, even this late in the summer and in the gloom of a heavy overcast; the passenger wondered how that could be, when so much of the talk in Lume for the past few seasons had been of crop failures and famine.

The coach jolted over some unevenness in the road, and Anrel Murau braced himself against the window frame as he gazed out at a harvested field. He could not tell what had been grown there, or how much the land had yielded, but the rain-darkened earth certainly looked rich and fertile—as it should. After all, this was Aulix, one of the richest provinces in the Walasian Empire. A famine in Walasia, the heart of the Bound Lands—could that really be possible? This was the realm where the forces of nature had been brought under control, where the Mother and the Father looked kindly upon humanity and its sorceries. It wasn't some wild hinterland like the outer reaches of Quand, or the Ermetian mystery lands, where days might be different lengths from one to the next, or monsters might prowl the fields, or snow might fall in midsummer, if the seasons were even regular enough to *have* a summer. No, this was a land of order and stability, where farmers had been feeding the population reliably for centuries, where sorcerers regulated the weather, where most of the wild spirits and negative forces that plagued the Unbound Lands had long since been banished. What could have changed, to allow food shortages to occur?

Nothing he saw from the coach window gave him any hint. The fields rolling by, whether still green or stripped bare, all *looked* fertile enough.

They also looked simultaneously familiar and strange. He had spent his entire childhood in this region, but after his four years in the capital the countryside seemed vaguely unreal, like a nostalgic dream rather than a present reality. The placid, rain-washed green hills and brown fields, virtually empty of human life, were so very different from the crowded, stone-paved streets of Lume. Here there were no pleading beggars, no hungry men clustered around notice boards looking for work, no coachmen with whips clearing the way for their vehicles, no scowling watchmen patrolling their elevated walkways.

Here in the country sorcerers looked after their subjects, as they ought to—or at least, that was how he remembered it, and he hoped *that* had not changed while he was studying history and law in the court schools. The most powerful magicians were the landgraves who ruled the empire's sixteen provinces, but every town or village was under the benevolent rule of a burgrave, every border was guarded by a margrave, and lesser sorcerers served as magistrates and administrators, devoting their magic to the public good.

At least in theory. Anrel knew all too well that sorcerers were merely human.

Some of Anrel's fellow students had insisted that discontent was widespread throughout the empire, that high taxes and tariffs were ruining trade, that sorcerers were too caught up in their own magic and their intrigues to attend to their duties, but Anrel chose not to believe it. People had always complained, and young men, he knew from his history books, always thought they were coming of age in a time of crisis and impending collapse. They wanted to save the world, and that meant the world had to need saving.

Anrel had no interest in saving the world, and did not think anyone needed to. He merely wanted to find a place in it.

He *hoped* the world didn't need saving, but matters did seem to have deteriorated in Lume during his time there. The burgrave of Lume's guards and the Emperor's Watch had been called out to put down riots more in the past season than in the entire previous year, which had already been an unusually violent one.

Surely, though, that was a temporary aberration.

Temporary or not, it had nothing to do with matters here in Aulix. The coach had taken him from the unhappy ferment of Lume through Beynos, where the streets had been only slightly troubled, and then Orlias, and Kevár, and all the other villages along the route, each calmer than the town before, until finally Kuriel had appeared so placid that Anrel had wondered if the inhabitants might have been enchanted. It was as if the coach had been carrying him back into his childhood, when he was blithely unaware of any political issues or unrest at all.

Not that his childhood had been unmarked by tragedy. He remembered the first time he had ridden a coach along this road, eighteen years ago; he had been a child of only four, but the memory was indelibly fixed in his head. He had been newly orphaned, on his way to live with a widowed uncle he had never met; of course he remembered it! He had been frightened and lost and alone, mere days from the horror of discovering what was left of his parents after a spell had gone wrong, and he had known, even at that tender age, that the coach was taking him to a new and different life, that he would never return to the house where he was born.

That new life had been pleasant enough. Lord Dorias Adirane, burgrave of Alzur, had been kind to him, and Anrel had spent fourteen happy years in his uncle's home before being sent off to Lume to complete his education.

Now he was once again on his way to his uncle's mansion.

He wished he could be more certain of his reception. Uncle Dorias's letters had not seemed very enthusiastic about his nephew's plans—what few plans he had, as he had to admit he was somewhat vague about his future. Anrel hoped to find some employment appropriate for a young man of his station, a young man without magic but with the best education the court schools of Lume could provide. As for the precise *nature* of this employment—well, he had not satisfied his uncle on that account.

He had not satisfied himself, either.

In truth, it was unlikely he would find a suitable post in Alzur; the village had no use for a scholar. Anrel had the impression Lord Dorias had expected him to find a position in Lume, or perhaps one of the other cities of the empire, rather than returning to his uncle's estate, but the old man had not come out and said so, and no such employment had manifested itself, as yet.

Uncle Dorias had made plain that he had no intention of supporting Anrel's studies beyond the customary four years, and with no prospects in Lume Anrel had had little choice but to return to Alzur, but he did not regret that in the least. For one thing, he had a notion that his uncle's fosterling and former apprentice Valin—*Lord* Valin—might have found himself a position where a skilled clerk would be useful. Settling down as his childhood companion's aide had a great deal to recommend it, Anrel thought. A few quiet rooms somewhere working for his friend, and eventually a wife, perhaps children—that was a life that would suit Anrel well. He had no desire to change the world or achieve great things.

He looked out at the countryside, and hoped his modest ambitions could be realized. He could see from the scenery that the coach was nearing the village of Alzur; he leaned out the window and peered at the hills ahead, trying to make out his uncle's house.

He spotted it readily enough. Although Lord Dorias was burgrave of Alzur, he did not actually live inside the village's iron pale, as a burgrave should; his manor stood instead atop one of the higher hills in the vicinity, roughly two miles south of the village square.

Anrel recalled that he hadn't known that when he had first come to Alzur as a child. He had mistaken the far larger estate of Lord Allutar Hezir, a mile north of town, for his uncle's home, and had been confused when he was instead taken back across the bridge to the southern bank of the Raish River.

Even now, eighteen years later, he didn't understand why Lord Allutar, the landgrave of Aulix, chose to make his seat at a village like Alzur, instead of at Naith, the provincial capital. Alzur was a modest collection of shops and homes stretching along half a mile of riverbank between the two sorcerers' mansions, while Naith, a dozen miles farther west, was a thriving city that seemed a far more sensible place for the landgrave to live. All the other provincial officials, from the lowliest clerk to the Lords Magistrate, lived in Naith, but the landgrave himself dwelt in Alzur.

Anrel would have much preferred Lord Allutar to live elsewhere, but it was not up to him. He pulled his head in and settled down in his seat to wait, leaning back against the worn leather.

He hoped that his uncle would be there to meet him; Anrel had said, in his last letter, which coach he would be on. If Lord Dorias was waiting for him, that would be an indication that the coldness Anrel had thought he'd perceived in recent correspondence was merely a figment of his imagination.

Then the coach was across the bridge and rumbling up the streets into Alzur proper.

A moment later the coachman called to his team, and the vehicle rolled to a stop on the wet cobbles of the town's only square. "Alzur!" the driver called as he set the brake. "This is Alzur!"

Anrel sat up and fumbled with the latch, and the door banged open. He thrust out his head and looked around. "Indeed it *is* Alzur," he said aloud, addressing the air. "It hasn't changed a bit, has it?" The town was exactly as he remembered it. Just now everything was damp from the recent rain, water dripping from the eaves and trickling down the streets, but otherwise it could have been any day since he had first seen the place eighteen years before.

But then, why would a sleepy village in Aulix look any different? The rabble-rousers of Lume might claim great changes were afoot in the world, but Anrel thought they would hardly reach a place like this.

He looked around and saw no sign of his uncle. He did, however, see a young man in a green frock coat trotting across the cobbles and waving to him. "Anrel!" this person called. "You've made it!"

The traveler looked down at his dearest friend and smiled broadly. "Hello, Valin," he said, clambering quickly down from the coach. "It's good to see you!"

"Very good indeed!" Valin replied, stepping forward, his own grin as broad as the traveler's.

The two men embraced, and when they separated Anrel said, "You haven't changed any more than Alzur has, I see."

"Ah, so it might appear to the casual glance," Lord Valin said, clapping his friend on the back, "but I believe that when we have a chance to talk a little you'll see just how different I have become. When you left I was little more than a child, and I like to think I am rather more than that now."

Anrel's smile broadened. Valin was his senior by more than a year, but in truth, had never in Anrel's memory seemed the more mature of the pair. Perhaps, though, he really *had* changed during Anrel's absence this time; his sparse letters provided no compelling evidence either way. "I'm eager to hear all about it," he said.

"And *I* am eager to hear all the news from Lume," Valin answered. "What's happening there? Is there much excitement about the calling of the Grand Council?"

Anrel's smile dimmed. Not two minutes out of the coach, and Valin was asking him about political affairs. Pleased as he was to see him apparently unchanged, Anrel had hoped that Valin's obsession with wild schemes to change the world had faded. He was as bad as the firebrands of Lume, and with far less justification.

Indeed, it was largely his familiarity with Valin that had led him to dismiss the beliefs of the agitators, idealists, and theorists of the court schools as unfounded.

"I am not sure I would call it excitement so much as uncertainty," Anrel said. He glanced over to see that the coachman had already exchanged the day's incoming and outgoing mail with Alzur's postmistress, the same plump little woman who had held the position when Anrel departed four years before—Oria Neynar, was it? Yes, that was her name. She was trotting off with the dispatch case in hand while the driver proceeded around toward the back of the coach. "But let us retrieve my baggage and be on our way, so that this good man can get on with his business."

"Yes, to be sure," Valin agreed.

A few fresh raindrops spattered the pavement just then, and Anrel glanced at the sky. He hoped it was just a final sprinkle, and not the start of a fresh downpour. "I think we should make haste," he said. He turned to the driver, who had untied the protective canvas and was heaving a leather-bound traveling case to the cobbles.

"Of course!" Valin said, hurrying to snatch up the first bag.

The coachman handed the next bag, a battered valise, directly to Anrel, who nodded, and passed the man a coin in exchange—a sixpence, one-tenth of a guilder, which was generous, but the man had made good time and kept the ride reasonably smooth, and there were no other passengers to contribute to his pay.

The coachman smiled and tipped his hat, then turned to secure the coach for the next leg of his run. Fat drops began to darken the canvas as the driver tied it back in place, and Anrel looked up again. The sky did not look promising.

"Is this everything?" Valin asked, hefting the traveling case.

"Indeed it is," Anrel said, turning his attention to his friend. "I am, after all, only a poor student, not a mighty sorcerer like yourself." The statement was made in jest, but it was also the simple truth—Valin *was* a sorcerer, where Anrel was not.

Valin punched him lightly on the shoulder. "Sorcerer, pfah! I am a man like yourself, Anrel. Are we not all the children of the Father and the Mother, and heirs of the Old Empire?" He began marching south across the square.

"Some of us are the more favored heirs, Valin, while others are but despised cousins," Anrel said, following his companion. "Your magic gives you a status most of us can never aspire to."

Lord Valin glanced back over his shoulder. "*Never* aspire to? I think you may misjudge the situation, my friend. What our fathers dared not dream of, our sons may take for granted. Changes are coming, Anrel! Surely, if I have heard as much in the taverns of Naith, you have heard it in the capital!"

Anrel did not need to ask what he meant, since he had indeed heard these utopian schemes bruited about in Lume. He did not put much stock in them, but kept his opinion to himself. Instead, hoping to divert the discussion away from the capital and toward Valin's own situation, he said, "You have certainly achieved what *your* father did not."

"Pfah!" Valin waved his free hand in dismissal. "I can take little pleasure in a fortunate accident of birth. I was merely . . ."

At that point, with no further warning, the skies opened anew, and rain deluged upon the pair, turning the world gray and wet. Water poured from the eaves on every side, and the spaces between cobbles all seemed to fill instantly.

"Over there!" Anrel shouted over the drumming of the torrent, as he pointed toward a pair of small tables set beneath a broad sky-blue awning. The awning was already soaked, but it was still the closest shelter; the two men ran for it.

A moment later the two of them had ducked beneath the sagging awning, and turned to stare out at the downpour.

"It would seem that the spirits of air and water do not want me to rush to my uncle's hearth," Anrel said.

"Indeed," Valin agreed.

"This is not the homecoming I had hoped for," Anrel said. He meant not merely the weather, but the fact that Valin had come alone to meet him. His uncle's presence would have been very welcome, or that of Anrel's cousin, Lady Saria. Lord Dorias's only child had been a baby when Anrel first came to Alzur, and was only just blossoming into womanhood when he left for Lume. He wondered what she looked like now; she had shown signs of becoming a beauty. How much had she changed in his absence?

He would see her soon enough, he supposed, but he wished she had come to meet him and welcome him home. He would have found it reassuring.

But at least someone from the Adirane household was here, even if Valin was not actually a member of the family. It was very good to see Valin again, and to know at least *someone* welcomed his return.

2

In Which Lord Valin Learns of an Apparent Injustice

The two young men beneath the awning gazed silently out at the rain for a few seconds; then Anrel turned and reached for a chair. Valin followed his example, and the pair settled at one of the tables, setting Anrel's drenched luggage to one side.

"I expect it will let up in due time," Valin said.

"Eventually, it must," Anrel agreed. "I doubt the Father has decided to drown us all."

Valin smiled, and shook the water from his hat.

Anrel glanced at his companion. There were a thousand things he wanted to ask Valin, so many he scarcely knew where to begin, about Valin's situation, and Lord Dorias, and Lady Saria, and everything that had happened in Alzur in his absence, but he was puzzled. He would have expected Valin to talk about all that without prompting. Why was the fellow so quiet? His only questions so far had been about luggage and matters in Lume; he had not so much as asked after Anrel's health. It would seem he really *had* changed, and not for the better.

Lord Valin li-Tarbek was no kin to Anrel or the Adiranes; he had been born to a family of commoners, but had demonstrated a talent for magic as a child. He had undergone the trials and had been determined to be a sorcerer, and therefore had been made a noble of the empire. But he had needed training if he was to do anything with his sorcery, training his own family could not provide. Uncle Dorias had generously accepted him as a fosterling and an apprentice, and had raised him alongside Anrel and Saria.

Valin and Anrel had been almost inseparable as boys, despite the difference in their rank and background—in fact, Anrel had sometimes wondered whether Uncle Dorias had taken Valin in just to give Anrel a playmate.

Their personalities were utterly different, though. Anrel had been happy as a student, spending hours poring over dusty books, while he suspected Valin would not have lasted a single season in the court schools before going mad with boredom—either that, or he would have spent all his time arguing in the capital's innumerable taverns, forcing his tutors to expel him.

They had been fast friends all the same, but Anrel's long absence seemed to have let them grow apart.

Anrel frowned. Perhaps a little further conversation would allow him to judge just how Lord Valin had changed. "You were saying, just before this deluge began, that you cannot take any great pleasure in an accident of birth," he said. "But surely you realize that a great many sorcerers do just that, particularly those who are heir to some specialty, some ancient binding or unique talent."

"They mark themselves as fools thereby," Valin replied. "The Father and Mother give each of us gifts at birth, and those say nothing of who we are, or what our worth might be. It is what we *do* with those gifts that makes us deserving of respect. That I was given the gift of sorcery, when none of my ancestors had it, when none of my siblings are so blessed, does not make me a better man than they."

"It makes you a noble of the empire," Anrel pointed out, "and entitles you to call yourself Lord Valin. It opens many doors, gives you access to rights and privileges denied to the rest of us. There are many who take pride in that distinction."

Valin shook his head. "Fools. And their folly may soon be demonstrated, should the Grand Council so choose."

Anrel grimaced. He had heard this sort of nonsense in Lume, and had hoped he would not hear it again once he left the student community behind. The emperor's announcement that he would summon a second Grand Council was just a ruse, Anrel was sure; it meant nothing. "I think you wildly misjudge the situation if you consider so radical a change to be likely."

Valin leaned closer. "You do not? What is the news, then, in Lume? Has the emperor said how the delegates are to be chosen?"

Anrel suppressed a sigh. He was quite sure that it did not matter what process was used; the Grand Council would be impotent. That was not what his friend wanted to hear, though, and Anrel did not want to antagonize Valin.

"On the contrary," Anrel said, "the emperor has continued to change his mind with every shift of the wind, but his latest proclamation says that each province, each city or town, is to decide upon its own method of selection, just as was done when first the Grand Council met, some six centuries ago."

"Well, then," Valin said, straightening again. "Do you not think—"

"Valin," Anrel interrupted wearily, "do you not see what will happen? The people of the provinces are scattered, and unaccustomed to any meddling in civic affairs. They will do as they have always done, and leave it to the landgraves to choose their representatives, and the landgraves, protecting their own interests, will appoint delegates who will see to it that nothing changes. Likewise, the people of the marches must always defer to their margraves, who they depend upon to guard the borders. Only in the towns is there any possibility that the selection will be left to commoners, and even there, who's to say they won't name whomsoever the burgraves suggest?"

Lord Valin shook his head. "Anrel, you have been locked up in the courts and schools for four years; I think you underestimate the discontent of the populace. Food is in short supply, and most of my fellow sorcerers do nothing to alleviate the shortages. There are beggars in the streets of Naith where there were none when I was a child. When crops fail, the lords shrug and say it's the will of the Mother. The magic that might help feed the hungry is devoted instead to extravagant displays intended to assert status within the government—and that doesn't even mention what is sometimes done to ordinary people to *power* that magic. These things *must* change!"

Anrel turned up empty hands. "While I concede that times are hard and many unhappy, this is how our society has conducted its affairs since the Old Empire fell," he said. "The realm needs magic to function, so those who have magic have power, and those who do not have none—save for the emperor, of course. A few misfortunes, a few bad years, won't alter that. It's how the world works."

"But it doesn't need to be like this!" Valin insisted. "Look at Quand, where there is no link between magic and nobility, and where the people choose their leaders. Look at Ermetia, with its two sets of nobles, terrestrial and arcane."

"What do you know of Quand or Ermetia?" Anrel asked, startled. Valin had never shown the slightest interest in reading about foreign lands—or much of anything else, for that matter. "Have you been traveling while I was in Lume?"

Valin shook his head. "No farther than Naith, but I have spoken with travelers. There is a Quandishman called Lord Blackfield who came to visit with your uncle not long ago, and who I believe is now Lord Allutar's guest; he has told me a great deal about the world beyond the empire's borders."

Lord Blackfield's name was vaguely familiar, but Anrel could not place it at first, though he didn't suppose it mattered. He should have realized that Valin would put his trust in such a source. "You believed every word he said, of course. We all know how utterly reliable and impartial foreign barbarians are."

"Now, that was uncalled for," Valin protested. "I am no child, to accept nonsense without question."

"Ah, that's right," Anrel replied. "You did say you had changed."

"Anrel!" Valin appeared genuinely annoyed.

Anrel held up a hand. "Yes, I know, I have overstepped the bounds of decency. I apologize, dear Valin; I have no business questioning my superiors."

"Even your apology contains more sarcasm than contrition!"

"It does, doesn't it? I *am* sorry, Valin. I fear it's just my nature." He smiled. "Does it not strike you as odd, though, that you, a Walasian sorcerer lord, should be arguing for the abolition of the system that has elevated you to a rank your ancestors could never achieve, while I, the outcast spawn of two sorcerers who somehow remained a mere commoner myself, should be arguing to retain the privileges of the magically gifted?"

"I do not think you *want* to be a lord, Anrel. I think you were relieved when you failed that trial."

That came uncomfortably close to matters Anrel did not want to discuss. "Can you wonder at that, given my parents' fate?" he said. He shook his head. "No, I am content to be a clerk or a scholar, well outside the corridors of power and privilege, answerable to no one but myself and perhaps a burgrave, or some lesser lord."

"But a man of your intelligence—what a shame that you have no magic! Perhaps I should put *your* name forward as a delegate to the Grand Council."

That notion horrified Anrel. "Oh, you will do no such thing! I would be of no use there; I would merely poke holes in everyone else's ideas, while putting forth none of my own." Before Valin could reply, Anrel changed the subject. "This Quandishman, Lord Blackfield—what is he doing here? Is he a sorcerer?"

"He is, yes. He is on a campaign to stamp out black magic, it seems—he and a few of his foreign friends. They call themselves the Lantern Society, shining a light in darkness."

"Darkness? They consider the Walasian Empire benighted?"

"Only in our use of black magic, I think."

Anrel cocked his head. "*Black* magic?"

"Magic that draws power from blood, pain, or death, or that requires unwilling participants, or that exists only to cause harm. In Quand, it seems they divide magic into various colors—black, white, and gray, for the most part. Black magic has been outlawed entirely, Lord Blackfield says, much as we have outlawed witchcraft."

"Ah, I've heard something of that." In fact, Anrel had read the statute itself during his studies, but in the original tongue. He had not immediately recognized the Walasian term, though, as he had mentally translated the Quandish as "malevolent magic," rather than the literal "black magic," and he had not taken any particular note of the regulation.

"The Ermetians impose similar limitations on themselves," he added. "So do some of the Cousins—in Skarl, I believe, and perhaps Andegor."

"There are said to be some Ermetians among Lord Blackfield's group," Valin acknowledged. "I have heard nothing of anyone from the Cousins, though, and I have met only Blackfield himself."

Anrel considered for a moment, then asked, "Who decides which magic is black? It's simple enough to determine whether a Walasian magician is a sorcerer or a witch simply by consulting the Great List, but how does one judge whether a particular spell is malign?"

"I told you—if it draws upon blood or pain, or causes harm."

"*All* magic that draws blood is forbidden? Wouldn't that outlaw most fertility spells?"

"I suppose it would, yes."

Anrel shook his head. "They're foolish idealists," he said. "When social rank is determined by magical power, one can hardly expect sorcerers to set arbitrary limits upon themselves."

"But these limits are hardly arbitrary!" Valin protested. "And if all are bound equally by them, how can they interfere with the determination of status?" He sighed. "For that matter, have I not just been arguing that we should abandon using sorcerous talent to determine rank?"

"Were we to do so, we would hardly be Walasians," Anrel said. "The system has been in place for centuries, Valin—just as the Quandish have maintained their bizarre arrangements for centuries, and the Ermetians theirs. Ours works best for us. The situation is stable as it is, and change can only bring grief."

"Ah, but change is surely coming! The emperor has called the Grand Council, for only the second time in our history. It was the Grand Council that created the system, and the Grand Council that has the power to alter it—if only we can send the right delegates to Lume."

This theme again. Valin's bizarre enthusiasm for the Grand Council and its supposed transformative effect annoyed Anrel. "The emperor seeks only to revise the tax system, to pay his debts," he said. "He will not welcome any meddling beyond that."

"But the Grand Council outranks even the emperor himself!" Valin insisted. "It was the first Grand Council that established the imperial family and set the first emperor upon the throne, and the second Grand Council will have the authority to remove the present incumbent, should he resist whatever changes the council sees fit to make."

"Father and Mother, Valin, I would hope that you have not suggested anything so treasonous where anyone else might hear it!"

"It has been mentioned in the taverns and teahouses of Naith," Valin said, a trifle defensively.

Anrel stared at his companion in amazement. "In Lume," he said, "such talk might well see you dragged off by the Emperor's Watch and cast into one of their dungeons, or simply hanged as a traitor."

Valin turned his head, rather than meet his friend's intense gaze, and looked out at the square. "The rain is lessening," he said.

"Good!" Anrel said, straightening. "Then we can go home, and I can see my uncle."

Before Valin could reply, a woman in a white apron came bustling up to their table and said breathlessly, "Lord Valin! I'm so sorry; I didn't think anyone would be out in this rain. How can I serve you?"

Anrel noticed she was focused entirely on the sorcerer, ignoring the poor student. That was no surprise. The only surprise was that he did not recognize her; when last he had been in Alzur this café had been the property of the widowed Dailur Harrea. Master Harrea had apparently died, remarried, or sold the business in the interim.

Valin, Anrel noticed, did not bother to introduce them. Instead he looked questioningly at his companion. "We are here," he said. "Shall we have a little something while we wait out these last few drops?"

"I dined at the Kuriel way station," Anrel said. "Just a little wine to wash the road dust from my throat would be fine."

"A bottle of Lithrayn red, then," Valin said to the woman. "And a plate of sausages, and some of those lovely seedcakes from—" He stopped, frowning. He had turned to point to a nearby shop, but now he broke off in midsentence and asked, "Is the bakery closed?"

The woman followed his gaze and said, "Hadn't you heard? Lord Allutar caught the baker's son stealing from his herb garden, and has sentenced him to death." Anrel noticed that she pronounced the landgrave's name much as she might speak of some detestable vermin. "The whole family is up at the landgrave's house now, pleading for his life."

"I was aware of some commotion as I came into town, but I had no idea!" Valin said, horrified. "I was too eager to welcome my old friend home to ask what it was about."

"Very unfortunate," Anrel said.

"Unfortunate!" Valin turned to face him, shocked. "*Unfortunate*? A young man's life is at issue here!"

"A thief's life, from the sound of it."

"Still, a human life! Over a few herbs?"

"A *sorcerer's* herbs, Valin. *Lord Allutar's* herbs. Lord Allutar is still landgrave of Aulix, is he not?"

"Of course he is."

"Then he has the power of high and low justice over all the commoners in the province, and stealing from the landgrave's own garden is the height of suicidal folly. The baker's son is doomed, and his removal can only improve the species."

Valin recoiled. "Anrel, how can you be so cold? Is that what they taught you at the court schools? This is a human being, a young man with almost his whole life yet to be lived! He's this woman's neighbor! He's the baker's son! He has friends and family who are about to be arbitrarily deprived of his presence, who will grieve over his loss—"

"Who, it would seem, did nothing to prevent him from stealing from a sorcerer's garden." As it happened, since the baker had only one son, Anrel knew exactly who the youth was—Urunar Kazien. He had known the boy when they were children, though they had little contact after Valin's arrival. This acquaintance did not incline him to any special sympathy; he had never liked Urunar. "Valin, really! Those herbs might well be magical, for all we know, and what would happen if ordinary folk, those whose true names are unknown, began meddling with magical powers? That would be witchcraft, and witches are hanged; executing the thief before he can do any harm does not change the outcome, but merely avoids any possible damage to others." He saw Valin start to protest, and hastily concluded, "In any case, what can we do about it? What's done is done."

"But he isn't dead yet, and while he lives, there is hope." Valin turned to the woman. "You said his family is pleading for his life?"

"So I've heard, my lord."

Valin thrust back his chair and got to his feet. "Then let us go add our own voices to theirs, Anrel! Let us make clear to Lord Allutar that it is not merely the family who wants to see the boy's life spared, but every soul whose heart holds a trace of common humanity."

Anrel grimaced. "I think you may find, Valin, that there are not as many of those as you would like to believe—that common humanity is, in truth, not common at all." He remained seated.

Valin glowered at him. "I think *you* may find, Anrel, that your pessimism is unfounded. Surely, a spark of decency must flicker even in Lord Allutar's breast, and it is our duty, as citizens of the empire, to fan it into flame. *I* am going, even if you are not!" He turned and hurried out into the rain.

With a sigh, Anrel arose. "Your pardon, mistress," he said, with a tip of his sodden student's cap. "I'm afraid we won't be having that wine and sausage just yet, nor shall I be going to see my uncle—I must first save Lord Valin from his folly. I can only hope we will be back soon." He glanced down, and added, "If you could look after my luggage, I would be in your debt." A coin appeared in his hand—a penny this time, not a sixpence—and was passed to hers. She bobbed in acknowledgment, and Anrel set out on his friend's heels, leaving the two traveling cases behind.

This was *definitely* not how he had envisioned his return to Alzur.

3

In Which Attempts Are Made to Dissuade Lord Allutar from His Intentions

By the time Anrel caught up to Valin they had rounded the corner by the clockmaker's shop. The rain had lessened to a thin drizzle, but still continued.

Valin glanced at his companion, but said nothing.

Anrel remarked, "I confess, this is not quite the homecoming I imagined."

Valin smiled at that. "I am sure it's not," he said. "I suppose you expected a leisurely walk in the opposite direction."

Anrel smiled ruefully in return. "In fact, I flattered myself that Lord Dorias might have met me himself, rather than sending you. Perhaps if he had, you would not be rushing off on this fool's errand."

"Ah, Anrel! I'm afraid our dear patron said he was not well, and did not feel himself up to the journey."

"What?" Anrel stopped in his tracks. "Do you mean to tell me that you are marching us off to defend this thieving nobody, when your own guardian, my beloved uncle, is ill? Why did you not rush me to his bedside immediately, rain or no? Valin, I—"

Valin held up a hand, interrupting him. "No, no; the illness, such as it is, is not so severe as that. In truth, I think it as much a sour mood as any physical ailment. There is no danger whatsoever, I assure you, or indeed I *would* have rushed you to his bedside. As it is, were you at his bedside I fear you would find yourself alone, as when last I saw your uncle he was amusing himself in his orangery, viciously pruning any blossom that displeased him while complaining at length about the emperor's foolishness and your own perversity in choosing this particular time to return to Alzur. Lady Saria was present to provide an ear for his tirade, so I felt no need to remain there myself, nor to coax him to meet your coach."

"Ah." Anrel allowed himself to relax. "That does sound like him, and I can understand not wishing to interrupt him in such a situation." He began walking again, pulling his cap forward on his brow to better shield his face from the rain. "Let us allow him to cleanse the oranges of unhealthy blooms, then, while we waste our breath in asserting our own moral superiority to Lord Allutar."

"Father and Mother, Anrel," Valin said, falling in beside him. "Have you no sympathy for the baker's son?"

Anrel said, "Should I? He is no friend of mine. Would you have my heart bleed for every stranger who meets an unkind fate, from the sailor who drowns storm-tossed in the southern seas, to the peasant eaten by wolves in Noroda? I fear that such an excess of sympathy would leave me utterly exsanguinated in short order."

"Anrel, this man is one of our own neighbors, a Walasian and a citizen of Alzur, not some foreign barbarian."

"Oh? Tell me, Valin, do you know his name? I notice you call him the baker's son; do you even know the *baker's* name?"

"Kazien," Valin replied defensively.

"That's the family name, yes—I could have read the sign on the shop for myself to learn that much. But do you know either man's *personal* name?"

"No," Valin admitted. "And I am ashamed that I do not. I have spoken with both of them on more than one occasion, and should have learned their names."

"Ashamed? Valin, you are a sorcerer, a noble of the empire! You have a *true* name, recorded on the Great List. Why should you concern yourself with some ordinary tradesman's calling name?"

"Because he is a man, whether he has any talent for magic or not, and his humanity is deserving of respect. Should I deny my own father respect because he was no sorcerer? Should I disdain my mother's embrace because she cannot bind spirits to her will? Should I refuse *your* company, because you lack arcane skills?"

"Your parents deserve your respect because they are your parents, Valin, and I would hope that you take pleasure in my company, though I am, despite my heritage, but a scholar and no magician. We are your family and your friends—but this herb thief is not. By your own admission, in all the years you have lived in my uncle's home you have never troubled yourself to learn the baker's name, let alone that of his son, yet you are determined to antagonize the landgrave on his behalf. One thing I was taught in Lume is that we must choose where our efforts are best spent, that no one has the strength to fight every battle, nor study every field of learning. Do you really think this confrontation is the best use of your time and energy?"

"Yes, Anrel, I do," Valin said, as they passed the iron fence that marked the village boundary, and the limit of the burgrave's authority. Anrel could feel the faint tingle of his uncle's magic; Lord Dorias had, of course, set wards all along the pale, to defend Alzur from hostile influences—not that any hostile influences were likely to come from outside. "Confronting injustice is every man's duty, and to value a few herbs over a man's life is the grossest of injustices."

Anrel sighed, and looked up the hill ahead, past the neatly trimmed lawns, the carefully placed hedges, and the tidy rows of poplars, at the grand home of Lord Allutar Hezir, landgrave of Aulix. The white stone walls gleamed even in the rain, as water streamed from the turrets and gargoyles; the exterior of the house was designed to impress, to intimidate, but Valin did not seem deterred by its splendor.

Clearly, Valin was determined to see Lord Allutar and argue for the trespasser's life; further protest could accomplish nothing. Still, Anrel was not at all pleased by the prospect.

In truth, he did not care very much one way or another about the baker or his son; he would prefer to see the youth freed, if only to please Valin, but he did not think it would be possible to sway Lord Allutar. He did not particularly care to see everyone's time and effort wasted in a doomed attempt to do so.

Anrel did remember the baker and his children. That Valin did not made a point in Anrel's own mind about his friend's obliviousness. Anrel knew the baker's name was Darith Kazien, and while the man was a master of his craft, he was not a particularly pleasant individual in other ways. His son, Urunar, three years younger than Anrel and almost five years Valin's junior, had been an unhappy child with a streak of cruelty. Although they had seen little of each other and had never been friends, more than once Anrel had stopped Urunar from bullying younger children or tormenting stray animals.

But on occasion he had also seen Urunar comforting his sisters after their father had abused them, or after one of the girls had yet again burned her hand trying to help out at the bakery. The boy had not been without redeeming features. Despite his reluctance to intervene, Anrel had no desire to see him dead—but he did not find the prospect unthinkable, either.

Anrel was not surprised that Valin did not remember Urunar's name. Ever since Valin's magical talent had first manifested itself and his parents had sent him to be trained in sorcery and the social graces of the aristocracy by Lord Dorias, Valin had been a dreamer, too caught up in his hopes and schemes, too focused on grand ideas, to notice the details of the everyday world around him.

Furthermore, in their younger years, when Anrel and Lady Saria and the other children of the village had played together, Valin had often been kept in his guardian's home, studying the arcane arts. Dorias's tutelage had been strict and time-consuming. Valin had had far less contact with the other households in the area than had Anrel or his cousin.

That fact had done a great deal to please young Anrel with his own failure as a sorcerer; he had enjoyed his freedom. Lady Saria was a sorceress, of course, but had somehow managed to elude her lessons far more often than had Lord Valin.

That isolation, Anrel thought, might also explain why Valin had seemingly not guessed the greatest reason for Anrel's utter lack of enthusiasm for their errand. Simply put, Anrel had no desire to ever see Lord Allutar again, under any circumstances whatsoever. He did not wish to share a room with the sorcerer, nor breathe the same air. In their every previous encounter Lord Allutar had demonstrated himself to be arrogant, inconsiderate, and unpleasant, and to have a knack for causing Anrel, who normally prided himself on his cool equanimity, to lose his temper.

With that in mind, Anrel promised himself that he would say as little as possible on this occasion.

The footman at the mansion's door recognized Lord Valin, and allowed him in—one did not argue with sorcerers, even very minor ones. If Lord Valin was intruding, then it was up to another sorcerer, such as Lord Allutar, to stop him; it was not the place of a lowly servant unless specific orders had been given.

Anrel was admitted solely because he marched in so close on Valin's heels that the footman could not get the door closed quickly enough.

The footman did, however, manage to hurry past the visitors to announce them before they actually crossed the threshold of Lord Allutar's hall.

"Lord Valin li-Tarbek, fosterling of the House of Adirane," he said, a trifle breathlessly, "and Master Anrel Murau."

Anrel was mildly surprised the footman remembered his name, as it had not been mentioned at the door. He had expected to be "and companion," or ignored entirely. He nodded an acknowledgment to the footman, hanging back for a moment as Valin strode into the hall.

The room was large and magnificent; carved stone arches supported a high ceiling where golden stars gleamed on a deep blue background, and a long row of lancet windows admitted the gray light of day. Lush blue and gold carpets from somewhere in the Ermetian mystery lands covered most of the stone floor, while tapestries adorned the walls. Heavy tables were pushed back against the walls, leaving most of the room open; the hearth, cold and dark this time of year, occupied one end of the long room, while a dais filled the other. A homunculus somewhat larger than a man stood motionless in one corner, its back against the wall, its features utterly still and lifeless. Anrel gave it a curious glance; his uncle had never made or owned one, and the few Anrel had seen in Lume had been busy on their masters' business and had not provided him much of an opportunity for study, so he would have liked a chance to give the creature a close inspection.

But he was not here to study the homunculus; he was here to support Valin against the master of the hall.

Lord Allutar was seated upon a grand chair upon the dais—was it still a throne, Anrel wondered, when it was merely a landgrave's chair, rather than the seat of an emperor? It certainly *looked* like a throne. Allutar appeared as unpleasant as ever, glaring down his long nose at everyone.

A stranger was standing on the dais beside the throne, a tall blond man Anrel had never seen before—a foreigner, by the look of him, perhaps Quandish, or from somewhere in the Cousins. Anrel guessed this might be the Lord Blackfield Valin had mentioned.

Although he had not seen the Quandishman before, the stranger's presence jogged a memory loose—wasn't Lord Blackfield the name of one of the foreigners involved with the previous year's scandal surrounding Prince Sharal, and the murder of Lady Arissa Taline? Anrel could not recall the exact connection.

Whether this was the same man or not, he was standing beside Lord Allutar like a trusted friend.

The baker, Darith Kazien, knelt on the steps of the dais at Lord Allutar's feet; his wife and his two daughters knelt beside him. Several servants were standing attentively to one side or the other. There was no sign of Urunar himself.

Lord Valin, Anrel was dismayed to see, was marching across the room as if preparing to chastise a misbehaving dog. He stopped only when he could go no farther without kicking aside some member of the baker's family.

"Lord Valin," Allutar said, gazing mildly at the intruder. "What brings *you* barging into my home?"

"I have come to add my voice to those demanding that you free the baker's son!" Valin announced.

"Demanding? *Demanding?*" Anrel thought Allutar was genuinely surprised by this effrontery; the tone of his raised voice seemed to be more astonishment than anger. "By what authority can *you* possibly make demands of *me?*"

"By the authority of our shared humanity, and of common decency!" Valin cried.

"What authority is *that*?" Allutar asked, his astonishment turning to amusement. He leaned on one elbow, rested his chin on his hand, and stared at Valin.

"Lord Allutar, we are all brothers, as the deacons tell us," Valin proclaimed, "and as your brother, I have the right to ask you to show mercy to this unfortunate youth."

"The right to ask, perhaps, but hardly the authority to demand," Allutar said, straightening up again. "I am the landgrave of Aulix, appointed to that post by the emperor himself, after assessment by the Imperial College in Lume; that is *my* authority to do as I please with this thief. I think that sufficient."

"But you cannot just ignore the rights of a fellow human being!" Valin exclaimed.

"Oh? Are you claiming that these rights supersede the authority of the Walasian Empire?" Allutar shook his head. "I don't think you would find many who would agree with you—certainly not among the magistrates. The empire has far more men and horses and cannon enforcing the emperor's orders than you will find defending common decency. Not to mention that in addition to his soldiers, the emperor has magicians such as ourselves subject to his whims."

Valin appeared about to shout a response, and was taking a breath, when one of the baker's daughters—Felizza, was it?—looked up from where she crouched and murmured, "Please, Lord Valin, don't make him angry." Anrel did not think she intended it to be heard by anyone but Valin, but as fortune would have it the words emerged during one of those momentary silences that can occur in any conversation, and were clearly audible to everyone present.

Lord Allutar froze for an instant, then turned his gaze on the kneeling girl.

"I am not angry, child," he said. "Nor does this jumped-up imitation of a sorcerer have the power to anger me. I am not so easily troubled as that." He looked back to Valin. "However, I do not take kindly to my inferiors making demands of me."

Anrel watched Valin struggle with himself before he spoke, and could guess what his friend was thinking—he wanted to continue as he had begun, to denounce Lord Allutar as an insensitive monster, to argue with everything the man said, but he had heard the girl's protest, and knew that he might well be hurting his own cause were he to remain belligerent.

Circumspection, and the desire to save the youth's life, won out over Valin's righteous wrath.

"Your pardon, Landgrave," Valin said. "My emotions got the better of me. Perhaps *you* are always able to restrain your anger, but I fear in that respect, if no other, I may indeed confess myself the weaker man."

Allutar smiled a tight little smile of satisfaction, and nodded almost imperceptibly. "Well said," he acknowledged. "Now, I have been listening to the pleas of the scoundrel's family, and have been touched by them, if not yet swayed from my course. I have also heard some argument from my Quandish guest, Lord Blackfield." He gestured at the blond stranger. Anrel's guess of the man's identity had been correct.

"However," Allutar said, "no one has yet given me any reason to doubt that the boy did indeed trespass upon my private gardens and attempt to carry away a basketful of valuable herbs. No one has yet caused me to doubt the legality of putting him to death for this offense. I have heard a great deal about the supposed benefits of mercy, which I have countered with arguments I think just as sound on the deterrent effects of a strong and prompt punishment. Furthermore, as it happens I have a *use* for someone's death—there is a binding I would like to attempt that requires the sacrifice of a man or woman's lifeblood."

The Quandishman made an unhappy wordless noise at that; Allutar did not appear to notice. Such a sacrifice clearly fell into the category the Quandish considered black magic; Lord Blackfield's efforts had obviously not swayed his host.

"So," Allutar continued, "I find myself weighing these various elements. I believe I have every legal right to carry out this execution, and no one seems to be questioning that. The moral right is another matter, and I admit that is far less certain, but I am willing to risk the stain on my soul, and will leave any consequences in the hands of our ancestral spirits. With the legal and moral issues thus resolved to my satisfaction, that leaves practical considerations. Obviously, I have the physical capability of disposing of young Urunar as I see fit, but do the benefits to be achieved outweigh the costs? His family have presented their case for heavy emotional costs to themselves, and some small economic consequences to the village. They argue that showing mercy will enhance my reputation. I cannot deny any of these, but against them I set the costs of being thought foolishly lenient by other would-be thieves and trespassers—not a trivial matter in these unsettled times—and the sorcerous benefits I hope to derive from the planned blood sacrifice, not merely for myself but for our entire province. I find the balance still favors butchering the baker's boy." He smiled grimly at his little wordplay. "Lord Blackfield has suggested some potential risks in my proposed course of action, and some vague possible benefits of eschewing it, but frankly, I do not take these very seriously. Lord Blackfield and his friends have been presenting these same arguments here and there for several years now, and I remain unconvinced. So, Lord Valin—do you have any new factors to add to the equation? Have you new elements that might tip the balance the other way?"

Anrel suppressed a sigh. Lord Allutar had already won—not that there had ever been much doubt of his eventual victory. He had made himself out to be the voice of reason, the avatar of dispassionate logic, and Valin had allowed it to happen. Barring some miracle of eloquence, Valin could not hope to change anything now; no matter what arguments he might present, Allutar needed only to consider them for a moment, and then declare them insufficient.

But Valin did not seem to know that. He had not spent the last four years studying logic, rhetoric, and oratory in the court schools, as Anrel had.

"Why, I believe I do have another factor to add," Valin said. "I believe that the emperor himself has provided an element that you must consider before taking any hasty action."

Allutar's tight little smile vanished. "Oh?"

"My friend here is newly arrived from the courts of Lume, and he will confirm what I say," Valin said, gesturing at Anrel. "The emperor has summoned the Grand Council."

"That's hardly news," Allutar snapped. "We received word a quarter season past. What does *that* have to do with anything?"

"Why, you say you are acting on your authority as landgrave of Aulix, but when the Grand Council meets, it supersedes all other authority in the empire—the emperor himself is not safe on his throne, should the council decide to depose him. How do you know you will *remain* landgrave of Aulix? The council may not look kindly on those nobles who abuse their power by slaughtering harmless tradespeople."

Allutar stared at Valin for a moment in apparent disbelief, then chuckled.

"You're a fool, Valin," he said. "Why would the Grand Council care about a single thief? I intend to be *on* that council, and I assure you, I have no intention of prying into the household affairs of every landgrave in Walasia. The council is convening because the emperor wants to be bailed out of a century's debts accumulated by himself and his ancestors, not because he gives any credence to the fools who say we sorcerers have been ruling our lands too firmly."

"That may indeed be the emperor's reason," Valin said, "but once summoned, the Grand Council has the authority to do anything it pleases, and though he can call it, the emperor cannot dismiss it. The council may well see the wisdom in Lord Blackfield's arguments, and ban black magic. The council could throw out our entire outmoded system of government. The days when political power required magical power are gone, Lord Allutar. The council might well decide that magicians are more suited to service than supremacy. Some talented clerk might well be made landgrave of Aulix in your stead, and do a better job of administering the province because he would not be spending his time experimenting with sorcerous bindings and blood sacrifices when he should be overseeing his farmers."

Allutar laughed. "My dear Lord Valin, our current system has persisted for . . . let me see . . . five hundred and eighty-eight years, is it? Why, yes, I believe that's the number. It has functioned quite adequately for almost six centuries. Why, then, would the Grand Council change it? I admit that the council would have the power to do so, but I cannot see that it would have any *reason* to do so—especially since I expect the council to be made up of sorcerers and their dependents. Why in all the Bound Lands would they deliberately throw away their own positions?

And in any case, what the council *might* do is of no import here—the council has not yet met, and right now, I have the authority and the right to do as I please with this miscreant."

"The authority, but never the right," Valin replied. "To take away a man's entire existence because he picked a few plants cannot be right."

"It *is* my right, as landgrave," Allutar insisted. "I am working for the greater good, my lord, and the lives of every commoner in Aulix are at my disposal. My sorcery requires a death, and the Father has seen fit to deliver a criminal into my hands at this time; would you rather I chose some innocent and killed *him*?"

"Like Lord Blackfield, I would rather you abandoned the practice of black magic," Valin said. "The benefits it yields never justify the costs."

"What you seem to have missed," Allutar replied, "is that *I* won't be the one paying the cost, any more than you. Urunar Kazien will be."

"His death will not be the only cost," the Quandishman said, speaking for the first time since Anrel's arrival and startling everyone. His Walasian was clear and unaccented. "There are other, subtler costs, and at least some of those you *will* pay yourself."

"So you say," Allutar replied. "I cannot help but wonder, though, whether it's true, or whether, perhaps, you and your foreign friends are campaigning to see black magic outlawed in Walasia not out of any altruistic motive, but rather, to remove a significant weapon from the empire's arsenal. Our two nations have been at peace for forty years, but that peace may not last forever, and anything that might weaken Walasia would benefit Quand, in the unhappy event that war should break out."

Anrel noticed that Valin seemed shaken by this response; obviously, he had not thought of this possibility.

"I am no warmonger," Lord Blackfield protested. "I assure you, Lord Allutar, that I wish no harm to any living soul, Walasian or not."

"Can you prove it?" He waved a hand before Lord Blackfield could consider a response. "No, you cannot. No one can know what is in your mind. Were you a commoner I might be able to bind you to the truth, but you are a sorcerer, quite possibly as powerful a sorcerer as myself, which means no binding I can place upon you would be guaranteed of success."

"I give you my word, as a sorcerer and a Gatherman."

Allutar gazed curiously at the Quandishman. "Do you know your own mind that well, then? Do you know the hearts of every member of your Lantern Society, to be so certain that they have not played you for a fool? And present intent aside, can you be sure that abandoning the darker magic will not be seen as a sign of weakness and lead to an attack by Quand, or Ermetia, or some other power? No, I fear that the sorcerers of Walasia cannot afford to relinquish *any* sort of magic while we have foes on our borders."

"You are making foes of your own people, as well, then," the Quandishman said.

"Listen to him," Valin said. He gestured at the baker and his family. "These are *your people*—you should be protecting them, not murdering them!"

"I *am* protecting them. From each other," Allutar retorted. He sighed. "Has anyone else a fresh argument to present? Lord Valin? Lord Blackfield? You, Master Murau—you haven't said a word. Do *you* have anything to add?"

"No, Lord Allutar," Anrel said. "I am here to accompany Lord Valin, and nothing more."

"And do *you* think I should execute the thief?"

"I recognize your authority to do so," Anrel said. "I would prefer that you not exercise it."

This answer seemed to intrigue Allutar. He leaned forward and asked, "Why?"

Anrel sighed. "Because my friend wishes it. Because I enjoy the pastries and confections the baker sells, and would rather not see him suffer such a loss. Because as a child I saw Urunar comfort his sisters when they needed comfort."

Allutar clasped his hands and stared at Anrel. "You have no ideology to promote, then? You do not see in this case a reflection of some greater principle?"

Anrel shrugged. "I am just a young man without magic, my lord, not a philosopher. I have spent the last four years in Lume studying ideologies and principles, as well as history and literature and a great many other things, and I have come to realize that ideologies and principles are mere theory, while a father's sorrow and a sister's grief are facts. Likewise, the Grand Council is as yet a theory, while your power in Aulix is a fact. If I thought theories would sway you I would be happy to spout them at length, to argue every angle, but I believe you are a man who prefers facts, and I have none to present of which you are not already aware. The decision is yours to make. I will add my voice to those saying we would prefer you let the lad live, but beyond that, I have nothing to offer."

Allutar smiled, and pointed at Anrel. "You may not be a magician, Master Murau, but you are a man of sense. I commend you for it." He sat back on his throne. "Now, here is what I will do. For the greatest efficacy, my spell should be cast on the equinox, when day and night are of equal length, and I therefore intend to forgo the customary visit to the sacred grove, and remain here to execute my unhappy thief and perform this binding. That is some six days from now. During those six days, I will permit the family to speak with the prisoner as they please. I will accept any documents anyone may care to prepare in the case, arguing whatever grounds may present themselves. I will entertain requests for private audience. I may be swayed, should anyone produce arguments of sufficient power. If by some peculiar happenstance another, more heinous criminal shall be apprehended in that time, I will gladly put *him* to death instead, and set Master Kazien free—perhaps after a few strokes of the whip, but free he will be if a more suitable prisoner falls into my hands." Then he rose, and his voice became a bellow. "But I will *not* tolerate anyone, whether sorcerer or commoner, barging in here with baseless pleas or unjustified demands! You will respect my home, and set foot inside only when invited! Now, begone, all of you!"

The baker and his family groveled and began backing away, almost tripping Lord Valin; the young sorcerer began to protest, but Anrel stepped forward and caught him by the arm, pulling him hence.

"This is not the time," Anrel hissed in Valin's ear. "You have six days. Marshal your words and march them in proper order; don't send them charging forward unprepared and in disarray!"

"But . . ."

"The landgrave of Aulix has bidden us go," Anrel insisted. "We must go."

Valin hesitated, staring at Allutar, then tore his arm from Anrel's grip. "Fine!" he said. "Fine, then! Let us go."

He turned, and stamped out of the hall, with Anrel on his heels.

4

In Which Lord Dorias Welcomes Anrel Home

The sun was low in the west, and the clouds had diminished enough to leave its disk visible, by the time Valin and Anrel finally trudged up the granite steps and into Lord Dorias's home. Valin's mood had brightened considerably.

"It is true that Lord Allutar did not set the boy free," he said to Anrel as they reached the front door. "But to have the poor lad there in his home for six days, in abject terror—I think that must certainly soften the landgrave's heart, to observe such suffering. Indeed, I think his refusal to yield the point immediately must have been merely to save face; surely, he cannot be so inhuman as to carry out this execution!"

"It is a shame you have not studied more history," Anrel said, as he stepped across the threshold. "If you had, you would know that even respectable, civilized men are capable of the most appalling barbarities."

Valin opened his mouth to reply, but before he could speak a female voice shrieked.

"*Anrel!* You're home!"

Before Anrel could respond his cousin had bounded down the stairs and flung herself at him, embracing him so vigorously that he could scarcely find the breath to speak.

"Father and Mother, Saria, you'll injure him if you aren't careful!" Valin said.

"What *took* you so long?" Saria demanded. "The coach was due hours ago! Did it break a wheel, perhaps, or did one of the horses go lame? You didn't encounter bandits?"

"No, nothing like that," Anrel assured her as he gently disentangled himself. "But we decided to wait out the rain at Master Harrea's cookshop, and then Lord Valin set out to play the hero and rescue a young man from a bitter fate."

"Valin, a hero?" She glanced from one young man to the other. "What was this?"

"Lord Allutar has condemned the baker's son to death for trespassing and theft," Valin said. "I had hoped to convince him to commute the sentence."

"The baker's son?"

"Urunar Kazien," Anrel said. "You remember him?"

"The bully? Of course I do! How generous of you, Valin, to speak on his behalf. I assume it was no use?"

Valin looked hurt. "Do you think so little of my persuasive abilities, then?"

"By no means! It is not that I think your words inadequate to such a task in the ordinary way of things, but that I know Lord Allutar to not be easily swayed." Anrel thought he heard something unspoken in the tone of her voice—admiration, perhaps? "He has spoken of late of the need for firm discipline, given the shortages."

Somewhat mollified by her words, Valin said, "The matter is not yet decided. Lord Allutar has said he will consider the circumstances for another six days; it seems he wishes to use the death in a spell, and the equinox is the most propitious time for it."

"Is he making heartsblood wine, then?" Saria asked.

"He spoke of a binding," Anrel replied.

"Whatever his intention, he may yet reconsider," Valin said.

"I do not think it likely," Anrel said, as he removed his cap and tried to impose some order on his damp hair. "Do not raise your hopes too high, Valin, lest they crush you when they fall."

"Ah, you are always the voice of despair, Anrel," Valin said. "I had forgotten how gloomy you are, and how your presence makes the rest of the world seem brighter by contrast."

"Nonsense!" Saria said. "My cousin merely refuses to blind himself to unpleasant truths."

Anrel bowed to her. "I thank you for your defense, Cousin."

"The family forms a united front against me," Valin said. "But I tell you, someday you will see me proven right—we can make the world a better place, one where we need not tolerate the abuses of men like Lord Allutar. Lord Blackfield and his friends have the right of it; nothing good can come of black magic, and we must stamp it out."

"Lord Blackfield is a very pleasant fellow," Saria said, "but even he acknowledges that his Lantern Society is making little headway."

"Then you've met him?" Anrel asked, as he peeled off his coat.

"Oh, he stayed here for several days," Saria said. "Not that it took him that long to convince my father of anything; he had made his case *there* before his first night here was out. You know how Father dislikes using *any* magic; convincing him not to work black magic, which I don't believe he has ever attempted, was no great challenge. But Lord Blackfield remained our guest until he was able to coax an invitation from the landgrave, and you can guess how difficult *that* was."

"And how *is* your father?" Anrel asked. "Valin told me he was rather out of sorts today."

"The rain depressed him, I think," Saria said. "His mood has been foul all day. He sent the servants off on various errands, saying he wanted them where they wouldn't bother him. He's well enough, though. He says the dampness troubles his joints, but he always says that."

Anrel had wondered why none of the household staff had been in evidence, and was relieved by this explanation; he had feared financial reverses or some other disaster.

As for the painful joints, those were indeed a familiar story, but that did not mean they were not real. "It may always be true, when he says it," Anrel said. "What do we know of the innermost working of the human knee, or how our fingers are assembled? Perhaps there are tissues that swell in wet weather, and the swelling pains Uncle Dorias. May I see him, do you think?"

"Of course! He was waiting for you, you know. He refused to leave the house until he had word of your safe arrival. That dreadful Master

Pollibiel who claims to speak for the shopkeepers wanted to talk to him about something earlier; he was quite disagreeable, and Father sent the man away, told him that it could wait until tomorrow, whatever it was."

"Then let us find my uncle at once, before he dismisses an imperial messenger or an Ermetian envoy; I would not care to be responsible for any shirking of his duties as burgrave of Alzur."

With that, the three of them made their way down the passage and through the salon into the kitchens, where they found Lord Dorias arranging biscuits on a table.

"Keeping them dry," he explained, before anyone asked. "So they won't get moldy."

"Of course, Uncle," Anrel said.

"So you're finally back from Lume," the master of the house grumbled.

"Yes, Uncle."

"I wasn't entirely sure you wouldn't find employment there, and stay there."

"Alas, no such opportunity presented itself."

"Then did you learn anything worth knowing there, or was that all just a waste of your four years and my five thousand guilders?"

"I think I learned a great deal, actually," Anrel said. "How much of it will prove to be of any use remains to be seen."

"You learned nothing of sorcery, I suppose."

"Only a little history and theory, Uncle. Nothing has happened to change the results of my trials."

"That's a shame," Dorias said. "Such a shame. My sister was a talented sorceress, and that husband of hers was not totally useless. How the two of them could produce a child with no arcane skill whatsoever remains a mystery to me."

"Yet for my own part, Uncle, when I remember my parents as I last saw them, or when I see how troublesome your duties as burgrave are, I find myself unable to regret having failed that examination. Not everyone can be a sorcerer, and I am content to be among the ungifted majority, unencumbered by the risks and duties of the magician."

"Humph." Dorias placed the final biscuit, then looked up from his array and met Anrel's eye. "I confess, it's good to see you again, Anrel, sorcerer or not, and employed or not."

"I assure you, Uncle, any pleasure you take in my return is as nothing compared to my own delight at being once more beneath your roof." He stepped forward, and Dorias accepted a brief, restrained embrace, his reaction far less enthusiastic than his daughter's, but no less sincere, Anrel was sure.

"I might ask," Dorias said, when they had separated, "why, if you are so happy to be here, you were not here sooner."

"Ah, Uncle, we were caught in the rain, and took shelter in town."

"The rain ended hours ago!"

"Lord Valin had an errand to run," Anrel said. "I accompanied him, in hopes I might be of some use."

Dorias turned to glare at Valin, but still directed his question at Anrel. "I *knew* I should have come to meet you myself, despite my pains. And what errand did my erstwhile apprentice think was so urgent?"

"He needed to speak with Lord Allutar," Anrel said.

"About *what*?" Dorias demanded. "Valin, what business did you have with the landgrave?"

"I sought to save a man's life," Valin said. "I hope I may yet manage it."

"What man?"

"Urunar Kazien," Anrel said.

"The baker's boy?" Dorias asked. "What's he done now?"

"He is accused of stealing herbs from the landgrave's garden," Valin replied.

Dorias snorted. "I'm sure he did, the little fool. And Allutar means to put him to death?"

"He does," Valin said.

"More specifically, Uncle, he proposes to sacrifice the lad on the autumnal equinox, in hopes of working a spell of some sort," Anrel explained.

"Does he?" Dorias shook his head. "Well, then, I suppose the poor boy is doomed. His parents must be miserable."

"Magister, I have—" Valin began.

"Oh, dear Mother," Dorias interrupted.

Disconcerted, Valin said, "What?"

"Any time you call me Magister, I know you're about to ask something dreadful. You are well past the age of apprenticeship, after all, even if I don't think you ever really properly completed your studies."

Valin frowned. "And what else should I call you?"

"Unless you want something, you generally don't bother to call me *anything*. Should you choose to do so, you know the proper forms of address, or at least you ought to. 'My lord' would serve, or 'Lord Dorias,' or 'Burgrave'—but go on, then, what were you going to ask?"

"I was going to suggest, Magis—my lord, that you might perhaps intercede on the boy's behalf. After all, you *are* burgrave of Alzur; as a resident of Alzur, is he not one of your own dependents?"

"Of course he is, and now that you mention it, I can require that Lord Allutar compensate his parents, if he has not already arranged to do so—I believe the appropriate amount under the law would be four hundred guilders. But if the boy stole from the landgrave, or was apprehended outside the pale, then I'm afraid I have no claim on his life."

"But cannot you *ask* Lord Allutar to reconsider?"

Dorias snorted. "I can, and Lord Allutar can then tell me to mind my own business. As I have no doubt he will."

"But can't you make a case somehow, Magister? Perhaps say that you suspect the boy of having a talent for magic—a sorcerer cannot be put to death without the emperor's consent, you know that."

"But I do *not* suspect the boy of having a talent for magic. Mischief, yes—this is hardly the first time he's embarrassed himself—but not magic."

"But then why did he want the herbs in the first place?"

"I would assume he intended to bake something with them. Herbs have a great many uses other than sorcery. In fact, if he *was* using them for magic, since he has passed no trial he would not be a sorcerer but a witch, and witchcraft is punishable by death just as certainly as any theft."

"Oh, I don't mean he's *performing* magic, just that he has a natural talent that led him to the herbs."

"That's nonsense, Valin. You must know that."

"But isn't it enough to suggest the *possibility* of magical ability?"

"Valin, if I go to the landgrave and say the boy may have the talent to be a sorcerer, he will simply administer a few tests, and the matter will be settled. You are raising false hope. People like you, sorcerers born to commoners, are very rare, my lad, and I assure you, I have heard not the slightest rumor, nor seen the least sign, that Urunar Kazien might be one of those exotic individuals."

"But Magis—my lord, Lord Allutar said that he would listen to arguments for the six days left to the boy. Can't you at least speak to him, and urge him to reconsider, on grounds of simple humanity? Or suggest that putting the boy to death will stir up unrest?"

Dorias sighed. He looked at his daughter and nephew. Saria was obviously not interested; Anrel, as he so often was, was unreadable. Still, neither seemed disposed to argue against Valin's position.

"The day after tomorrow," the burgrave said. "If the weather isn't too unpleasant, and my stomach isn't troubling me, I will speak with Lord Allutar the day after tomorrow."

"Not tomorrow?" Valin asked.

"Not tomorrow," Dorias replied firmly. "I intend to spend much of tomorrow becoming reacquainted with our returned scholar, since he is here, and hearing all the latest gossip from the emperor's court."

"I was hardly an intimate to the court," Anrel protested.

"But you were in the capital, and I'm sure you heard a few tales, didn't you? The empress, for example—is she truly the mad, bad Ermetian ogre some of the stories would have her?"

Anrel smothered a sigh. "I haven't met her, Uncle."

"But you've heard stories?"

"A few," Anrel reluctantly admitted.

"There! You'll tell me all of them, then. And the day *after* tomorrow, I shall speak to Lord Allutar about various matters, and I will make certain to inquire after the Kazien boy, and to urge leniency."

"And suggest he might be a magician?" Valin said.

"I hardly . . . oh, very well. I'll suggest it."

"Shall I come with you, to add my voice?"

"I think Lord Allutar has heard all he wants of your voice," Anrel said, before Lord Dorias could respond.

Valin opened his mouth to protest, then closed it again. Saria laughed.

"It's no laughing matter," Valin reproached her. "A man's life is at stake."

"Then if you are determined to save him, I would listen to Anrel," Saria said. "He may be the only one here who is not a sorcerer, but I think he may have the most sense of us all."

"Perhaps that was how the Mother compensated me for my lack of arcane skill," Anrel said, bowing an acknowledgment to his cousin.

"Quite possibly," Dorias said. "We can include the question in our prayers at the next change of the seasons; perhaps the spirits will give us a sign."

"I would not trouble any spirits with such questions," Anrel said. "I am content to know that I am thought sensible by those I love, and need no explanation of how I came to be so fortunate."

"If it is good sense to leave the baker's son to die, then I thank the Father and Mother I was not so blessed!" Valin said, raising his nose.

"Oh, will you please be silent about that accursed boy?" Dorias snapped. "I have said I will plead for him two days hence, and the equinox is yet six days away; there's no need for his fate to so dominate our conversation! I would much rather hear what Anrel has to say about his time in Lume. Is it true that the emperor's palace is lit so brightly these days the very walls seem to glow?"

"Not that I noticed when I happened by it," Anrel said. "It is still very much as you saw it four years ago."

"Did you ever see the emperor?" Saria asked.

"Only from a great distance," Anrel told her. "During a procession."

"But you saw him!"

"Yes," Anrel admitted.

"Then tell us about it!" Saria insisted.

"Yes, do," Dorias said. He took a final glance at his biscuits, then swept them aside. "Let us sit in the parlor and hear all about it!"

With that, the four of them left the kitchen, and the subject of the impending execution was not mentioned again that night.

5

In Which Anrel Finds Himself at Home

Fitting back into the routine in his uncle's home was more difficult than Anrel had expected. Now that Lord Valin had completed his studies in sorcery, or at any rate ended them, and Lady Saria was old enough to make her own arrangements, Lord Dorias no longer had a schedule to maintain, and had allowed his habits to become somewhat eccentric. He did not arise until midmorning, while Anrel, accustomed to the strictures of the court schools, was up and dressed by sunrise.

Anrel was therefore able to spend some time reacquainting himself with his uncle's staff and looking over the burgrave's estate before joining the family for a late breakfast and extended conversation.

At the table he gave them an impassioned account of the hardships of a student's lot, as well as the glories of the libraries and museums in Lume. He described several of his professors and tutors, and something of the capital's architecture and fashionable inhabitants. He mentioned the forbidding aspect of the city's extensive walls and defenses, and the air of mystery that still clung to some of the standing ruins, where traces of the strange magic of the Old Empire's long-vanished wizards still lingered.

He did not mention the beggars in the streets, or the countless whores desperate enough to pursue even poverty-stricken students. He made no mention of the watch patrolling atop their arches and rooftop catwalks, nor the seething unrest in the Pensioners' Quarter and the angry mood of the general populace. He described the emperor's palace, with its glittering spires and magnificent carvings, for Lady Saria, but said nothing of the red-painted cannon on its ramparts, manned and aimed at the crowds in the surrounding streets whenever the people of the capital gathered to protest the high taxes, food shortages, and other misfortunes they laid at the government's feet. All of those unhappy details could be introduced when he had had more time to settle in, and had reacquainted himself with the political leanings of his uncle, his cousin, and his friend.

Prior to his stay in Lume Anrel had taken no interest in politics, and had therefore noticed little of the politics of those around him. He would have preferred to continue in that fashion. Four years in the capital, though, especially four years such as those just ending, would force *anyone* to acquire a basic knowledge of the issues confronting the empire, and to form opinions about them.

The dominant opinion Anrel had formed was that however unjust and miserable the present situation might be, none of the proposed changes would be any better, no matter what faction might be making the proposals. Every utopian scheme Anrel heard propounded seemed to him to depend on people ceasing to act like people, which is to say, every plan assumed that ordinary men and women would henceforth be free of stupidity, greed, venality, and other widespread human characteristics. Since he could not bring himself to believe that such traits were going to miraculously vanish, Anrel concluded that every such solution to the empire's problems was doomed to failure, and that the best anyone could hope for was that the present system would somehow muddle through, since at least the problems inherent in it were known and familiar.

This was not an opinion that a student could safely voice in the court schools, so Anrel had developed the habit of saying nothing that might trigger a political debate of any sort. That habit had survived the journey back to Alzur.

So he neglected to mention the sick, starving masses he had seen in the streets of Lume, or the petty bullying of the Emperor's Watch, or any number of other things he had encountered, and he said nothing when Lord Dorias complained about the demands the emperor placed on the administrators of his realm, the landgraves and burgraves and margraves. He did not argue with Lord Valin's speeches about the nobility of the common man. He ignored Lady Saria's snide rejoinders suggesting that Valin only loved the common man because he wasn't one, and that if Valin had not escaped his own common background he would be less enthusiastic about his fellows.

Valin, however, looked uncomfortably at Anrel after one of Saria's remarks.

"Pay no attention to her, Anrel," he said.

Anrel smiled wryly. "Oh, I'm sure my dear cousin did not mean to include *me* in her dismissal of most of our species as little more than beasts," he said.

"But you aren't common at all, Anrel!" Saria protested. "You're a scholar, and born of sorcerers, even if you haven't any magical skill of your own."

"Walasian law recognizes only two categories of citizens," Anrel pointed out. "One is a sorcerer, or one is not. Sorcerers are entitled to own land and administer the empire, and commoners are not."

"The *emperor* isn't a sorcerer," Saria retorted. "Are you calling him and his family commoners?"

"Indeed, our ancestors determined to avoid competition for the throne by saying no sorcerer could have it," Anrel agreed. "I concede that the imperial family is in a third category. I am not, however, a member of that illustrious clan."

"You're a member of *our* clan," Saria insisted. "The House of Adirane. We are not commoners."

"I am a Murau," Anrel corrected her. "My mother was an Adirane, but I took my father's name."

"Adirane or Murau, both are noble families—and do you really mean to disclaim our kinship, Cousin? After my father took you in and raised you, as if you were my own brother?"

"Of course he's an Adirane, whatever his name may be," Dorias proclaimed. "But he's no sorcerer, you know that, so he's quite right in saying he's a commoner."

"But he's my own cousin!"

"There's no shame in being a commoner, Saria," Dorias said. "The Mother and Father made him as he is, and it's not for us to question it."

"Indeed, if there is shame to be found on either side of the divide, I would look among sorcerers," Valin said. "What use have we made of our gifts? Many of us have aggrandized ourselves at the expense of the unfortunates we are supposed to be protecting. Look at Lord Allutar, preparing to slaughter a young man in pursuit of some spell!"

"Do you even know *what* spell, Valin?" Saria demanded. "For all we know, it may be an accomplishment well worth the expenditure of a human life—if you can in fact call Urunar Kazien human, which I consider open to debate."

Anrel was startled by her vehemence. "You seem to have a low opinion of the lad."

"I had a few encounters with Master Kazien while you were in Lume, and while Lord Valin was carousing in Naith," Saria said. "My opinion is low, yes—indeed, it's subterranean."

Anrel smiled.

"I was hardly *carousing*!" Valin protested. "I was seeking a position for myself. Since I have been blessed with sorcerous ability, I would prefer to employ it for the benefit of others, and there's no need for more sorcerers in so small a town as Alzur. Your father and Lord Allutar, whatever differences I may have with them, are beyond question competent in their roles."

"Did you find a position?" Anrel asked with sudden interest. "You hadn't mentioned any of this yesterday."

"It's not settled, as yet," Valin said sullenly. "The First Lord Magistrate is looking into some possibilities."

"For half a season now," Saria said.

"I'm sure Lord Neriam will find you something," Dorias said.

"Indeed," Anrel said, "where administrators are involved, a delay of a season or two is scarcely worthy of mention."

"Especially when one has so little to offer," Saria said.

Valin opened his mouth to protest, but the master of the house cut him off. "Enough of this!" Dorias said. "I want to hear more about

Anrel's education in Lume, not about politics or executions or you two squabbling."

With that, the conversation returned to safer subjects.

As the day wore on, Anrel began to suspect that there were things the two other young members of the household were not telling him; Valin seemed reluctant to say much about his prospects in Naith, and Saria's attitude seemed to be somehow odd, in a way Anrel could not quite grasp. Her bickering with Valin seemed less playful and more serious than he recalled.

Lord Dorias, however, was much as he had always been, and gave no sign of any secrets.

Even his uncle, though, could be disconcerting. At one point Anrel mused briefly about his own future, and Dorias cut him off sharply with, "There will be time to speak of that later."

There had been several hints that Anrel would have been well-advised to find a position in Lume, rather than returning to Alzur at all, and in truth, Anrel did not know what was to become of him. There was no place for a scholar in a village like Alzur, but he had no connections anywhere else. He knew he should have tried to make some influential friends during his time in Lume, but he had not managed it; he had spent his time in the company of impecunious scholars like himself. He had a first-rate education that would fit him for clerking or even the practice of law in any city large enough to house a magistrate's court, but he had no patron to aid him in establishing himself in such a position. His uncle's support might prove sufficient, but he was by no means certain of that—and Dorias's dismissal of the subject did not bode well.

He had thought that perhaps he might follow Valin into service somewhere, but Valin did not seem to have found a place for himself as yet, either.

On the other hand, Lord Dorias had given no sign that he intended to stop supporting Anrel anytime soon. Anrel's self-respect would not permit him to remain a parasite on his uncle's goodwill indefinitely, but another season or two would be tolerable.

At midafternoon Anrel felt he needed a respite from his family's attentions, and took a walk, saying he was in the mood for fresh air. He waved to Ziral the butler as he ambled out the front door and down the granite steps to the graveled path.

He paused at the edge of the lawn to look back at the house. It was far less grand than Lord Allutar's; the walls were rough gray stone rather than white and polished, and the roof slates were all a plain dark gray rather than patterned in three colors. There were no turrets, and ivy obscured the few carved figures. Still, Anrel loved the old manor, and it was certainly far finer than his rented room on the Court of the Red Serpent in Lume.

It was, in fact, finer than he deserved. He had done nothing to earn a place here.

He frowned, and turned his gaze north, toward the village.

He had originally intended to walk into the square and perhaps drink wine or tea, but now he suddenly did not want to face any of the villagers. Although he hated to admit it, even to himself, he was afraid Alzur would, upon closer inspection, turn out to have changed in his absence. He did not want to see beggars in the square, or people who fell silent whenever a stranger passed for fear that stranger was an informant for the watch. He could not imagine how such things could have come here, but he did not want to risk it.

Rather more likely, and still not something he wanted to deal with, was the possibility that the townsfolk would try to involve him further in the matter of Urunar Kazien. He was not sure which would be worse, villagers pleading with him to do what he could to save the thief, or applauding the spell Lord Allutar intended to cast with Urunar's lifeblood.

Instead he turned west, toward the little patch of woods that crowned a nearby hill. The hill was outside Alzur's pale, but on the Adirane family lands, and therefore under his uncle's jurisdiction. Lord Dorias had forbidden the local farmers to clear that land, despite many requests, rejecting arguments that every acre was needed in this era of poor crops, and that outlaws hid among the trees. The burgrave had insisted that the village needed the forest to shelter game and provide firewood.

It also provided pleasant shade on hot days, and Anrel had spent many hours there as a child. Although the rains had passed and the day was sunny, it was not especially hot; nonetheless, the idea of strolling in that cool green grove, renewing his acquaintance with it, was very appealing. He ambled up the slope toward the trees.

As he did he heard a sound that he did not immediately identify, a rhythmic thumping. He paid no attention at first, but then realized it was growing louder as he walked; it came from the grove.

That was the clue that caused him to recognize the sound of an axe chopping wood. Anrel frowned. His uncle never set the foresters to work until after the equinox. The villagers were welcome to gather any windfall firewood they could find, but not to cut their own. Perhaps a large limb, or an entire tree, had fallen, and someone was cutting it up for ease in hauling?

Whomever it was, it would do no harm to exchange a few pleasantries; Anrel directed his steps toward the sound.

He had passed through much of the grove before he finally spotted a man swinging a long-handled axe.

The man was dressed in the well-worn woolens of an ordinary workman—a brown jacket and gray trousers. His old brown boots were wrapped in dirty rags that held sole and upper together, and a faded blue scarf kept twigs and chips from falling down his collar; he wore no hat, and his hair was long, tangled, and none too clean. He was hacking away not at a fallen limb, but at a standing ash tree, and he was not making a very good job of it; his cut was ragged, and wider than it needed to be. He was clearly not a trained forester, nor did he appear particularly strong or well fed. Judging by the hay cart that stood a few yards away, Anrel guessed him to be a farmer.

"Hello, sir!" Anrel called, as the man raised the axe for another blow.

Startled, the axe-man stopped midswing and turned. "Who are *you*?" he exclaimed.

Anrel had worn his student's cap out of habit, even though he was back home and had access to a more extensive wardrobe than he had maintained in Lume; now he doffed the cap and bowed. "Anrel Murau," he said. "At your service. And might I ask *your* name?"

"None of your business," the man replied, shifting his grip on the axe. "Be on about your own affairs, and leave me to mine."

Anrel straightened, replaced his cap, and stepped closer. "I fear, sir, that this may *be* my affair. How is it you are attempting to fell one of my uncle's trees?"

"Your uncle?" The man glanced in the direction of Lord Dorias's house.

"Indeed," Anrel said.

The man looked at Anrel, then down at the axe he held, then at the ash tree he had scarred, then back at Anrel.

Then, without warning, he charged at Anrel, lifting the axe as he came.

Anrel had feared such an attack; he dove sideways, clutching at the ground.

The first blow missed Anrel's left foot by a few inches, and the axe head bit into the earth. The axe-man promptly snatched it back and raised it to strike again.

Anrel had rolled aside; now he came back up to one knee and flung a handful of dirt and dust in his attacker's eyes. Then he went down again as his enraged opponent swung the axe in a swooping horizontal arc that skimmed just above his shoulders.

Anrel had always avoided fights whenever possible, but he had been an ordinary child, and he had spent four years in the student courts of Lume. He had been in a few childhood tussles and half a dozen tavern brawls, and had twice confronted would-be robbers. After taking a beating or two he had applied himself to improving the odds of preventing a recurrence, and had worked out a few simple rules.

The first was, don't be where your opponent expects you to be. In one memorable dispute in Lume, that had meant leaping up on a table and grabbing for the chandelier, but the best solution, if one couldn't avoid the fight entirely, was usually to drop down and move sideways, as he had done here.

The second rule was to use whatever tools came to hand, as he had with the handful of dirt.

His third rule was to do whatever he could to avoid his opponent's weapons. If his foe held a knife, that meant getting out of reach; on the other hand, if his foe wielded a weapon that used a longer reach, such as a sword or whip, it was better to get in so close that the weapon could not be used effectively.

And his final rule was, where possible, to fight to disarm, not to hurt. A swordsman with no sword was generally at a loss, where the same man might still be a serious threat after a blow to the head or a slash on the arm. A robber without his cosh would seek easier prey, where an elbow in the gut might only anger him. Few were capable of killing a grown man with their bare hands; removing weapons generally meant removing the risk of death.

Therefore, rather than ducking away, or trying to regain his feet, or looking for a weapon of his own, he launched himself at the axe-man's knees, timing his lunge so that he struck just as the axe reached the end of its arc, before the man could turn it around and swing it back, when he was most likely to be off balance.

The tactic worked; the man stumbled and fell backward, one hand coming off the axe handle to fend Anrel off.

Anrel ignored that hand and grabbed for the axe, not trying yet to pull it away, but only to push it back where his opponent could not use it. He missed, but his fingers closed on his assailant's wrist.

Anrel was not a particularly large man, but neither was he small, and his strength was considerable; he was able to force the axe, and the hand that held it, up by his opponent's left ear. Then he brought his own left hand across, grabbed the axe handle, and twisted it upward, breaking the man's grip.

Anrel made no attempt to use the axe himself; instead he flung it awkwardly aside, out of reach, and shoved his left forearm under his foe's nose, pushing upward hard, forcing the man's head back. A moment later he had the man down on his back, head and left hand pinned to the ground, right hand clutching at Anrel's throat. Anrel made no serious effort to dislodge it; the one hand could cause him considerable discomfort, but unless the man was clever enough to press on a major blood vessel, no more than that.

He did not appear to be very clever, nor, judging by his grip, very strong.

"Now, sir," Anrel said, "let us discuss your presence in my uncle's grove. You are obviously not here by invitation."

"Let me go!" the man managed to say, despite Anrel's arm across his face.

"I think not. You are trespassing, are you not?"

"I'm trying to feed my family!"

"You also attempted to kill me!"

"No! I—" He stopped, apparently realizing he could not defend that position. He also realized his struggles were useless. His right hand fell from Anrel's throat. "Let me up."

"In good time. Tell me, have you ever heard of one Urunar Kazien?"

The man frowned. "Who?"

"He is the baker's son, here in Alzur. He is to be executed on the equinox for stealing a handful of Lord Allutar's herbs. His blood will be used in a spell the landgrave wishes to attempt."

"I don't . . ." The man looked confused.

"Tell me, do you think the penalty for stealing an entire tree from the burgrave of Alzur would be any less?"

"I don't . . . I wasn't . . ." The downed man swallowed uneasily.

"The landgrave suggested that he would spare the boy, if a more deserving criminal could be found to die in his stead."

His eyes widened. "I meant no harm!"

"What were you hoping to do with that ash?"

"I . . ."

"I would strongly advise an honest answer."

"I was going to sell it to a sawyer in Kuriel. For the cabinetmakers."

Anrel was startled. "You came all the way *here* for that?"

"The woods around Kuriel are all guarded now."

Anrel drew back his arm. "Are they?" He tried to remember what he had seen from the coach. Kuriel had seemed quiet, but he had not visited any groves or woodlots.

"Yes. The ones that haven't been cut down, anyway."

"Are circumstances as bad as that, then?"

"You know they are, surely."

"No," Anrel said, releasing the man's wrist. "I have been away."

"Half of Aulix is starving," the man said, making no attempt to rise.

"The landgrave sends our crops to Lume, and leaves us with nothing. Though I've heard it's even worse in some of the other provinces."

Anrel had no reply to that; he had no idea how much truth there was in the man's claims. He sat up.

"Are you going to hand me over to the burgrave, then?"

Anrel shook his head. He knew Uncle Dorias would refer the matter to Lord Allutar, and Allutar would most likely sentence the man to death.

Whether he would then allow Urunar Kazien to live, Anrel could not say; he certainly did not want to rely upon the landgrave's good faith. Giving him an alternative would only complicate matters. One death was enough; Anrel did not care to risk the possibility that Allutar would execute them both, and could not guess how Valin would react to any of this if he were to learn of it. "The tree still stands," he said. "You are indeed trespassing, though, and I expect you to remove yourself, your cart, and your axe from these lands immediately."

The axe-man blinked up at him. "You're letting me go?"

"I am. I am no watchman or magistrate."

"But you said . . . the burgrave is your uncle? You're a sorcerer?"

"The burgrave is my uncle, but I am no sorcerer. I am a man without magic, much like yourself, save for my good fortune in choosing my family. Now, be off with you, before I change my mind."

"Yes, my lord . . . I mean, yes, sir." Both men got to their feet, brushing dirt and dead leaves from their clothes. The axe-man gave Anrel a wary glance, then retrieved his axe, being careful to hold it just below the head, in as unthreatening a manner as possible. As Anrel watched, he tossed the axe in the hay cart and began maneuvering it around.

"A moment," Anrel said, raising a hand. He slid the other hand in his pocket. If he was going to let this would-be thief go, he did not want him to simply find something else to steal.

"What?"

"I want an agreement from you," Anrel said. "In exchange for your life and freedom."

The man eyed him warily. "What sort of agreement?"

"I want it understood clearly that you will not return to this grove, nor to Alzur."

The axe-man grimaced. "Agreed."

"You will not speak of this afternoon's events to anyone, nor shall I."

"As you wish."

"And I ask you to take this, to seal our agreement," Anrel said, as he drew a coin from his pocket and tossed it to the axe-man.

He reached up and caught the coin, and started to say something, then stopped as he felt the size and weight of Anrel's gift. He looked down at his hand, and stared.

"This is a guilder," he said. "I saw one once, when I was a boy."

"Yes, it is," Anrel acknowledged. "I think it sufficient."

"More than sufficient! Thank you, my lord!" This time he made no effort to correct himself as he bowed, twice, to Anrel before stuffing the coin in his jacket. Then he turned, hurrying to get away before the over-generous madman could change his mind. A guilder could feed his family for a few days, at least.

Anrel watched him go, then turned back toward his uncle's house. The notion of walking farther had lost its appeal, and his clothes were a mess.

Back in Lume he could not have thrown guilders about so carelessly, but here—here, he lived on his uncle's generosity with no clear limits.

As he walked home, he wondered whether the man had been telling the truth about conditions in Kuriel and the rest of Aulix. It was possible that matters had indeed reached as sorry a state as he described, but Anrel sincerely hoped the rascal had exaggerated.

Not that there was anything to be done about it, of course, even if every word was true.

Anrel retired that night enjoying the comforts of his old home, but not entirely at ease about any number of things.

6

In Which Anrel Learns of Lady Saria's Hopes

The following morning Lord Dorias was as good as his word, and set out immediately after breakfast for the short trip across the river, through the village, and up the hill to Lord Allutar's estate. He traveled in the company of two of his four footmen, leaving his family at home.

Valin announced his intention to pursue some errand of his own, which left Anrel and Saria in each other's company for much of the morning.

Saria did not share her uncle's fascination with the court schools, nor Valin's interest in politics, but she did want to know what the fashionable ladies of Lume had been wearing. Anrel did his best to satisfy her curiosity, but eventually he was forced to remind her, "I did not spend much time among the elite, dear Saria. I was, after all, only a student and a commoner."

"I do wish you would stop reminding us that you are technically a commoner." Saria pouted.

"I wish you would not make it necessary to remind you," Anrel retorted.

"So you did not go to fancy balls at the palace?"

"By no means. Generous as your father's stipend was, by the time I paid for my room, my books, and my professors' fees, I had enough trouble keeping food in my belly and shoes on my feet. I attended no cotillions, danced at no balls, and never set foot inside the emperor's palace. On those occasions when my funds extended to anything beyond necessities, I generally made do with a glass of wine at one of the taverns in the courts, and perhaps a few songs with my fellow students."

"You did not entertain the ladies of the capital, then?"

"I am afraid I did not."

"Really, Anrel, have you no *interest* in the other members of my sex?"

"Oh, I assure you, dear cousin, I *watched* the women of Lume with great interest, but with my limited funds I could do little more than watch."

"And here I had wondered whether you might not bring home a wife, or at least inform us of a betrothal."

Anrel snorted derisively. "I think you have a very unrealistic idea of my circumstances in Lume—and for that matter, anywhere. Much as I might wish otherwise, I am a young man without magic, and with no family trade but sorcery; what do *I* have to offer a bride?"

"A charming manner, when you trouble to use it, as well as a quick wit, and a face that is pleasant enough to look upon."

"But no employment, nor any great prospects. No lands, nor mastery of any art or trade. A family of some note, true, but one from which I am of necessity outcast."

"Anrel! You are no outcast."

"You asked me to stop reminding you that I am a commoner, yet once again you force me to do so. In all our extended family, whether Adirane or Murau, is there another commoner to be found? How can I *not* be considered an outcast?"

That could hardly be argued, but Saria was not to be deterred so easily. "That doesn't make you an outcast—but I concede it does alter the situation somewhat. Still, you are an educated man, one whom several sorcerers look upon with favor even if you are no sorcerer yourself—what young woman would not be willing to at least look at you?"

"A great many, to judge by my experience in Lume."

"They are all fools in Lume, it would seem."

Anrel decided he had had enough of defending his own position, and that the time had come to turn from defense to offense. "And you, Cousin—do you have some young man you hope to wed?"

He had an idea of what answer he might expect, so her blush was not a great surprise, but her words destroyed his theory completely.

"Not a *young* man," she said.

Momentarily at a loss, he stared at her for a few seconds before asking, "Who might this fortunate man be, then?"

"Can you not guess? After all, Anrel, if I am to avoid scandal I must marry a sorcerer, and I have had little opportunity to travel beyond the limits of my father's burgravate."

"Indeed," Anrel said. "I had thought that the obvious match would therefore be yourself and our own Lord Valin."

The blush vanished, and Saria's jaw dropped. "Valin?" she said. "You thought I might marry *Valin*?"

"I fail to see why this should so astonish you," Anrel said.

"But he's been like a *brother* to me!" she protested. "I could no more marry him than I could marry *you*!"

"On the contrary," Anrel said. "There is no legal impediment whatsoever to marrying him, whereas I am quite out of the question. He is a sorcerer, as I am not; he is unrelated by blood, while I am your first cousin, a degree of consanguinity that would require an imperial decree of license to allow marriage. To marry me is twice impossible; to marry Valin would be entirely permissible."

"But we grew up together!" Saria said. "You don't really think I could stand to share my bed with *him*, do you?" She shuddered with disgust.

"I had not thought the matter so obvious as you do, to say the least," Anrel said. "It would seem I badly misjudged the situation."

"I should say you did. Marry *Valin*! Augh! Why not just auction me off, like some old-fashioned peasant?"

"I scarcely think marrying your father's fosterling is equivalent to a bridal auction. In any event, if not Valin, then who is your intended spouse?"

"Anrel, don't play the fool." She glared at him. "What other sorcerer is there in the vicinity of Alzur?"

Anrel stared at her in dawning horror. "Surely, you don't mean Lord Allutar?"

She lifted her nose. "And why not? Do you think me unworthy of him?"

"On the contrary, I think *him* very obviously unworthy of *you*. He is twice your age!"

"What of it? Do you think I would prefer an untried boy to a mature adult?"

"He is a vile, unmannered lout!"

"He is plainspoken at times, perhaps."

"He intends to murder a young man four days from now—does that not trouble you at all?"

"He is attempting powerful sorcery. That is entirely fitting for a landgrave of the empire. And he is dispensing justice, which is also appropriate."

Anrel could find no further words, but merely stared at her in awkward silence, marveling at how little he really knew her. Had she changed so much in the four years he was gone? Perhaps she had; four years was a significant amount of time, after all, especially for one as young as Saria. Those four years were a fifth of her life.

This, at least, explained some of her behavior in the previous day's debate over Urunar Kazien's impending doom. Anrel had taken that for a means of trying herself against Valin; now he saw that she had instead been defending the man she hoped to wed.

He tried unsuccessfully to grasp the idea. She really wanted to marry Lord Allutar? Had she not once shared his own loathing for the man? Allutar was arrogant, heartless, condescending—but perhaps not to her. Anrel thought back, reviewing his contacts with the landgrave that had formed his opinions, and realized that Saria had not been present for most of them. Lord Allutar had often been rude to Anrel—but Anrel was an orphan and a commoner. Saria was the burgrave's daughter, and a competent sorceress.

Lord Allutar was wealthy, powerful, respected, and inasmuch as Anrel was any judge of such things, not unpleasant in appearance—his skin was clear, his hair and beard clean and well maintained, his shoulders broad, his belly flat, his features regular and well-balanced, and he was tall enough to be commanding without being freakish. Was it really so strange that Saria might find him desirable? Anrel's own dislike of the man was so strong that the possibility had never occurred to him, but now that he thought about it he could see nothing unreasonable about it.

He could not even be sure he found the idea entirely disagreeable. Allutar was going to continue to live on the hill above Alzur in any case, and Saria might prove a moderating influence upon him. On a purely instinctual, emotional level the notion of Saria sharing Allutar's bed was nauseating, but on a rational level Anrel had to admit that was her concern, and not his own.

This might also explain why the constant rivalry between Valin and Saria had acquired a sharper edge—Valin and Allutar despised each other.

The silence had grown awkward, but it was Saria who broke it. "How long do the ladies of Lume wear their hair these days?" she asked.

"Shorter than those out here in the countryside," Anrel replied, relieved to have the conversation once more on safe ground. "Indeed, scarcely past the collar, in some cases, but tightly curled."

Some minutes later, to Anrel's relief, a footman called them to lunch.

After they had eaten, Saria retired upstairs, while Anrel took a book to the parlor. He had read several chapters when he looked up to see Lord Valin marching in.

"Ho!" Anrel said. "The conquering hero has returned!"

"I am in no mood for your badinage," Valin replied.

"Then I shall not trouble you with it," Anrel said. "Is there something you would like to say, or shall I continue with my reading?"

"By all means, read on," Valin said. "I will not be fit company for some time yet."

Anrel's curiosity was aroused, but he did not ask for explanation; instead he shrugged, and opened his book anew.

Valin found a volume of his own on the shelves, and sank into a chair.

The two of them sat thus, in silence interrupted by the rustling of turned pages and an occasional quiet remark, for the better part of an hour. They were still thus engaged when the master of the house returned, his presence announced by the stamping of feet and the slamming of doors.

Lord Dorias was smiling broadly as he walked into his parlor, which Valin and Anrel took as an encouraging sign. The two of them had both put down their books in anticipation of the burgrave's arrival.

"What news, then, Uncle?" Anrel asked.

"Ah, my lads, Lord Allutar has agreed to call on Saria on the morrow."

Valin frowned. "What?"

Anrel glanced at his friend. Perhaps Anrel had not been the only member of the household unaware of Saria's romantic interest in the landgrave.

"We have an understanding, he and I," Dorias said. "I have made plain that I have no objections to the match, and he has expressed an interest in becoming better acquainted with Saria. Naturally, nothing is finalized yet—"

"That is not what concerns me," Valin interrupted. "What of the baker's son? Were you not going to argue for his life?"

"What? Oh, yes." The burgrave's smile dimmed. "I'm afraid I could do nothing. My plea for simple mercy was refused. I did bring up your absurd contention that stealing those herbs indicated an interest in magic, and although the landgrave thinks it ridiculous, he has agreed that if the boy wants to claim a talent for sorcery he may be tested—after all, he must have a true name for the sacrifice in any case, so the test will add little inconvenience. But if he does not make such a claim, or if he fails the tests, the sacrifice will take place at midday on the equinox, as planned. Beyond that, there was nothing more I could say."

"Nothing? You could devise no threat, no entreaty, that would help? It hardly seems you tried, if you have consented to allow Lord Allutar within these walls tomorrow!"

"Valin, I was not about to risk my daughter's future on behalf of a common thief!" He looked around. "Where is Saria, then?"

"In her room, I believe," Anrel said—but just then the door burst open and Saria entered.

"What did he say, Father?" she asked breathlessly.

"He will pay his respects tomorrow," Dorias told her.

"Oh, wonderful!" She scampered across the room and embraced her father, and his smile was renewed, brighter than ever.

"I will speak with him here, then," Valin said. "The baker's son—"

"You will *not*, Lord Valin li-Tarbek!" Saria snapped, releasing her father and whirling to face Valin. "You will not harass him when he comes courting me!" She turned back to Dorias. "Father, make him stop!"

"But—" Valin began.

"Did you ask him what the spell is, Father?" Saria asked, interrupting Valin.

"Yes, I did," Dorias replied. "He hopes to bind an earth spirit with the boy's blood, to restore the fertility of the fields in the Raish Valley from Kulimir to Tereth din-Sal. The yields there have been very poor in recent years; several of the farmers have been suffering greatly. We believe this has contributed heavily to the outlawry and general unhappiness in the vicinity."

"There, you see?" Saria said to Valin. "He is trying to feed his people, as a landgrave must!"

"But an innocent boy's life—"

"Urunar Kazien is no innocent," Saria replied sharply. "He is a thief, a seducer, and a scoundrel, and if his blood can revive the fields of the Raish Valley, it will be well spent."

Anrel heard her words with an odd sort of relief; since his encounter in the grove he had sometimes wondered whether he should after all have delivered the stranger to Lord Dorias in exchange for Urunar Kazien, but it was clear that at least one member of the household would not think so.

"But to *kill* a man for a binding—" Valin began.

"Valin, you will *not* interfere with Lord Allutar when he comes calling!" Saria announced.

Valin stared at her in silent, frustrated fury.

"Perhaps, Valin," Lord Dorias said gently, "tomorrow might be a good day to visit Naith, for the latest news of the planning for the Grand Council."

"I do not understand how you can all accept this . . . this *abomination* so calmly!" Valin burst out.

"Naith. You will leave for Naith at first light." Dorias's tone was much less gentle now.

Valin glared at him.

"Perhaps Anrel will accompany you," Dorias said. "He has not seen Naith in four years."

"I would be happy to," Anrel volunteered.

Valin swallowed. "Yes, my lord," he said.

7

In Which Lord Valin Introduces Anrel to the Society of Aulix Square

The provincial capital was much as Anrel remembered it; Naith yet stood atop its hill, behind its massive walls, overlooking the surrounding country as it had for generations.

The streets and squares that had seemed so large and crowded when Anrel was a boy were far less impressive after his years in Lume, though, and there were far more beggars than he recalled. He gave a few coins to some of the most pitiful. The general population seemed less cheerful, as well; he saw very few smiles.

Lord Valin moved through the streets with the ease of familiarity, and seemed to not notice the crowds and beggars at all. Anrel commented, "I take it you come here often."

"Often enough," Valin said. "At least I can sometimes find an intelligent conversation here, which is by no means likely in Alzur. Really, Anrel, I sometimes wonder how we managed to grow up with our brains still functional after so long in that dismal little town!"

"We had each other," Anrel pointed out. "Perhaps that was enough."

They passed through the largest of the several plazas within the city walls, Aulix Square, where assorted statuary stood between the courthouse and the Provincial College of Sorcerers, and Valin led the way to a wine garden just beyond the square, a few paces from one gargoyle-carved corner of the college. There he took a seat at a table, and gestured for Anrel to do the same.

"I assume, since you have brought us directly here, without so much as a glance elsewhere, that you had some particular destination and purpose in mind," Anrel remarked.

Valin shrugged. "Lord Dorias said we should gather the latest news. This is an excellent place to do so."

"I would have thought a visit to the notice board on the courthouse wall might also have been appropriate," Anrel said mildly.

Valin shrugged again. "Here we will get the real story; the notice board says only what the lords and magistrates wish us to believe. Besides, the wine here is very reasonable—or if you've developed exotic habits during your stay in Lume, they serve Quandish ale, as well, and even some outlandish brew from the Cousins."

"I would be content with tea," Anrel said. He looked up; the sun was still at least an hour short of its zenith, which seemed to him too early to be drinking wine.

"Then tea you shall have," Valin said, rapping the table.

A girl in a wine-stained apron, her thick black hair already beginning to come down over one ear, hurried over at the sound. "Lord Valin!" she said. "A pleasure to see you again. Your usual?"

"That would be fine, Binna," Valin said.

"And for your friend?" She turned to Anrel.

"You have tea?"

"The very best Ermetian leaf . . ." She hesitated, then said, "my lord."

Anrel smiled wryly.

"No, I'm afraid not," he said.

Binna flushed slightly. "Sir," she said.

"You know they do not grow the tea in Ermetia?" Anrel remarked. "The Ermetians import it from somewhere in the mystery lands."

Binna looked puzzled. "We buy it from an Ermetian merchant, sir, wherever it's grown. It's really excellent, I assure you."

"Then I will have some of this excellent tea, thank you," Anrel said.

Binna bobbed at the knee, then hurried away.

Anrel watched her go, then turned back to his companion. "Your usual?" he said, eyeing Valin.

"A modest white wine," Valin replied. "She knows which vintage and which vineyard."

"You *do* come here often."

"And here is one of the reasons I do," Valin said, starting to rise.

Anrel turned, startled, to find two young men approaching the table. One was tall, handsome, and athletically built, and wore a blue brocade jacket cut unfashionably short; the other was of medium height and softer in face and form, but superbly turned out in white linen and yellow silk.

"Lord Valin!" the shorter one called. "I had not expected to see you back here so soon!"

"I had not expected to *be* here so soon," Valin answered. "My guardian insisted."

"Did he? You will have to tell us more," the new arrival said. He glanced at Anrel. "Who's your friend?"

"This is my guardian's nephew, and my dearest friend in all Alzur, Anrel Murau," Valin explained. "He has just returned from four years of study at the court schools in Lume."

Anrel rose to greet the pair, hand outstretched. As he took the first man's hand Valin said, "Anrel, these are Derhin li-Parsil, clerk to the second magistrate, and Amanir tel-Kabanim, assistant to the housemaster at the College of Sorcerers."

"I am delighted to make your acquaintance," Anrel said with a bow. He noticed that although they were well dressed, neither man appeared to hold noble rank; there were no badges of office nor family crests to be seen, and in the introductions Valin had not called them lords. Valin's professed interest in commoners, it would seem, was not limited to theory, or to condemned criminals.

"The court schools?" Derhin said, speaking for the first time. "Are you looking for a position with the magistrates, then?"

"I have not yet settled on a course of action," Anrel said.

"I want to hear why Lord Valin's guardian sent him to Naith," Amanir said.

"He is entertaining a guest I despise, and he feared I might make a scene," Valin said.

"And would you have done so, given a chance?"

"Almost certainly," Valin admitted. "The man is unspeakable."

"Who is this regrettable guest, then?"

"Lord Allutar."

Derhin choked. "The landgrave?"

"None other."

Amanir chuckled nervously. "You speak very freely, dear Valin, to call him unspeakable."

"Why should I not? We are Walasians. We are civilized men, free to speak our minds. I say only what everyone in Naith believes, whether they would admit it or not."

Anrel almost protested, despite his own dislike for Allutar, but held his tongue; he did not as yet know these people well enough to talk so openly with them.

"I think you misjudge," Derhin said. "A great many people still think him a fine man and a worthy one, despite the sorry condition of the province. Those who have had dealings with him may know otherwise, but most of the citizens of Aulix have not had that misfortune."

"I think you could name at least *one* person in Alzur who has had dealings with him who yet thinks him a fine man," Anrel suggested.

"Don't remind me," Valin said, clapping a hand to his temple.

At that point the serving girl returned with Valin's wine and Anrel's tea; Derhin and Amanir sent her off to fetch another bottle and two more glasses.

The interruption had broken the thread of the conversation. When she had left, the four seated themselves and resumed speaking, but not about Lord Allutar himself; instead they discussed the Grand Council, and the eighteen seats that were rumored to be designated for Aulix.

"Four for Naith, I heard," Derhin said. "Fourteen more for the rest of the province. And Lord Allutar will probably take it upon himself to name all eighteen."

"That must not be allowed!" Valin said.

"It won't be," Amanir said. "The college will insist on the right to name at least one. I would expect the magistrates to have their say, as well."

"The magistrates will name whoever Allutar wants them to name," Derhin said. "There isn't a man among them with the courage or ambition to do otherwise."

"What about the burgraves?" Amanir asked. "Will they also all yield to Allutar, do you think?"

"Does it matter?" Valin demanded. "They're all of a kind."

"Even your guardian?" Derhin said.

"He is even now closeted with Lord Allutar, auctioning off his daughter's virginity," Valin replied. "I think that says all we need know."

"You are speaking of my uncle," Anrel reminded him sharply. "The man who raised me, who paid for my education, and who trained you in the arcane arts."

Valin turned to him. "But look at what he's done, Anrel! He has not only failed to persuade the landgrave to free the baker's son, but has instead offered him his daughter! The man has no integrity, no sense of justice. He cares only for his own place in society, and his daughter's."

"The baker's son?" Derhin inquired.

"Offered him his daughter?" Amanir asked.

Anrel sighed, and Valin launched into a highly colored account of the last few days.

When all had been made clear, and the first bottle of wine had been consumed, the conversation came back to the question of who might be sent to the Grand Council. A few names were suggested, none of them familiar to Anrel; then Derhin said, "Perhaps Lord Dorias will see to it that *you* are named to the council, Valin."

Valin snorted. "Why would he do that? We agree on nothing."

"But it would get you out of Alzur, where you could no longer interfere with his plans for Lady Saria."

Valin started to retort, then stopped. His expression turned thoughtful. "Alzur *is* entitled to a representative, isn't it?"

"Of course it is," Amanir replied. "At least one."

"And the burgrave would choose him?"

"That isn't as clear," Derhin said. "Especially since Lord Allutar makes his home there."

"Surely Lord Allutar won't begrudge Lord Dorias one selection!"

Amanir said. "Especially if it clears the way for his own courtship of Lady Saria."

"Are you seriously considering this, or is it the wine talking?" Anrel asked.

"Why not?" Valin said, turning to Anrel. "Your uncle doesn't care a crumb about politics, not really—he gripes about the emperor, but beyond that, he doesn't concern himself with the empire's affairs. He hasn't set foot in his family's house in Lume since he delivered you to school four years ago. He probably cares more about getting me out from underfoot than he does about the imperial accounts, or crop failures, or the abuse of black magic, or anything else the council is likely to consider."

Anrel could not argue with that. "But the landgrave . . ."

"The landgrave will have several of the other seats under his control, I am sure. He can surely spare one to please his intended father-in-law."

"And would you *want* a seat, under such circumstances? I thought you wanted the *commoners* to choose their representatives, not Lord Allutar and Uncle Dorias."

"But think about it, Anrel! If I am the representative for Alzur, I will have a chance to speak *for* the commoners. I can make certain that their voice is heard, through me!"

"But you, *Lord* Valin, are not a commoner at all," Anrel pointed out. "How can you speak with their voice? Were you not saying that the commoners of Alzur should choose one of their own?"

"And have you not been telling me that would not be possible? Here, then, is a compromise!"

"He's right, though, Valin," Amanir said. "You *aren't* a commoner."

"I was until I was twelve," Valin said. "Even now, while I am called 'lord,' other sorcerers see me as the lowest of their class—I have no family ties, no hereditary lands or talents. My magical skills, while real enough, are dismissed as hopelessly inadequate for any great rank or important post."

"Are they?" Derhin asked. "I hadn't realized."

"I can cast a decent ward," Valin said defensively. "I can manage any of the simple bindings. I can do as much as half the lords in the college here. But no, I cannot perform the sort of grand magic that caused the emperor to name Lord Allutar a landgrave, nor the complex wardings that my guardian maintains around Alzur. His ancestors have built those up over the last two centuries; they're in his blood, while in my own veins flows the blood of shopkeepers."

That speech made clear to Anrel a few things he had not entirely understood about his friend Valin. Yes, Valin had made the jump from commoner to nobleman—but as he saw it, only to the bottommost rung of the nobility. That seemed to rankle.

"At any rate, if the representatives are to be appointed by the nobility, as seems so inevitable to many, can you name a *better* choice than myself?" Valin demanded.

"No," Derhin said mildly, "but I would still prefer to let the people choose their own representatives. Even if they make a worse choice, it will be *theirs,* and not the whim of aristocrats foisted upon them."

"Pfah," Amanir said. "If the right choice is made, does it matter who made it?"

"Exactly," Valin said.

At that same instant Derhin said, "Yes," and the two turned to glare at each other.

Anrel beckoned to the serving girl for more tea.

The discussion continued through much of the day; on occasion other young men joined in, either taking seats at the table when there was room, or crowding around to listen and comment. It became clear that a great many people in Naith knew Valin, and that most of them seemed to think highly of him.

Anrel wondered at that; for his part, he did not find much wisdom in Valin's words. Derhin seemed to have done a better job of thinking through his positions, and keeping them consistent, than either Valin or Amanir, but when disagreements arose, most of the audience tended to side with Valin.

Listening to them, Anrel came to suspect that this was because he was *Lord* Valin, while the others were all commoners. Valin might feel that he was not respected by other sorcerers, but it would seem that he needed no distinguished family or powerful magic to impress the people of Naith; the bare title was enough.

Although Valin had claimed to have come here in pursuit of the latest news, Anrel heard little evidence that anything under discussion was based on more than gossip. No one cited sources; simply saying, "I've heard," seemed to be sufficient grounds to treat a statement as proven fact. In some cases the tales obviously originated from the provincial magistrates, or members of the College of Sorcerers, but others gave every sign of being pure speculation and wild fancy.

As the crowd around the table grew, Anrel grew steadily more nervous. In Lume a gathering like this would have long since drawn the attention of the Emperor's Watch; there would be bowmen atop the nearest arch, and a sergeant coming to break it up. Naith had no network of arches, and no one here would answer directly to the emperor, but surely, there must be watchmen who would take a dim view of what amounted to sedition, should they realize what was being said. When his concern became unbearable Anrel tried to push back from the table and dissociate himself from the conversation, letting another young man take his place while he moved his teacup to a low wall, away from Valin's table.

Once he had settled in this new position he sat silently, declining to contribute further. He refused offers of wine, restricting himself to tea and some lovely sweet rolls. When the others ordered a midday meal of stewed beef, complaining mightily about the price as they did so, Anrel made do with a mild onion soup.

The conversation rambled on, across a variety of inflammatory topics—the food shortages, the emperor's debts, why there were rumored to be hired magicians from the Cousins at the imperial court, why the money that paid for those magicians was not being used to import food or pay the imperial debts instead, the lingering mystery and scandal surrounding the gruesome death of Lady Arissa Taline, and half a dozen others—but in truth, none of these discussions were anything new to Anrel. He had heard all of the complaints and accusations, and many more, in Lume, in the taverns and common rooms. They had never been aired as openly as this, out in the streets, though, nor with so large a crowd in attendance.

As it happened, Anrel knew beyond question that there really were hired magicians at court; a season or so back he had been introduced to one, a fellow from Azuria by the name of Garzan tel-Barragun, during a meeting with one of his professors, and had exchanged a few polite words with the man. He knew that at least eight magicians of various schools, from various nations in the Cousins, had been brought in at the request of the Empress Annineia, who was of Ermetian birth and did not trust Walasian sorcerers. All the same, he said nothing. He did not care to become involved in the conversation to that extent.

A few of the discussions involved outright lies. In Lume the students would have picked these apart and, if no authority could be named, dismissed them as nonsense, but here many absurdities were accepted almost without question.

The story of the empress driving her carriage over starving children, crushing them, Anrel knew to be a fabrication; had such a thing happened the news would have been all over Lume in hours, and there would have been riots. No such event had occurred. The closest anything had come, and perhaps the origin of the tale, had been when a magistrate's coachman had whipped an urchin hard enough to crack bone, and that had triggered a small disturbance, if not quite a riot.

The empress had not been involved, and the magistrate, Lord Orvaz Pol, had eventually appeased the mob by paying a physician to attend the boy and make sure that the injury would not cripple him. As told in Naith, though, the empress had merely laughed and driven on, leaving dead and dying children in the road.

Anrel had avoided commenting on the foreign sorcerers, but the blithe acceptance of this account was too much; he spoke up, saying the tale was nonsense, only to be told by Amanir, "I suppose they hushed it up somehow."

Others were more realistic, and agreed that Anrel was probably right, and that particular story was at best an exaggeration.

Anrel did not consider it a mere exaggeration, but he had no interest in arguing with these people. He said no more, allowing the arguments to continue without his interference.

The entire experience amazed him. He had always assumed that the debates in the student-haunted taverns of Lume were a manifestation of the sophistication and perversity of the capital's educated elite; to hear the people of Naith spouting the same seditious talk astonished him. While he had known that times were hard, and that some honest peasants had been driven to begging and thievery, the discontent of the empire's people obviously ran much deeper than Anrel had thought.

That was a troubling realization, and Anrel was uneasy as he drank tea and listened.

Most troubling of all, though, was the realization that Valin was the ringleader of this treasonous gathering.

At last Derhin glanced up at the position of the sun and said, "I must get back to work. The afternoon session will be starting." He rose, then turned to Anrel. "It was a pleasure meeting you, Master Murau."

Anrel shook his hand, and watched him go.

Several members of the crowd took note of his departure, and scattered as well. Many of them headed for the courthouse, as Derhin had.

"Fine men, all of them," Amanir remarked.

"They are the future of the empire," Valin said.

Somehow, Anrel thought that unlikely. However clever and impassioned these people might be, they were mere commoners in a provincial capital, and he thought it far more likely that the future of the empire would be shaped by the sorcerers of Lume.

8

In Which the House of Adirane Celebrates the Equinox

Lord Allutar was still in Lord Dorias's parlor when Valin and Anrel returned from Naith, though the evening was well advanced. He did not linger; he nodded an acknowledgment of the new arrivals, then took his leave of Lady Saria and departed.

Saria's face was flushed, Anrel noticed, though he could not have said precisely why. Whether it was perplexity or passion he could not guess, and his cousin did not volunteer an explanation.

"Is Naith as you remembered it, Anrel?" she asked.

"In most respects, yes," he said. "It is I who have changed; I see it with more educated eyes now."

"Oh?"

"Saria," Valin said, interrupting, "I trust today's visit from your suitor went well?"

"Well enough," Saria said.

"Did you think, perhaps, to ask him to spare the baker's son? Perhaps he would do so to please you, as a courting gift—surely, you would prefer not to wed a murderer."

Saria's flush deepened. "No, I did not ask, Lord Valin. I have no interest in seeing Urunar Kazien's life spared."

"No? And what has Master Kazien done to you, that you would see him dead?" Valin demanded.

"Not to me, but to Mistress Lenzinir," Saria snapped. "I was merely one of those who sought to comfort her; I did not share her misfortune."

Taken aback, Valin said, "What?"

"Do you pay *no* attention to what happens in Alzur, then?" Saria asked. "Is our little town so utterly beneath your notice, my lord? Or is it only the women you ignore?"

"I don't . . . who is Mistress Lenzinir?"

"Gei Lenzinir, the weaver's apprentice," Saria said. "From Orlias, originally, though she has lived here in Alzur for three years now."

That relieved Anrel's mind; he had been trying unsuccessfully to place the name, but if she had only dwelt in Alzur for three years, then he would have had no opportunity to meet her. "Valin," he murmured, "I think you had best drop the subject."

Valin looked from Saria to Anrel and back, then retreated in confusion, leaving the parlor to the two cousins.

"What does he *do* in Naith?" Saria asked, after a moment of silent consideration. "What does he find so fascinating there?"

"He sits at a table in Aulix Square, drinking cheap wine and debating politics with his friends," Anrel said. "The fascination would seem to lie in the admiring audience these discussions attract."

"He was not talking to prospective employers?"

"No."

"Then how does he ever hope to find employment? He has no land, and no chance of an imperial appointment; he needs to earn a living if he is not to remain dependent upon my father forever."

Anrel smiled wryly. "He has decided he wants a seat on the Grand Council," he said. "It was suggested that you and your father might want to arrange it merely to get him out of Alzur, and away from Lord Allutar."

Saria started. "What an outrageous notion!" she said.

"Indeed."

Saria looked at Anrel, realized he was serious, then turned to stare at the doorway where Valin had departed. "I sometimes wonder how the mind of someone who has lived in my home since I was a child can be such a mystery to me."

"He lived his first twelve years as a shopkeeper's son," Anrel said. "And he does not share our blood."

"Even so."

Anrel nodded. "How *did* the visit from Lord Allutar go?"

"Oh, wonderfully well, really."

"I'm pleased for you," Anrel said sincerely.

She looked him in the eye. "I believe you are," she said. "I know you dislike Lord Allutar, but you mean it all the same, don't you?"

"Whatever my opinion of the landgrave, Cousin, I love *you*, and I wish you to be happy. If you want Lord Allutar as your husband, then I hope you shall have him." He smiled. "Do not expect frequent visits from me, however, should you achieve your goal."

"I can only hope you will give him a chance to change your estimation of his character," Saria said.

"I will do my best, for your sake."

With that, they parted.

Over the course of the next four days Lord Valin continued to campaign for Urunar Kazien's life by every means at his disposal—and furthermore, he did indeed introduce the notion that he might represent Alzur in the Grand Council. To the dismay of Anrel and Lady Saria, Lord Dorias did not dismiss the notion out of hand.

There was no evidence that Lord Allutar had relented, but Valin seemed to have convinced himself that the baker's son would be allowed to live. Anrel worried about how his friend would react should his optimism prove unfounded.

Anrel also troubled himself uselessly over having let the axe-wielding stranger go, rather than at least attempting to trade his life for Urunar's—but then, had the exchange been made, would Valin have taken up the axe-man's cause, as he had the baker's son's? True, the Kazien family lived in Alzur, while the would-be wood thief did not, but would that have mattered to Valin? It was not as if he actually knew Urunar any better than he knew the stranger. Valin would probably have fought as hard for any commoner's life.

In any case, Anrel realized there was no point in questioning his impulsive actions; what he had done was done, and could not be undone.

Still, his mind was accustomed to activity, and when given little else to engage his thoughts he found himself returning to this subject again and again.

On the day of the solstice the household gathered, then trudged over the hill to the ancient shrine of the Adirane family, where one by one they knelt before the phalloliths and made their personal prayers to the ancestral spirits. Although Anrel had proclaimed himself a Murau rather than an Adirane, he took his own turn, as he always had, acknowledging his mother's blood.

He had not been here in four years, instead making his quarterly obeisance in the temples of Lume, but as he knelt he thought he could feel the divine presence, as if he had never gone. That presence had been perceptible in most of his youthful visits as well, though not, perhaps, in all of them.

He murmured his true name, so there could be no mistake of who was speaking; the one good thing to have come from his sorcery trials, in his opinion, was that he now had a true name that he could use at moments such as this. He then apologized, as he always did, for forsaking his heritage and failing to prove himself a sorcerer. He prayed for the safety and happiness of his family, and of his friend Valin, and of some half-dozen comrades he had known in Lume, and for the welfare of Alzur and all the empire.

Finally, he acknowledged the inadequacy of his own wisdom, and wished for the affairs of Lord Allutar, Urunar Kazien, Lord Valin, and Lady Saria to resolve themselves in the best possible fashion, whatever that might be.

He felt a sudden darkness and oppression at that moment, and he shuddered, unsure what that might mean. Was this the response to his prayer?

Then the sunlight seemed to return and the air to lighten, and he arose, still puzzled, making way for Valin. Valin was no Adirane, by any stretch of the imagination, but as a former apprentice of Lord Dorias who still remained in the household, he was permitted to attend services with the family.

After Valin would come the three servants who had accompanied the party—the senior footman Ollith Tuir, and his wife and daughter, who were respectively the housekeeper and the upstairs maid. The other four members of the household staff had gone to their own places of reverence, whatever those might be. Anrel walked back up the hill to where Dorias and Saria waited, trying to think what that peculiar psychic darkness might have meant.

Then he realized what it must have been.

"You felt that?" Saria asked as he approached.

"Yes," Anrel said. "Valin will not be pleased."

"Then you think Urunar Kazien is dead?"

"Of course. I have little experience of black sorcery, but what else could it have been?"

"For it to be felt so strongly here—that was powerful magic, indeed!"

Anrel shrugged. "No one has ever questioned Lord Allutar's sorcerous prowess."

"Do you think it worked?"

"We may not know that until next year's harvest."

"Let us hope it worked," Dorias said. "It's been several years now since the Raish Valley could feed as many as it should."

"I would not want Master Kazien to have died in vain," Anrel replied.

"I wonder," Saria said, "whether there was anything left over to make heartsblood wine."

Anrel glanced at her, but did not ask why. His grasp of the exact nature of the notorious magical decoction was vague, but he knew it could be used to bind lovers indissolubly; perhaps she was thinking of her intended marriage.

A few moments later Valin joined them, but no one spoke; Anrel did not know what to say, under the circumstances. He was unsure whether Valin had realized the situation.

The four of them stood in awkward silence while the servants took their turns before the sacred stones. After that the main ceremony began, with Lord Dorias serving as deacon, leading the party in the traditional prayers of thanksgiving to the Father and the Mother, the sky and the earth, and then reciting the catalogue of wonders, from seas and stars down to the salt of the earth, that had been given to humankind. That was followed by the customary brief sermon about the shortening days and growing nights, and the celebrants' faith that the annual cycle would proceed as it had ever since the great wizards of old first brought these lands out of chaos and bound them to a stable form and a regular calendar. Throughout this speech, no one had the opportunity to say anything other than the words of the ritual.

Finally, as the sun neared the crown of the hill to the west, Lord Dorias gave the final benediction, and the entire party started back toward the house. Anrel eyed Valin uncertainly as they walked, but it was Saria who finally murmured something in his ear.

Valin turned to look at her. "Are you sure?" he asked, loud enough for everyone to hear.

"What else could it have been?"

Anrel did not hear Valin's reply; the conversation with Saria sank to a whisper.

They arrived safely home, where the cook had already returned from her own rites and was preparing the autumnal breakfast. Valin seemed unnaturally quiet as they settled in and awaited the call to the table.

He remained thoughtful and reserved throughout the meal, and ate sparingly.

As they pushed back from the table, though, Valin announced, "I must speak with Lord Allutar."

"Not tonight," Dorias said. "Not at this hour. Not on the equinox."

There was really little argument Valin could make to that. "In the morning, then," he said.

"I cannot stop you," Dorias said. "I would advise against it, however."

The next day Anrel awoke, dressed, and came downstairs to discover that Valin had already left, perhaps a quarter hour before, intent on seeing Lord Allutar.

Anrel hesitated, then grabbed his hat and set out after his friend.

He had expected to go through the village and up to the landgrave's home, but that proved unnecessary; he found Lord Valin sitting at a table in the town square, talking to the big, well-dressed Quandishman, Lord Blackfield.

Relieved to find Valin alive and calm, Anrel ambled over and asked, "May I join you?"

"By all means," Valin said, gesturing to an empty chair. "Lord Blackfield is waiting for the next westbound coach, and I am keeping him company until it arrives."

Anrel considered for a moment, and looked at the eastern sky, where the sun was not yet clear of the rooftops. The morning coach started from Kuriel at first light, when the driver could manage it.

"It should be here any minute," he said.

"That was my opinion, as well," Valin said.

"Then you are leaving us, Lord Blackfield?" Anrel said, taking the proffered seat.

"I am afraid so," the Quandishman said.

"We have had no chance to speak. I am Anrel Murau."

"I am delighted to make your acquaintance, Master Murau, however briefly." He offered a hand, which Anrel shook. "I am Barzal of Blackfield. You spoke most pragmatically at that gathering in the landgrave's hall the other day."

"I had no reason to do otherwise," Anrel said, noting that Lord Blackfield's name and title followed the Quandish rules, and indicated that he was not merely a lord, but the head of his family. Otherwise he would have been "Lord Barzal."

Walasian nobles made no such distinction, of course, or else Uncle Dorias would have been "Lord Adirane."

"I knew nothing *I* could say would sway Lord Allutar," Anrel added.

"Indeed, we none of us swayed him in the slightest, did we?" Lord Blackfield sighed. "The boy is dead. His heart was cut out, and his blood offered to the spirits of the earth."

"I believe we felt something of the spell's impact," Anrel remarked.

"Most probably. Dark sorcery reaches far and wide, and has subtler effects than its practitioners know." He shook his head. "I tell you, your Walasian sorcerers do not understand what they are doing, experimenting with such magic."

National pride swelled in Anrel's breast. "But surely, our magicians know as much of magic as anyone! Is not ours the heartland of the Old Empire that was home to the mightiest wizards of the ancient world?"

"Oh, the Walasian Empire is unquestionably the core of the Bound Lands, but the wizards of old vanished, and took much of their knowledge with them," Lord Blackfield said. "I do not deny the remarkable abilities of your sorcerers, who have done their best to preserve and expand their magical heritage, but I think they have become overconfident *because* they live in the heart of the Bound Lands. Walasia is too safe, too stable, the ancient bindings too strong, to let your magicians remember what magic can do. Here the sun rises on schedule every morning, and sets in its proper place each evening; it is always the same color, the same size. Throughout the empire each season is ninety-one days, year after year, without change. Every animal brings forth its own kind; every seed bears the appropriate fruit. In Quand this is not always the case; while the Quandish Peninsula is partially in the Bound Lands and quite stable, there are islands in the outer reaches of the Quandish Archipelago where a season may last no more than a single afternoon, where a cow may bear kittens and calves grow on trees. We have constant reminders of what can happen when magic is not properly controlled."

"But this is *not* the archipelago, nor the Ermetian mystery lands, nor anywhere else on the fringes of the world," Anrel protested. "We are safely in the Bound Lands."

Lord Blackfield shook his head. "Even here, black magic cannot be trusted; there are always hidden costs, as there are not in the straightforward bindings and wardings of everyday spells."

"Lord Allutar thought you exaggerated these costs," Valin said.

"I can only hope, for his sake, that he is right and I am wrong. I was certainly unable to convince him of my position."

"Is that why you're leaving, then?" Anrel asked.

"In part."

"Where are you bound?"

"I will be making one more call in Kerdery, at a village called Darmolir, and then heading back home to Quand."

"Darmolir? I don't believe I know it," Valin said.

"It's not on the well-trodden path," the Quandishman acknowledged. "Indeed, there are no public coaches that go there; I have sent for my own coachman to meet me in Lower Pelzin."

"What takes you to Darmolir?" Anrel asked. "Are there no more black sorcerers to discourage here in Aulix?"

"There may be," Lord Blackfield said. "But I am tired, and intend to make only this one more visit before returning home for the winter."

"A sorcerer in Darmolir? The burgrave, perhaps?"

"A good guess, Master Murau. Yes, Lord Salchen Elbar is the burgrave of Darmolir."

"Is he planning to eviscerate someone for the solstice, then?"

Lord Blackfield gave a bray of laughter. "You have a harsh wit, Master Murau," he said. "No, Lord Salchen's experiments in black sorcery have drawn on other sources of power than death, and his cruelties have been subtler—though perhaps all the more effective for that."

At that moment all three men heard a rattle, and looked up to see the westbound coach entering the square, wheels and hooves clattering on the cobbles. The Quandishman rose.

"I'm told the coachman is impatient of delays," he said. "I hope you will forgive me if I take my leave in haste."

"Of course," Valin said. He, too, got to his feet. "Let us accompany you to the coach, at least. Shall I carry that bag for you?"

"That would be most kind."

A moment later, the trio approached the coach. The driver saw them as he clambered down from his perch. "Ah, masters," he said. "I have messages from Lume for Lord Allutar and Lord Dorias; could you tell me who I must see to ensure they are received?"

Startled, Anrel and Valin exchanged glances.

"I am Lord Valin," Valin said. "I can take the messages."

"I am Lord Dorias's nephew," Anrel said. "I can accept his, if you would like."

"And I am a passenger bound for Lower Pelzin," Lord Blackfield said, "so I cannot help, other than to assure you that these two are indeed who they claim to be."

"Thank you, sir," the driver said. "Lower Pelzin is a day and a half from here, but we can get you there."

"Excellent."

"The messages?" Valin said.

"A moment," the coachman said. He made his way to the rear of his vehicle, and proceeded to open several locks and latches before producing two envelopes. He handed one to Valin, the other to Anrel.

"That's the emperor's seal," Anrel said, looking at his prize.

"But the emperor sends messengers!" Valin protested. "He doesn't just post a letter!"

"He did this time," the driver said, as he closed up the locks. "Or someone did. Perhaps there aren't enough messengers in Lume to have carried all of these—there's a letter there for every burgrave on my route, and for the landgrave of Kerdery, and for the margrave of Kallai. I'd guess the lords along the other coach roads are getting letters, as well."

"But only imperial officials?" Valin asked. "Not every noble?"

"Only the landgraves, the burgraves, and the margrave," the driver said, as he loaded Lord Blackfield's luggage. "No one else. Not even the Lords Magistrate."

"That's quite enough," Anrel said. "Is it about the Grand Council?"

"I wouldn't know, sir. I know better than to open a sorcerer's mail, and I can't wait around until the lords open their own; I have a schedule to keep." He finished lashing the canvas in place, closed the door behind Lord Blackfield, and swung himself up onto his bench.

Valin and Anrel stepped back out of his way, and watched silently as the driver shook out the reins, called to his team, and got the coach rolling. They waved a farewell to Lord Blackfield, and waited as the vehicle rattled out of the square.

Then Valin looked down at the envelope he held.

"It would seem I have more business with Lord Allutar than I had thought," he said.

"I'll come with you," Anrel said.

"What of the message for Lord Dorias?"

"I think my uncle can wait."

"And you think I am likely to cause trouble if I confront the landgrave alone."

"The possibility had occurred to me, yes."

Valin smiled. "Come along, then. Let us not keep the great man waiting!"

9

In Which Lord Valin Delivers a Message from the Emperor

The footman who answered the door did not admit the two visitors immediately.

"Lord Allutar was quite emphatic about it, my lord," he told Valin. "I am to admit no one without his explicit command."

"We have a message for him from the emperor," Valin said, holding up the envelope.

"I can see that he gets it, my lord . . ."

"No," Valin said, "*I* shall see that he receives it, directly from my own hand. I assured the coachman that I would make certain it reached its destination."

The footman frowned. "If you would wait here, my lord?"

"Very well."

The footman closed the door, leaving the two standing in the portico, and Anrel remarked, "You could have just handed it to the man."

"But I prefer to see for myself that Lord Allutar receives it," Valin replied with a smile.

Anrel shook his head. He knew perfectly well that Valin was hoping for a confrontation over Urunar's death, and the emperor's letter was merely an excuse.

A moment later the footman reappeared. "This way, my lord," he said. He hesitated when Anrel followed Valin inside, then shrugged and led both of them to a small, bare room Anrel did not recall ever having seen before.

"The landgrave will join you shortly," the footman said. Then he departed, closing the door behind him, leaving the two men alone.

Anrel glanced around, and realized there was nowhere to sit. "Lord Allutar is not exactly putting any great effort into hospitality today, is he?" he said wryly.

The room consisted of four bare stone walls, a single diamond-paned casement, a tile floor, two heavy wooden doors, and a vaulted ceiling; there were no furnishings at all. A less welcoming prospect was difficult to imagine.

"Perhaps he wants to be sure we won't pocket the silver," Valin answered.

Before Anrel could respond, one of the doors opened and Lord Allutar appeared. He looked tired, as if he had not slept well, and his collar was askew.

"Lord Valin," he said. "Hollem tells me you have something of mine?"

"A message from the emperor, newly arrived on the morning stage," Valin said, displaying the envelope. "I assured the coachman I would see that it reached you."

"Then see that it reaches me," Allutar said, holding out a hand.

"Of course," Valin said, making no move to deliver the envelope. "Might I ask, though, how you feel this morning? Frankly, you do not appear to be at your best."

"My well-being is no concern of yours, my lord," Allutar said.

"On the contrary, my lord, I am a resident of Aulix, and you are the landgrave of Aulix. Your health is very much the concern of everyone in the province."

Allutar gazed calmly at him. "My health is excellent, Lord Valin."

"Then you were not troubled by cutting the still-beating heart out of a man's chest yesterday?"

Anrel drew in his breath, but Allutar gave no sign of annoyance. The landgrave answered in calm, measured tones, "I was revolted by the experience, my lord, but I felt it necessary. I do not regret my actions."

"And you still believe that black magic is an appropriate employment of your skills?"

"I do, my lord. My letter?"

"You felt no ill effects from the spell?"

"What I felt or did not feel is my business. The letter, please." His outstretched hand still waited.

Valin began to say something else, but Anrel could stand it no longer. "Father and Mother, Valin, give him the blasted letter!"

Startled, Valin turned to look at his companion, and Allutar snatched the envelope from his hand. Before either Anrel or Valin could say another word, he tore it open and pulled out the letter inside. He read it quickly—Anrel could see that there were only a few lines of text.

Allutar frowned. He held the paper up to the light from the casement. "It appears genuine," he said.

"The possibility of fraud had not occurred to me," Valin said.

"That does not surprise me," Allutar retorted. He looked Valin in the eye. "Have you read it?"

Valin lifted his chin haughtily. "I am not in the habit of reading the private correspondence of others," he said.

"No, you are in the habit of sitting in wineshops in Naith and holding forth on subjects of which you know nothing," Allutar retorted. "However, one can occasionally do things other than the habitual."

Stung, Valin drew himself up to his full height. "I delivered the letter still sealed," he said. "Unopened and unread."

"You claim to be a sorcerer," Allutar said. "Any magician worthy of the name could have restored the seal after reading this."

"I give you my word I did not," Valin said coldly.

"Then you do not know what it says?"

"I do not."

Allutar stared at Valin for a moment, then shrugged. "You will know soon enough; I might as well tell you, though it will undoubtedly please you."

"I doubt anything you might say would please me," Valin replied.

"But it is the emperor who says this, my lord. He has changed his mind again, and put an end to the confusion regarding the makeup of the Grand Council."

"Oh?"

"In the interests of avoiding strife, he says, he commands that every landgrave, every margrave, and every burgrave shall appoint a single representative to the Grand Council, in conference with the other nobles in his demesne."

"That hardly pleases me," Valin said.

"Nor did I think otherwise," Allutar said. "But he likewise commands that the commoners in each jurisdiction shall elect one of their own number, so that fully one-half the council will be commoners, chosen by commoners." He flung the letter at Valin. "See for yourself."

Valin caught the letter and turned it. He read hastily.

"How are these elections to be managed, my lord?" Anrel asked. "Is that set forth?"

"No, it is not," Allutar said. "I am to use whatever means I find at my discretion to be sure that each male head of household shall have the opportunity to cast a vote, but what means those might be, or how the candidates are to be chosen, is not mentioned." He smiled. "Perhaps this is not as pleasant for Lord Valin as I first thought; it would appear to me to be within my authority to choose the candidates for whom the people will be permitted to vote."

"Naturally, that would occur to you," Valin said, looking up from the letter.

"I believe I am generally cognizant of how best to defend my own interests, yes."

"And you see nothing reprehensible about asserting your own authority regardless of the cost to others, do you?"

"Lord Valin, my own interests are likewise the interests of all Aulix, and indeed of all Walasia. I would much prefer to be landgrave of a prosperous and happy province, rather than lording over a cowed and starving populace. I think it better to live in an empire that is flourishing than one in decline. I take no pleasure in the suffering of others; on the contrary, it pains me to observe it, and so I act to prevent it where possible. If this sometimes means that I must harm an individual for the good of the community, I do so, much as I would choose to suffer the pain of extracting a splinter over the possibility of infection. What is reprehensible in that?"

"You see nothing wrong in refusing others the freedom to speak for themselves?"

"When they would speak foolishly and to their own detriment? Indeed, I do not."

"You will not allow the commoners to choose their own representatives freely?"

"What do commoners know of governance? They would vote for the well-spoken over the truly wise, I would think."

"You are not so easily fooled, then?"

"I like to think I am not, my lord."

Anrel listened to this brisk exchange with something not unlike despair. He was quite certain that neither commoners nor sorcerers had any monopoly on wisdom, nor even a sufficiency of that particular virtue, and in specific he was convinced that very few men of any station possessed the wisdom to recognize wisdom in others. These two magicians were arguing over whether the blind or the smitten were more suited to objectively judging the beauty of women.

"You are so certain of your own virtue, then?" Valin demanded.

"I am certain that the emperor saw fit to confirm me in my position as landgrave of Aulix, and that it is both my responsibility and my privilege to govern the province as I judge best. Whether that is how the commoners would judge best does not trouble me; let their grandchildren say whether I governed poorly or well, when time has shown the consequences of my actions."

"Time, my lord, will undoubtedly show that you lacked the imagination to help guide the empire into a new era of equality, liberty, and glory. Don't you see that if the commoners are given a voice, they will be inspired to greater things? They have hearts and minds that could be put to the service of the empire, but because they have no magic we tell them, no, you are nothing, you are the dirt beneath our heels, to be trodden upon as we please, and you can never be anything more. If we allowed them the opportunity to rise above their present station, we would in all probability encourage them to heights we cannot now imagine!"

"I hardly think that commoners are so disheartened as you seem to believe, Lord Valin. Have you ever seen the homes of the great merchants and bankers in Lume? They are flourishing without being permitted any voice in government."

"But they could do so much more!"

Allutar spread his hands. "Have you the slightest shred of evidence to support this claim? If a commoner has it in him to create some magnificent enterprise, then what would stop him from creating it?"

"The fear that he might be seen as a threat, and be called a criminal, perhaps accused of trespassing or theft with no witness but the man who has the power to decide his guilt and order him executed."

"Valin!" Anrel said warningly.

Allutar did not reply; he stared balefully at Valin for a moment, then snatched the paper from his hands and turned away. "You have delivered the emperor's letter," he said. "Hollem will see you out."

Valin started to protest, but Anrel held him back as Allutar strode out of the room and slammed the door behind himself.

"Valin," Anrel said, "you came near to accusing the landgrave of perjury and murder."

"Did I?" Valin spat on the floor. "And what if he *is* a perjurer and murderer? Should I say nothing?"

"You have no evidence to support such a claim." He glanced at the closed door. "I like Lord Allutar no more than you do, but he has all the law and custom on his side, and you have no evidence that he has done anything outside his authority."

"I do not acknowledge his authority to kill a man for no reason."

"He *had* a reason, Valin. He had two—Urunar Kazien was a thief, and Lord Allutar needed a sacrifice for his spell. Either one would suffice under the law. I do not even mention other crimes of which Master Kazien was accused, but which were never proven to the landgrave's satisfaction."

"I do not see those reasons as even remotely sufficient," Valin proclaimed defiantly.

"All the emperors, from the first through the current incumbent, would disagree with you, my lord. Landgraves have the power of life and death over the commoners in their provinces."

"That does not make it *right*, Anrel."

Anrel sighed. "I might find it easier to support you in this had Master Kazien been a better person—"

He might have said more, but the door opened and the footman reappeared. "This way, please," he said.

The two visitors followed him silently back to the front door; they had both stepped outside when the footman leaned over and said, "A moment, Master Murau."

Valin turned, curious.

"A personal matter, sir," the footman said. "Could I see you inside, for just a moment?"

Anrel hesitated, and glanced at Valin.

"Just you, sir," the footman said. "I'm afraid Lord Allutar has made it plain that Lord Valin is not welcome in this house."

"Shall I wait for you?" Valin asked.

"No," Anrel said. "Go on without me. I'll be along shortly."

Valin nodded, and walked away. For a second or two Anrel watched him go; then he shrugged and followed the footman back inside.

Lord Allutar was waiting in the foyer.

"My lord," Anrel said, unsurprised. He bowed.

"Master Murau," Allutar replied.

"I take it, my lord, that it was you, rather than the estimable Hollem, who wished a word with me in private?"

"Indeed." Allutar frowned. "I remember you as a boy, Master Murau, and I did not think much of you then, but it seems to me you have grown up considerably during your four years in Lume. Your uncle has told me that your professors spoke well of you in their letters reporting your progress, and your academic performance was, by all accounts, excellent. You seem to me to have become a young man of considerable sense—unlike your friend."

"You flatter me, my lord."

"False modesty does not become you, Master Murau."

"Then I will merely thank you for the observation, my lord. I hope you're right."

"I hope so, as well. Right or wrong, that assessment is why I choose to give you this warning, rather than addressing it directly to Lord Valin. I believe he would take it as a challenge, whereas you may see that it is nothing of the sort."

"Warning, my lord?"

"To date, I have restrained myself for several reasons—a general desire to avoid strife, my respect for your uncle, and to avoid displeasing your cousin, to name three. I am telling you now, though, that your friend Lord Valin has pushed me to the limits of my toleration. You heard him a few minutes ago, when he all but called me a liar to my face."

"I did," Anrel admitted.

"He is obsessed with this Urunar Kazien. He doubts his guilt—but he has not even asked about the facts of the case. Lord Valin's claim that there were no witnesses is baseless and offensive. I do not deign to explain myself to him, but perhaps you might explain to him that he is in error. It was not *I* who caught Master Kazien stealing herbs from my garden; it was my gardener, Guldim li-Forsha. An examination of the Kazien family bakery discovered a large cache of my herbs—it seems Darith Kazien has been using them in his herb bread for some time. I could have had the entire family put to death; I did not. Nor was this the first complaint against Urunar Kazien; he has previously been accused more than once of grievous assault, but there was insufficient evidence in every prior instance. I may be a tyrant, sir, but I am not an *arbitrary* tyrant, nor am I merciless. I would thank you to convey this to your companion."

"I will try, my lord."

"I trust you will succeed, Master Murau, because I warn you now that despite my love for Lord Dorias, and my hopes for Lady Saria, I will not tolerate any further insolence from your uncle's erstwhile apprentice. If he troubles me further, there will be dire consequences."

Anrel hesitated.

"Is there something you would say, Master Murau?"

"My lord," Anrel said, "even if Val—Lord Valin abandons the case of the late Urunar Kazien, you and he have many other disagreements, as well. From your comment a few moments ago I take it you are aware that he has become a radical populist, and holds forth on politics in the taverns and squares of Naith in much the same fashion he spoke to you today. I think it possible he will come to your attention further on this account, and I hope you will not consider this to be intended to disturb *you*, in particular."

"His *intention* is not at issue, Master Murau. I can forgive a certain amount of youthful idealism, but there are very definite limits to that amount, especially in times as uncertain as these."

"I am sure it is indeed just youthful folly, my lord, and that nothing will come of it."

"See that it does not, Master Murau."

"I will do my best to restrain him, my lord."

"I have quite enough to concern me as it is, Master Murau—crop failures in the Raish Valley, this Grand Council that will most probably require an extended stay in Lume, petty crime in a dozen villages, and crimes more than petty in the streets of Naith. I am not looking for ways to busy myself at your friend's expense, but neither am I oversupplied with patience at present. Do I make myself clear?"

"You do, my lord, and I thank you for the warning."

"Do your best to make him heed it."

"I will do what I can, my lord, but Lord Valin has his own mind."

"I will not hold you personally to account should my warnings be ignored; you need not trouble yourself about that. It is only Lord Valin who is at risk, so far."

"Thank you, my lord."

"That will be all, then." He turned away.

"Thank you," Anrel said again, as Hollem opened the door to usher him out.

And then he was standing in the portico as the door closed in his face.

He shuddered, and turned to hurry after Valin.

10

In Which Lord Dorias Makes His Selection

Lord Dorias read the emperor's letter slowly and carefully, seeming to pause over every word. Valin waited patiently, leaning against the door frame, while his guardian absorbed the missive; Anrel, having delivered his burden, settled into a velvet-upholstered armchair and let his chin sink to his breast as he tried to think how best to prevent a disastrous confrontation between Valin and Allutar.

"So I am to choose a delegate to the Grand Council?" Lord Dorias said, looking up from the paper at last.

"Uncle, we have not read the letter," Anrel said. "We cannot tell you what it means."

"Then take it and read it!" Dorias snapped, thrusting the letter into Anrel's face.

Anrel's head jerked up, and he snatched the paper before Valin could reach for it. He clutched it in both hands and read it carefully.

"Whereas our Ministers have brought to Our Attention," it read, "that Certain Elements have taken Advantage of Our Generosity in allowing the Citizens of the Empire to select their Representatives as they might see fit, and created Strife amongst the Populace regarding the Exact Methods to be employed, THEREFORE do We hereby set forth THE METHOD whereby All Representatives to the Grand Council shall be Selected.

"FIRSTLY, each Landgrave of All Our several Provinces shall designate One Person, of Whatever Rank He shall see fit, to represent the Province;

this Individual to be chosen purely at the discretion of the LANDGRAVE, without Restriction;

"SECONDLY, each Burgrave of All Our several Municipalities shall designate One Person, of Whatever Rank He shall see fit, to represent that Municipality; this Individual to be chosen purely at the discretion of the BURGRAVE, without Restriction;

"THIRDLY, each Margrave who guards Our Borders shall designate One Person, of Whatever Rank He shall see fit, to represent Himself and those Persons under His Protection and under His Command; this Individual to be chosen purely at the discretion of the MARGRAVE, without Restriction;

"FOURTHLY and FINALLY, the common people of each Province shall choose by the Vote of every Male Head of Household, under the Supervision of the Landgrave of that Province and His Designees, Representatives equal in number to the Total of the Landgrave and All the Burgraves and Margraves of that Province, these Representatives to be of COMMON RANK, viz., possessing no Title of Nobility, nor Talent for Sorcery, nor Government Office. Let no Person interfere with the proper Conduct of this Election; We reserve the Right to weigh any Penalty, up to and including Death, upon any who shall impede the proper Selection of these Representatives.

"Thus shall One-Half of the GRAND COUNCIL consist of Representatives chosen by Sorcerers, and One-Half of the GRAND COUNCIL consist of Representatives chosen by the Common People under the Administration of the Landgraves, to reflect the Diversity of Our Empire.

"All those Representatives thus chosen shall present themselves at the Imperial Offices in Lume, to assume their Duties, no later than Sunset upon the Winter Solstice in this Year.

"By Our Command, and with Our Seal, upon this Eighty-Sixth Day of Summer in the Twenty-Third Year of Our Reign."

Below that was the emperor's seal, but no actual signature; Anrel supposed some secretary had been given the task of writing these out. Sixteen provinces, eleven margravates, and the Father alone knew how many municipalities—no one would expect the emperor himself to waste time signing so many letters.

"It seems clear," Anrel remarked. He had certainly read far more opaque documents in the course of his education.

"Then explain it to me!" Dorias said. "Give me something for my five thousand guilders!"

"It is as you thought," he said. "You are to name a representative to the Grand Council, and you are forbidden to interfere in the election of the commoners who will serve on the council."

"I'm forbidden to interfere? I am not required to do anything in this election?"

"Indeed not," Anrel said, folding up the letter. "That is quite explicitly left to the landgrave and the commoners. Your only role is the selection of your own delegate, who will represent Alzur."

"I don't want to choose a delegate, though! I had every intention of leaving the entire matter to Lord Allutar."

"Uncle Dorias, please don't let this trouble you," Anrel said. "You need merely name someone, *anyone*, to go to Lume and sit on the council."

"But how am I to choose? I know nothing of statecraft!"

Anrel shrugged. "Few men do, including many who would practice the trade. Honestly, Uncle, I do not think the representative of Alzur will be called upon to do much; for that matter, I have serious doubts about whether the Grand Council as a whole will accomplish much. Send anyone who will not embarrass you."

"Such as yourself, perhaps?"

Anrel paled. "Father and Mother, Uncle, no! I have just come back from Lume; I have no desire to return there. And I have been four years away from Alzur; how could I represent the town's concerns adequately?"

"I would be willing," Valin said.

Dorias turned to see that Valin had straightened, removing himself from the door frame. He stood erect, eyes bright.

"I know Alzur well," Valin said. "I have lived here half my life, after all. And they will expect you to send a sorcerer—with half the council made up of commoners, I think every noble will name a sorcerer as his delegate, and it would seem odd were you to do otherwise. What other sorcerer could you choose?"

Dorias hesitated.

"I have little to keep me here," Valin continued. "You have made it clear—oh, only most subtly and politely, but clear!—that you are displeased I have found no appropriate employment, and I, too, chafe at my enforced idleness; here, then, is a way to put me to work. More, I have spoken at length with scholars and others in Naith regarding the issues the Grand Council will address; you could find no one better prepared than I. Further, you know that I have little love for Lord Allutar, and I believe Lady Saria has hopes that he will be spending more time under this roof in the future; would it not be more pleasant for all concerned if I am gainfully occupied elsewhere? And finally, Magister, I would enjoy an opportunity to see the capital and its wonders for more than the few days I have been able to visit there."

Anrel sat and stared at his stunned uncle, trying to decide whether he should say anything. All Valin's reasons were true—in fact, Anrel was startled at Valin's honesty in presenting them all so openly. But there were strong reasons that Valin should *not* be named to the council, as well, beginning with Anrel's conviction that his friend, much as he loved him, was an idealistic fool.

As for avoiding Lord Allutar, the landgrave had clearly implied that he would be choosing *himself* as his delegate. Putting Valin and Allutar in the same deliberative body would not be conducive to any sort of peaceful negotiation, especially in light of Lord Allutar's warning, given little more than an hour earlier.

But on the other hand, the Walasian Empire held sixteen provinces, eleven margravates, and some hundreds of towns; the Grand Council would be made up of twice that number. It would not be impossible for the two men to avoid each other in such a crowd.

Valin's idealism, too, would surely be rendered harmless in such a crowd . . .

"Done," Dorias said, holding out his hand to his fosterling. "You shall be my delegate to the Grand Council. And *that* is one less foolish concern troubling me!"

"Uncle," Anrel said, "there is no need for haste—"

"Nor is there any reason for delay," Valin said. "Thank you, Magister!" He bowed.

"Let him have plenty of time to get ready," Dorias said to Anrel. "After all, he needs to be in Lume in less than a season."

"He can be ready in a day, and reach Lume in five!" Anrel protested. "But why rush so?"

"Exactly, my lord—why rush? At least give it a day's thought . . ."

"Anrel," Valin said, his tone hurt, "I thought you would be pleased on my behalf."

"I am!" Anrel said, startled. "But I . . . I am of a cautious disposition in such matters, and would not see you caught up in something you may later regret. Could you not both give this a day's thought, before determining it so definitely?"

"No need!" Dorias said, clapping Anrel on the shoulder. "I know a good idea when I hear it, and this one has all the earmarks. You turned the position down, Anrel; I would say that forfeits any claim you might have to a say in who takes it."

"I do not question—" He broke off in midsentence, and sighed. "As you will, then, Uncle. I have no desire to vex you. I confess, I can see every argument in favor of such a choice, while those opposed seem hazy and ill-defined; I assure you, it is only my natural caution and my love for you both that impels me to ask whether there may be risks or drawbacks we have not yet considered."

"Caution is a worthy trait," Dorias said, "but there are times when boldness and instinct will serve as well. I am content with my choice. It relieves my mind. I prefer to have it over and done, and so it is."

"As you say, Uncle."

"That's settled, then." Dorias plucked the letter from Anrel's hand and tossed it on a table, then strode out of the room, smiling.

"Anrel, why did you—" Valin began, stepping over toward Anrel.

"I will miss you, Valin," Anrel interrupted.

Valin stopped. "Oh," he said.

"If we are both to spend years in Lume, I would have preferred that those years coincide," Anrel said. "Alas, they will not."

"Perhaps you can come to Lume to clerk for me," Valin said. "Or perhaps you might be chosen as one of the commoners."

Anrel shook his head. "No. I would not accept such a choice. I am very tired of Lume, Valin, and of the empire's politics. Four years there was more than enough for me, at least for the present. Even the pleasure of your company cannot draw me back there so soon."

"Oh," Valin said again.

"There is something more," Anrel said. "You realize that Lord Allutar's selection is to be the landgrave himself? The two of you will be serving together in the delegation from Aulix. For the sake of the House of Adirane and the people of Alzur, you must restrain your feelings toward the man and present a united front to the world."

"He chooses *himself*? Is that what that footman told you?" Valin grimaced. "The man has no shame."

"He certainly does not bother with false modesty," Anrel said, noting without surprise that Valin had failed to register Lord Allutar's intention.

"It's good, then, that I will be there to remind him that he is merely mortal," Valin said with a wolfish grin.

"Oh, no," Anrel said warningly. "He is still the landgrave of Aulix. Do not vex him needlessly."

"Needlessly? But I think such arrogance *does* need to be punctured."

"Valin, as long as you remain tied to Alzur, you will have to live with Lord Allutar; surely it would be better to have peace between you!"

"No, I do not think it would," Valin replied, still smiling. "A man can be judged by his foes, don't you think? One who never makes an enemy can hardly be much of a man at all! Let all see that I have chosen the very essence of sorcerous pride as my nemesis, and that I fear him not a whit."

"Perhaps you *should* fear him!"

"I fear no one, Anrel, not even the emperor himself. I have right on my side, and the spirits of our ancestors, human and divine, will see that I thrive thereby."

"Father and Mother, Valin, you make such a claim, and then you say *Lord Allutar* is arrogant?"

Valin laughed. "You catch me out, Anrel! Yet I *do* believe I am fully in the right in what I am undertaking. The empire's structure is rotten, can you not see that? The bad wood needs to be cut away, and fresh wood set in its place, and I have no doubt that Lord Allutar represents the very worst sort of decay."

"I know you believe that," Anrel said. "For my own part, I am not entirely convinced. And even if it is the simple truth, be wary that you do not bring it all down upon your head when you tap repeatedly at that rotted beam. Remember what befell Uru—the baker's son."

Valin's laughter faded. "*That* is why I can never live in peace with Lord Allutar," he said. "He killed a boy for a spell!"

"A spell that may have saved the livelihoods of many farmers, and perhaps filled hundreds of hungry bellies."

"A few missed meals to save a man's life? I think that a bad bargain."

"I think you misjudge the severity of the crop failures." In fact, Anrel suspected that Valin, despite his commoner heritage, had no real concept of what true hunger was like, or that those failed harvests would cost real lives. Anrel might not have understood the reality himself if he had not seen some of what he had seen in Lume, and had not fought the axe-wielding thief in the Adiranes' grove.

"Why are you determined to make excuses for the man?" Valin asked, annoyed. "You claim to dislike him as much as I do, yet you constantly argue on his behalf!"

"I am striving for objectivity, as I have been trained to do," Anrel said. "You seem determined to condemn him, so when speaking with you I look for extenuating circumstances. To my cousin, who seems to see Lord Allutar through a golden haze, I am more likely to focus on his shortcomings."

"Ah, then you are determined to *disagree* with everyone, rather than to take any specific position! I hardly think that is the sort of objectivity your professors had in mind. Do you think there is no actual right or wrong here, no just assessment of the facts?"

"I do not think either you or Lady Saria has arrived at so flawless a view that I should not quibble. Lord Allutar is neither hero nor monster, but a man like the rest of us." He could not help smiling and adding, "Albeit a most aggravating one."

"And arrogant, Anrel. It is the sheer *gall* of the man that affronts me."

"And arrogant, yes. But he is the landgrave of Aulix, and likely to remain so. He is, like yourself, to be a member of the Grand Council, and as you have told me yourself, there can be no higher authority in Walasia than the council. He is a powerful sorcerer, a man of ancient and honorable family, holder of extensive lands, and rumored to be the heir to certain unique talents and bindings. His mind and will are strong, and he has the emperor's favor. His arrogance is not empty. If you truly wish to aid the people of Alzur and the rest of Aulix, then it does not serve you well to antagonize their master."

Valin stared at him for a moment before replying, "They taught you well in Lume—I cannot but acknowledge that you have a point." He shrugged. "Perhaps a majority of the council will see him as I do, and strip him of his lands and titles—but for now, you are right. I should not go out of my way to trouble him, and for your sake, for Lady Saria's sake, and for the sake of the people of Alzur, I will not, I promise you. But note, I say 'go out of my way.' I cannot hold my tongue should he commit some other enormity, nor will I."

"I would not ask it," Anrel said.

"Then we understand each other."

"And that being said, shall we go find Ziral, and see if he can find us some entertaining beverage with which to celebrate your appointment to the Grand Council?"

"An excellent idea, my dear Anrel!"

With that, the two of them headed for the kitchens, in search of the butler and his key to the wine cellar.

11

In Which Lord Valin Breaks His Promise

The following day a message arrived for Lord Dorias, saying that Lord Allutar hoped to call on him and his daughter that evening. Dorias promptly sent a reply assuring the landgrave that he would be made welcome.

He then summoned Anrel.

"Yes, Uncle?" Anrel said, as he entered Dorias's study.

"Anrel, my dear boy," Dorias said, shifting in his chair so that the leather upholstery creaked. "While I am delighted to have you here, do you not find the quiet evenings here tedious, after the excitements of Lume?"

Anrel considered this for a moment, debating whether or not he should pretend to be unaware of his uncle's purpose, and decided to save everyone some time and avoid the possibility of misunderstanding, at the cost of any pretense of civility.

"Not in the least," he said, "but I take your true intent to be to ask that I take Valin elsewhere this evening, so that he and Lord Allutar might more readily avoid each other."

Dorias blinked, then seemed to sag in his chair. "Yes," he said. "You're right. I don't know what it is with that young man; he seems to take an unnatural delight in angering the landgrave."

"I think he has appointed himself Urunar Kazien's avenger, Uncle," Anrel said. "Though why he feels that troublesome youth deserves avenging I am not entirely sure. Perhaps Valin took too much to heart Lord Blackfield's admonitions against black magic."

"Perhaps so. Trust a Quandishman to stir up trouble, eh? At any rate, I would very much prefer that Lord Allutar hear of Valin's selection as my delegate from me, rather than from Valin."

"A worthy goal, my lord uncle." He sketched a bow. "I will do what I can to keep Lord Valin entertained elsewhere."

"Thank you, Anrel." Dorias shook his head. "There are times I think it very perverse of the Father and Mother to have given Valin sorcery, and left you with none."

"I am quite content with my lot, Uncle," Anrel replied, retreating a step. "Remember what befell my parents—do you know, my very earliest memory is of stepping in their blood, and not understanding what it was? I know I then looked up and saw their bodies, and I am told I began screaming uncontrollably, but I do not recall that; I only remember feeling the sticky wetness under my shoe, and looking down to see what caused it." He shuddered. "If sorcery carries such risks, I am just as pleased to live without it."

"Oh, but!" Dorias protested. "Really, Anrel, you know better than that. You have lived with me for these, what, almost eighteen years—well, thirteen or fourteen, I suppose, if one doesn't count your time in Lume. You have seen me perform any number of wardings and bindings. You have seen Lady Saria, little more than a child, and Lord Valin, who you know to sometimes show all the sense of a sparrow, cast any number of spells without suffering any harm. You have felt the resonances when Lord Allutar works enchantments that cover the entire province. Has any of us come to any harm thereby? What happened to your dear parents was a horror—I miss your mother to this day—and yes, it was to all appearances caused by sorcery gone wrong, but it was an almost unique tragedy. Its very nature remains a mystery. You might just as well fear walking out of doors lest you be struck by lightning."

"There are those who will not walk in the rain for that very fear, Uncle," Anrel replied.

"Which is completely foolish! Can you name a single other sorcerer who has been harmed by his magic?"

Anrel knew the question was rhetorical, but could not resist answering, "Lady Arissa Taline."

"Lady . . . ?" Lord Dorias drew back his head and frowned for a moment, then shook it. "No, no, Anrel—I said by *his own* magic! Lady Arissa was murdered."

"There is still no solid proof of that."

"Every witness and divination says it must be so, though."

"Witnesses and divinations may err."

Lord Dorias hemmed and hawed briefly, then waved the matter away. "I think we cannot count her case for *either* side, then," he said. "It's of no matter. I tell you, Anrel, sorcery is a blessing."

"Uncle, why would you have me think so, when I have failed the trial given me when I was little more than half my present age? What good can it do me to wish for it?"

"Oh, none, none! I just—" Dorias stopped and frowned, as he realized the uselessness of the argument.

"Suffice it to say, Uncle, that because I remember what I do, I do not in the least regret having failed the trial. Everything you say may be true, sorcery may be the greatest gift any can inherit from the Mother and Father of us all, but no matter what reason and logic may say, there is yet a terrified child in my heart who is very glad indeed that I could not cast a ward for the Lady Examiner, nor break the binding she placed upon me."

Dorias sighed. "As you will, then. Will you keep Lord Valin elsewhere this evening?"

"I have said I will, Uncle."

"Oh, of course you did. Thank you."

"Was there anything else?"

"No, no. Thank you, that's all."

"Then I take my leave." Anrel bowed, and left the room.

It seemed as if keeping Valin out of trouble was becoming a full-time occupation, a duty that both Lord Allutar and Lord Dorias laid upon him. This was hardly a career he would have chosen, but at least he was making himself useful, after a fashion. He was beginning to wonder how Valin had ever survived the four years of his absence.

There was no point in putting off his assigned task; it was not as if he found Valin's company disagreeable. He had a good idea where he might find the young sorcerer, so he turned his footsteps toward the south terrace. As he had expected, he found Valin there, looking out across the hills from a wrought-iron chair, a glass of wine in his hand, a mostly empty bottle by his foot.

"Hello, Anrel," Valin said, glancing up.

"Hello, Valin," Anrel replied. He found another chair, and settled beside his friend. "Enjoying the weather?"

"Thinking about the future, rather," Valin said. "Imagining what will become of all this when the old hierarchies are swept away."

"I would say, *if* the old hierarchies are swept away," Anrel answered. "Even with your appointment to the Grand Council, I hardly consider it a certainty that anything significant will change."

"But it must! A system where men like Lord Allutar, ruthless killers with no thought for the lives of their people, rise to the top, cannot be permitted to stand."

"It has stood for half a millennium."

"Too long! Far, far too long!"

Anrel sighed. "You should read more history," he said. "Consider Ermetia, where the kings and lords have no magic of their own; do you think their rulers have proven any less cruel than our own, or any less ruthless?"

Valin frowned.

"Or look at the Cousins, where most titles of nobility are entirely a matter of ancestry, often unconnected to sorcerous ability. In terms of vicious stupidity, pointless wars, and brutal savagery, there has been little to choose between those noblemen who perform their own magic, and those who must hire others to do it for them."

"But those are barbarians," Valin said. "What of Quand?"

Anrel hesitated. "Though I learned the language, I read only a little Quandish history in Lume," he said. "Quandish authors seem oddly reticent about their nation's past. Perhaps they prefer to keep their internal quarrels on their own side of the Dragonlands."

"Or perhaps they have found a system that rewards character and ability, and has no room for petty tyrants."

"They're still human, Valin," Anrel said. "Most of them, at any rate—there are questions about some. Nor is their history entirely free of needless cruelty, by any means. Have you ever heard of Lord Westmoor? Or the Archmage Fimbin?"

"No," Valin admitted.

"Along the western shores, I am told, they still use Westmoor's name to frighten children. And they still haven't found all of Fimbin's bones, after better than a hundred years—a knucklebone turned up about eight years ago, completing the left hand, but half the right and several ribs are still lacking."

Valin smiled indulgently. "You always had a fondness for stories, Anrel, while I prefer to study how the world works, so that I might see how to better it. The Quandish elect their rulers, and have outlawed black magic, and to me those seem to be improvements—improvements I would like to see made here in Walasia."

"But they are not *improvements* in Quand, Valin! The Quandish have *always* chosen their Gathermen, and have *never* permitted dark sorcery. Those work for them, yes, because they are the way Quand has always been; here in Walasia, though, we have always done it *our* way."

"Perhaps, though, it is time to try theirs," Valin replied. "We are on the verge of famine, our emperor says he is bankrupt—is our situation so glorious that we really want to preserve it just as it is?"

"So you want to sweep away five hundred years of history, and make the Grand Council into a Walasian version of the Quandish Gathering?"

"Why not?" he demanded. "We might bring the empire to new heights of glory! With the unity of purpose an elected government can bring we might be able to reconquer Ermetia and the western Cousins, and finally restore the boundaries of the Old Empire."

"Unity of purpose?" Anrel blinked in astonishment. "Valin, you and Lord Allutar are both going to be on the Grand Council—do you think you have any commonality of intent?"

Valin hesitated. "I suppose we both wish to see the empire prosperous—but *he* hasn't been elected by anyone but himself."

"And the emperor."

"Yes, the emperor, true. But still, he was not chosen by popular vote."

"Neither were you. Do you think it impossible, though, that both of you might have won election, were the entire Grand Council to be chosen thus?"

Valin paused, considering that.

"I do not think an elected government must have unity of purpose at all," Anrel said. "The people of Walasia have no unity of purpose; why should their representatives? Are we no different here in Aulix from the people of Lithrayn, or Pirienna, or Agrivar?"

Valin frowned. "You may be right," he conceded. "I had been thinking that the elective process would winnow out those ideas and behaviors that disrupt our national thinking—that each representative would become a reflection of the purified will of the majority, and as such, would each share the same goals and beliefs as the population as a whole. But I see now that in practice, the system must work with human frailty, and must take regional variation into account, so the purification cannot be complete."

Anrel did not dare reply to this nonsense with more than a simple, "Yes."

"An interesting point. I shall want to hear what Derhin has to say about it."

"Have we time to ask him today?"

Startled, Valin, who had been staring off at the horizon, turned to stare at Anrel. "I hardly think so," he said. "Derhin is in Naith." He glanced at the sun. "It's too late to make the trip today."

"Is it?"

"Anrel, are you mad? Of course it is!"

"The sun is not yet at its zenith."

"But the morning coach has been gone an hour!"

"There are other ways to travel, my lord."

"Do you propose to *walk* such a distance?"

"My uncle would surely lend us horses, should we ask."

Valin looked distinctly uncomfortable. "A twelve-mile ride would be a wearisome effort to make merely to see what Derhin thinks of our discussion."

It was clear to Anrel that Valin did not want to go to Naith, and would find excuses at every turn—perhaps he had drunk enough to make the long ride awkward. Anrel abandoned that approach. "Still, it is too pleasant a day to remain here at home! Let us at least walk into Alzur—I never did get the wine and sausages you promised me when I first returned. Perhaps we can find a decent luncheon there, and in any case, it will give you an opportunity to become better acquainted with the people you are to represent in Lume."

Valin considered that for a moment, then nodded. "If it would please you, Anrel, then let us go."

"It would indeed please me."

"Then let us be off!"

An hour later the two were seated beneath the awning in the town square, giving their order to the same woman who had told them of Urunar Kazien's doom several days before. As they did, Valin glared past her at the black mourning bunting that draped the bakery's sign, and frowned deeply.

When he had proposed this outing Anrel had not considered that they would be sitting near the bakery, reminding Valin of his inability to save the late thief's life. That had clearly been an error on Anrel's part. He wished that Valin had been interested in visiting Naith, which would have avoided the issue.

He had not expected the somber draperies, either, and they certainly aggravated the situation, making it impossible to pretend everything here was as it had been before.

Another potentially troublesome matter was that this square lay directly on the most natural route from Lord Allutar's home to Lord Dorias's. If the landgrave happened to pass through while Valin was here, questions and recriminations might arise.

Since Lord Allutar was not expected at the house for several hours yet, that danger was not immediate, but Anrel had observed in Naith that Valin was capable of sitting at a table for an entire day. He would need to pry his friend away by midafternoon. He could not hope that Valin would restrain himself; after all, Valin had already been drinking for some time.

"I'll have that for you in a moment," the woman said, when Anrel had agreed with Valin's choice of beverage. She turned and hurried away.

Anrel watched her go, and therefore did not notice immediately when Valin's gaze turned hard. The young sorcerer said nothing, but stared intently past his friend.

And when Anrel's own attention returned to the table, he saw that intensity instantly; Valin was staring at the bakery with a fierceness Anrel found startling.

"What is it?" Anrel asked, turning to see what Valin saw.

The door of the bakery stood open, and a man in a cloak was in the doorway, his back to them. He wore a fine hat. Two other men stood nearby, and with a sinking sensation Anrel recognized their livery.

"How dare he?" Valin said. "How *dare* he intrude on the family's grief? Is he buying a dozen biscuits there as if he had never wronged them, as if he had not snatched their son from their arms?"

"I doubt it," Anrel said. "He would have sent a servant for that."

"Then what is he doing there?"

"I don't know," Anrel admitted.

Valin stood so abruptly that his chair fell backward; he did not seem to notice.

"Valin," Anrel said warningly.

Valin paid no attention; he marched around the table, past Anrel, and toward the bakery.

Anrel rose and grabbed his friend's sleeve. "You promised you would not trouble him."

"I promised I would not go out of my way to do so if he committed no new atrocity, but look at him, Anrel!" He gestured wildly toward the black-draped bakery. "He affronts the boy's memory by daring to set foot in a house of mourning."

"It's a *shop*, Valin, not a house," Anrel said, "and for all you know he is there to apologize, to offer his respects!"

"That would require some sense of decency, and Lord Allutar has none." He pulled his sleeve from Anrel's grasp and stalked toward the bakery.

Anrel followed, trying to think of words that might dissuade his friend, and watched in horror as the cloaked figure turned and stepped out of the bakery. It was indeed Lord Allutar, who now stood calmly watching as Lord Valin marched up to him.

"You unspeakable *monster*," Valin said without preamble, loudly enough to be heard throughout the square. Half a dozen villagers turned, startled.

"A pleasant day to you, Lord Valin," Allutar replied calmly.

"How can you barge in on them like this, when their son's body is scarcely cold?" Valin demanded.

"I understand you knew Master Kazien, Lord Valin, and so I will pardon your rudeness," Allutar said. "I came here to personally deliver my apologies, and the compensation required by law and custom; the sum was large enough that I preferred to present it myself, rather than tempt an underling."

"You think money can make up for the loss of a *human life*?" Valin shouted. "Do you think they will be *grateful* for your miserable attempt at charity?"

Allutar's mouth tightened. "No, my lord, I do not," he said. "I am quite sure that the loss of their son will affect them deeply for as long as they live, and that they will in all probability never forgive me. Nonetheless, I am required by law and my own conscience to make this payment so that at least, while they will yet inevitably suffer, that suffering will not be compounded by any risk of financial ruin." He sighed. "I could have had the entire matter attended to by my servants, or by other go-betweens, but I prefer to think myself enough of a man to run my own errands when they are as distasteful as this."

Allutar's calm seemed to infuriate Valin—a reaction Anrel understood, as he had experienced it himself on more than one occasion in the past. Oddly, this time he felt no outrage at all, a fact that troubled him—had his years in Lume hardened him? Or was it that, for once, Lord Allutar was behaving with appropriate dignity and grace?

Certainly his behavior was better than Valin's.

"You foul, heartless creature!" Valin shouted. "It is a disgrace to the empire that you are called a landgrave!"

Allutar's expression hardened. "Guard your words, my lord," he said.

"Guard my words? Oh, you would have me silence myself, and bow to your vaunted authority? I think not, Allutar Hezir! I am a delegate to the Grand Council now, as much as you are yourself, and I will see to it that all Lume knows you for the appalling beast you are!"

Allutar blinked. "What did you say?"

"I said I will denounce you before the council and the emperor; I will see your title stripped from you, your lands confiscated, your name disgraced. I will see you cast down from your high place, into the mud where you belong."

"*You* are to be on the Grand Council?" He looked past Valin at Anrel, who could only stand in horror-stricken silence, hands spread.

"My guardian has granted me that honor, yes," Valin said. "I am to represent Alzur on the council, on behalf of the burgrave."

Still looking at Anrel, Allutar demanded, "Is this true?"

"Yes, my lord," Anrel said, his heart sinking and his gorge rising.

"You call me a liar, now?" Valin demanded.

"The possibility that you are mad had not escaped me," Allutar replied. "Indeed, I had *hoped* your appointment was a mere delusion." He shook his head. "I am most disappointed in Lord Dorias."

"Disappointed that he dared make his own choice, rather than toadying to you? I remind you, Allutar, that the emperor has forbidden interference in the elections. Do not think yourself free to cozen my guardian."

"You will address me properly, young man," Allutar snapped.

" 'Lord' is a title of respect, is it not? I have no respect for you."

"I am still the landgrave of Aulix, Lord Valin, and you will address me accordingly."

"You have no right to be any sort of noble!"

A sudden stillness seemed to settle over Allutar's features, and a chill closed on Anrel's heart.

"Are you challenging my right to my position?" Allutar asked, calm once again.

"Of course I am! Haven't you heard what I've been saying?"

Allutar spoke very clearly and precisely as he said, "You are a sorcerer of the empire, challenging me to demonstrate my fitness to be landgrave of Aulix?"

Anrel's blood seemed to freeze in his veins. He recognized that formula, as Valin almost certainly did not. He wanted to call out, to warn his friend, but Valin replied before Anrel could speak.

"Yes!" he said.

Anrel's heart sank. The challenge had been made; any warning now would be useless.

Allutar turned to the two men who had accompanied him. "You have heard this?" he asked.

The two exchanged glances; then one of them nodded, and said, "Yes, my lord."

The other hesitated another moment under Allutar's intense scrutiny before finally saying, very quietly, "Yes."

"Good!" Allutar said. He turned back to Valin. "I accept the challenge. My seconds will call on you in the morning to arrange the details." He looked over Valin's shoulder. "Master Murau!"

"Wait—you what?" Valin said, baffled.

"Yes, my lord?" Anrel said, dreading what was to come.

"I am afraid that I must change my plans for this evening. Would you please inform your uncle and your lovely cousin that I will not be calling on them, after all?"

"Yes, my lord."

"Does Lord Valin have friends who can act as his seconds?"

Anrel hesitated a fraction of a second before replying, "He has me, my lord."

"More than he deserves, I think." He turned back to Valin and stared at him for a long moment—silently, as under the law he could no longer speak to him. Then he tugged at his cloak and turned away.

"Wait," Valin said.

Allutar ignored him; Anrel grabbed Valin's sleeve again. "Not another word!" he said.

The two men stood, Anrel clutching Valin's sleeve, as Allutar and his two attendants marched away, across the square and up the hill toward the landgrave's estate. When they were gone, Valin asked plaintively, "What happened? What did I do?"

Anrel stared at him. "You really don't know?"

"No," Valin said. "What did I do?"

Anrel sighed. "You challenged Lord Allutar to trial by sorcery," he said. "The winner shall be landgrave of Aulix."

"I . . . what?" Valin whirled and stared after the departing sorcerer.

Anrel did not bother to repeat himself.

"And . . . and the loser?" Valin asked, still watching Lord Allutar.

"That is up to the winner," Anrel said. "Assuming, of course, that the loser survives the trial."

12

In Which Matters Are Arranged to Resolve Lord Valin's Challenge

"This can't be happening," Lord Dorias said, his head in his hands. "It can't be!"

"I'm sorry, Magister," Valin said, eyes downcast. "I had not intended my words—"

"Anrel," Dorias interrupted, ignoring Valin, "didn't I ask you to keep Valin *away* from Lord Allutar?"

Anrel saw the look of stunned dismay that flickered across Valin's face, and considered lying—Valin might believe old Dorias was even more confused than usual—but decided there was no point in deception. "I said I would keep him occupied elsewhere this evening, yes, but evening had not come, and I had not anticipated Lord Allutar's presence in the town square."

"Do you know how long it has been since there has been a formal challenge in Aulix?"

"Thirty-eight years," Anrel replied immediately. "Lord Nerval Cherneth challenged the sitting burgrave of Paldis, a Lord Kordomir, and defeated him easily."

"How do you . . . oh, never mind. It doesn't matter." Dorias sighed. "Even if Lord Allutar chooses not to do you any permanent physical harm, Valin, and I doubt you will be so fortunate as that, do you know what this will do to your reputation? You are a sorcerer, yes, but against Lord Allutar you are a child with a stick fighting a skilled swordsman, and this trial will make you look like a complete fool. This cannot end well."

Stung, Valin began, "I am not completely without ability—"

Dorias cut him off. "I *trained* you," he said. "I know your abilities quite well. You have the talent to be a . . . a functionary, a warder perhaps, even a magistrate. But a landgrave? No." He shook his head. "It is not possible."

"Fine, then!" Valin said, flinging his head back. "I will do my best, and I will be defeated, and honor will be served."

"And for the rest of your life, people will whisper behind their hands, saying, 'There goes the fool who challenged Lord Allutar!' Do you think you have had difficulty in finding a position *now*? It will be a thousand times worse when the news gets out. And all this assumes that you *survive* this confrontation, which is by no means certain, and are not crippled. As Anrel can tell you, sorcery can kill."

Anrel's mouth tightened, and he resisted the temptation to throw his uncle's earlier words about the blessings of sorcery back in his face.

"And if I survive I will go to Lume as your delegate, Magister," Valin said, "and I will do what I can there to make a record that will make them all forget my moment of folly."

"Let us hope that you will be so fortunate!"

"Perhaps this will put paid to the quarrel between them, Uncle," Anrel said. "It may even prove a blessing in the end—the conflict will be resolved, honor satisfied, and our two houses reconciled thereby, to the benefit of"—he caught himself before implying something indelicate about Lady Saria, and concluded—"of all concerned."

"Perhaps," Dorias said, in tones of unrelieved woe that made plain his disbelief. He turned to Valin. "You will need seconds."

"I am unfamiliar with the protocol," Valin admitted.

"You will need companions who will serve as your aides," Dorias explained. "The seconds serve as go-betweens between the two principals, since they are forbidden to speak to each other, lest their words be subtle spells. The seconds also serve as judges, to ensure an honest competition, and to decide the victor should the outcome not be immediately obvious. The seconds are responsible for acknowledging defeat, should they deem their principal unable to continue."

"I have no one in Alzur I would trust to serve such a role, save Anrel and yourself," Valin said.

"Could you perhaps send to Naith for your friends there?" Anrel suggested. "I do not believe the trial need take place immediately."

"I fear that the challenged party sets the time and place," Dorias said. "If Lord Allutar chooses, the trial may be held tomorrow morning. By custom he must allow you one night to put your affairs in order, but no more than that. You must have a second in place by morning, to receive the terms."

"Magister, would you do me the honor?"

"No," Dorias said unhappily. "I cannot. As burgrave of Alzur, where the challenge was given and accepted, I must remain neutral."

Valin turned to Anrel.

Anrel turned to Dorias. "Is it not customary for the seconds to be sorcerers themselves, to prevent trickery?"

"Customary, but not required," Dorias replied. "As long as they are of good family and reputation, any may serve."

"And there *are* no sorcerers in Alzur save Allutar, Saria, Dorias, and myself," Valin said. "I do not seem to have the option of following custom."

"Lady Saria—" Anrel began, then stopped. "No, I suppose not." He could hardly expect Saria to choose sides between her father's fosterling and her own suitor.

"Write to your friends in Naith," Dorias said. "I will have Ollith deliver the letter to the College of Sorcerers there, and if Lord Allutar allows time, those friends may come to Alzur to support you. They will be made welcome in my home."

"A letter?" Valin frowned. "I cannot go myself, I suppose."

"You cannot leave my jurisdiction without Lord Allutar's permission," Dorias said. "The challenge has been made and accepted, and you are now bound by laws as old as the empire."

"A pity. I would be more persuasive in person, I am sure." He turned to Anrel again. "Will you serve as my second, then, until such time as I can find a sorcerer to aid me?"

"Of course," Anrel said, trying to conceal his misgivings. A thought struck him. "I wonder who Lord Allutar will choose as his seconds. As you observed, there are no other sorcerers in Alzur."

"I would guess his messenger is already on the road to Naith," Dorias said.

"Then let us set ours on his heels," Valin said. "I will write the letter at once." He turned and hurried from the room.

Dorias stared after him for a moment, then turned to Anrel. "He does not seem to understand the gravity of the situation," Dorias said.

"I am not sure *I* understand the gravity of the situation," Anrel admitted. "Although I have of course read about them, the only sorcerous trial I have ever seen was my own. What is likely to come of this challenge?"

"Whatever Lord Allutar pleases," Dorias said. "In truth, Valin's magic is weak, and he has never applied himself to his studies, despite my encouragements. The form of the thing is this: Each party is given time to prepare whatever wardings he may choose, using whatever devices he has brought with him, and to work whatever defensive bindings he may be able. Then, when all is agreed to be in readiness, each party is free to attack the other by any magical means whatsoever, until such time as one party shall fall, with wards broken. The assault is then to stop immediately—if the attacker does not realize at once that the wards are lost, the seconds must inform him. Any attack after the wards are known to be gone is a crime, but there is no requirement to withdraw any previous spells; there are tales of trials conducted in this manner of old where the loser suffered the most embarrassing enchantments for days afterward. Lord Abizien of Agrivar allegedly once turned a challenger into a pig, and left him in that form permanently; I don't think Lord Allutar could manage a binding of *that* complexity, but there is no question he could kill or maim Valin, should he choose to do so."

Anrel had indeed read several such accounts of challenges and trials, but he had hoped that there might have been changes to bring them more into accord with modern sensibilities. Apparently, there had not. "Valin could die."

"If Lord Allutar wishes, yes. Easily."

Anrel shuddered.

But then he reconsidered. Surely, Lord Allutar would not kill Valin.

True, he had put Urunar Kazien to death, but Valin li-Tarbek, whatever his family, was a sorcerer, not a commoner, and one who had committed no crime beyond speaking foolishly. Further, to murder a fosterling of his intended bride's father would hardly endear him to her.

No, Lord Allutar would humble Valin, not kill him. Anrel was sure of it.

At least, he tried to tell himself he was sure of it. As he lay in his bed that night, unable to sleep, he said quietly to the canopy above his bed, "All will be well. Valin will live, and learn to curb his tongue. It will be a salutary lesson for him."

He hoped he spoke the truth.

The following morning Anrel had scarcely finished dressing when he heard the thud of the big door-knocker, followed by low voices. He hurried downstairs.

Dolz, one of the footmen, had answered the knock, and was speaking with two well-dressed men in the foyer. The gaze of one of the visitors fell on Anrel, and Dolz turned.

"Master Murau!" he said. "These lords say that they must speak with Lord Valin's seconds."

"I am Lord Valin's second," Anrel said, striding into the foyer. He stopped, and bowed to the pair.

They exchanged glances, then essayed rudimentary bows in return. "*Master* Murau?" one of them asked. "You are not a sorcerer?"

"I am not," Anrel confirmed. "My parents were, but I was not fortunate enough to inherit their skills. My true name is not entered in the Great List, nor can I cast so much as a simple ward. It is my understanding, however, that in these matters the seconds are not actually *required* to be sorcerers themselves."

"Your understanding is correct, sir," the visitor acknowledged.

"Lord Valin has sent word of his situation to Naith, and hopes that other friends may attend him later, but for now, I am his only representative in this affair," Anrel said. "My name is Anrel Murau, son of Lord Beniaz Murau and Lady Gava Adirane, and I speak for the interests of Lord Valin li-Tarbek, who is the apprentice and fosterling of my uncle, Lord Dorias Adirane, burgrave of Alzur, and who is also the burgrave's designee for Alzur's appointed place on the Grand Council. May I ask who I have the honor of addressing?"

"I am Neriam Kadara, First Lord Magistrate of the Landgrave's Court in Naith," the speaker said. "My companion is Lord Lindred Palonin, chief warder of the College of Sorcerers. We represent the interests of the landgrave of Aulix, Lord Allutar Hezir, in the matter of Lord Valin's challenge to his position."

"I am at your service, my lords," Anrel said with a bow.

"It is the landgrave's desire that this matter be concluded as swiftly as possible," Lord Neriam said. "It serves no one to draw it out."

"I believe my principal feels much the same," Anrel said. Valin had said the previous night, after dispatching his letter, that he wanted the whole thing over with. "What do you propose?"

"It is necessary, of course, that the trial be held on neutral ground, and therefore it can be neither on Lord Allutar's personal estate proper nor anywhere in the demesne of the burgrave of Alzur, since the burgrave is Lord Valin's guardian. You accept this?"

"Absolutely, my lords. It is beyond question."

"Then are you familiar with a small ash grove overlooking the Raish River, roughly a mile east of the Alzur Pale?"

Anrel knew it; it was technically on Lord Allutar's lands, as the grove where he had encountered the axe-man was on Lord Dorias's, but since most of Aulix was likewise the landgrave's property, that was probably unavoidable. "I believe I know the spot. I do not think Lord Valin will make any objection to meeting there."

"At midday today, then, the contest to begin when the sun is at its zenith?"

"We will be entirely at your disposal at that time and in that place, my lords."

"And Lord Valin understands the terms of the contest?"

"While I believe he does, I would not be averse to hearing your own understanding of them, my lord, so that we may be certain there is no disagreement."

Lord Neriam nodded. "Lord Valin has given challenge, questioning Lord Allutar's right to call himself landgrave of Aulix. Under our ancient custom, as set down by the Grand Council in the founding days of the Walasian Empire, any sorcerer may so challenge the holder of any office or title higher than his own, and that challenge, once given and accepted, cannot be withdrawn—only the emperor's own direct intervention may revoke it."

"I wonder why the Grand Council chose to make such challenges irrevocable," Anrel said.

"Oh, we have their explanation," Lord Lindred said, speaking for the first time. His voice was a nasal tenor. "It was recorded and disseminated. They did not want challenges made lightly, nor did they want disputes of this nature to go unresolved, or to recur, because that might interfere with the administration of the province. The emperor's right to overrule a challenge was included so that his chosen and trusted officials could not be removed against his will."

"Yes," Lord Neriam said, with a slightly irked glance at his companion. "At any rate, challenge was made and accepted, yesterday in Alzur's town square, before witnesses, and therefore these two sorcerers must meet and test themselves against each other. There are no restrictions on what preparations they make, save that they cannot carry anything more to the trial than they can lift with one hand, and no independent entities, human or otherwise, are permitted to assist them once all parties have arrived at the agreed-upon site."

"No homunculi or demons or spirits brought along to help, then," Anrel said.

"Unless Lord Valin can conjure one on the spot, no, no homunculus or spirit would be permitted to interfere," Lindred said.

"Once the signal to begin is given, the two shall use whatever methods they please upon each other, save that neither shall physically touch the other, with hand, weapon, or tool," Neriam continued. "When one man falls the contest is ended, and the man still standing shall be declared the victor, and shall be the landgrave of Aulix thereafter."

"What would happen should both men fall?" Anrel asked.

Lindred and Neriam glanced at each other. "Most unlikely," Neriam said.

"Under the law," Lindred said, "the first to rise and demonstrate himself to be in possession of his faculties would be considered the winner. If there is any doubt, the seconds would confer to settle the matter. In the event there is no clear resolution possible even then, the incumbent remains landgrave, but the challenger may petition the emperor for further consideration."

Anrel nodded. "You will forgive me, my lords, if I trouble you with a brief summary—I am, as you noted, not a sorcerer, and therefore not familiar with matters of this sort. My friend Lord Valin is to present himself at the ash grove overlooking the river east of Alzur no later than midday today, with whatever magical preparations he can manage, and there he and Lord Allutar will contest to see whose sorcery is more potent, the victor to henceforth be landgrave of Aulix. That is the gist of it?"

"Yes, Master Murau," Neriam said.

"And is there anything else we need know? Any customs of which we might be ignorant, given that I am no sorcerer, and Lord Valin was born of commoners?"

Neriam looked at Lindred, who frowned thoughtfully.

"I cannot think of any," Lindred said.

"Very good, then; we will be at the grove by midday." He bowed.

The two lords bowed in return.

A moment later, when the footman had ushered them out, Anrel stared at the closed door and murmured, "May all our ancestors protect him."

13

In Which the Challenge Is Concluded

Although the sun was bright in the southern sky, there was a slight chill in the air, unusual for so early in the autumn. Anrel refused to allow himself to shiver, though; the other men would misinterpret it. He walked out into the grove while Lord Valin waited behind, as protocol required.

No other seconds had arrived to support Valin; if his letter had reached Naith, it had not yielded any results. Anrel and Valin had come alone.

Valin was terrified, though he was trying very hard to hide it. When Anrel had asked him if he wanted to ask for a postponement, so that another second might be found, Valin had shaken his head and said through clenched teeth, "If we delay, I fear I might faint, or flee. Let us get on with it."

Neriam and Lindred walked into the grove from the other side; beyond them Anrel could see Lord Allutar's coach, the door standing open. A coachman sat on the driver's bench, and two footmen stood close by. Anrel recognized one of them as Hollem, who had admitted him to Lord Allutar's home a few days ago.

Lord Allutar himself was not in sight. Anrel assumed he was in the carriage.

Anrel stopped at what he judged to be the center of the grove, and waited while Neriam and Lindred came up to him.

"Master Murau," Neriam said, with an exaggerated nod that was still clearly not a bow.

"Lord Neriam."

"Is your man ready, then?"

"He is. And the landgrave?"

"Quite prepared, thank you."

Anrel hesitated. "May I ask whether Lord Allutar has said anything of his intentions toward Lord Valin, in the event he is victorious?"

Lord Neriam and Lord Lindred exchanged glances. "I am afraid that it is not our place to say," Neriam replied.

"The question is entirely inappropriate," Lindred added.

Anrel nodded. "I feared as much. Then what is the next step, my lords? You will forgive me, but I am not entirely certain of the procedures."

"Of course; I would judge there hasn't been a true challenge in your lifetime." Neriam glanced at Lindred again; Lindred said nothing. "The principals must take up positions and await the signal to begin. There should be no obstructions, and everyone else must stand well clear."

Anrel nodded again. "What is the signal, and who is to give it?"

"That is for the three of us to decide. Ordinarily it would be the challenged incumbent whose seconds would give the signal, but this contest is sufficiently—" He grimaced as he groped for a word.

"Unbalanced?" Anrel suggested.

"Yes, thank you. Sufficiently unbalanced, that Lord Allutar has suggested that you should give the signal. The word 'begin' should serve nicely."

Anrel nodded. "I will raise my hand, and call out 'begin' when I drop it. Would that suit the landgrave?"

"Most excellently, sir. Thank you."

"Then let us position the participants to our mutual satisfaction."

"Excellent." Neriam nodded again. "Lord Lindred?"

Lindred raised a hand in acknowledgment, then turned and trotted back to the coach. A moment later, as Anrel began guiding Valin to his chosen spot between two large ash trees, Lord Allutar emerged.

He was wearing the full regalia of his office, which Anrel had never seen before. An ankle-length cloak of wine red velvet draped his shoulders; a peaked red hat trimmed in ermine adorned his head. This attire would have been impressive in a more appropriate setting, but here in the sun-dappled ash grove it looked bizarre, almost dreamlike, and Anrel found himself staring.

Then he remembered his role and turned his attention to Valin, who was wearing a good blue frock coat, a white ruffled shirt, and soft leather breeches. "Over here," he said. "You have your wards in place?"

"As best I know how," Valin said. His voice was not entirely steady, but he was able to speak clearly enough.

"And protective bindings?"

"I don't know any. I tried; there was one Lord Dorias taught me, tried to teach me, years ago, but I couldn't remember it—" His voice rose, then broke off.

Anrel held up a hand. "Don't let it trouble you, dear Valin." He thought, but did not say aloud, that no binding Valin could have worked would make any real difference in any case. "Come this way."

"I'm going to die, Anrel." Valin's voice was thin and unsteady.

"I sincerely hope not," Anrel replied, wishing he could say something more reassuring. He felt slightly ill, and imagined Valin's own terror was far worse.

He could not help wondering whether he had somehow contributed to this disaster. Could he not have somehow kept Valin away from Allutar? Might he have saved Urunar somehow? Would Valin have been so outraged and foolish if that stranger with the axe had been executed, instead of the baker's son?

He had done what seemed best at the time at every step, yet here they were, rendering his own judgment almost as suspect as Valin's.

Suppressing a sigh, Anrel carefully positioned Valin beneath the arching branches of two trees, very similar to the post Lord Allutar had chosen. Anrel had no conscious memories from before his parents' deaths, but he had spent his entire life in the homes of sorcerers, or at schools that taught magic alongside the history and logic he had studied, so he knew something of how magic worked. A curve overhead would have some very slight protective value, and the trees themselves were a link to the Mother's good earth; being centered between two trees would help keep Valin's energies in balance.

"Stand ready," Anrel said.

Valin nodded, and raised his hands in a warding. He spoke a word of the old Imperial tongue, and Anrel felt the air ripple.

That was good; Valin had *some* power at his command, anyway.

Anrel turned, and saw Lord Allutar standing in his chosen spot. His hands were not in a ward, but spread wide, palms up, ready to draw power from the sky above.

That was *not* good. If Allutar only meant to break Valin's wards, he would have no need to draw down energy—surely, the landgrave knew how badly he outclassed his opponent.

But there was no turning back now. Anrel looked to the south, up at the sun.

It was approaching its zenith.

"Are you ready, Valin?" Anrel asked.

Valin nodded, unable to speak.

Anrel stepped away, moving well clear, then turned and called, "Lord Neriam."

"The landgrave is ready, Master Murau."

"Then when I drop my hand and say 'begin,' let this unfortunate business be done."

"As you say."

Anrel marched away from Valin, away from the two ash trees, then turned and raised his right hand above his head.

Then he let it fall and shouted, "Begin!"

Valin's hands and lips began to move, though Anrel could hear no words and feel no effects; then Lord Allutar brought his outspread hands together before his face and spoke a single word, a word that Anrel could never have pronounced, could never remember, and could not imagine being represented in any human alphabet.

The air between the two sorcerers seemed to split in half; for an instant the whole world seemed to be doubled in Anrel's vision, and then a thunderclap and a rush of wind slammed him backward.

He kept his eyes on Valin, though, and saw that burst of wind or energy or raw magic, whatever it was, tear Valin's coat and shirt open, baring his chest—and then tear open the skin of his chest, as well. Blood sprayed out, and Valin crumpled, falling slowly backward from the knees.

The entire thing had taken no more than a few seconds.

Anrel screamed something, probably his friend's name, and ran to Valin, reaching him as he hit the soft ground. Blood was spilling upward in a horribly unnatural fashion, like a sort of red mist, from a gaping split in the young sorcerer's chest.

"Stop it!" Anrel shrieked as he ran. "Stop! He's down! You've won!"

Lord Allutar lowered his hands to his sides, and stood unmoving between his two ash trees. He said nothing.

Valin was gasping for breath as Anrel knelt beside him.

"Valin," Anrel said, "can you hear me? Can you heal this?"

Valin gasped wordlessly, his fingers clutching at air. The flow of blood from the wound had changed to a more natural form; a pool of rich red was filling in the tear in the flesh, covering up what Anrel realized were exposed bones.

"Help him!" Anrel said, looking up at the three sorcerers standing on the other side of the clearing. "Help him, please!"

"We are forbidden to interfere," Lindred called. "Seconds can only attend their own principal."

"Lord Allutar isn't forbidden!" Anrel cried. "Please, you've won—don't let him die! You don't need to kill him!"

Allutar stared at him for a moment, then turned and headed back toward his coach without a word.

Anrel stared a precious few seconds in disbelief, then turned back to Valin. He pulled at the torn remains of his friend's shirt, trying to stanch the bleeding. "Valin!" he called. "Bind it! He unbound your flesh—bind it back!"

"I . . . never was good at bindings . . ." Valin gasped, as he held up shaking hands, trying to form the gestures he needed.

"No, listen," Anrel said, then stopped.

He had no words that would help, even if Valin heeded them. Valin was a sorcerer, and had been trained in bindings; Anrel had failed his trial and never learned a spell. He could not guide Valin.

But he raised his own hands, curled his middle fingers in, and tried to gather power from the earth, tried to channel it. He didn't know the right words, so he spoke his own. "Close, bind, heal," he murmured. "Be one flesh again."

Anrel brought his hands down and together, trying to close up the ghastly wound with the magic he had denied for so long, the magic he had deliberately rejected when he was twelve, the magic that he had refused because of what had happened to his parents.

He could feel the power; he could sense it flowing through him—but it then spilled out aimlessly. He could not direct it, could not bind up Valin's chest, could not undo what Lord Allutar had done. Blood continued to bubble up from the wound; it had filled the entire gash from end to end and was dribbling out, running down either side of Valin's neck and trickling onto the earth, and the power Anrel summoned could not stop it.

"Cold," Valin said, his head falling back, his left hand sagging to the side.

"No, Valin!" Anrel said. "No, no, no!" He reached down and put both hands on Valin's chest, trying to press the wound closed; the pooled blood rose up and spilled to either side. Anrel tried to push magic into the gap, to bind up the flesh, but the power seemed to squirm and twist and slip away.

Valin's right hand fell; he coughed, and blood seeped from his nose and mouth.

And then the flow stopped, and Anrel realized he could no longer feel a heartbeat beneath his hands. Valin's eyes were open, but unseeing.

Anrel pulled his hands away. They were covered in blood; blood had soaked into his shirt cuffs, and one knee had Valin's blood on it, as well, where he had knelt in the spreading pool.

He looked up.

Lord Allutar's coach was still there, the door still open. Lord Neriam was standing by, watching Anrel; Lord Lindred was walking back toward the carriage.

"You could have saved him," Anrel said.

Lindred paused and looked back over his shoulder.

Anrel rose from his dead friend's side and repeated more loudly, "You could have saved him!"

"I take it Lord Valin is dead?" Neriam asked.

"You know he is!" Anrel shouted.

"Then our business here is done. Shall I have your uncle send men out to collect the remains?"

Anrel stared at him in horror, then glanced back at Valin's corpse.

He could not answer—and there was nothing more he could do to help Lord Valin. Instead he turned and marched through the center of the grove, toward the landgrave's coach.

Neriam and Lindred made no move to stop him, but the two footmen closed ranks, blocking the carriage door.

"Allutar!" Anrel cried. "Why did you *kill* him? You didn't need to do that!"

Allutar turned in his seat and looked calmly out at Anrel. "He challenged me," the landgrave said. "I was within my rights to use whatever means I chose to defeat him."

"But there was no *reason* to kill him!"

"Of course there was," Allutar retorted. "He was hounding me to no purpose, and he had made clear that he intended to *continue* hounding me, both here and in Lume. I warned you that I would not tolerate it. I asked you to restrain him. You did not—for which I do not fault you, Master Murau; I have no doubt you did your best. Lord Valin was a man of high ideals, great determination, and very little sense. The empire does not need idealistic young fools like that making impassioned speeches in the Grand Council, wasting everyone's time and giving the peasants impossible notions. Better for everyone if he's dead."

"Better for *him*?" Anrel demanded. "For me? Do you think Lady Saria and Lord Dorias will look kindly on the man who killed his fosterling?"

"Your uncle and your cousin are sensible people, Master Murau. They will recognize that your late friend brought this on himself with his populist rantings."

"Could you find no other way to silence him than to *kill* him? You didn't need to let him lie there and bleed to death!"

"You think a mere defeat would have silenced him? That he would have been sufficiently chastised if I had torn him open, and then closed the wound back up? That I should have waited until he could fetch sorcerers here to be his seconds, so that *they* might have kept him alive?" Allutar shook his head. "I think you misjudge your friend. I do not believe he would have been cowed. He always knew that his magic was weak—I think that was why he fought so hard against the system that has served us so well for so long. If I merely demonstrated that I could best him in a duel of sorcery, that would convince him of nothing; if I then healed him and left him alive, do you honestly think he would not return to preaching his nonsense? If anything, I would expect him to redouble his efforts."

"I don't . . ." Anrel hesitated.

"He was a stubborn man, and a man of strong will," Allutar said. "I don't know whether you could feel it, unskilled as you are—I suppose you could not—but right to the end he was still trying to draw power from the earth, so that he might close the wound with it. He was unable to direct it, but I could sense the flow of magic from here."

"That was . . . I—" Anrel stopped. He had assumed that he had given away his own secret, after keeping it safe for a decade, but apparently Allutar had thought *Valin* was the one failing to heal the wound.

Although it seemed utterly unimportant in comparison with Valin's death, some tiny portion of Anrel's mind realized that this was to his benefit. He would not need to explain his ability. He would not need to make up some lie about developing it late, and hope that would be accepted. No one would suspect that he had hidden his talents, such as they were, deliberately. Hiding magical ability was a crime, a serious crime. So was using that hidden skill. For anyone but an untested child or an acknowledged sorcerer to work magic, however ineptly, was witchcraft, and witchcraft carried the death penalty.

If Lord Allutar and his seconds thought that was *Valin's* magic, then Anrel need not fear being hanged as a witch, nor, if he gave lying explanations that were believed, would he have to allow himself to be made a lord and a sorcerer. He could remain the commoner he had always been, untainted by power.

"Your friend fought hard to live," Allutar said, bringing Anrel's thoughts back to Valin's death. "Harder than I expected. It's a shame that such potential was so utterly wasted."

"*You* wasted it!" Anrel said. "There was no need to kill him. If you had dropped your spell the instant he fell—"

"I did," Allutar interrupted. "No, I did not immediately lower my hands, because I thought he might manage a counter, but I did nothing after the first instant of unbinding."

"So you claim." Anrel turned. "Lord Neriam, I say that Lord Allutar failed to cease his attack as required by the rules of the challenge. Doesn't that make this a case of murder?"

Neriam sighed. "Lord Allutar did not continue his attack. I am a sorcerer myself, Master Murau, and I can assure you, the attack ceased instantly."

"He killed Lord Valin needlessly! He could have won without killing him!"

"He is the landgrave of Aulix, with the power of high and low justice. If he thought lethal power was necessary to defeat the challenge, he had the right to use it."

"The power of high and low justice over commoners, perhaps, but Lord Valin was a sorcerer . . ."

"Which means he was entitled to *high* justice, rather than low, but a landgrave is empowered for both."

"Lord Valin was to be Alzur's delegate to the Grand Council," Anrel said. "Doesn't that matter? The emperor's letter forbade interference in the selection of delegates."

"Lord Allutar did not interfere in any selection. He defended himself against a challenge. Really, Master Murau, while I understand your grief, Lord Allutar has committed no crime. You do yourself, and your friend's memory, no service with these empty accusations."

"He didn't kill Valin because of any challenge," Anrel insisted. "That was an excuse. He killed Lord Valin because Valin *annoyed* him. Because he thought Lord Valin's politics were a nuisance, perhaps dangerous!"

"Lord Valin challenged Lord Allutar's right to the office of landgrave, before witnesses," Lord Lindred said, as he stepped past Anrel and clambered into the coach. "The reason for Lord Allutar's acceptance of that challenge is irrelevant."

Anrel glared at both Allutar's seconds in turn, then turned back to the landgrave.

"You killed my friend to silence him," he said. "I swear to you, Lord Allutar, that you have not silenced him. Lord Valin's voice will be heard. His death will gain you nothing, I promise you that."

"I would advise you, Master Murau," Allutar said quietly, "to make no threats. Threatening the emperor's appointed officials can be construed as treason. I have already killed two of your friends in the last several days; I would prefer not to kill again, but I will not be threatened."

Lord Neriam climbed into the coach, blocking the door for a moment; when the way was clear and Anrel could see Lord Allutar again, he said, "Urunar Kazien was no friend of mine, and his death was no great crime, but this attempt to silence Lord Valin li-Tarbek—that was *wrong*, my lord. You will yet hear his voice."

"Only necromancers can hear the voices of the dead, Master Murau, and under the enlightened laws of the Walasian Empire, necromancy is illegal." Allutar gestured, and the coach door swung closed. "We will inform Lord Dorias where he can find his fosterling's remains. I will not insult you by wishing you a good day, Master Murau, but I assure you, I wish you no further ill."

With that, he rapped on the roof of the coach, and the driver shook out the reins. The two footmen jumped for the rear platform as the carriage began rolling.

Anrel stood and watched as the coach turned and headed back toward Alzur. He watched until it was a hundred yards away, almost out of sight among the trees.

Then he turned and walked back through the grove to sit with his friend's body until the burgrave's men arrived.

14

In Which Anrel Makes Good His Promise

For the two days leading up to Lord Valin's funeral, Anrel spent most of his time in his room. His uncle and cousin, both miserable themselves at Valin's death, scarcely noticed his absence, but so far as they were aware of his isolation they assumed he was lost in grief. They would have been astonished to see that he was instead devoting every second to reading from a variety of books, or writing draft after draft of a speech.

Anrel had promised that Valin's voice would be heard, and he intended to keep that promise. He would not be able to speak to the Grand Council, as Valin would have, but he could still see to it that *someone* heard the words Lord Allutar had sought to silence.

He judged he would probably only have one chance to speak out. Oh, he could have simply taken Valin's place in the wine-garden discussions behind Aulix Square, but that was not enough; he could not speak with conviction in such a setting, since he did not in fact believe most of the populist nonsense Valin had espoused, and such idle conversation accomplished little. Valin's words had been heard there, and had meant nothing. No, if he was to disturb Lord Allutar's calm Anrel needed to do something more, something that would draw the attention of people who would never have listened to a bunch of idealistic young fools chatting idly in a tavern.

Not all that attention would be favorable, so he would need to have his words planned out, so that he could say what he had to say quickly and then leave quickly.

He hoped that he could make his speech without being recognized, but he had to consider the possibility that that would not happen. He had to be prepared for the consequences. It might well be necessary to flee the area temporarily, rather than return immediately to his uncle's house. With that in mind he made a few preparations in addition to his speech, gathering and concealing his personal fortune, such as it was—all of it, he knew, given him by Lord Dorias; he owed his uncle debts he could never repay.

"Your voice will be heard," he muttered to himself more than once.

At the burial itself, when it came Anrel's turn to speak a few words, he stood up and said, "My friend and childhood companion was murdered by Lord Allutar so that his voice would not be heard by the people of Aulix. I want you all to know that his voice *will* be heard. I did not believe the things Valin believed; I did not share his idealism; but I will not permit those beliefs and ideals to die with my friend. To do so would be to betray him, and that I will not do. We bury the body of Lord Valin li-Tarbek today, but his words will live on."

Then he sat down. This was not the time or place to make his stand; there were no more than thirty people in attendance, most of them servants. Lord Allutar, of course, was not in attendance, as his presence could only have been considered a deliberate insult to Valin's memory.

Lord Dorias clearly found Anrel's brief speech disconcerting; Lady Saria, red-eyed and weeping, seemed baffled by it. Their own eulogies were far more traditional, extolling Valin's compassion and good humor.

Valin's parents, brother, and sisters, however, appeared to be frightened by Anrel's words, and refused to speak to him afterward. Anrel regretted that; he had only met them once or twice before, years earlier, and would have liked a chance to share their grief. He did not pretend, however, that he did not understand their reluctance; they had heard him call the landgrave of Aulix a murderer, and wanted no part of such sedition. Their son and brother was dead, but they were not, and they preferred to keep it that way.

After the service, after the li-Tarbeks had turned away, declined an invitation from Lord Dorias, and left for home, Anrel went directly to his room and shut the door, not speaking to anyone.

The following morning, immediately after breakfast, he set out for Naith. He had chosen his attire carefully, to be tasteful without being particularly distinctive—he wanted to look like a man to be taken seriously, but not one who would stand out immediately. He wore a fine brown velvet coat and fawn-colored breeches, and had replaced his customary student's cap with a broad-brimmed traveler's hat. In case he should be caught and searched he had concealed a good part of his funds by sewing coins into his coat, under the lining, each one suspended by just a few threads.

He made his way to Aulix Square, following the route Valin had shown him, and found the square just as he remembered it. He walked around the perimeter, considering it all carefully, choosing the best spot to carry out his plans.

The north end of the square was taken up by the courthouse, the center of government for the entire province, an imposing building in the simple, elegant style of the late Old Empire; legend had it that the original courthouse had been converted from a wizard's abandoned villa after the Old Empire's fall, but the structure had been expanded many times over the centuries, and Anrel doubted much remained of that ancient estate. Elaborate warding spells kept its polished stone façade clean.

The south side of the square was completely filled by the Provincial College of Sorcerers, a dark contrast to the clean, straight lines of the courthouse; the college had been built three hundred years before, in the ornate fashion of the time, and had been blackened by centuries of smoke and filth that clung to the porous gray stone and accumulated in the niches and crannies—no wards had been devoted to appearances here, though Anrel had no doubt the structure's magical protections were otherwise formidable. Twisted spires thrust up from every corner and portico, and gargoyles clung to every cornice, their carved faces glowering down at the crowds in the square.

To the west the square was bound by a row of grand houses—Anrel counted five. Most were of recent vintage, going by the architecture. Anrel considered the grand balcony on the central one thoughtfully before moving on.

The eastern side of the square was made up of shops—vintners, restaurants, a bookshop, a bakery, and half a dozen others—with two or three floors of rooms and apartments above each one. The wine garden where he had spent the day with Valin was not technically on the square itself, but just around the corner at the southern end of this row.

Down the center of Aulix Square was a line, north to south, of sculpture. At either end of this was a fountain—a round stone pool, perhaps twenty feet in diameter, with water spraying up from the center. Between the fountains stood several carved stone benches, facing east and west, and between the benches, upon sturdy marble pedestals, were statues of famous men—though in truth, Anrel did not recognize most of them.

And at the midpoint of this line, in the exact center of the square, was a broad plinth, perhaps fifteen feet square and four feet high, supporting a grand pedestal that held a statue of the First Emperor, in his robe and crown, holding up a golden sphere in his right hand, a sphere that shone so brightly with magic that the glow was dimly visible even in daylight.

Anrel considered that balcony, and the courthouse steps, and the central portico of the college, and even the arbor over the entrance of a restaurant, but in the end there really wasn't any other choice. As the midday crowds began to fill the square he threw himself atop the central plinth, then grabbed the First Emperor's leg and heaved himself up onto the great man's pedestal, where he reached up and steadied himself by holding that outstretched right arm. He tugged his hat forward to shadow his face—while it was unlikely anyone from Alzur would be here and recognize him, he had been introduced to several people in the wine garden. There was no need to make his features too visible.

"People of Aulix!" he shouted.

A few faces turned up to look at him; one or two people pointed him out to companions, and someone laughed.

"People of Aulix," Anrel repeated, "you stand at a crossroads of history!"

"Who are *you*?" someone called.

"You have an opportunity to remake your province, the empire, the *world*!" Anrel proclaimed. "It is within your grasp; you need merely reach out and take it!"

"What's he talking about?"

"Is he a sorcerer?"

"I don't understand."

"Who *are* you?"

"*Who are you?*"

Anrel looked down at his audience and decided he needed a name, but even if he were to admit his identity, who would listen to Anrel Murau, the obscure young scholar, the failed son of dead sorcerers? "Call me Alvos," he said, using a word for "speaker" from the ancient Imperial tongue. "I speak for all of you—not only for those who are here today, but for those who have died, and those yet to be born. I speak for all Walasians everywhere, throughout the empire!"

"He's mad," a woman's voice called.

"Let him talk," someone answered.

"You all know that the emperor has summoned the Grand Council," Anrel shouted. "You know he has said that half the representatives are to be chosen by the common people of the empire. But do you understand what that means?"

The crowd of upturned faces was growing; more and more of the people in the square were gathering about him, and listening to his words. Anrel thought he saw familiar features here and there, people who had listened to Valin hold forth at the wine garden.

"The first Grand Council *made* the empire!" Anrel said. "The Old Empire had fallen, the ancient wizards had vanished, and the survivors, the original Walasians, gathered in the Grand Council to create a *new* empire. It was the Grand Council that first decreed that all sorcerers and only sorcerers would be nobles of the empire. It was the Grand Council that decreed that to lessen the risk of assassinations and struggles for the throne, the emperor could *not* be a magician. It was the Grand Council that chose the First Emperor, whose image you see here behind me, and decreed that he and his family would rule. There is no higher human authority than the Grand Council. There can *be* no higher human authority than the Grand Council. The Grand Council *is* the empire." He paused dramatically, then continued, "And now, after almost six hundred years, the emperor has commanded the reinstatement of the Grand Council, and *you,* people of Aulix, are to choose members of the Grand Council. *You* are to choose the men who will determine your fate." He pointed at one face after another. "*You*, and *you*, and *you—you* will decide the fate of the empire! *You* have the power to send our arrogant spendthrift empress back to her Ermetian family! *You* have the power to remove the wastrel emperor from his throne and set another in his place! *You* have the power to dismiss Lord Allutar and name a new landgrave of Aulix—or to do away with sorcerers and landgraves and provinces altogether! It is for *you* to decide! I am not telling you what the Grand Council should do, because that is not for me to say—I have no more right to direct it than *you* do, each and every one of you! Do you understand that? *Do you?*"

A few voices called out something that might have been agreement.

"That part is simple enough—you don't know who I am, and I'm just another citizen," Anrel continued. "But here's the part you may not have grasped yet. *Lord Allutar* has no more right to direct the Grand Council than you do! The burgrave of Naith has no more right than you do!" He pointed first at the courthouse, and then at the college. "The Lords Magistrate, the entire College of Sorcerers—*they* have no more say than any of *you* once the Grand Council convenes in Lume, unless—" He paused again, looking out over the crowd.

Hundreds of faces were turned up toward him now; hundreds of voices were hushed in anticipation. Anrel glanced toward the courthouse, and as he had expected, there were men in the uniform of the city watch conferring on the courthouse steps. He might not have much time left to speak.

He turned his attention back to the crowd below him. "*Unless you give it to them!*" he shouted. "That's right, all power in the empire comes from *you*, but the sorcerers will be only happy to take it from you if you let them. You must choose *your own* delegates! Don't let Lord Allutar handpick his own lackeys as your representatives—choose *your own* men, men of goodwill and stout heart, men who will stand up for the rights of every citizen of the empire, whether he has a true name and wears silks and velvets, or scarcely knows his own father and goes barefoot in rags! All of us have rights, *all* of us! We are *all* the heirs of the Father and the Mother; we are all the heirs of the Old Empire. The empire belongs to *all* of us, from the mightiest lord to the poorest beggar. Our ancestors gave the sorcerers their privileges so that they would use their magic to help the empire thrive, but have they *earned* those privileges of late? Has *your* family been thriving? Has their sorcery helped *you*, or are you worried about what your children will eat this winter? Have the sorcerers earned our loyalty? Do we still *need* their magic? Do they use it for the good of the empire, or for their *own* ends? Perhaps it's time for the Grand Council to take those privileges back!" He gestured broadly, but then drew his arm back to his chest, his hand in a fist. "Or perhaps not. Perhaps we do still want the sorcerers to tell us what to do. It's not for *me* to say. But I do say that *you* must choose delegates who will have the courage, the *audacity*, to do whatever is right, to think the unthinkable, to consider *every* option, and to do *whatever it takes* to make the empire flourish and see that every belly is filled, regardless of who they may need to defy, what power they may need to cast down, to see that it's done!"

"And who would *that* be?" someone called from the crowd. "You?"

"Me?" Anrel laughed. "*Me?* No, I am only a speaker, I am merely Alvos—I don't have the integrity, the courage, the learning to represent you on the Grand Council. No, you must choose men who have studied the issues, men who know and understand the ways of the world, men with the vision to see what the empire can become. Men like Derhin li-Parsil or Amanir tel-Kabanim." His smile vanished as he said, "A few days ago, my friends, I might have named Lord Valin li-Tarbek; indeed, Lord Dorias, the burgrave of Alzur, *had* named Lord Valin as Alzur's appointed delegate. Lord Allutar was not happy with that choice, and four days ago he *killed* Lord Valin, so that his voice would not be heard in Lume. He silenced one of the finest voices in this province so that he might substitute a man more to his liking. I implore you, people of Aulix, do not allow this injustice, this tyranny, to stand! Do not vote for any candidate Lord Allutar might name; vote instead for the likes of Derhin li-Parsil, for the voices that will speak up for freedom and justice and prosperity! Demand that your burgraves choose *good* men, not toadies and lickspittles!"

"That's enough of that!" someone shouted from somewhere to the north. Anrel turned.

Lord Neriam was walking across the square, with a line of a dozen of the city's watchmen moving ahead of him, pressing the crowd back.

And what's more, it was obvious from the magistrate's expression that he had recognized Anrel.

So much for any hope of anonymity. Anrel had gambled, and he had lost. How seriously his crime would be taken remained to be seen, but he was now a known criminal.

"Lord Allutar's lackeys are coming to silence me," Anrel called. "In a moment I'll be gone—but remember what I've told you! Remember, the Grand Council is yours! It represents *you*, the people of the empire! Not the sorcerers or the emperor or any mere *part* of the empire, but *all* of you! Don't let them tell you otherwise! Don't let them choose *for* you! It's *yours*!"

"Get down from there!" one of the watchmen bellowed.

"Why should he?" someone in the crowd shouted back.

"Let him speak!"

Anrel had no intention of speaking any further, though—he had done what he set out to do, and it was time to get down and see if he could get away unscathed. What would become of him he did not know, but staying here could only mean disaster. Still, he hesitated, watching to see what would happen. Would the watchmen try to force their way into the crowd? There were twelve of them, with Lord Neriam's sorcery supporting them, against several hundred citizens of every age, sex, and condition.

"Step aside!"

Then someone shoved one of the watchmen, and a truncheon swung, aimed at a bare head but striking only a shoulder. Blades appeared—and to Anrel's surprise, not only in the watchmen's hands.

"Alvos! This way!" someone called up to him.

He turned to see a woman beckoning to him. He took one final glance at the line of watchmen—now not so much a line as a huddle—and the mob that was encircling them, and then jumped down from his place on the First Emperor's foot, to the plinth and then to the surrounding pavement, where several hands quickly grasped his own hands, arms, and coat. He found himself being hustled away by a score of people who seemed to know what they were doing. He put up no resistance, but let himself be led away.

Before he was able to see clearly where he was, he had been pushed through a door, which had then slammed shut behind him; he was in a narrow corridor, and a woman in a red bonnet and white blouse was pulling him toward a stairway leading up.

"Hurry," she said. "The watchmen may have been too busy to see where you went, but their spies will know."

"Where is this?" Anrel asked.

"It's a way out, nothing more," she said. "Up here, then across, and out through the back garden."

Anrel glanced back at the closed door. He could hear shouting, but could make out no words.

"Hurry!" the woman repeated, and Anrel yielded, rushing up the stairs.

They climbed three flights in all, then ran through an empty room and out through a tall casement onto a narrow balcony. At the woman's urging Anrel leapt from it to an adjoining balcony, one building north; there he found an open window leading back inside, and made his way back down to ground level, where an unlocked door let him out into a surprisingly large and well-kept garden. A brick walkway led him to the back gate, where he lifted the latch and slipped out into a quiet alleyway.

The shouting from Aulix Square had not abated with his escape. Indeed, it had escalated to screaming, and as he stood by the garden gate he heard the unmistakable sound of shattering glass.

It would seem he had started something a little more violent than he had intended. He had thought the crowd of listeners would disperse when the watchmen arrived, and the entire affair would be a minor incident, but from the sound it seemed he had started a riot, with the crowds fighting the watchmen vigorously. He tried to decide whether he regretted that, and concluded that he probably did not. This would make his appearance that much more memorable; his words, his attempt to sum up Valin's most important political position in a single brief speech, were more likely to be remembered and spread this way.

Of course, it might also mean that the authorities would take it that much more seriously, making his own escape more difficult, but those mysterious people who had rushed him out of Aulix Square had given him a good start.

He wondered who they were. Had they improvised their actions on the spot, or were they an organization of some sort, prepared for such eventualities as slipping a man out of the square mere yards ahead of the city watch?

He might never know, and it didn't really matter. He had done his part, made good on his promise, and he was done with politics. It was time to leave.

He turned and trotted down the alley, looking for a way out of Naith.

15

In Which Anrel's Departure Proves Difficult

Anrel was not entirely surprised, upon reaching the city's northeastern gate, to discover that the portcullis had been lowered, and the guards were questioning all travelers before allowing them in or out through the narrow postern. Had his little speech gone as he had expected, and resulted in little more than gossip and a few shouted insults, Anrel doubted that anyone would have bothered with such measures. Since he had apparently started a good-sized riot, though, the magistrates were taking matters more seriously.

This did complicate his situation. If he tried to walk out, even giving a false name and fabricated background, they would almost certainly see that he matched the description of the rabble-rousing speaker—brown velvet coat, fawn breeches, broad-brimmed hat. He needed to change his appearance, or find another way out.

Discarding his hat would be simple enough, though he hated to lose it—it was a good hat. The coat and breeches would be more difficult to disguise; a man without a coat would stand out even more than one in brown velvet.

Better, then, if he could find another way out of the town.

That woman who had shown him the back way out of Aulix Square—might she know a way out of Naith? Or might someone be able to provide him with a change of clothing?

In Lume he would have known where to go; there was a row of

shops in the Catseye district, just outside the Pensioners' Quarter, where the merchants were known for their discretion. They would sell the same item, whether a frock coat or a letter of introduction or a sound dagger, for either of two prices—a low one for those who could afford nothing more, or a much higher one that would come with the certainty that they would tell neither the city watch nor the Emperor's Watch anything, should they be questioned. While these businesses dealt primarily with Lume's more unsavory inhabitants, students sometimes had reason to shop there, as well, and Anrel had on occasion seen one nobleman or another, usually wrapped in a cloak and with his hat pulled down, hurrying along that block.

Anrel supposed that Naith must have something similar, but he had no idea where it might be.

One of the guards at the gate was looking at him, and Anrel realized he had been standing in the same place, staring at the postern, for a minute or so. He waved, and turned away.

He was a good half mile from Aulix Square, but he could still hear the shouting of many voices—the disturbance was continuing, and had perhaps even spread. He had not anticipated that. He had expected a few people to argue with the watchmen, perhaps, but no more. He had thought anyone who took his words seriously would digest them, then go peaceably about their business until the election.

A full-fledged riot had come as a complete surprise.

As the noise continued, he found it more distressing. Yes, he wanted his words—or Valin's words—to be remembered, but if this went on people would be hurt, property destroyed, to no purpose. He did not want that.

He was not sure what he *did* want. He did not really think that the empire would be improved if the sorcerers lost their exclusive hold on power; the injustices and abuses of authority came about because the rulers were human, not because they were sorcerers. He had made his speech to give voice to his dead friend's beliefs, not his own. He did not really care who was elected or appointed to the Grand Council, or what they might do once the council met, but Valin had cared, or at least had claimed to.

Lord Allutar had cared enough to silence Valin permanently. Anrel had done his best to ensure that did the landgrave no good, and in so doing had, beyond any reasonable doubt, branded himself a criminal. Despite the false name he had used, he knew he had not gone unrecognized. Even if Lord Neriam had somehow failed to identify him, which seemed vanishingly unlikely, or if the magistrate took a blow to the head in the rioting that knocked Anrel's name from his lips, many of Valin's friends had seen Anrel and heard that name in the wine garden a few days before, and many of them had undoubtedly been in the square today, listening to Alvos.

He had expected that when he planned his little adventure, of course. He had thought they might keep the information to themselves, out of sympathy to Valin's cause, but that was when he assumed he was just someone making a foolish speech. Now that he was the instigator of a riot, a preacher of sedition, it seemed likely that someone would inform the authorities of his actual identity.

Until he knew more of what was being said and done he did not dare go home to Alzur, nor could he stay in Naith. He had to get out of the city somehow, and then get well away as quickly as he could—probably out of the province. Lord Allutar could not very well pursue him into Kerdery or Demerren. If he could remain free for a few days, until the initial excitement had passed, he thought he would be able to manage a quiet return to his uncle's home, but first he had to survive those few days.

Now that he took a moment to think, he knew where he should go. His most sensible destination was Lume. It was the only place in the empire he knew well enough to hide in effectively, and in that seething mass of humanity, who would notice one more face? He could presume upon the hospitality of some of his friends in the student courts and write Lord Dorias a letter to let his uncle know he was well. If he could find some way to receive a message, Uncle Dorias could tell him when it was safe to go home.

Or it might not be necessary to go so far as Lume; perhaps a few miles up the road he might find a refuge that would shelter him until the furor subsided. He could stop at an inn, and talk to a few travelers;

he had more than enough money in his purse to cover his expenses for several days. If Naith calmed quickly he could return without going all the way to Lume.

But first he had to get out of Naith. Trying to hide here, where he knew only a handful of people and none of them well, was foolish. He had no idea how thorough the city watch might be in trying to find the man who had incited the riots, but their efforts might well be more thorough than he could elude.

Getting out of the city undetected, however, presented a challenge. None of the five gates was likely to serve—if this one was closed and guarded, they presumably all were. Still, while Naith was a big enough town to have a real city wall, unlike Alzur's symbolic iron pale, that wall was relatively small, nothing like the massive and magnificent ramparts surrounding Lume. Anrel thought there should be some way out of the city other than through the gates.

The obvious possibility was the canal. Naith was built on hills, not on a river, but there was a barge canal two or three miles long that stepped its way down the hillside and linked the city to the Raish River, near where the Raish flowed into the Galdin. Anrel had only seen the canal from a distance, but he knew it existed, and that barges unloaded inside the city walls. That meant there had to be a way for those barges to pass in and out.

He took a moment to orient himself, estimating where the confluence of the Raish and Galdin would be, and where the canal would presumably be. Then he turned and began making his way in that direction, wishing he knew the winding streets better.

Half an hour later he stood on the canal wall below the city ramparts, looking down at the water gate. Dodging watchmen had delayed him, and he had made a few wrong turns, but he had eventually found it.

The gate was well below street level; there were three locks, each with its elaborate framework of doors and spillways, one after another, between the basin where barges unloaded and the city wall. Altogether the three locks dropped barges a good thirty feet, perhaps more, below the surrounding surface; the water gate through which the canal passed was not really a gate so much as a tunnel through the city wall. This steep descent was necessary because the city stood well above the surrounding terrain; while the walls were perhaps fifteen or twenty feet high on the inside, the exterior of this portion was a sheer drop of at least fifty. That height required a thick, solid structure to support it, and a barrier that thick required a tunnel.

There was no way Anrel could see to climb down to the tunnel, nor was there any towpath to walk on. He supposed one might dive into the canal, and then swim out—if one knew how to make so long a dive safely, and could swim well enough, which Anrel did not and could not. He could swim after a fashion, but making his way through that tunnel, especially fully dressed, was not something he cared to attempt.

But if he could get onto a barge . . .

The hard part would be getting a barge crew to cooperate. He knew a sorcerer could have compelled obedience with a simple spell, and even made the bargemen forget afterward that he had ever been there, but Anrel was no sorcerer. His unsuccessful attempt to save Valin's life had been the first time he had tried to use magic since he had failed the trial when he was twelve, and had shown him anew the limits of his ability. Yes, he *could* sense magic and draw the energy into himself from either earth or sky, despite the lies he had told everyone after his parents died, but he could not *use* it. He was utterly untrained, and had no idea how he might go about ensorceling anyone.

Under other circumstances he might have also worried about the fact that for any Walasian whose true name was not duly recorded on the Great List to use magic constituted the crime of witchcraft, which carried a death penalty. Having overheard some of the watchmen he avoided while looking for the canal, though, he suspected he was already facing execution for sedition should the city watch catch him, and if so, then committing witchcraft could hardly make matters worse.

He was not entirely sure just how he had come to this. He had given a speech to honor Valin's memory and frustrate his killer, and this had transformed him into a wanted criminal—and not wanted for some paltry indiscretion, but for sedition and incitement to riot.

But it had been mere words! He had done no harm to anyone. He had not even told his listeners to harm anyone. He had simply delivered aloud the same sort of idealistic nonsense Valin and his friends had spoken across their table in the wine garden.

Apparently Valin had not been the only one who took all this far too seriously.

However it had come about, it had happened, and he needed to get out of Naith, and those barges looked like his best means of egress.

Money might compel the cooperation of a barge crew, but Anrel's funds were limited. His only income, since childhood, had been the allowance Lord Dorias granted him, and while he had saved up almost a hundred guilders, and had been bright enough to bring it all with him, that was all he had, with no prospects for obtaining more. Using it to bribe a bargeman—well, it might be worth trying as a last resort.

A threat might be more effective. He frowned. He was of only average size, not a violent man, nor particularly skilled with weapons, but he was young and strong. He had a dagger in his boot, an inheritance from his father, to defend himself in an emergency; he carried nothing else in the way of arms. He was not one of the swaggering dandies of Lume who paraded through the streets with swords on their hips; he had been a mere scholar, so that even the dagger was unusual, as the more customary weapon for students at the court schools was a cosh, a little bag of lead suitable for cracking an assailant over the head. Anrel had just enough family pride to have kept his father's dagger instead.

A dagger would be better than a cosh for intimidating bargemen, but not by much. He needed a sword, or a small crossbow, or perhaps one of those newfangled hand-cannons with which the Emperor's Watch was rumored to be experimenting.

Or perhaps, he thought, he was being too pessimistic. Perhaps he could *hide* on a barge, unknown to the crew. The vessels were simple and not overlarge, but there might be spaces in among the cargo where he could conceal himself.

He turned his steps toward the basin and docks at the head of the canal, and realized as he did that he could still hear fighting, off toward the center of town. Uncomfortably, he wondered what he had done. It *couldn't* have just been his words that provoked so sustained a reaction; Naith must have been brimming with anger and sedition beforehand.

He should have guessed that, he told himself. He had seen the crowd that gathered around Lord Valin. He had heard the conversations in the wine garden. He had encountered those people with their planned escape routes out of Aulix Square, ready for his use.

For that matter, Valin's wild ideas had not come out of nowhere; in the four years that Anrel was in Lume Valin had gone from mild discontent and wistful idealism to passionate, radical populism, and it had apparently been his frequent visits to Naith that had brought about this transformation. The city must have been a tinderbox, ready to burst into flame.

And Anrel had provided the spark that set it ablaze, triggering an uprising that the city watch had not yet entirely suppressed.

It occurred to him that a good many watchmen must be employed in guarding the gates, rather than trying to put down the riot; he wondered whose decision that was, and whether it was a wise one.

Then he came within sight of the docks around the basin, and discovered that there were several watchmen here, too, keeping an eye on the activity. How many men, he wondered, were *in* Naith's city watch? Where did the burgrave find the money to pay them all? Why did he think he needed them?

No wonder the citizens of Naith felt themselves ill-used, to be taxed heavily enough to fund such a force.

Anrel did not allow himself to hesitate at the sight of uniforms; that would have drawn their attention immediately. Instead he ambled on toward the docks, where several sturdy wooden cranes were hoisting bundles out of a line of barges. He came to a bridge across the canal, just above the highest lock, and walked up onto it, then turned and leaned upon the rail.

A guardsman glanced up at him, then turned his attention back to the barges.

Anrel watched for a few minutes, taking in the situation. The head of the canal was a modest basin, about as wide as four barges side by side, and long enough for three to pull up to either side. Three sides of the basin were straight, and low enough for people to climb easily in and out of the barges, while the fourth tapered into the top lock, ending just at Anrel's feet, and was somewhat higher. The surrounding streets and lots were higher, as well. The cranes were mounted on these higher surfaces, but their arms were long enough to reach out over the basin. There were several other structures and mechanisms here, most of which Anrel did not recognize; the whole thing was a triumph of modern imperial engineering.

At the moment there were four barges in sight, two on each side of the basin, and four of the six cranes were in use, heaving the cargo up from the barges, then swinging around to deposit the bales or bundles on the surrounding pavement. Each crane seemed to have a crew of four, hauling on various ropes and levers, while each barge held anywhere from two men to half a dozen.

Eight or nine watchmen strolled around, watching the laborers but doing nothing to help. A few other people stood about, as well, talking or watching or dealing with their own business; some of these appeared to be merchants, presumably the owners of the arriving or departing cargoes.

No one paid any attention to Anrel. The guards seemed to be focused entirely on the barges, and Anrel guessed that they were there to make sure no one left the city by barge other than the legitimate crews of those barges.

One of the barges had been completely emptied now, and men were shouting orders back and forth. Anrel watched with interest as cargo began to be loaded; he had not realized that the barges carried finished goods from the town's workshops out, as well as bringing food and fuel and raw materials in. This particular barge was receiving roll after roll of fabric, presumably the products of the city's weavers. He wondered where it was bound.

He also wondered just how much room there was inside one of those big rolls. That might be his way out. The fabric seemed to have been hauled out of a warehouse just across a broad pavement from the docks. Anrel straightened up and began walking again, toward that warehouse.

No one paid him any attention at first, but when he reached the warehouse door he found a man standing guard—not a watchman, but a big man in a black broadcloth coat, holding a good-sized bludgeon. Presumably the owner of the goods being loaded on the barge was concerned about the possibility of theft.

This fellow watched Anrel approach, and nodded to him as he drew near. Anrel nodded in return, and kept walking; asking any questions would draw unwanted attention. He did glance into the warehouse as he went past, though.

There were several people in there; it wouldn't be practical to wrap himself up in one of the bolts of cloth.

He heard shouting—not the distant sound of the brawl in and around Aulix Square, but something calmer and closer at hand. He turned to see one of the barges, fully loaded, pushing off. The shouting was instructions from the tillerman to the other members of the crew, who were propelling the barge with long poles that ended in big leather pads. They pressed the pads against the walls of the canal, then pushed, driving the barge out and forward.

Anrel watched with interest. While most of the bargemen stood along the left-hand side—port, was it?—one man was waiting in the starboard bow, his pole ready to fend off when they came within reach of the far side.

His leather pad thumped against the wall, and the prow of the barge swung back to port, aiming directly into the uppermost lock. Anrel watched as it slid into place, the bargemen quickly repositioning themselves to keep the barge from bumping into the sides of the lock, or the downstream gates.

Four of the men who had been loading cargo were now up on the walls of the lock, two on each side; they leaned against the massive wooden beams that were mounted to the upstream gates, heaving them closed.

The huge wooden doors thumped together, closing the lock off from the basin; then one of the men on each side ran to the downstream end of the lock, and each of them threw his weight onto a rope, pulling up the hatches on the spillways. Water began to drain from the lock, lowering the barge. In just a moment, far faster than Anrel had expected, the barge and its crew were entirely out of sight of everyone except the four lockkeepers.

Those four, however, were watching the descent, moving slowly into position to open the downstream gates. If Anrel were to get onto a barge he would need to hide; those lockkeepers would see him if he stood there with a sword at someone's throat, and could simply refuse to open the gates.

The four of them began heaving at the second set of gates, opening it to allow the barge into the second lock. As they did one of the watchmen came strolling up onto the lock wall, peering down into the lock.

No, threats were not going to work.

"Excuse me, sir," one of the lockkeepers said. The watchman's foot was in the path of the huge lever that worked the gate on that side.

The watchman glanced at the lockkeeper and stepped aside, allowing the gate to be swung open, but it was notably out of time with its mate by then. Anrel didn't suppose it really mattered, but it seemed less *elegant* to have the doors so uncoordinated.

He heard the thump of leather on stone as the bargemen began poling their craft forward into the second lock. A moment later the lockkeepers had come around to the other side of the levers, ready to close the doors—or rather, three of them had; the watchman was in the fourth man's way, and in no hurry to move.

Anrel half expected the lockkeeper to say something rude, but he did not; his manner was deferential as he said, "Pardon me, sir." The watchman glanced at him as Anrel might glance at a rat in the gutter, then moved out of the way.

That disdainful glance gave Anrel an idea. He was accustomed to keeping company with the nobility, to whom watchmen were just another category of servant, or with students, for whom watchmen were a despised nuisance. The workingmen of Naith, however, seemed to consider the city watch their betters. That automatic deference was something he could use.

Anrel turned and walked away, doing his best to look casual.

16

In Which Anrel Makes Good His Escape

No one paid any attention to Anrel as he ambled away.

It was entirely possible that these watchmen had been given a description of the treasonous Alvos, or even been told Anrel's real name, and yet had entirely failed to recognize Anrel as their target because they were looking for someone running or skulking, not a well-dressed fellow out for a stroll. After all, he had done nothing to disguise himself except to behave as if he could not possibly be their quarry.

He rounded a corner, walked up to the next street, then turned left. He made his way up that street, turned left again, and a moment later was approaching the docks once more, but from a different direction.

He paused in a doorway, where he doffed his hat and coat; then he walked onward—or rather, staggered. He stumbled, and stopped when he came within sight of the docks—and of a watchman guarding them. *One* watchman; Anrel had positioned himself carefully. He leaned against the wall of a warehouse and made a noise, a sort of retching sound. The watchman glanced over and noticed him.

Anrel beckoned.

He could see the guard hesitate.

"Officer of the watch?" Anrel called—not too loudly, as he did not want an entire crowd of them, and keeping his voice ragged, as if he had been injured.

The watchman glanced back toward the docks, then turned his attention to Anrel. He drew his sword and came trotting up the street. "Is something wrong here?" he called. Anrel was pleased to see that the man was roughly the same size and build as Anrel himself.

"That man—he took my coat and my bag," Anrel said, pointing back to the street he had just come from. He put a hand to the side of his head and winced. "He hit me with . . . with something."

"Where?" the watchman asked. "Where did this happen, and when?"

"Just now, around the corner there. He caught me off guard, the little thief."

"Show me," the watchman said, turning a wary gaze up the street.

"Around the corner." Anrel pointed again.

The guardsman trotted up to the corner and peered around the bricks as Anrel came up behind him.

"Where?" he said again.

Whereupon Anrel pulled the dagger from his boot and brought the pommel down hard on the back of the watchman's head, striking as hard as he dared. He did not want to kill the man, only to stun him.

To his surprise, the guardsman did not drop his sword, but he did stagger, somewhat dazed. Apparently, rendering a man unconscious was not as easy as the stories made it sound. Anrel hit him again, harder this time, and he went down.

Even as he delivered the blow, Anrel found himself marveling at what he was doing. He was not a violent man, and he had never thought of himself as a criminal, yet here he was, assaulting an innocent man—and not just any man, but a watchman. He had never done anything like this before.

He wished he had no reason to do it now, but it was already too late to turn back. He quickly pulled the sword from the fallen watchman's hand, then grabbed his arms and dragged him around the corner, into the mouth of a narrow alley.

The man was still conscious, though dazed, so Anrel held the dagger to his throat. "One sound out of you," he said, "and I'll slit your gullet."

The watchman said nothing; he merely blinked.

"Take off your clothes. Now," Anrel ordered.

"I don't . . ." The man's words were slurred, and he was unable to finish the sentence; Anrel hoped his blows had not done any permanent damage. He set both sword and dagger aside, and set to stripping off the watchman's uniform himself. The watchman did not resist, but sat limply as Anrel tugged at his garments.

By the time Anrel was done and dressed in the blue and white coat and breeches, the man's grogginess was passing; he was sitting up in his underclothes and looking frightened.

"Just stay quiet and I won't hurt you," Anrel said, snatching up his stolen sword and holding it at the watchman's throat. "Call out, and I'll kill you."

The watchman nodded. He remained silently cooperative as Anrel used his own belt to tie his captive's wrists behind him, and then his own fawn breeches to bind the man's ankles. Finally, he stuffed a handkerchief in the watchman's mouth.

He made sure the bindings were as secure as he could make them, and that the man was well out of sight of the main street; he did not want the watchman getting loose or being found too soon.

Then he stood and finished buttoning and belting himself into the watchman's uniform. He slid the sword back into the sheath on his stolen belt, and tucked the dagger back into his boot—the finely made weapon wasn't something a real watchman was likely to have, but he could not bring himself to leave it behind.

He had kept his own boots. The watchman's would not have fit properly; he could see that at a glance. He thought his own were similar enough to pass a casual inspection.

Once again fully dressed he stopped at that doorway to retrieve his velvet coat and traveler's hat, which he stuffed into the watchman's almost-empty rucksack. That rucksack might prove very convenient at some point, Anrel thought.

Aware that his captive might work his way free very quickly, Anrel wasted no more time. He clapped the watchman's hat on his head and marched down toward the docks, deliberately letting his sword rattle.

As he entered the square several pairs of eyes turned toward him, and he spoke before anyone else could.

"Orders from Lord Neriam," he said, as he marched toward the docks. "I'm to ride the next barge down and make sure none of the conspirators have gotten at the locks. Can't afford to have the canal out of service."

"I think we'd have seen if anyone did anything," one of the other watchmen replied.

Anrel shrugged. "I didn't give the orders. Take it up with the magistrates." He looked at the barges. "Which one's leaving next?"

For a moment no one answered; then a bargeman pointed, and Anrel strode briskly to the indicated craft. "Where can I stand?" he demanded, as he set one foot on the gunwale.

The crew of the barge all stopped what they were doing to stare at him; Anrel suppressed the urge to either run away or demand to know what they were staring at.

"I'm to ride down the canal with you," he said. "Where can I stand?"

"Over there," the tillerman replied, bemused. He gestured toward a clear space near the bow.

Anrel resisted the temptation to say thank you; it seemed out of character for his role. Instead he stepped down into the barge without another word and made his way to the spot the tillerman had indicated, where he would be out of the way of the four men with barge poles.

None of them spoke to him; they watched silently as he passed, then returned to their labors.

Anrel took up his position and stood there, looking conspicuously useless, as the crew finished loading the barge.

To every outward appearance he was calm, even bored, but in his heart Anrel was almost mad with impatience and worry—at any moment the watchman he had robbed might work his way free and come denounce Anrel as an imposter. Anrel wanted to shout at the men to hurry up, to get the barge moving, to get him out of the city, but he could not do so without giving himself away, so he forced himself to stand idle, weight on one leg, hands on his hips.

At last, though, the barge seemed to be full, yet no one made a move to push off. "What are you people waiting for?" he demanded.

"The lock's still filling," the nearest bargeman said smugly.

Anrel turned. Sure enough, the big doors were still closed, and the water beyond was still a couple of feet below the level of the basin.

"Right," Anrel said. "Carry on."

"Yes indeed, sir." The bargemen exchanged amused glances. Anrel resisted the temptation to make some ill-tempered comment; it would have been in character, but he did not want to be drawn into any conversations, as they might go in directions for which he was not prepared.

Eventually the water level on both sides of the gates equalized, and the lockkeepers heaved at the beams, forcing the valves open. The tillerman barked an order, and the bargemen lifted their poles and pushed off.

Anrel watched with feigned indifference as the barge slid through into the lock, and the doors closed behind it. Up until now, if a band of watchmen had come after him, he could have jumped overboard and made a run for it. Once the spillways were opened, though, and the barge began to descend, the jump from barge to wall grew rapidly and steadily more difficult; if his deception was detected before the barge passed under the city wall he could easily be trapped.

"What was it you wanted to see, sir?" one of the forward bargemen asked.

Anrel turned to look at him. "What concern is it of yours?"

"Well, sir, we know the canal better than you do. I thought I might be able to point things out to you."

Anrel considered that, then nodded. "Lord Neriam's secretary heard a rumor that someone was cutting a hole down into the tunnel," he said.

The bargemen exchanged glances. "You mean the passage under the city wall?"

"Yes."

"I don't see how that would be possible, sir."

Anrel allowed himself a smile. "I don't, either," he said, "but looking for signs of it is an easier way for me to earn today's pay than fighting rioters in Aulix Square."

"Rioters? Is that what all that noise was?"

Startled, Anrel asked, "You hadn't heard?"

"The lieutenant said there was trouble, but he didn't say what kind."

"Oh. Then perhaps I shouldn't, either."

"But we're on our way out of the city, sir—look, they're opening the doors to the next lock. Poles up, boys!"

For the next few minutes the bargemen were too busy maneuvering their craft safely into the next compartment to ask any more questions, or listen to any more answers. Once the doors had closed behind them, though, they turned their attention back to Anrel.

"Now, sir, what's this about rioters?" the nearest man asked. "Was it something about the grain shipments?"

"Grain? No, nothing like that," Anrel said. "Just some damned idiot making ridiculous speeches and getting everyone stirred up."

The clang of the spillway doors opening echoed from the stone walls of the lock, and Anrel looked up at the lockkeepers, standing a dozen feet above him. The sky had shrunk down to a rectangle, and as the water drained out from beneath them and the barge sank downward it contracted still further.

"Speeches?"

"About the Grand Council, I heard," Anrel said. "I don't know the details."

"You said there were conspirators?"

"Must have been," Anrel said. "*Someone* spirited our orator out of Aulix Square before he could be arrested. They say that the crowd in the square seemed organized, too, as if they had planned their actions in advance." He hoped desperately that this didn't contradict anything these people had heard earlier.

It seemed to satisfy the bargemen; they did not question him further, but merely watched the walls sliding up around them.

At last the roar of water through the spillways trailed off to nothing, and a moment later the doors ahead of the barge swung open. Four barge poles thumped against the walls of the lock, and the craft slid forward, into the third and final lock.

Anrel looked up at the lockkeepers, far above. Not much longer, and he would be safe. If his deception held until he was in the tunnel, that was all he needed.

The doors thumped shut behind them, and the lockkeepers opened the final spillways, which drained not into the lower canal, but into underground holding tanks, whence it could be pumped back up to refill the locks. Again, the barge descended.

No one seemed to have anything to say this time, though.

Finally the last pair of doors swung open, and the poles thumped on the walls, and the barge slid forward into the tunnel that led out of Naith. Anrel looked up at the lockkeepers one last time.

Someone shouted, and the lockkeepers all turned to see what was happening. Anrel guessed that his captive had finally freed himself. He started to say something to the bargemen, to urge them to greater speed, but he caught himself in time—they were through the doors, and there was no way the lockkeepers could stop the barge now. Closing the doors would merely speed them forward a little.

"Wonder what that's about?" one of the bargemen said, glancing up.

"Nothing to do with us," another replied, before Anrel could respond.

And then the barge slipped into the gloom ahead. The sky overhead vanished, taking the lockkeepers and the city watch with it, and the barge, its cargo, and the six men aboard it were surrounded by the arched stone of the tunnel. A half circle of daylight, perhaps a hundred feet away, provided most of the illumination and beckoned them onward.

17

In Which Anrel Takes to the Water

When the barge finally emerged from the tunnel into the afternoon sun the glare was almost blinding; Anrel shaded his eyes as best he could, but still had to blink and squint. The bargemen didn't seem to do much better.

One of them turned and smiled at Anrel. "I didn't see any holes, sir—did you?"

"No," Anrel admitted. "You can put me ashore . . ." Then he stopped as he looked at his surroundings.

The canal here was cut deep into the earth; the barge was being poled along between high stone walls. There was no shore, no bank, to put him on. The walls towered a good ten feet above his head.

Behind him the ramparts of Naith rose even higher, easily sixty feet from the barge's deck, and as he looked he saw heads appearing atop the wall, peering down at him.

"Fend off!" the tillerman called, and Anrel whirled around to see that another barge was heading directly toward them, on its way into Naith. He stared at it in horror, expecting a collision—surely, the canal wasn't wide enough here for the two barges to pass!

But it was. The barge poles were pulled in on one side, pushed hard on the other, and the two craft slid past each other, with less than a foot of clearance between them, and less than a foot between the gunwale and the wall of the canal.

The bargemen on the starboard side stood with their poles raised straight up, and greeted the other barge's crew as the two passed; it was clear they all knew one another.

"Hey, Orlin, still seeing that girl in Kuriel?" one man asked, and a young man on the other barge blushed bright red.

"Does she have a sister?" another man asked, and everyone laughed.

The people atop the city ramparts were shouting now, but their words were unintelligible over the laughter, the thump of barge poles on stone and wood, the echoes from the smooth stone walls. The tillerman looked up over his shoulder and muttered something Anrel could not make out.

If the words from above did manage to be heard, Anrel knew he was in trouble. He could still be trapped here, in this barge, in this canal. His hand fell to the hilt of his stolen sword.

"Those fools up there seem to be shouting at *us*," a bargeman remarked, looking up at Naith.

"Probably telling us they caught someone," Anrel said.

The bow of the barge was well clear of the other craft now, and the forward starboard bargeman had lowered his pole back to the horizontal, ready to resume pushing; the aft starboard bargeman was still waiting for the other boat's stern to be entirely clear, and the tillermen were calling their respects to each other. Anrel's hand closed on the sword.

He had taken a few lessons in swordsmanship during his years in Lume—not so much because he intended to ever use them, but merely to impress the local women. He had learned enough to know that he wasn't actually very good with a blade. His instructor had said he showed some talent, but he had never applied himself seriously to the study, preferring to devote his time to history and law, which he expected to be more valuable in finding employment.

Taking on five large, muscular opponents, four of whom held barge poles that could make very serviceable weapons, would be suicide.

Surrendering to the magistrates of Naith would be equally suicidal, though—there could be no doubt that if he was caught here and now, while memories were still fresh and fires still burning, and while still wearing his stolen uniform, he would be hanged for sedition or treason. He needed time for things to cool down.

He looked up, trying to judge the height of the walls of the canal. That height was dropping down toward the canal's level as the barge made its way out of the hillside toward the river, but it was still much too far to leap, and probably farther than he could hope to climb. The joints between stones did not seem to provide many handholds.

"Stop!" The single word, called from the ramparts, was finally understandable, where the earlier shouting was not. The other barge was well clear, and at that moment none of the poles happened to be thudding against the walls, nothing happened to be splashing, no one was speaking. The lower walls here produced fewer echoes to obscure the sound, which more than made up for the increased distance.

"Do they mean us?" one of the bargemen asked, looking up.

"He's pointing at us," another replied.

". . . not a watchman!" came the cry from above.

It took a second for the words to penetrate; then five faces turned toward Anrel. The tiller and the four poles were held motionless, leaving the craft to drift gently on the calm water of the canal.

In the sudden silence, the next shout was clear: "Hold him there!"

Anrel smiled. His sword would not save him here, but his words still might.

"It's true," he said. "I'm not a watchman. I stole this uniform I'm wearing. They were hunting for me, and the canal was the only way I could hope to escape the city, so I knocked a watchman on the head and took his clothes. I didn't kill him; I didn't hurt him any more than I had to. I tied him up, but it seems he got loose and raised the alarm."

The bargemen exchanged uncertain glances.

"Now, the five of you have a decision to make," Anrel said, pulling the sword halfway from its sheath. "You can fight me, five against one, and probably win, but I do have this sword, and I've studied swordsmanship, so I could probably hurt two or three of you before you take me down—maybe even kill one or two. It would be messy."

Again, uncertain glances, a little more worried this time.

"Or you could keep poling us along, pretend you couldn't hear, until we get to a point where I can get off the barge, off the canal, and make a run for it. If you do that, why, I've no reason to hurt anyone, and when they ask you why you let me go, you can just say you didn't know any better. Or if you think it would be more convincing, you could say I threatened you all with the sword, and demonstrated such amazing skill with a blade that you did not think your numbers would be sufficient to overcome me—I'd be happy with that, too, as it might intimidate anyone they send after me."

"And why shouldn't we just knock you off the boat with a barge pole and leave you to drown?" the tillerman asked.

"You might be able to do that," Anrel conceded. "Or I might dodge better than you think, and then, as I said, it would be messy. Still, I can see why you'd think it was worth a try. Bear with me for just a moment more, though, and let me tell you *why* they're hunting for me."

The bargemen exchanged glances. "Well, boys, should we hear him out?" the tillerman asked.

"*I* say we should," the man closest to Anrel's sword said, with a significant glance at Anrel's hand on the hilt.

"Why not?"

"As you please—I don't care."

"All right, stranger," the tillerman said. "Tell us why you're here."

"Because Lord Allutar killed a friend of mine," Anrel said. "He tore my friend's chest open with his foul sorcery. The magistrates said there was nothing I could do about it, because Lord Allutar is the landgrave of Aulix and has the right to do anything he pleases, even if it means the death of an innocent man. So I stood up on the statue of the First Emperor in Aulix Square, and I told the people of Naith the truth, and for that Lord Neriam declared me a traitor, closed the gates, and set the watch on me. I robbed no one; I harmed no one, save the man I hit over the head to get this uniform. I spoke the truth, nothing more, and for that they mean to kill me."

The bargemen did not seem entirely convinced.

"What's going on down there?" someone called from above.

"Was that what started the fighting we heard about?" one of the bargemen asked.

"The city watch came out into Aulix Square to break up the crowd, and the crowd fought back," Anrel explained. "I didn't ask them to, but it seems I'm not the only one who's had his fill of sorcerers playing their games while the ordinary people of the empire starve."

"You aren't," one bargeman muttered.

One of the others turned to the tillerman. "We aren't watchmen," he said. "Why should we do their work for them, then? I want to get this cargo down the river while there's still daylight!"

The tillerman looked at his four crewmen and saw general agreement. "All right, lads," he said. "It seems we didn't hear the shouting correctly, and thought we were supposed to deliver this fellow to the lockkeeper at number four, and how were we to guess he'd jump for it and run before we got there?"

"Right you are!" a bargeman said, as the others nodded.

"Now then, sir, which side would you like to jump for and run on?" the tillerman asked.

Anrel smiled, looked up at the sky to orient himself, concluded that he couldn't tell which way would be a better route for Lume, and then said, "I'm afraid I'm not sure which would be best, so whichever would be easier for you will suit me."

"Fair enough, sir," the tillerman said. "You just be ready, then. I suspect they have men on the way down."

"I'm sure they do," Anrel agreed. "Thank you for your concern."

"All right, lads, both sides, best speed!" the tillerman called, and all four poles swung into position. Four leather pads thumped on stone, and the barge shot forward.

Someone shouted from the ramparts, but the thumping, the rush of water, and the increasing distance rendered it unintelligible.

Moments later the walls on either side dropped down far enough that Anrel could see over them. He looked to the right, and saw figures approaching at a run across the harvested fields.

"To port, please, Master Tillerman?" he called, as he crossed to the port bow.

"Aye, sir." The boat's path began to veer to the left.

Anrel looked ahead; the walls dropped to waist-high ahead, then leveled out, to maintain a surface for the poles to push against, while the ground beyond them sank lower. The fourth of the canal's five locks, dropping it down another few feet closer to the level of the river, was perhaps two hundred yards away; he would need to be off the barge before it reached the gates. A waist-high barrier would not be insuperable if he could get close enough . . .

"Poles in to port, lads!" the tillerman called. "Get ready, sir!"

"Stop!" someone called from the right bank.

The tillerman grinned. "You heard the man, boys!" The poles began braking, rather than driving the craft forward.

That, Anrel saw, would make the jump much easier. "My thanks to all of you," he said. Then, as the boat came to a near standstill mere inches from the port side, he leapt.

He had slightly misjudged the height, the distance, and how much the barge would give beneath him; he slammed his left knee into the stone, and his boots splashed into the canal, but his upper body draped itself across the top of the wall and he was able to quickly drag himself up and over. He tumbled to the ground, landing on the black earth of a recently harvested hay field, then untangled himself and got to his feet.

The barge was gliding smoothly onward, toward lock number four; half a dozen men, most of them in the uniforms of Naith's city watch, were running toward the far side of the canal, shouting incoherently. More men were standing atop the distant city wall; if they were still shouting Anrel could not hear it from so far away.

The canal was not a true barrier; his pursuers could cross it easily at the lock. Anrel saw he had no time to waste and began running, with no destination in mind but simply trying to put more distance between himself and his foes.

He passed a line of trees on the far side of the hay field, and paused long enough to glance back and catch his breath.

His pursuers were at the lock, but had not yet crossed the canal, so far as he could see. The barge he had ridden was also at the lock, and some argument appeared to be taking place. Anrel did not stop to try to interpret that, but began running again, a little less desperately, across the next field.

Off to his right he could see a farmhouse, and a road and river beyond; to his left the hill sloped up to Naith's city walls. Ahead were more fields, more farmhouses, and a patch of woods; he headed for the trees, hoping to get out of sight.

Once he reached the grove he turned right, toward the river; he knew he had to cross the water somewhere if he was to get to Lume. He was fairly certain that this was the Raish, and that if he followed it far enough upstream he would find himself back in Alzur, which would not do at all. If he could find a way across, though, and then get to the Galdin River, he could follow that upstream all the way to the capital.

As he walked quickly through the trees he straightened his belt, made sure the sword was securely in place, then brushed dust and hay from his stolen jacket. His boots were drying quickly; they had only dabbled in the canal briefly.

He debated whether to stay in the stolen watchman's coat or change back into his own. A watchman would not ordinarily be seen outside the walls of Naith, but might be all the more intimidating because of that very fact.

On the other hand, if the word spread quickly that someone was abroad in stolen watchman's garb, there could be little question that he was that man. In a brown coat and traveler's hat he might match the description of the escaped traitor, but there would be room for doubt.

Perhaps he might contrive a compromise. He reached up and pulled the watchman's cap from his head and tossed it aside, then swung his rucksack around and fished out his broad-brimmed hat, all without stopping.

The velvet coat was more distinctive than the hat, so he left that in the pack for now, but he slid the watchman's jacket off, and drew the dagger from his boot. He had to slow his pace somewhat, but he kept walking as he first cut the epaulets from the jacket's shoulders, and then pried the white panels from the lapels, leaving blue broadcloth. He cast aside the bits he had removed.

It was still recognizably a watchman's jacket if one looked closely, but it was no longer so obvious. He pulled the garment back on, and hurried on, emerging from the woods onto the riverside road.

A farmhouse stood by the road just ahead on the left, a smaller structure on the right, between the road and the river; Anrel was mildly wary of passing between them, but saw no sensible alternative. He looked at the smaller building as he passed, then stopped in his tracks as he realized what it was.

It was a boathouse.

That was hardly surprising, really, but he had somehow not expected it. He had not been thinking clearly; the need to escape pursuit had driven much of his usual common sense from his head. Now, though, the boathouse presented an obvious opportunity. He quickly circled around until he found a door.

It was locked, but that was no real obstacle for a desperate man with a dagger and a good pair of boots; he kicked the door hard enough to loosen the lock, then used the knife to pry it open the rest of the way.

The dim, damp interior held two small boats—a flat-bottomed skiff, suitable for fishing in the shallows or gathering frogs along the bank, and a somewhat sturdier rowboat.

Anrel smiled as he sheathed his dagger; then he hurried to the rowboat. It was heavier than it looked, and he was unable to lift it, but he did manage to drag it to the edge of the boathouse floor and heave it over the side.

There were two pairs of oars resting on the tie beams overhead; he slid one set down and lowered them into the boat, then climbed in after them. A few minutes later he was rowing out onto the Raish, and discovering that working the oars was more difficult than it looked, and required the use of muscles from which he did not generally demand much. Still, he was able to keep his craft moving and under control, which was all he required. He turned the little boat's prow to starboard, heading downstream toward the confluence of the Raish and the Galdin, ignoring the few other boats in the area—most of which were barges bound to or from Naith.

He had an uncomfortable moment when a search party came hurrying along the road along the riverbank not more than a hundred yards away, but while they saw him, they did not recognize him in his traveler's hat and altered jacket.

One man did pause to stare at him, and Anrel released one oar long enough to wave cheerily. He was fairly sure they would not expect a desperate fugitive to do anything like that. They would also not expect such a fugitive to head downstream, back toward the canal mouth and Naith, rather than fleeing farther upstream, toward Alzur. It seemed unlikely that they would identify this boatman as their quarry.

Besides, even if they did realize who he was, they would need to find a boat of their own to come after him, and if he saw that happening he would pull as hard as he could for the far shore and resort to his feet once again. He wondered whether he should have disabled the skiff when he had the chance, but decided he had been right not to bother—it would have wasted time, and would have left evidence that he was not just an innocent man who happened to be on the river when the city guards were searching for an escaped traitor.

After the first party let him go by, each subsequent patrolling guardsman seemed that much less menacing, that much less likely to raise the alarm and send pursuit onto the river—after all, if the man in the rowboat was anyone suspicious, wouldn't the others upstream have stopped him?

So Anrel was able to row calmly past the canal mouth, past barges heading into Naith, and out onto the Galdin, where he turned his little boat upstream and rowed as hard as he could, trying to cover as much distance as possible while the light lasted.

18

In Which Anrel Makes the Acquaintance of Certain Travelers

Anrel had rowed for as long as he could see, well after most of the other boats on the river had anchored or put ashore, and had then made for the northern bank, where he secured his vessel to a tree, curled himself up in the bottom, and went to sleep. He awoke with the sunrise, retrieved the oars, and continued his journey up the Galdin.

He rowed as much as he could, but sometimes found it necessary to tie up and rest his arms; he deliberately chose to make these stops as far from any town as possible, instead using overhanging trees or farmers' fishing piers as his anchorage. He ignored the growing discomfort in his belly; he had not eaten since the previous midday. He did not want to risk going ashore to find food yet. Instead he rowed on.

This gave him plenty of time to think, as rowing a boat up the Galdin did not require a great deal of his attention; the motion, while vigorous, was simple and repetitive, and the river was wide enough and slow enough that traffic and current were of almost no concern.

He found himself wondering what he had done. He had risked his life to defend a man who was already dead. Nothing he had done would benefit Valin; that worthy's soul had already joined his ancestors in the afterlife, and would be judged entirely on what Valin himself had done in life, not for anything Anrel did in his behalf.

It was possible that his actions would seriously discommode Lord

Allutar, and might therefore punish him for Valin's murder, but even that seemed unlikely. Really, the more he thought about it, the more Anrel saw his speech as an empty gesture, a meaningless act that would do nothing to improve anyone's circumstances, and which had made his own situation desperate indeed. When he was planning it, and when he was speaking, he had thought of it as a tribute to Valin's memory that would create a brief stir and nothing more, but now, looking back, he realized it had been far more than that.

He had started a riot—unintentionally, but nonetheless, he *had* started a riot. He had delivered a speech that Lord Allutar and his minions would almost certainly label seditious or treasonous; the authorities in Naith had been surprisingly tolerant of young men talking rebellious nonsense in taverns, but those same words delivered from the First Emperor's statue could not be so readily ignored.

What's more, he had assaulted a watchman, stolen his uniform and sword, and commandeered a barge. Even if his speech was dismissed as meaningless, he had *assaulted a watchman.*

And he had stolen a boat.

He was a criminal; there could be no real argument. He had committed real crimes in his determination to ensure that Valin's words were heard. He had not *planned* to commit assault or theft or impersonation of a watchman; it had all just happened as he proceeded from one step to the next.

It might well take considerably more than a few days for this to blow over. He might need to pay fines, at the very least. He might need to throw himself on the notoriously skimpy mercy of the magistrates in Naith. He might need to convince his uncle to beg for his life—and even that might not be enough.

He might never be able to go home to Alzur again.

He would take shelter somewhere, he told himself—in Lume, perhaps, or some convenient town. He would use a false name, and write letters, asking friends and family for their assessment of his situation. It might not be as bad as he feared.

Or it might be even worse. Depending on just how much damage the rioting had caused, and how determined the landgrave and his magistrates were for a scapegoat, he might even now be the subject of a manhunt, with a death warrant sworn out against him by Lord Neriam.

He might well have thrown away his entire life in his attempt to make Lord Allutar regret Valin's death.

Logically, he should not have done it. It had been a foolish, romantic, impulsive thing to do.

And he knew that given a chance, he would almost certainly do it again. Anything less would have been a surrender to the appalling Lord Allutar, and a disgrace to Valin's memory, a betrayal of their long friendship. Allutar had killed Valin to silence him; therefore, justice had required that Valin's voice be heard.

Alas, that it had fallen to Anrel to speak with that voice, saying words he did not believe and sacrificing his own well-being in the process. If there had been some other way to avenge Valin—well, Anrel had been unable to think of one. He was no assassin, to take Allutar's life in revenge, nor a thief to take anything else in compensation—or at least, he told himself, looking down at the boat, until yesterday he had not been a thief.

But he had learned to speak persuasively in the court schools, and had done his best with the skills he had.

Now his greatest regret was that he did not have greater skill with a pair of oars.

He shrugged. If he had indeed thrown away his old life, he would need to make himself a new one—but he still had hopes of salvaging something from the old, if he could find refuge in his familiar haunts in Lume and somehow make contact with his uncle.

By midday of that second day on the water, though, Anrel knew he could not possibly row all the way to Lume. He had covered only a few miles, but his arms were losing their strength; he needed food and water and rest. He had nothing to eat, and his only water source was the river itself; every so often he strained a little water through a handkerchief into his hand, removing the worst of the contaminants, and drank the result, but that was not really satisfactory. He had hoped the boat's rightful owner might have left a few supplies hidden somewhere aboard the craft, but a careful search had found nothing; the boat had been completely empty when he stole it. There was no water, no preserved food, no fishing gear.

What's more, people on docks and other boats seemed to be taking altogether too much interest in him; some appeared to be referring to papers of some sort, so Anrel guessed that his description was being circulated.

Since no one pointed and shouted, and no boats came rowing out after him, he suspected it wasn't a very *good* description. Still, he thought that putting ashore anywhere densely populated would be unwise.

Staying on the river indefinitely was not possible—he did need food and rest. And he did not think sleeping in the boat again would be safe; he had managed it without incident the first night, but he could not rely on doing so again. He might well wake up to find himself looking up at guardsmen holding one of those papers.

Because of the stares and papers, he intended to go ashore somewhere more or less uninhabited. That proved surprisingly difficult; the banks of the Galdin seemed to hold an amazing number of villages. He was scarcely ever out of sight of a town, and when he was, the river's shores were still lined with farmers' fields that would provide no cover, and which had mostly already been harvested, which meant they would do little to feed him.

Finally, though, when the sun was low in the west, a cluster of trees appeared on the bank ahead, and Anrel steered for this promising destination.

Much of that promise faded when he got close enough to see why no farm or village occupied this spot, though; the ground, what there was of it, appeared to be black muck. Still, it was somewhere he could go ashore unseen, even if it meant wading through mud and perhaps ruining his boots.

He ran his boat as far aground as he could, digging the oar blades into the muddy river bottom to gain the last few feet; then he clambered overboard, and after some awkward splashing and floundering managed to find solid footing on half-buried tree roots under knee-deep water. He was able to work his way up out of the water, pulling the boat after him. In fact, he contrived to heave the boat out of the water entirely, and drag it behind two trees that were growing close together. He stowed the oars carefully, then turned his steps inland, intent on finding food. Perhaps a few nuts, even some low-hanging fruit . . .

Unfortunately, the grove he had landed in was comprised mostly of ash and willow. Exposed willow roots provided decent footing, so the black mud was less trouble than he had anticipated, but these trees produced nothing edible.

The sun was down now, and shadows were gathering; reluctantly, Anrel concluded that he would need to find other people if he was to obtain any supper. He had deliberately chosen his landing to be as far away from any villages or farms as possible, but he knew that was not actually very far. If he could find his way out to a road he could claim to be an ordinary traveler. He had plenty of money for a room and meal at an inn.

Explaining how he came to be wearing a watchman's sword might be a little difficult. He looked down at the weapon, trying to decide whether it was distinctively a *watchman's* sword, and did not reach a firm conclusion. He told himself that he would abandon the sword if necessary, but hoped it would not come to that—a weapon might be useful.

Even when he had moved out of sight of the water he could orient himself easily by the sunset's glow reflecting from the river; that golden light still filtered through the trees, and guided him as he trudged up the bank at an angle, still moving upstream.

He saw a light ahead, barely visible in the fading daylight, that was not the sunset, and headed toward it, guessing it to be a farmhouse—perhaps daylight reflecting from a glass window, or a lantern hung by a door.

Fairly quickly, though, as the sky dimmed and he drew nearer, he realized that he was seeing the light of a fire, and one that was nearer than he had initially believed. That, he thought, was worth a closer look, at any rate. He approached cautiously, trying not to step on anything that would rustle, or that might cling and make noise when he pulled his foot free. He had just gotten to a point where he could see the fire, at least two or three figures seated around it, and what appeared to be a wagon of some sort, when he felt the ward.

Anrel was not a sorcerer, but he had grown up among sorcerers, and despite years of denial he had some innate magical talent himself; he knew a warding spell when he sensed one, and he had very definitely encountered a ward—a weak one, badly done, sufficient only to alert its creator to an intruder's presence, not a real defense at all, but nonetheless, a ward.

He stopped dead in his tracks, holding his breath, not daring to move, as he tried to think what it could mean. What would a sorcerer be doing out here, in a marshy riverside grove at sunset?

Or had the wards been set some time ago, perhaps? Was this merely a boundary marker, an indication of the edge of some nobleman's property?

But if so, why were those people camping *inside* it?

And why were they sitting so very still? From the instant he first felt the touch of magic, they had frozen in place, motionless as statues—much as he was himself.

Then one of them rose, and turned to look directly at him—a woman, though he could not make out her features in the shadows, with the firelight behind her. "Who's there?" she called quietly.

There was no point in pretending further; he raised his hands to show himself unarmed, and began walking again, no longer concerned with disturbing fallen leaves. "Just a traveler," he answered.

"Come where we can see you," she said, peering in his direction.

Annoyed with himself, Anrel realized that he was still deep in the shadows of the grove, and in all likelihood she could not actually see him at all; he could probably have slipped away safely if he had tried.

It was too late now, though. "I'm coming," he said.

Now the other figures around the fire were getting to their feet as well, and turning to watch him. There were more of them than he had thought. One was a big man—tall, broad in the shoulders, and obviously not a man who missed many meals, though Anrel judged him to have as much muscle as fat on his generous frame. He wore a battered hat not unlike Anrel's own in design, but showing every sign of long, hard use.

The others all seemed to be women—four in all, counting the one who had first addressed him, all of them wearing simple country dresses.

None of the five appeared to be especially well attired, which was puzzling; which of them was the sorcerer who had placed the wards? Perhaps the man was some eccentric noble who had decided to try roughing it for a few days, and had brought along a few of his maids to help him.

The wagon, though, was not by any stretch of the imagination a nobleman's coach; it was little more than a rather battered box on wheels, with a canvas cover stretched across an arched frame over the top. A lone horse stood a few yards away, almost invisible in the twilight and apparently asleep. Surely, even the most eccentric sorcerer would not have trusted himself and four others to a single draft horse?

"Who are you?" the big man demanded.

"My name is . . . is Dyssan," Anrel said, remembering at the last instant to give a name that he could be reasonably sure was not that of a known fugitive. "Dyssan Adirane." He emerged into the light of the fire, hands still raised.

There was a pot on the fire, he saw, and he could smell something cooking. His mouth watered.

The big man glanced at one of the women, then back at Anrel. "What do you want here?" he asked.

"To dry my boots by your fire, if I may," Anrel said.

"You're wearing a sword."

"Indeed I am. Despite the landgrave's best efforts, brigands are not unknown in Aulix," Anrel replied dryly.

Something brushed against him then, something intangible, something he could not name and could not explain. He started, but kept his hands up.

Two of the women exchanged startled glances.

The big man turned and asked, "Well, ladies? What do you think?"

"Let him come," one of them said.

"I don't think we could stop him," another added.

"Oh?" The man gave Anrel a wary glance.

"He's a sorcerer," she explained.

The big man turned and studied Anrel, taking in the torn fabric on his shoulders and lapels and the mud on his boots, but also the quality of the leather beneath the mud. "A sorcerer? Then by all means, my lord, feel free to join us."

"Thank you," Anrel said, lowering his hands and advancing further into the firelight. He was unsure what to say about being called a sorcerer and addressed as "my lord." Instead, he asked, "Whose company do I have the pleasure of joining?"

"Just a family of travelers, like yourself," the man replied. He gestured at the nearest woman, then at the others. "This is my wife, and these are my daughters."

Anrel took note of the lack of names. "I am delighted to make your acquaintance," he said with a bow, doffing his hat. "Pray, do not stand on my account."

"You heard him, girls," the man said. "Sit down."

Slowly, the four women resumed their places around the fire; the man stepped aside and gestured for Anrel to take his own spot, while he moved farther around to one side.

"Would you care to share our supper, my lord?" one of the women asked. Anrel was now able to see their faces, and he judged her to be the oldest of the daughters—a young woman perhaps his own age. She was, he was fairly certain, the one who had called him a sorcerer.

"I would," he said. "I regret that I have no food nor drink of my own to offer in return, but perhaps I can make recompense in some other fashion."

"No need, my lord," the big man assured him.

Anrel hesitated, then asked, "Forgive me, but why do you call me a sorcerer?"

The man turned to look at his wife; she and the eldest daughter exchanged looks of surprise.

"Because you *are* a sorcerer," the daughter said.

"What makes you think so?"

"You felt the wards! And the binding I tried to use!" As the girl spoke her mother was desperately gesturing for silence, but her attention was fixed on Anrel, and she did not see this attempt at parental guidance.

Anrel looked at her without speaking for a long moment as he considered what this meant.

This woman had used magic, but she did not appear to be a sorceress. She was traveling with her parents and sisters, but no attendants, and her attire was plain and of no more than middling quality. This was hardly the behavior of a noblewoman, nor would a noblewoman's family have declined to give names.

Although he had never before met any, Anrel had of course heard of people who used magic illicitly—people who, for one reason or another, had not faced the trials, and had not had their true names inscribed in the Great List. They had not been acknowledged as magicians, had not been trained in sorcery, and had not been given the rank of lord or lady.

They were called witches, and in the Walasian Empire the penalty for witchcraft was death by hanging.

From what he had been told in the court schools, witches were tolerated in Quand and Ermetia, and in the Cousins their fate might depend on the whim of the local lord, but in Walasia they were condemned to the noose. The empire did not allow its people any magic outside the established aristocracy. Historically, Anrel had read during his studies in Lume, magic had been rare and precious, and vital to the nation's survival. Withholding it from the public had therefore become a crime.

Anrel had wondered why anyone else would refuse an opportunity to become a noble, and as a child he had sometimes even doubted that witches really existed, yet here was at least one—and of course, he realized, he himself might be considered a witch. He had taken the trials when he was twelve, but had failed them deliberately, and his true name had not been sent to the scribes in Lume. It had never occurred to him that anyone else might have done that, but perhaps it was more common than he had suspected.

He turned to the girl's mother, who was sitting motionless, holding her breath, waiting to see what the sorcerer who now held her daughter's life in his hands would say.

"You need have no fear, mistress," Anrel said. "Yes, I see that your daughter is a witch, but she is wrong in calling me a sorcerer. I am no sorcerer." He paused, and took a deep breath, then said, "It seems I am a witch, as well."

19

In Which the Travelers Come to Certain Understandings

For a long moment no one spoke; then at last the father said, "Well, this is an interesting situation. Then you are not Lord Dyssan, but Master Adirane?"

"Master Murau, actually," Anrel said. "I borrowed my uncle's name a moment ago, but I think I have no further need of it."

"And why would you do that? Why give a false name?"

"Have I not just said that I am a witch? Does that not make me an outlaw by definition? Would you really expect an outlaw to give his correct name when asked?"

"Then why do you claim to give it now?"

"Because now, sir, I know that you dare not deliver me to the authorities, since I would then denounce your daughter as a witch—and I suspect, from the looks they exchanged, that your wife is not unacquainted with the arcane arts, as well. Better that we should trust one another, as we are now in a position to give the hangman a few necks upon which to practice his art if that trust is betrayed."

"There is some logic to your words," the big man reluctantly admitted. He frowned. "What would you have of us, then, Master Witch?"

"For the moment, I would be content with some of that stew I smell," Anrel replied, gesturing toward the pot on the fire. "There will be time to discuss our situation further once we have all eaten; I find negotiations always seem to go better on a full belly."

The big man's frown faded. "Hungry, are you? Well, even if I did sire a witch, I am not so lost to common decency to refuse a hungry man some common hospitality. Tazia, serve us out a bowl apiece, won't you?"

One of the other daughters fetched wooden bowls and a ladle from a box nearby, and began scooping stew from the pot into the bowls, glancing occasionally at their guest. The youngest daughter then distributed the bowls. Anrel watched with interest, and eagerly accepted the bowl she proffered him. He was aware that there were still several important questions that should be asked and answered, but the yawning emptiness in his belly took priority.

"Thank you," he said, as he set the bowl of stew on his lap. He then realized he had not been provided with a spoon; he hesitated only briefly before drawing the dagger from his boot and spearing a chunk of pinkish meat with it. He tore off a bite and chewed enthusiastically.

The meat was rabbit, and it might have been better had it stewed a little longer, but in his famished state Anrel found it quite satisfactory just as it was.

When everyone had a bowl in hand, and had taken at least a few bites, the father of the family set his bowl down for a moment and said, "Now, Reva, suppose you explain to your father why you thought our guest was a sorcerer, and why you were so open about your own unfortunate situation."

Anrel was startled by the man's tone, which seemed to carry an undercurrent of menace.

The eldest daughter looked uneasy; she glanced from her father to her mother, then at Anrel, then back to her father. "He could feel the binding we tried," she said. "That meant he was a magician, and I never thought we would meet another witch in a place like this, so I called him a sorcerer."

"And why, daughter, did you say this *out loud*, and announce to the world that you're a witch?"

"Because he already *knew*, Father! He had felt the wards, and the binding—he *knew* there was magic here, and he saw Mother and me react, so he knew we were the magicians. There was no way to hide it."

The father shook his head sadly. "Haven't I told you, girl, how easy it is to persuade people that they did not see or feel what they have just seen or felt? We might have talked our way out of it, if you hadn't proclaimed the truth as you did." He turned to Anrel. "Tell me, sir, *did* you realize she was a witch before she said she had set wards and attempted a binding?"

"I certainly knew magic was in use," Anrel said, as he speared half a carrot with his dagger. "I had not yet identified her beyond doubt as the source." He took a bite. "But I think I would have in another moment."

"Well, perhaps you would have, and perhaps you wouldn't. I see you're enjoying your supper."

"Very much, sir."

"Tell us, then, as payment for your meal, how you come to be wandering about these woods, alone, on foot, and by the look of it, half starved."

Anrel swallowed, looked regretfully at the remaining chunk of carrot on the point of his knife, then set down his bowl.

"My name is Anrel Murau," he said. "I lived much of my life in the village of Alzur, a few miles up the Raish Valley, where Lord Allutar, the landgrave of Aulix, makes his home, away from the noise and stench of Naith. My dearest friend in Alzur was my uncle's fosterling, Valin li-Tarbek, a young man with an unfortunate tendency to speak his mind; a few days ago he indulged this tendency in a manner that infuriated Lord Allutar, and the landgrave retaliated by killing Valin. Oh, he arranged a legal pretext, so that the magistrates accepted it as the proper exercise of Lord Allutar's authority, but in truth it was at best little more than simple murder." Anrel closed his fists and his eyes as he remembered Valin dying in his arms, and paused for a moment, unable to continue.

"I see," the father said. "And you did something foolish in response?"

"I gave a speech," Anrel said. "In Aulix Square, in Naith. I explained Valin's beliefs to the crowd, and told them that Allutar had murdered him for espousing those beliefs. While I did not stay to hear the magistrates explain exactly what I was being charged with, it appears my little talk was deemed criminal. I fled, and stole a small boat, and put ashore in these trees so that I could hide that boat, and then I saw the light of your fire, and here I am."

"A speech? I'd have cut his throat!" the big man bellowed.

Anrel shook his head. "Lord Allutar is a powerful sorcerer," he said. "I could not have just walked through *his* wards as I did through yours. Besides, he killed Valin to silence him, so it was fitting that Valin's words be spoken, even if not by himself."

"You said you're a witch," the youngest daughter said.

"Yes."

"Then why didn't you use magic against him? Yes, he's more powerful, but couldn't you have found some way around, and caught him off guard?"

"I don't know how," Anrel admitted. "I have some talent for magic—not very much, I don't think—but I don't know how to use it."

The sisters exchanged glances.

"How did *that* happen?" their father demanded.

Anrel sighed. "I took the trials to become a sorcerer when I was twelve," he said, "but at the time I did not *want* to be a sorcerer, so I deliberately failed them. Since then I have done my best to never admit having any magic at all, not even to myself, even though a young man without magic has few prospects in Alzur. Only when Valin lay dying, and I tried to heal him, did I finally want to use my talent again; before that I had not touched the power since I was a child. That attempt, useless and inept as it was, seems to have reawakened what little natural ability I have; a season ago I doubt I would have noticed the ward you had set."

"So you *aren't* really a witch," Tazia, the middle daughter, said, looking at him with an expression Anrel found unreadable.

"Perhaps not," Anrel acknowledged. "I am a man with a completely untrained talent for magic, though—is that not enough to make me a witch?"

"To the magistrates, maybe," the father said.

"I am, I believe, already condemned as a traitor," Anrel said. "Calling myself a witch can scarcely make matters any worse."

"Oh, I wouldn't say that," the mother said. "There are other dangers besides the law."

"The law is quite enough for me," Anrel replied. He looked around at the family. "Now, perhaps you would like to introduce yourselves, and tell me how *you* came to be camped in this place."

"Our tale is far more ordinary than your own," the mother said. "When I was a girl I was frightened of sorcerers, even though my mother said my late father had been one, so I never dared apply for the trials. In truth, I did not even think of what I felt and did as magic; it was not until I was married that I realized that it was, that I should have put aside my fears and faced the trials, and by then it was too late. Even if I had somehow managed to claim I had not known the truth, I was married to a commoner, and therefore could not be a sorceress; instead I learned a few simple spells, little things that the nobles can't be bothered with, and began selling them."

"As you can imagine, I was not pleased to learn this," her husband said, and the mother flinched at that. "I had not realized I was marrying an outlaw. But we made the best of it."

"I thought we might keep it a secret," his wife said. "But somehow everyone found out."

"Of course, we couldn't stay in one place after that," the man said. "Sooner or later someone would have been jealous, or sought to avoid paying us, and would have turned us in. Besides, one little village doesn't need enough magic to keep a witch busy year-round. So we began traveling."

"We've been traveling ever since," the mother continued. "In time our girls started to show their talents, as well, but we couldn't send them for trials, not without risking our own necks, so we've kept them with us."

"We didn't want to go anywhere else," Reva said. "Not when we were of an age to be examined."

Anrel saw Tazia throw her sister a glance that implied perhaps Reva was not speaking for all of them, but she said nothing.

Indeed, Anrel had his doubts about some details of the account. He knew that sometimes talented children of commoners were missed, especially girls; parents were often reluctant to face the possibility of sending a daughter away to be fostered by sorcerers, since there were rumors about the uses sorcerers might have for young women, rumors that Anrel believed had some basis in fact.

But the law took that reluctance into account, and as long as a child, or even a young adult, had not been deliberately using magic illicitly, he or she could still take the trials, regardless of age. Nor did a commoner spouse make it impossible; while sorcerers generally married other sorcerers, Anrel did not believe it was actually required by law—not in all sixteen provinces, anyway. This woman *could* have presented herself to the authorities at any time, and become a lady of the empire—right up until she first accepted payment for performing witchcraft.

Now, of course, it was too late.

"Are all three of your daughters witches, then?" he asked.

"Yes, they are," the mother said, with a note of pride in her voice.

"And you, sir?" Anrel asked, looking at the father.

"No," he said. "I am merely an ordinary man who happened to marry the wrong woman—but I suspect that would be enough to put my head in a noose." He held out a hand. "My name is Garras Lir, by the way."

"Anrel Murau," Anrel said, accepting the hand. "As I said."

"My wife, Nivain," Garras said, gesturing. "And my daughters, Reva, Tazia, and Perynis."

"It is a pleasure to meet you all," Anrel said, doffing his hat and nodding at the women. Then he clapped the hat back on his head, and picked up his bowl of stew.

Garras waited until Anrel had eaten a few more bites, then asked, "Where are you bound, Master Murau? You said you came from Alzur?"

"Thence I came, yes, but that is not where I'm bound," Anrel replied. "I was heading for Lume; I have friends there I hope will shelter me until I can make more permanent arrangements."

"Lume? Ah, we won't go there," Garras said. "Too many watchmen, between the emperor's men and the burgrave's, and the city has its own witches and no need of us."

Anrel nodded. "Where *are* you going, then?"

"Oh, working our way up the Galdin, village by village," Garras said. "Then when we reach Beynos we'll cross the bridge and begin working our way back down the far side."

"Beynos?" Anrel knew the name, and had even visited the town a few times—if one could consider riding the coach through the town square "visiting." Beynos was a fair-sized town just two or three hours outside the walls of the capital, and to the best of his knowledge had nothing to especially recommend it other than its location. He could remember few noteworthy features; there was a very good bridge across the Galdin there, and several fine houses, but he could not recall any other particularly distinctive details.

Still, it was mere hours from Lume.

"If you are bound for Beynos, perhaps we might travel together," he suggested.

Garras looked at him warily. "And why would we want to do that?"

"I will tell you frankly what *I* hope to gain from it," Anrel said. "The landgrave's men are looking for a lone traveler; if I am a part of your company, and you swear I have been with you since the equinox, why, even if they stop us and question us, they will not know me and will not haul me back to Naith for trial and execution. What's more, I will have company, and space in your wagon, and a share of your fine cooking." He held up his mostly empty bowl.

"While I am sure this would make *your* situation easier," Garras said, "how would it benefit *me*?"

"You will have another pair of willing hands for whatever task you might care to set them to," Anrel said, "and my sword to defend your family. What's more, while I am not wealthy, and left most of my worldly possessions in my uncle's house, I *do* have my purse, and it is not completely empty. I could pay a little something to cover any expenses you might incur by my presence." He was not trusting or foolish enough to mention that his purse was in fact rather plump, or that he had additional coins hidden elsewhere; he might yet need most of that money.

"Ah," Garras said thoughtfully.

"I am sure I need not remind you of the risks you take, should you refuse me, and should I be captured," Anrel added.

"And the risks *you* face?"

"Well, let us just agree that we are safer together than apart."

"I suppose we are," Garras said, studying Anrel's calm features.

"It would only be as far as Beynos," Anrel said. "After that, I will continue on to Lume on my own."

Garras stroked his close-trimmed beard. "You understand, we are in no hurry," he said. "We intend to stop at every village along the way, and try to earn a few guilders in each."

"I am in no hurry myself," Anrel said. "I have no long-term goal in mind, as yet, beyond my own survival. Perhaps such an extended journey would provide an opportunity for your wife and daughters to teach me a little witchcraft—for a fee, of course! In exchange, I will gladly teach them whatever I can recall of sorcery—which, I concede, will be very little, but my uncle is the burgrave of Alzur, and while I was never trained in the arcane arts myself, I did sometimes overhear the lessons he gave his apprentice and his daughter."

"Your uncle is a burgrave?" Nivain asked, startled.

"Yes, he is," Anrel said. "Lord Dorias Adirane, burgrave of Alzur. My mother was his younger sister."

"Yet you hide here in these woods, like a common outlaw?"

"I *am* a common outlaw," Anrel said. "Guilty of sedition, theft, and witchcraft."

"But . . . can your uncle not plead for you?"

Anrel shook his head. "Lord Allutar is not so easily swayed. I have seen the landgrave kill two young men against my uncle's wishes; I have no desire to be a third. I intend to make contact with my uncle at the earliest opportunity and ask for his assistance, but I dare not return to Alzur until I have his assurance that I won't find the hangman waiting for me. I hope this will be just a few days, but I am resigned to staying away indefinitely, should it prove necessary."

"But I never heard of such a thing!" Nivain exclaimed. "A man of good family like yourself?"

"Oh, the sorcerers feud among themselves, like any other men," Garras said, trying on an air of calm wisdom. "Undoubtedly this uncle has fallen afoul of Lord Allutar in some fashion."

"On the contrary," Anrel said. "He is doing all he can to stay in Lord Allutar's good graces, for reasons that seem good to him, and he was willing to sacrifice his fosterling to that cause. I do not know that his nephew will fare any better."

Even as he said this, Anrel wondered whether it was entirely true.

Dorias had indeed let Valin go to his death, but Valin had not asked him to intervene, and it had been a matter of honor. Dorias and Saria had appeared to grieve for Valin, and Anrel had not seen them speak to Lord Allutar after Valin's death; perhaps they *had* given up any thought of an alliance between the son of Hezir and the daughter of Adirane.

And after Valin's death Anrel had not informed his uncle of his own intentions. Dorias had been given no opportunity to defend Anrel from Lord Neriam and the Naith Watch, or to speak on his nephew's behalf. Perhaps even now the old man was demanding the charges against Anrel be dropped.

In time, when the situation in Naith had calmed down, perhaps when the Grand Council had done its business and disbanded, Anrel would send word to his uncle and ask for his help in resolving the situation. Perhaps there might be some way to obtain a pardon.

His old life might not all be irretrievably lost. For the present, though, accompanying these people to Beynos and then making his way into Lume still seemed his best course; he simply didn't know what the situation was in Alzur or Naith.

"How dreadful!" Tazia said, as she took Anrel's empty bowl and brought his thoughts back to the present. Her fingers brushed his hand as she did.

"I do not fault him for it," Anrel said. "He took me in when my parents died, and raised me as best he could; that I chose to fling caution aside and lay myself open to a charge of treason was in no way his responsibility."

"Still, it doesn't seem right," Nivain said.

Tazia handed Anrel his bowl, which she had refilled from the stew pot. "It's all so sad! What did you *say*, that so angered the magistrates?"

"Oh, a lot of nonsense, for the most part," Anrel said, accepting the stew. "Valin had this theory that the Grand Council the emperor has called can reshape the entire empire into something wonderful and new, if the common people choose the right delegates."

"You say that's nonsense?" Garras asked warily.

"Those in power will never relinquish it peacefully," Anrel said, "and what can commoners do against sorcerers? The emperor has the Great

List, but the Grand Council will have nothing but words, and what good are words against magic?" He shook his head. "Everything will go on much as it has for centuries, and that's just as well—the sorcerers may be as venal and selfish as anyone else, but at least they have had some practice in running the empire, and they *do* have their magic."

Garras studied Anrel's face in the firelight, then nodded. "I would be glad of your company on our way to Beynos, Master Murau," he said. "You can tell us more about these theories of yours, and your friend's theories, as well." He smiled. "Your company, and of course, your coin."

"Of course," Anrel said, as he lifted his bowl to drink the broth. "Shall we say, three guilders?"

"For the entire journey? I had rather more in mind."

With that, the negotiations began in earnest.

20

In Which Anrel Becomes Acquainted with His Companions, and Their Work

The journey upriver took longer than Anrel had expected, despite Garras's warning that they would be stopping at every village along the way. Anrel had envisioned "every village" to mean every town big enough to have a wall or paling of some sort, but in fact it also meant every wide spot in the road where half a dozen houses huddled around an inn or a forge. Likewise, he had thought "stop" meant a stay of a night or at most two, when many of these visits lasted four, five, even ten or twelve days—however long it might take for the four witches to perform every love spell, prognostication, or healing that the villagers were willing to pay for. Merely dowsing for a well might take the better part of an afternoon, and treating a flock of sheep for scrapie or murrain could consume a full day.

And finally, Anrel had assumed that their route would closely parallel the riverbank, but instead they zigzagged across the landscape, over hills and through valleys, anywhere that Garras and Nivain thought there might be people in need of a witch's services.

What's more, even when moving they traveled slowly. The family's single horse was a sturdy animal, a heavily built gelding named Lolo, but asking him to haul the entire party and all their belongings would have been unreasonable; instead Garras generally drove, maintaining a leisurely pace, while Anrel and the four women walked alongside. Sometimes one of the women would be given a turn with the reins, and a chance to rest her feet, but this rarely lasted more than a mile or so; Garras clearly did not enjoy the exercise.

This arrangement was not what Anrel had hoped for, to say the least, but it was not entirely without its benefits. He had plenty of opportunity to talk with the women as they walked, and in fact the promised instruction in witchcraft, and his own accounts of the workings of sorcery, largely took place while trudging along the highway.

He found himself speaking most often with Tazia, the middle daughter, whom he found very pleasant company. She was quick-witted and charming, with a sly sense of humor. He thought she seemed to seek out his company, as well, indicating that his attentions were not unwelcome.

Her appearance was perhaps not as striking as her sisters', but she was comely enough. Anrel enjoyed passing the days walking beside her, even as he grew concerned with how slowly he was putting distance between Naith and himself.

The elections for the Grand Council came and went while Anrel and company were making their way from one village to the next; Anrel was able to observe the procedures in a village called Mizir, where the townsfolk lined up to drop red baked-clay disks in earthenware jars marked with the names of the various candidates, but of course he was not allowed to participate directly.

Other towns used various other methods—written ballots, colored chits, and so on. Every town big enough to have a burgrave held an election of some sort, choosing from one, two, three, or more candidates.

Because of his own fears of being recognized as the orator who had stirred up so much trouble in Naith, Anrel generally stayed out of sight as much as was practical during their stays in the several villages. On those occasions when he did accompany one of the women and observe her witchcraft in action he usually wore a large cape of Nivain's, with a generous cowl that hid his face. Nonetheless, despite shunning strangers, he did hear news and gossip now and then, and that was almost as educational as his training in forbidden magic.

Apparently his speech in Aulix Square had not been forgotten, as he had hoped it might be; instead, the tale had grown in the telling, as such things often did. The mysterious Alvos the orator was now said to have spoken for hours to a cheering crowd of thousands, setting forth the means by which the Walasian Empire might be transformed into an earthly paradise, before being forced to flee from a legion of the emperor's own elite guards, who then conducted a house-to-house search of the entire city, raping and pillaging as they went.

But they never found Alvos, who had been spirited away by his allies. Just who these allies might be was not generally agreed upon; theories varied from a few trusted friends operating in secret to a vast international conspiracy of powerful magicians—perhaps even wizards of the Old Empire who had been in hiding for centuries, manipulating events from behind the scenes.

Somehow, Anrel did not think these stories were going to fade in a few days and permit him to return to Alzur. Barring a miracle, his old life *was* gone. He needed to build a new one.

In truth, that prospect was not wholly unpleasant. The idea of making a new life as a witch had a certain appeal, especially if it was to be a life shared with Tazia.

Still, he was not ready to entirely abandon the past, so he listened to the stories about Alvos with an ear to finding some way to redeem himself and return to the Adirane estate. He noticed that his real name was never mentioned, though it must surely be known to many people; none of the stories gave any hint that Lord Neriam had come to any harm that might have caused him to forget Anrel's name. That gave him a faint but persistent flicker of hope, even while he told himself it was meaningless.

He was not the only one listening to the rumors and legends, of course. The several members of the Lir family were not stupid, and recognized the similarity of these stories to Anrel's account of his own reason for fleeing. At first nothing was said, but one night, some time after Anrel had joined the company, as the six of them sat gathered around a campfire after eating their evening meal, Garras straightened up, looked at Anrel, and said, "You're Alvos, aren't you?"

Anrel considered for a moment before answering. A flat denial would not be believed, but how he presented the truth might be important.

"I gave that name when I spoke in Aulix Square," he said. "The stories seem to have become greatly exaggerated, however—I barely recognize myself in some of the accounts we've heard of late."

"They call you a hero," Garras said.

"I was a fool," Anrel said. "I suspect the categories overlap considerably."

"Half the delegates to the Grand Council were chosen with your speech in mind."

"In Aulix, perhaps, but there are fifteen other provinces. It won't matter."

Garras studied him thoughtfully in the firelight. Uncomfortable under his scrutiny, Anrel looked around at the women.

Nivain's eyes were downcast; Reva was watching her father warily. Perynis was looking back and forth from Anrel to Garras, as if unsure she understood what was being said.

And Tazia's gaze was fixed adoringly on Anrel—not the shy half-smile she had given him so often on the road, but a wide-eyed adulation that made him nervous. He turned quickly away from her radiant face. He did not want to see such worship; he was sure it was based on the absurd stories she had heard about the legendary Alvos, rather than anything the flesh and blood Anrel had done.

"I would guess, Master Murau, that you were right in saying your uncle could not have saved you," Garras said. "When we first met that seemed unlikely, that a burgrave could not intervene on his nephew's behalf, but now? Now I am surprised you escaped at all."

Anrel felt himself flush, though he hoped it would not be visible in the red glow of the flames.

And that was that; the subject was not discussed openly again, though after that the women all made a point of telling Anrel whatever bits of political news they happened to hear, about elections and candidates' preparations and various speeches. Anrel tried unsuccessfully to convince them that he did not particularly care about politics, but he was not surprised by his failure; after all, how could the great Alvos not want to hear every detail of the gathering of the Grand Council?

He tried to distract them by talking about other matters—witchcraft, sorcery, and their own lives, for the most part.

By this time he had learned the basics of witchcraft; the four women had taken turns teaching him what they knew. He was not particularly surprised to learn that most of the witchcraft these people sold was really the same thing as the sorcery the nobles of the empire employed. Love spells were emotional bindings, nothing more, and the potions sometimes dispensed to enhance them were merely herbal brews that made the subject more receptive to the binding. They would have worked just as well for any other compulsion as they did for provoking lust or devotion.

Healing was the same healing that sorcerers did—bindings to repair torn flesh, wards to drive off poisons and evil influences, and perhaps a little infusion of earthly energy to help the body recover its strength. This was at least as likely to be used on livestock as on the villagers themselves.

Witches were consulted to locate new wells or latrines, and that was done by sensing the flow of energy beneath the soil, just as a sorcerer would have done, had any sorcerer ever troubled himself with so mundane a task.

And prognostication, which the witches and peasants usually called fortune-telling, was almost completely fraudulent. These witches could no more see the future than could anyone else. They could, however, use their magic to make their customers more suggestible, and to read subtle clues that would guide them in telling their customers what they wanted to hear. A few vaguely worded predictions, some clever guessing, and the eager buyers would believe that the witches had read the contents of their hearts, had seen their pasts, and could foretell their futures.

That was perhaps the biggest surprise—that so much of witchcraft was made up of lies and deception. Sorcery certainly had its failings, most particularly in the sort of black sorcery that Lord Blackfield and the others of the Lantern Society campaigned against, but it was still more honest than witchcraft. The witches took credit for anything that could possibly be attributed to magic; common coincidences were claimed as subtle spells, good luck was the result of a witch's blessing, and misfortune was a sign that someone had been cursed—though of course, never by the witch pointing out the supposed curse.

"For a small fee, I could try to remove the curse," the witch would say, "but of course, I can't offer any guarantees—the witch who laid this curse upon you may have powers greater than my own."

There was never any curse. In fact, Reva admitted that none of them even knew whether curses were actually possible.

"I would think that certain bindings could reasonably be considered curses," Anrel told her. "But I have no idea how one would cast them."

Reva shrugged. "Who would want to?"

Anrel had no answer for that.

The journey was slow, but Anrel stayed with the witches. He could, at any of several stops along the way, have simply paid the fare and caught a coach to Lume, but he did not do so; he knew from the stories about Alvos that he could not yet hope to return to Alzur, and Lume was not intended as his final destination, so there was no hurry about reaching the capital. He was learning witchcraft, keeping track of the wild stories about his alter ego, and enjoying the company of his fellow travelers. A coach might take him to Lume in a matter of three or four days, but it would not bring him any understanding of how to use his magical abilities, and he thought it very unlikely that he would find himself with any companions more pleasant than Tazia and her sisters.

As well as his education in witchcraft and politics, Anrel learned a great deal about the Lirs themselves.

Nivain, the mother of the family, eventually admitted that when she had spoken of her "late father," she had probably lied. She did not know whether her father was alive or dead, nor exactly who he had been. Her mother had been a shopkeeper's daughter who accepted the advances of a handsome young man who had claimed to be a sorcerer—Lord Perlitoun, he had called himself, according to Nivain's mother, but no one in the family knew whether that was really his name, where he was from, or where he had gone. He had appeared in her town, stayed for a season or so, and then departed, never to be seen again. Two and a half seasons later, Nivain had been born.

Her talent for magic had manifested fairly early, lending support to her father's claims of nobility, but her mother had done everything possible to keep that talent a secret.

"She was afraid that if I let anyone know about it, they would take me away from her," Nivain explained. "She thought my father might come back and claim me if I was acknowledged to be a sorceress. She didn't want that—I was all she had. She wasn't so foolish as to think that he might marry her, after so long, nor even foolish enough to *want* him to marry her. He had deserted her, and that had been enough to end her infatuation with him; she said he was a selfish, empty-headed fop, and she would not marry until she could do better for herself." Nivain sighed. "She never did—at least, she had not married when last we spoke."

Nivain herself, on the other hand, had married Garras when she was sixteen. He had been a big, strong, handsome, well-spoken man, and she had been eager to get away from her mother's rather overwhelming attentions. That he had no trade, and no sorcerer had leased him land to farm, had not troubled her, as she had been sure that in time the Mother and Father would provide him with something suitable. That he was short-tempered and given to boastful exaggeration she had not noticed until after they were wed. She had kept her magic hidden from him for almost a year, but at last the secret had slipped out.

She had thought he would be furious with her for withholding this information, that he would either forbid her to use it or want her to face the sorcery trials, but he had surprised her; it was his suggestion to take up witchcraft and travel. Ever since, they had wandered back and forth across the empire, from Kerdery to Tralmei and Hallin to Pirienna, selling her services.

"For twenty-four years now, my home has been a wagon," she said. She gestured at the vehicle Lolo pulled. "This one is our third."

Reva had been born in their first wagon some twenty-three years ago, making her a year or so older than Anrel himself, and very nearly Valin's age. Like her mother she had shown magical ability at an early age, and the question of whether or not she should face the trials had arisen. Garras had finally settled the matter—the risk was too great. If Reva were to become a sorceress, it was all too likely that she would attract official attention to the rest of her family that would eventually put Nivain's neck in a noose.

The others had followed the same path. Tazia turned nineteen just three days after Anrel first met her, and Perynis would turn seventeen eight days after the solstice, but neither had ever considered the trials.

Reva took little interest in talking to Anrel, either on the road or when they had stopped for the night; she was more concerned with her own plans. She was saving up money and intended to strike out on her own, and anything that did not bring her closer to that goal did not command her attention.

Tazia, on the other hand, sought Anrel out at every opportunity, even before he admitted to being Alvos. She seemed fascinated by every mention of his past life; oddly, at least from Anrel's point of view, she seemed to find the details of his life in Alzur, living in his uncle's house, more intriguing than his adventures as a student in Lume. A simple description of leaving boots by the door for the servants to tend held greater appeal for her than the tale of how he had caught a drunken friend diving off one of the watchmen's arches not a hundred feet from the emperor's palace.

She was reluctant to say anything about herself, though Anrel coaxed her to do so.

Perynis fell between these two extremes; she would chatter cheerfully with Anrel about whatever came into her head, whether that meant telling a story about helping Nivain deliver a baby, or pondering what the squirrels by the road might say if they could speak, or questioning Anrel about the construction of the boat he had stolen from the boathouse on the Raish and abandoned in the woods on the Galdin. Anrel thought, though, that she might have been equally happy speaking to one of her sisters, or even to old Lolo.

Reva was tall and stately, with straight dark hair to her waist, though she usually kept it tied back in a thick braid; her face was strong and elegant, with dark eyes and prominent cheekbones. Perynis was second in height, matching her mother, and despite her youth she was the most buxom of the lot, her curling hair tumbling over lush and generous curves. Tazia was shorter and plainer, but Anrel found her charming all the same—her constant attentiveness was a part of that, of course, but he also admired the smile that seemed to make her whole face glow, and the soft laugh that so often accompanied that smile. Her hair was as dark as Reva's, but almost as curly as Perynis's locks.

Anrel also noticed that Tazia alone of the three daughters took after her mother in one regard—Tazia and Nivain were by far the gentler and more considerate healers of the four, and seemed as concerned with making sure their patients were calm and comfortable as with the actual magic. Reva could not be bothered with such niceties, and for that reason was generally given other work; she reportedly excelled at love spells and other coercion, and was always responsible for setting wards when the family retired for the night, to warn them of any intruders. Perynis seemed concerned with her patients, but had, as yet, no knack for comforting or reassuring them.

All three daughters were definitely practicing witches, though—which meant, Anrel knew, that all three might well find themselves on a gallows someday, alongside the mother who had taught them their trade. That prospect did not please him at all, especially when he considered that he might well be up there with them.

Four witches in a single family also meant that finding work for all of them in a small village was not likely; this was a large part of why Reva intended to leave. As it was, the younger girls sometimes found themselves reduced to healing torn ears on injured house cats, or setting wards merely to protect woolens from moths.

This meant that Anrel's payments into the family coffers, which amounted in all to eleven guilders, were very welcome. It also meant that the family got very tired of rabbit stew, though once winter closed in and rabbits could no longer be readily snared they would undoubtedly look back on those thin and tiresome stews fondly. Food was not plentiful; the harvest had been poor for the sixth year running, so prices were high, and villagers less generous in paying the witches than they had been in good times. A good deal of grumbling was directed at the nobility for allowing this state of affairs to continue—surely there was *something* their sorcery could do! The protests by some sorcerers that they were trying their best with fertility spells were dismissed as self-serving exaggeration or outright lies. There was also much discussion of what would be the most efficacious way to phrase the prayers to the Father, the Mother, and all the ancestral spirits at the solstice rites.

The weather grew steadily colder as autumn wore on and the solstice approached; more than once Lolo's hooves crunched through ice as he pulled the wagon along the rutted roads, and a few brief flurries left the brown fields speckled with white. Between villages Nivain's cape, which Anrel wore to disguise himself when observing the witches at work, was (quite appropriately) wrapped around its rightful owner, so when the family was on the road Anrel wore his brown velvet coat over his blue jacket and kept his hat tugged down over his ears, more concerned with warmth than appearance, and wished that he had the good gray wool cloak that had seen him through four winters in Lume, and which he had left folded in a trunk in his uncle's house—not to mention the fur-lined gloves that his cousin Saria had given him as a going-away present when he first left to take up his studies in the capital.

When the solstice finally arrived Anrel was startled to discover that the Lir women did not celebrate it—they said no special prayers, made no obeisance, and did not divert themselves from their regular route in order to visit a sacred site or family shrine. When he remonstrated with Garras, his answer was a cold stare and a flat, "We don't have time for that."

He began a reply, then cut it off short, before the first word had finished leaving his lips. It was none of his business. Still, it troubled him that women who had so obviously benefited from the Mother's gifts would make no expression of gratitude.

They arrived that night in the town of Kolizand, home to some three hundred souls, of whom about a dozen were down with fever. Since the local burgrave had dismissed this illness as beneath his notice it would keep the witches nicely busy for two or three days, and then, if nothing else demanded their attention, they would move on.

"And that will be that," Garras said, as they sat around the hearth in Kolizand's one ramshackle inn, where they had paid for a night's lodging by blessing the wine, so that it would not turn to vinegar before spring. The "blessing" was a ward against further fermentation, a spell which might or might not actually last out the winter.

"That will be what?" Anrel asked.

"That will be the end of our association," Garras replied. "Didn't you know? The next town beyond this is Beynos, where we cross the river and you leave us."

"Ah," Anrel said. He glanced at Tazia, who blushed and dropped her gaze.

Garras seemed to take it for granted that they would be abiding by the original agreement they had made the night Anrel first met the Lirs, but Anrel himself was not so sure. Not for the first time, he wondered whether he *wanted* to leave the witches.

21

In Which Anrel Arrives at His Expected Destination in Unexpected Circumstances

The fever proved more intractable than expected; it was four long, exhausting days before the Lir women had finally restored all the people of Kolizand to health, and Anrel found himself musing whether the burgrave had misjudged the severity of the illness, or simply hadn't wanted to be bothered with such unpleasant matters.

After all, great things were happening in the world. Anrel's first day in Kolizand was also the first day the Grand Council finally met, less than a full day's travel to the east, in the ancient city of Lume, the eternal heart of the Walasian Empire. Who would blame the burgrave of Kolizand if he was preoccupied with following the news from the capital, and not interested in the boring business of running his own town?

Rumor had it that the makeup of the council was not what the emperor had wanted—he had hoped for a calm, cooperative group that he could direct as he pleased, and had called for the election of commoners believing that they would be overawed by his presence and too ignorant, too naïve, to present any resistance to his plans for revamping the tax laws. Instead, thanks to the work of agitators and revolutionaries like the mysterious Alvos of Naith, half the council was said to be made up of rabble-rousers and firebrands, eager to immediately right all the perceived wrongs of the empire.

The empress, who was due to bear her first child any day now, was said to be downright horrified by what had become of her husband's scheme, and had allegedly told him the council should not be permitted to meet at all. His Imperial Majesty had known better than that; he had convened the council, and once that was done, he did not have the authority to undo it. His wife, being Ermetian by birth, did not appreciate just how impossible it was to refuse this most sacred of all Walasian institutions.

Anrel found that perversely amusing; he suspected that two years ago most Walasians had never *heard* of the Grand Council, yet now it was a sacred institution. Two years ago most of those who did know of the Grand Council had probably considered it an irrelevant historical curiosity, yet now it was seen as the very foundation of the empire.

Of course, Anrel's studies in history had taught him that the original Grand Council really *was* the foundation of the empire. It had been the mechanism by which the ancient Walasian sorcerers were able to restore some semblance of order after the Old Empire disintegrated. The wizards who had created the Old Empire, and the bureaucrats who had administered it, had all vanished over a period of half a season, never to be seen again, and it had been the Grand Council that had created the Walasian Empire in their stead.

But that council had disbanded centuries ago, and had been all but forgotten until the emperor decided he needed some way to make demands of the nobility that were not permitted under the existing laws and covenants. To Anrel, this new Grand Council seemed little more than a sham, a shabby stunt on the emperor's part. If it was not working out quite as the emperor wanted, that was just as well.

By the time he and the Lir family finally made their preparations to depart Kolizand, though, the news from Lume had turned more dismaying. The emperor had refused to allow the Grand Council to meet in the palace, or any other official building, claiming that he did not want their deliberations to be influenced by the existing bureaucracy. Instead, they had been sent to an ancient, crumbling, little-used building, a relic of the Old Empire—a bathhouse, originally, though the plumbing that had once kept the baths filled, and the mechanisms that had heated the water, had all long ago corroded into uselessness. It was said to be haunted, though no one seemed to think that was a serious concern.

The more extreme populist members of the council had used this exile as evidence of the utter corruption of the empire's present government, and delegates who had previously espoused moderation seemed more inclined to listen to their radical compatriots now.

The rumors about Empress Annineia had turned darker, as well—she was now said to have a coterie of hired necromancers from the Cousins acting as her personal guards, brought in with the Ermetian physicians who had come to help with the impending birth. It was even said that demons, presumably summoned by her foreign magicians, had been glimpsed in the streets around the palace, though anyone with any sense dismissed that as absurd.

Anrel was more disturbed by this than he cared to admit. He had always assumed that the empire's governance was as solid and certain as the land itself. He had taken it for granted that the emperor would muddle through his economic woes somehow and retire his grandfather's debts, that the recent crop failures would end, and that everything would then return to the same sort of peace and prosperity that the empire had enjoyed for half a millennium. Now, though, things seemed to be slipping further and further out of control, further and further away from the old norm. Necromancers in the palace, and demons in the streets of Lume? The Grand Council made up largely of disgruntled commoners, and meeting in a haunted ruin? Returning to normal from *this* might not be as certain as Anrel had thought.

And to some extent, this was *his fault*. He had climbed up on that statue in Aulix Square and given his speech, meaning only to honor Valin's memory and anger Lord Allutar, and it was as if he had struck sparks into the sawdust on a carpenter's floor—flames smoldering everywhere and every so often flaring up unexpectedly.

He had never before thought the actions of an ordinary man could really matter, but that conviction was shaken. If he had not spoken, surely the news from Lume would be less disconcerting.

He began to wonder whether his hope of hiding in Lume until Lord Dorias could intervene on his behalf still had even the faintest possibility of realization. Alvos the orator was not just guilty of a dangerous prank, but of subverting the order of the empire. If the mad stories about Alvos continued to circulate, and the authorities in Aulix held all of Alvos's crimes against Anrel, an ordinary burgrave of no particular reputation could not save the notorious criminal from the consequences of his actions.

Furthermore, Lume was no longer a refuge where people could be relied upon not to ask a stranger his business. If the streets were full of foreign magicians and their demons, and nervous watchmen, and Grand Councillors, all of them familiar with the name Alvos, staying just another anonymous young man without magic might not be possible.

Perhaps, Anrel thought, not for the first time, he should simply stay with the Lir family. He might take his courtship of Tazia further; up until now he had tried to keep their growing friendship and mutual respect from turning into a firm commitment, since he had intended to leave her behind, with her parents and sisters, when he made his way to the capital, but now he was considering other possibilities. He was technically a witch himself, though he had performed little magic, so why not marry a witch, and take up her peripatetic lifestyle permanently? He thought Tazia would welcome his advances.

No, he told himself; to be honest, he *knew* she would welcome his advances.

Garras might not be so pleased, of course. He had allowed Anrel to accompany the family partly because of the threat of mutual destruction, but more important, because of that eleven guilders Anrel had contributed to the family's finances. That money was gone, and while Anrel still had a significant sum hidden away, he had not let any of the others know that. So far as they were aware his purse was now empty, every coin spent.

What's more, Anrel and Garras had, over the past half season or so, realized that they did not much like each other. Garras did no witchcraft, had no magic of any kind, yet it was usually he who collected the fees from the family's customers, only reluctantly doling out the pennies the women needed for their own expenses. He drove the wagon, leaving his women to walk; when they were not moving, Reva maintained the wagon, while Tazia and Perynis tended to Lolo. Garras did not cook, did not clean, did not sew, did not hunt; he did bargain with villagers seeking the services of his wife and daughters, but that was all.

Yet Garras ruled his family with a firm hand. He controlled the money, determined their route, set their schedule; he was served first at every meal, and when he was present the women did not speak without his permission. It had long ago become clear that it was Garras, not Nivain, who had decided that the daughters would not be permitted to face the trials that might have made them noblewomen.

He was, in short, a petty tyrant, and Anrel had never thought much of tyrants.

For his own part, Garras had made it plain that he considered Anrel a reckless fool, with a dangerous wit and a misplaced sense of humor. Anrel had the definite impression that Garras had thought the presence of another man might further cow the four women, and had felt betrayed when Anrel instead treated the women with respect and consideration.

The two had been able to coexist peacefully thus far largely by ignoring each other as much as possible, but the knowledge that their relationship had a definite end in sight had made that easier. If Anrel announced he had changed his plans and intended to stay with the Lir family, Garras might not cooperate.

Or perhaps he might; it was hard to say.

And there was always a third possibility—that Anrel and Tazia might split off from the family, as Reva hoped to, and make their own way in the world. Anrel had told himself when he first fled Naith that he had to build himself a new life, and he now hoped to build it around Tazia. If she was willing to leave her parents behind, that might well be the best of all possible outcomes.

It bore some thought, and there was no need to rush into anything; they had spent the morning settling accounts and loading up the wagon, and were about to leave Kolizand for Beynos. The walk would take half the afternoon, and then when they reached Beynos they would settle in somewhere. Once that was done they would probably spend several days attending to customers, healing the sick and injured, calming the frightened, selling love charms and happy lies. Anrel could use that time to think over his situation, and perhaps discuss it with Tazia, or with Nivain, or even with Garras; if he decided to continue on to Lume he could leave at any time, but if he decided he wanted to stay with Tazia—well, he would have a few days to consider his options.

"Ready, Anrel?" Perynis asked, as Garras climbed onto the driver's bench and shook out the reins.

"Of course," Anrel and Tazia said simultaneously. Anrel smiled, and Tazia giggled, and Anrel reached out and caught Tazia's hand as they began walking.

They had scarcely taken a step when the first flakes of snow began to fall.

Kolizand was too small for an actual wall, but like Alzur it had an iron fence called a pale that marked its statutory limits and the extent of the burgrave's authority. It was less than a quarter mile from the inn on the village square to the southeastern gate, but by the time the wagon had covered even that distance the weather had gone from merely overcast to snowing heavily, and the brown fields beside the road were already turning white.

"Are you sure we want to travel in this?" Anrel called to Garras, standing to one side as Lolo pulled the wagon through the unguarded gate.

"Yes," Garras snapped. "It's not more than six or seven miles to Beynos, and if we're going to be snowbound, I'd much rather be there than here."

Anrel glanced back at the unprepossessing village where they had spent the last four days, and saw Garras's point. There was no further work for witches in Kolizand, and little to do there for anyone. Beynos was much larger, with a fine bridge across the Galdin, several grand houses, a paved square, and even a few paved streets.

Still, the snow was coming down fast, great fluffy white flakes that clung to his hat and coat.

"Let's hurry, then," Anrel said.

Garras snorted. "We will go as fast as Lolo will go," he called back over his shoulder. "I'm not going to kill our horse because you don't want snow in your beard."

Anrel hurried through the gate, close behind the wagon, still holding

Tazia's hand; he could not very well argue with Garras about Lolo's capabilities, but he still did not like the idea of traveling six miles in thick snow at their usual leisurely pace. He trotted alongside the wagon, catching up to Garras.

"Perhaps, sir," he said, "I might go on ahead, with whichever of your family might care to join me, to arrange our lodging, so that Lolo will be able to get in out of the snow that much sooner."

"Lolo? You mean so *you* can get out of the snow. What a sorry excuse for a man you are, Anrel, to be so frightened of a few flakes!"

"Not frightened, Master Lir, merely discomfited."

"You need not stay with us if you do not choose to do so, Master Murau. As I recall, our agreement was that you would accompany us to Beynos, where we would part our ways and trouble each other no further. Well, we are almost to Beynos, and if you would prefer to end our pact a few miles early, I certainly won't object."

That confounded Anrel for a moment; he glanced at Tazia.

"Father, you're being unkind," Tazia said. "Master Murau makes good sense—why not make sure a warm stall is waiting for Lolo, and a hot fire for the rest of us?"

Garras turned to glare at her, and noticed that Perynis and Nivain were both walking nearby and listening, as well.

"I am in no hurry to depart your company, sir," Anrel said. "In fact, I had hoped to speak to you about my future plans once we had reached Beynos, and ask your advice."

That drew Nivain's attention; she threw Tazia a glance that her daughter pointedly ignored.

Garras considered Anrel for a moment, and Anrel did his best to keep his expression open and honest—which meant letting snow blow into his eyes, causing him to blink uncontrollably. He suspected that made him look like a simpering fool, which was not the impression he had been aiming for.

"I cannot stop you from hurrying on ahead," Garras said at last, "and I will not insist that any such separation must be permanent. I would ask you, though, to leave my family with me."

Anrel hesitated, and again looked at Tazia.

"He's my father," she said quietly. "We'll be fine. We've traveled in snow before."

"I'll have the innkeeper make everything ready," he said. "A roaring fire, good wine, and a generous dinner will be waiting for you, if I can possibly manage it."

Tazia smiled at him.

His own words brought a question to mind, though; he turned back to Garras. "I have never stayed in Beynos, Master Lir, but I have passed through it, and seem to remember a multiplicity of signboards," he said. "Is there a particular inn you would prefer?"

Garras nodded thoughtfully. "A good question," he said. "In the past we've been made welcome at the Boar's Head, on Cobbler Street—try there first."

"We'll look for you there," Tazia said, releasing his hand.

"If circumstances allow, I may instead meet you at the gate," Anrel said. "But if not, then yes, look for me in Cobbler Street." He waved a salute to Nivain, and then to Garras, as he broke into a trot. He resisted the temptation to blow Tazia a kiss; he did not think Garras would appreciate such a gesture.

Old Lolo gave Anrel half an eye as Anrel passed, then returned to concentrating on his own feet, trudging steadily onward through the storm.

Anrel hoped that the horse knew the road well, because by the time he had gone a mile from Kolizand's gate the wheel ruts were full of snow and the highway and verge had turned equally white. Anrel could see no more than a dozen yards in any direction; the snowfall was astonishingly dense, as if the Father had decided to make up for a dry and snowless autumn by delivering an entire season's precipitation in a single storm. The sky was so thick with clouds and snow that even now, in the early afternoon, it was as dark as twilight.

Fortunately, the wind was neither strong nor especially cold—there was no chance that the snow would melt anytime soon, but neither did it bite through Anrel's doubled coats, or freeze his breath in his beard. There was little danger anyone would freeze to death in such weather, but losing one's way in the endless, featureless whiteness would be easy.

A glance over his shoulder revealed no trace of the Lir family or their wagon, nor could he distinguish any trace of Kolizand. He broke from his brisk trot into a full run, as much to keep warm as to reach Beynos the sooner.

Almost an hour later he was beginning to wonder whether he had somehow lost the road when he saw lights ahead. It was still midafternoon, but the darkness was apparently enough to cause lanterns to be lit. He slowed his pace and squinted into the swirling gloom, trying to identify the source of the light.

There was a stone wall, he realized—white trimmed with green. There were windows, and lights in the windows.

And directly ahead of him was a city gate, where stood a guard holding a pike. That was mildly unusual; gates were usually left open and untended these days.

Or rather, they had been in days recently past; now that the Grand Council was in session and demons had reportedly been seen on the streets of Lume, who knew what was normal?

"Who goes there?" the guard called as Anrel approached.

"Just a traveler seeking shelter," Anrel replied, stepping forward into the light of the lantern hung above the gate.

"Traveling in *this* weather? Are you mad?"

"It wasn't yet snowing when I left Kolizand," Anrel explained. "By the time I realized the storm's severity, it was as easy to press on as to turn back." He glanced up at the arch above the gate, but snow was plastered across the stone, and if there was any sign there, he could not read it. "Is this Beynos?"

"Yes, of course," the guard said. "Where else could it be?"

"In *this* weather? It could be Ondine, for all I know."

The guard laughed at that. "Well, it's Beynos," he said.

"I am delighted to hear it, Master Guardsman. May I be admitted to the city, then?"

"You're wearing a sword?"

"I have been traveling in lands less civilized than this one," Anrel said. "I would have put it in my pack when I left those barbarous realms, but it didn't fit."

"Fair enough—but then I'll need your name, and your destination. The burgrave is wary, in these unsettled times."

"I don't blame him," Anrel said. "My name is Dyssan Adirane, and I'm bound for the Boar's Head Inn, on Cobbler Street—a friend recommended it."

"How long will you be staying in Beynos, then?"

"Perhaps five or six days; then I'll probably go on to Lume, unless I should find reason to change my plans."

"Are you familiar with Lume?"

"I lived there for a time."

"You'll find it changed, I think. These are not happy days, Master Adirane."

"So I have heard." Anrel hesitated, then said, "By the bye, I passed a wagon on the road—a family of traveling peddlers, I think. They seemed no more inclined to turn back than I was. I spoke with them, and said I might meet them here. If they arrive, and ask after me, tell them where I've gone, would you?"

"The Boar's Head?"

"Exactly. Just to reassure them that I wasn't lost in the snow."

"Of course."

"Thank you." Anrel tipped his hat, then started through the gate.

The guard stepped aside to let him pass, but there was something else, something invisible, that held him back for a moment.

The burgrave of Beynos had apparently been tending to his business; Anrel recognized the hindrance as a powerful warding spell. He wondered just what characteristic of his own made it slow him; he was not here with hostile intent, and he was a loyal Walasian. Could it somehow sense that he was a thief? Anrel had never heard of a ward *that* sophisticated.

Then it yielded, and Anrel stepped through the wards into the city of Beynos.

22

In Which Anrel Arranges Lodging and Hears Certain News

Anrel said nothing to the gatekeeper about the wards; he was not sure whether an ordinary traveler would even have felt them. To him, though, their presence was unmistakable, and after he was through, Anrel thought he could sense their nature after all. He thought the spells were intended to keep unnatural creatures outside the walls of Beynos.

As an untrained magician Anrel had seemed unnatural enough for a brief delay, but no more.

What did the burgrave fear, to set such wards? What unnatural creatures were abroad? The demons that the empress's hirelings were rumored to have summoned?

Once past the gate and the wards, however, nothing seemed out of the ordinary. The snow-covered streets were deserted, though there were enough tracks, and enough mud and slush mixed with the snow, to make it clear that the townsfolk had not been driven indoors by the first flakes. Light shone from several windows, though it was still mid-afternoon.

Anrel hurried through the eerie silent streets, trying to remember whether he had ever known just where Cobbler Street was. He should have asked the guard at the gate for directions; he cursed himself for not having done so.

As he neared the plaza and bridge at the center of town he saw a few figures moving about—apparently not *all* the streets were deserted.

Admitting to himself that nothing looked familiar, and that he was not sure he would have done much better even without the snow blanketing everything, he resolved to ask one of these people for directions—but then he glimpsed a signboard swinging in the wind down a side street, and stopped to peer at it.

It showed an inverted shoe on a cobbler's last.

Some spirit was apparently feeling helpful. He turned down the side street—little more than an alley, really—and started looking at the other shop fronts.

Yes, they were shoemakers, bootmakers, and cobblers, and what's more, at the end of the little street was a wrought-iron archway surrounding an open gate, and at the peak of the arch was a black iron fantasia largely obscured by wet snow, but which had ears, tusks, and an unmistakable snout protruding from its white covering.

Anrel trotted down the alley and through the gate and found himself in a snowy stable yard; an animal snorted somewhere in the shadows to his right, and Anrel could smell leather and horses. Directly ahead a lantern glowed above a heavy oaken door; he hurried up to the door and knocked.

For a moment nothing happened; then a panel slid aside and a pair of eyes stared out at him, glinting in the lantern light.

"I seek food and lodging," Anrel said.

A deep voice said, "You're alone and on foot?"

"On foot, yes," Anrel said. "The rest of my party is an hour behind me—I came ahead to secure us lodging, for ourselves and our horse."

"How many?"

"Six of us in all, with a wagon, and a good-natured gelding; he'll give your stable hands no trouble."

The voice did not reply immediately, and Anrel added, "Garras Lir said he had been welcome here in the past."

The eyes narrowed. "You know Master Lir?"

"He and his family make up the rest of my party," Anrel said.

"You're traveling with the witches?"

It seemed that not only had the Lirs been here before, but the nature of their work was known. "I'm *courting* one of the witches," Anrel said. "Now, are we welcome here, or should I look elsewhere?"

The panel slid shut, and for a moment Anrel thought he was indeed being sent away, but then the latch rattled and the door swung in, revealing a big man a few years past his prime, his once-impressive muscles starting to give way to fat. "You're courting Reva, then?" he asked.

The Lirs *were* known here. "No, Tazia," Anrel said.

"Ah," the man said with a nod. "She hasn't her sister's looks, but I'll wager she's more pleasant company. You said they're an hour behind you?" He stepped aside and ushered Anrel in.

"About that," Anrel said, stepping into the warmth and light of the inn.

"You're wearing a sword," the man said disapprovingly, once he got a look at his new customer.

"The roads aren't as safe as they used to be," Anrel replied, looking around. "If you can assure me you'll keep it safe for me, I'll take it off."

He was standing in a modest wood-paneled room that held two long tables, one on either side, and accompanying benches. A row of hooks on the far wall held half a dozen damp cloaks—none of them of good quality or particularly new, but that was hardly surprising. Half a dozen candles burned in sconces, providing a warm glow; the two windows were shuttered. Four open doors led to other rooms, and Anrel could hear voices from at least one of them. The place smelled, not unpleasantly, of spilled beer, candle wax, and old varnish.

The doorkeeper considered that for a moment, then shrugged. "If you can assure me it will stay in its sheath, you needn't bother."

"I certainly have no intention of drawing it," Anrel replied.

"Good enough. You said a room and a meal, for the six of you?"

"Probably several meals, and a stall for our horse."

"Show me the color of your money, then."

That was not the response Anrel had hoped for. "Master Lir's credit isn't good?" he asked.

"You, my new friend, are not Master Lir—and in fact, no, his credit is not particularly good."

That was dismaying, though not entirely surprising after a season spent in Garras's company. Anrel had no intention of paying for the entire party, though; he was quite sure Garras would never repay him. "Alas, Master Lir has the money," he said. "I did not think to ask him for any, as I had thought he was respected here."

"Then I'm afraid you'll have to take off your sword after all; it will serve as surety."

That seemed a fair compromise. Anrel unbuckled his sword belt and handed it over.

"Thank you," the doorkeeper said. "I am Dorrin Kabrig, by the way; you are . . . ?"

"Dyssan Adirane," Anrel said. "A pleasure to make your acquaintance, Master Kabrig." He tipped his hat.

"Good to meet you, too." Dorrin glanced around. "As you may have gathered, this room and the front door are in my charge; through there you'll find the saloon, which is my wife's domain, and over there Master Issulien oversees the main dining room. Go through that door to the back, and Mistress Sharduil can see you to a room, or fetch Billin the stable boy for you. Master Sharduil is the landlord, but I would advise you not to seek him out."

"Thank you," Anrel said, doffing his hat entirely. "I think I'll have a word with Mistress Sharduil, then."

He suited his actions to his words. Mistress Sharduil was a sturdy woman of perhaps half a century's vintage, wearing an apron and mobcap, and affecting a brisk and businesslike manner. Anrel made sure she understood that the Lir family was coming. She assured him that she would have a large room warm and ready for the family, a clean stall prepared for Lolo, and a sheltered corner where the wagon could be stored.

"But if they don't arrive, you'll be responsible for the cost," she said.

"They'll be here soon."

"You're really sure they'll come, in this weather?" she asked, as she glanced out a rear window at the deepening snow.

"They were already on the road when the snow started," Anrel assured her. "I cannot think they would turn back."

"They might shelter along the way, and try to wait it out," Mistress Sharduil suggested.

"I cannot utterly rule that out," Anrel said, frowning, "but it seems most unlikely to me—and inconsiderate, as I told them I would try to meet them at the city gate."

"And when are you expecting them, then?"

"Very soon," Anrel said, glancing in his turn out the window.

"Then shouldn't you be on your way to the gate?"

"Indeed, mistress, I should," Anrel agreed. He essayed a deep bow to his hostess, then clapped his hat on his head and made his way out to the front of the inn, past Master Kabrig and out into the stable yard.

After spending several minutes in the warmth of the inn the cold outside seemed far worse than before—his exposed skin stung with it, and it seemed to seep quickly in through his two coats and sturdy shirt. He wondered whether the temperature was really dropping, or whether it was merely the contrast with the cheerful interior, and decided it was probably a little of both.

He hurried up Cobbler Street and out onto the main thoroughfare, where the snow was now several inches deep, over the toes of his boots, and where the wind, blowing more fiercely than before, could reach him more readily and snatch away what little heat might still linger.

He reached the gate without incident, startling the guard. The wards were still in place, as strong as ever; it was reassuring to know he hadn't imagined them.

"I thought you were bound for the Boar's Head," the watchman said. "Surely, it's not full up!"

"No, I've taken a room there," Anrel told him. "But I came back to meet that party of peddlers I mentioned, and see them safe."

"Ah." The guard glanced out at the dim white emptiness beyond the gate. "I've seen no sign of them as yet."

"Might I wait with you, then, at least for a time? There were women with the party, and I admit to some concern."

"I'd be glad of your company," the guard assured him. "There's a stove in the gatehouse, if you'd like to warm your hands."

"I would like that very much," Anrel confirmed.

A moment later the two men were seated on wooden stools to either side of an old iron stove, holding their hands above soot black metal streaked with brown rust and letting the fire's heat sink into their bones. The only light in the little room came from a barred window looking out at the road, and the fire's glow leaking through the seams in the stove. The lantern above the gate was still burning, but its light did not reach far in the swirling whiteness.

"I see your sword is gone," the guard remarked.

"I left it at the inn," Anrel said. He did not mention he had left it as surety against his bill.

"Probably wise," the guardsman said. "You won't need it in Beynos—especially not in weather like this."

"I'm glad to hear that," Anrel said. "How *are* matters in Beynos these days? It seemed to me that the faces I've seen have looked worried."

The guard shrugged. "Is it any different anywhere else in the empire? The tales we hear from the capital are hardly calculated to soothe anyone's nerves."

"Of course, the capital is close by," Anrel pointed out. "Perhaps out on the outskirts, in Pirienna or Hallin, such concerns carry less weight."

"Perhaps," the guard conceded, "but still, we're all subjects of the same emperor and empress, and all now under the authority of the Grand Council."

"I doubt a goatherd in the hills of Pirienna has any idea what the Grand Council is doing," Anrel said. "For that matter, I've been traveling—*I* have no idea what the Grand Council is doing, and thus have not been worried by it."

"So far, from what I hear, they have done little but argue amongst themselves," the guard said. "A good many delegates are the younger sons of various sorcerers, sent by their parents to ensure that the old order is preserved, but some of those young men have apparently decided to work for their own good more than their parents'—there are schemes to split up the great estates to ensure that every magician has a piece of land of his own, or to give themselves the keys to the imperial treasury. Not that there's much *in* that treasury anymore, by all accounts."

"That's ridiculous," Anrel said.

"Of course it is," the guard agreed. "*We* know that, but *they* apparently don't. Fortunately for all of us, there are a few voices of reason among the magicians—some of the great nobles came themselves, rather than trusting anyone else. Three of the sixteen landgraves are on the council, and a score or so of burgraves. And half the council was elected by commoners, of course, and those people certainly have no desire to reward a pack of greedy young sorcerers with land and privilege."

"You seem to know more about this than I would have expected," Anrel remarked. He had not heard this sort of detailed discussion in any of his previous stops; certainly no one in Kolizand had ever mentioned the precise number of landgraves on the council, nor schemes to split up large estates.

"Well, we have several councillors staying in Beynos," the guardsman said. "Lume is not a pleasant place for a visiting nobleman these days; the mobs can be ugly, and the streets dangerous. Many of the wealthier delegates have taken up lodgings in the surrounding towns, and retreat to them whenever the council is not in session."

"But the council only just convened a few days ago!"

"Yes, but the councillors have been arriving for half a season, to make themselves at home and get ready for their deliberations. And this morning a three-day recess was announced, in honor of the prince's birth."

Anrel blinked. "The prince?"

The guard slapped his own forehead. "Oh, of course you wouldn't have heard! Yes, the prince. The empress has borne a son—she began her labor yesterday morning, and the child was delivered last night, not long before midnight. By all reports he's healthy and strong, and his name has been announced as Lurias Temnir Kaseir Imbredar."

"Another Lurias," Anrel remarked.

"Oh, of course! Haven't most of our emperors been named Lurias?"

"About half of them, I think," Anrel said. "The name did not become quite so established until some three centuries back." He noticed the guard's expression and added, "I spent some time as a student in the court schools."

"A scholar!"

Anrel shook his head. "I might have hoped to earn that title once, but no more. I haven't the temperament for it. I'm just a young man without magic or family, trying to find a place for himself."

For a moment neither spoke. Then the guard shook himself and said, "Well, at any rate, Prince Lurias was born last night, and the emperor declared a three-day celebration, so the Grand Council agreed to a recess. I think the emperor expected the delegates to join in the happy gatherings at the palace, but from what I've seen, most of them promptly left the city. Certainly, we have our full complement here in Beynos for the moment."

"I saw no sign of them in the streets."

"In this weather? Of course not! They'll be indoors, in their grand houses, drinking fine wine and dancing with beautiful women." At the mention of the weather he glanced out the window. He stopped and squinted, then sighed. "Someone's coming," he said.

Anrel rose and peered out the window into the white blur beyond. Yes, something was moving out there, something large and dark.

The veil of swirling snow parted for an instant as the shape drew nearer, and Anrel recognized it.

"That's their horse," he said. "It's my friends."

"Then straighten your hat, and let us welcome them to Beynos," the guard replied, getting to his feet.

Together, the two men stepped out into the snow.

23

In Which Reva Finds Lucrative Employment

Mistress Sharduil had kept her promises; upon arriving at the Boar's Head the Lir family found their room and Lolo's stall waiting. Nivain and Perynis tended to the horse while Garras and his other two daughters carried luggage inside, inspected the room, and negotiated terms with the innkeeper's wife.

Anrel accompanied Garras and carried a share of the baggage, but said as little as possible. He was still uncertain of his own plans. He knew that he wanted his future to involve Tazia, but how, and how soon, he had not yet decided.

The room was surprisingly large and equipped with four beds, which meant none of the daughters would need to sleep on the floor; in fact, if Tazia and Perynis shared a bed, there would even be one for Anrel. He had no intention of asking the two to share, but on the other hand, they might choose to because of the room's greatest drawback—it was cold. It was built out over the open stable, the walls were thin and poorly chinked, and the stove was small. Even though someone had built a good fire in the stove, the room was dreadfully chilly. Sleeping two to a bed might be a welcome way to stay warm in such a drafty, ill-heated space.

Garras seemed unreasonably pleased with the room, and Anrel wondered why. Did he care nothing for his daughters' comfort? Surely he had noticed the cold. Yes, he had only just moments before arrived after a long journey through the snow, but to get to this room he had passed through the delightful warmth of the inn proper, and his senses should have adjusted.

Garras spoke quietly to Mistress Sharduil for what seemed an inordinately long time, too quietly for Anrel to hear what was being discussed; then Mistress Sharduil, with a final bow and with a half-guilder deposit in hand, took her leave. Once she was gone Garras exclaimed, "This place is *perfect* for talking to customers! It won't seem cramped; it has every appearance of privacy—that long walk through the upstairs corridor will make it seem almost secret."

"And no one will need to remove his coat," Reva added bitterly.

"Exactly!"

She gave her father a look of utter disgust, and tossed her bag on one of the beds. "This one is mine," she announced.

Anrel set down his own burden and watched silently as the others distributed luggage; when that was done Tazia said, "I'll fetch Mother." She smiled at Anrel, then headed for the door.

"We'll be downstairs," Garras called after her.

"Somewhere warm," Reva said.

"Somewhere customers can find us," her father said. "I told the landlady she need not wait before sending us anyone in need of witchcraft."

"I hope we can at least spare the time to shake the snow from our clothes and warm our hands at the fire!" Reva snapped.

"Keep a civil tongue in your head, woman!" Garras barked back.

The two glared at each other, then turned and marched after Tazia.

Anrel hesitated, then shrugged and followed them.

Later the entire party was gathered around a table in one of the inn's larger dining rooms, enjoying the heat of the nearby hearth and sampling the inn's ale, when a young woman approached. She hesitated, standing a few feet away, as if uncertain it would be safe to come any closer.

Garras noticed her, and prodded Reva's shoulder. "See there? Go make yourself useful," he said.

Reva glared at him, then rose and turned to greet the stranger.

"I am Reva Lir," she said, in a conversational tone. "Perhaps I can help you."

"Are you . . ." the woman began, then stopped. She took a deep breath and held out a hand. "I am Mimmin li-Dargalleis," she said. "I've heard you might indeed be able to help me." She glanced past Reva at the rest of the family, then asked, "Is there somewhere we could speak privately?"

"Of course," Reva said. "This way."

The others sat silently, carefully not watching, as Reva led her customer away; then Nivain said, "That's one; three of us remain."

"I hope no one has a fever," Perynis said. "I had my fill of that in Kolizand!"

"I'll take care of any fevers, then," Tazia said. She glanced at Anrel.

"I will be happy to help with the sick, should the occasion arise," Anrel said, smiling at Tazia. His motives were not entirely altruistic; he was hoping for an opportunity to talk to her without the possibility her parents would overhear.

"I'd rather tell fortunes," Perynis said.

"You're welcome to my share of those," Tazia told her.

"We will all do whatever we can," Nivain told her daughters. "In times such as these we need every penny we can earn."

"Beynos may be a little more profitable than usual, if you act quickly," Anrel remarked. "I am told that several noblemen and delegates to the Grand Council are in town while the council is in recess."

"Why is the council in recess?" Perynis asked.

"In honor of the birth of Prince Lurias last night."

"A prince has been born?" Nivain asked, startled.

"So the gatekeeper told me," Anrel said.

"We need to know about this," Perynis said. "It wouldn't do for witches to not know something so important. What if I were trying to tell someone's fortune, and this came up, and I hadn't heard?"

"I hadn't thought of that," Anrel said.

"You said his name is Lurias," Nivain said. "Is he healthy?"

"To the best of my knowledge, he is."

"Then the emperor has his heir, at last!"

"The emperor has two younger brothers," Anrel reminded her. "The dynasty was hardly in danger of extinction."

"Still, a prince! That's good news."

Anrel considered that for a moment, then asked, "Why?"

Nivain stared at him. "Because . . . because it is. The succession is secured. The empire will continue."

"Right now, an heir to the throne does not strike me as the empire's most urgent need," Anrel said. "I don't see how it feeds the hungry, or calms the mobs in the street, or makes the Grand Council any less likely to do something disastrously stupid."

"You . . . have you no appreciation of . . ." Nivain stopped, unable to find the words she wanted.

"Indeed, I do not," Anrel agreed, sparing her the trouble. He knew well enough what she meant. Any number of Walasians, of every rank and station, idolized the emperor, and indeed, the entire imperial family. Anrel did not share their reverence; after all, the emperor was, despite his exalted station, merely a man. He was a man who held a difficult and staggeringly important job, and who had for the most part carried it out adequately if unexceptionally, but still, he was only human.

And for the most part, his actions did little to affect the everyday life of the empire's citizens. The emperor did not bring forth the crops in the fields, nor build the houses that sheltered the people. While the watchmen in every town were nominally employed by the emperor, and sometimes wore the emperor's green and gold and styled themselves the Emperor's Watch, in plain fact everywhere but Lume they were all hired by the burgraves, and commanded by their own officers, quite independently of who happened to occupy the imperial throne at the moment. It did not matter to Anrel who the emperor was, so long as the empire continued to function. Whether the next emperor was the son, brother, or nephew of the present incumbent did not strike him as a matter of any real significance.

In fact, given some of the rumors about the empress, Anrel thought it more certain that those brothers were truly of the same blood than that this newborn child was, though he would certainly never dare to suggest such a thing in public.

"Is it not the emperor who has declared you outlaws?" Anrel said quietly. "Simply because you did not care to attempt the trials?"

"That's different," Nivain said. "That's not his fault. The law was made centuries ago, long before he was born."

"Yet he's done nothing to change it."

"You should still speak respectfully," Garras said, entering the conversation for the first time.

"My apologies, sir." He did not want to argue with Master Lir, or do anything that might antagonize Tazia's father.

"What else did the gatekeeper tell you?" Garras demanded.

Anrel hesitated, trying to remember what else the guardsman had said. "He said . . . that several members of the Grand Council have taken homes here in Beynos, and elsewhere in the surrounding towns, because the streets of Lume are not safe. Though they were invited to celebrate the prince's birth in the capital, most have instead retreated to these outlying communities for the three days."

Garras frowned. "Then there are more sorcerers in Beynos than usual?"

"Probably."

"It doesn't matter," Nivain said. "Noblemen can't be bothered with the sort of magic we do."

"True enough," Garras said. "But I wonder whether any of them brought their own witches with them."

"Sorcerers hire witches? Why would they do that?" Anrel asked.

"I don't know," Garras said, "but Lume has its share of witches. That's why we don't go there—the people prefer to hire the witches they know from their own neighborhoods, not travelers like us. If there are people from Lume here, perhaps they brought witches."

"I don't think it likely," Anrel said. "Lume has so many people that there's business for witches the year around, so why would they chase after the councillors fleeing the city?"

"Then you don't think any of those witches work for nobles, or their households?"

"Well, my uncle never hired witches," Anrel said.

"That you knew of."

"That I knew of," Anrel acknowledged. He was fairly certain he *would* have known, but again, he had no desire to antagonize Garras.

"*We've* never worked for a sorcerer," Perynis said.

"And that may be our misfortune," Garras said.

"I would worry that any sorcerer might have us all hanged when he was done with us," Anrel said.

"We have never been hanged yet," Garras said.

"Sorcerers are the ruling class, and you have never worked for them," Anrel said. "Commoners have no reason to wish us ill, but sorcerers might well see your daughters as not merely outlaws, but competition."

"That might be so, or it might not," Garras replied. "Perhaps someday we will have an opportunity to test your theory."

"I am in no hurry."

Garras laughed and took a swig of ale.

After that the conversation wandered, and Anrel found himself paying more attention to the sight and smell of Tazia, sitting across a corner of the table from him, than to what was being said. He had just taken her hand in his own when Reva returned.

For a moment everyone fell silent and simply watched as Reva walked up and resumed her seat. They watched as she straightened her hair, tossing it back over her shoulders.

Then Nivain said, "Well?"

"She wants a love spell," Reva said slowly. "She wants it cast on a wealthy delegate who has taken refuge here while the council is in recess. This man has caught her eye, and she would like to catch his fancy in return."

Something about her manner seemed slightly odd; her parents exchanged glances.

"That should be easy enough, shouldn't it?" Garras said.

"If she can get me close enough to the man in question, yes," Reva replied.

"A binding," Anrel murmured, as he realized what sort of magic Reva was planning. "Binding the two souls together."

"That's the sorcerer's word," Tazia whispered back. "We're witches. We call it a love spell."

"There is more than one way to work such a binding," Anrel said, more to himself than to anyone else.

Reva heard him. "Oh, she wants him completely under her thumb, of course," she said. "And I'll do my best to oblige her."

"An asymmetric binding isn't stable, though," Anrel said.

Reva shrugged. "I don't think she needs it to be."

"A what?" Perynis said.

"A lopsided spell," Nivain explained. "He's right—unbalanced magic doesn't keep its shape. The spell might fade away, or the balance might shift in one direction or the other—either she will fall more in love and his love will lessen, or it will cease to be love at all and turn to something else even less balanced. Obsession, perhaps, or hatred."

"Well, we'll be long gone before that happens," Garras said.

Anrel started to say something in protest of this callous statement, but caught himself. He did not want to argue with Tazia's family, not when he was still so unsure of his own plans.

It did trouble him, though, that they all seemed so undisturbed over some of the reckless magic they performed. The fraudulent prophecies were bad enough, but a misused emotional binding could easily ruin someone's life. And an *asymmetric* one, effectively giving one person control of the other temporarily, that would inevitably and unpredictably collapse into something else—that was simply cruel.

Yes, it might equalize itself, and leave the pair genuinely in love for the rest of their lives, but that was not the most probable outcome. If Anrel remembered correctly what Valin and Saria had told him of their lessons, it was *much* more likely that the binding would break, perhaps very suddenly, leaving this man, whoever he was, married to someone in whom he had no real interest, and with no understanding of why he had been infatuated with her, or why the infatuation had abruptly ended. That could be very unpleasant for everyone involved.

Anrel was beginning to have a certain sympathy with whoever had outlawed witchcraft in the first place. "Did Mistress li-Dargalleis say who her intended paramour is?" he asked.

Reva smiled and cocked her head to one side in a way Anrel had never before seen her do. "Oh, yes," she said. "And that's the best part—even given that I'm charging her the most I have ever yet asked for a spell, and she's agreed with hardly a word of protest. His identity is *why*

I'm charging her fifty guilders." Perynis and Tazia gasped at the sum. "You'll like this, Master Murau," Reva continued. "I'm sure you will."

Anrel did not like the sound of that at all. "Will I?" he asked.

"I think so. Oh, I really do think so."

"Out with it, woman!" Garras demanded. "I know it's in the feminine nature to tease at every opportunity, but have mercy on us and say the name!"

Reva's smile broadened. "She has asked me to enchant the landgrave of Aulix, Lord Allutar Hezir."

24

In Which Anrel Weighs His Future Choices

Anrel's blood seemed to freeze in his veins at Reva's words.

"Lord Allutar?" he said.

"That's right," Reva said, nodding vigorously. "Mistress li-Dargalleis wants me to make Lord Allutar fall madly in love with her. And she'll pay *fifty guilders*!"

There were so many concerns rushing through Anrel's thoughts at this that he needed a few seconds to decide which to mention. Allutar's heartless, murderous nature came to mind immediately as a good reason for Mistress li-Dargalleis to stay well clear of him. Anrel also recalled the landgrave's intention of marrying Lady Saria, but Anrel's cousin had presumably broken that off after Valin's death.

But really, there was one single fact that doomed the entire enterprise. "Mistress Reva," Anrel said slowly, "you do realize that Lord Allutar is a powerful sorcerer?"

"Of course I do!" Reva snapped, her smile vanishing. "So I'll need to be very careful, I know that."

"I am not sure it's *possible* to be that careful," Anrel said.

"Of course it is," Reva said. "I've enchanted sorcerers before. I made Lady Fuirel hire that silly Bethuin girl as her lady's maid, didn't I?"

"I don't know," Anrel said. "Perhaps you did. But Lady Fuirel is no landgrave, no Lord Allutar." In truth, he had no idea who Lady Fuirel was, but he was fairly certain she was not half the sorcerer Lord Allutar was. As a landgrave, Allutar was theoretically supposed to be one of the sixteen most powerful magicians in the empire. Making allowances for the political facts he might not actually be among the top sixteen, but he was unquestionably among the top hundred.

"A sorcerer is a sorcerer," Reva said angrily. "Are you trying to frighten me? Is there some reason you *want* me to remain poor?"

Anrel would not have minded if he had succeeded in frightening her, but it would hardly do to admit it. "By no means, Mistress Reva!" he said instead. "I merely warn you to be very cautious indeed in this undertaking. I have dealt with Lord Allutar, and he is not a forgiving man. I would not care to see you fall afoul of him."

In truth, Anrel feared that Reva had signed her own death warrant by accepting this commission, but he could not think of any way to convince her of her folly. He knew that she would not listen to him if he tried to argue further at present.

He was uncomfortably aware that he had fifty guilders of his own hidden away in the lining of his coat; he could perhaps pay Reva *not* to attempt the spell. Doing so, however, would reveal that he had lied to the Lirs, and would use up a large portion of his funds, and there was nothing to keep her from refusing his money—or worse, taking his money and then attempting the spell anyway, excusing it as fair repayment for Anrel's lies. After all, refusing the commission from Mistress li-Dargalleis at this point would not be good for Reva's reputation as a witch.

But he was very much afraid that the spell would utterly fail, that Lord Allutar would sense the attempt and follow the magic back to its source, and that Reva would suffer in consequence.

What's more, she might not be the only one. Her family was known here at the Boar's Head, and Lord Allutar might trace her back here and find Anrel. Anrel did not want anything to bring him to Lord Allutar's attention. Just knowing that the landgrave was within the same city walls was distressing; suppose they encountered each other on the street?

In fact, that might happen, if Anrel ever set foot outside the inn. Even narrow little Cobbler Street was not safe, as Allutar might well decide to have a pair of boots reheeled.

This was going to be severely limiting, perhaps even more limiting than the snow that was falling again. It would also complicate any attempt to woo Tazia, or to gain Garras's blessing for his interest in her—how much of a man could he look, when he did not dare to walk the streets openly?

That was trivial when Reva's very life was at risk, but still, he could not help thinking about it.

Perhaps, he thought despairingly, he should give up on Tazia and her family, let Reva destroy herself, then go on to Lume and hide there, as he had originally planned.

But he could not give up on Tazia. And besides, Lord Allutar walked the streets of Lume, as well. He was a member of the Grand Council.

But Lume was so much larger than Beynos, and there were undoubtedly places Allutar did not go. Anrel could not imagine him venturing into the treacherous alleys of the Pensioners' Quarter, or the rowdy taverns behind the court schools, or the stinking fish markets of the Galdin steps—and that was only in the visible and inhabited portions of the capital! The scattered ruins left by the Old Empire were largely shunned by modern-day Walasians, and no one but drunken idiots trying to prove their courage ever ventured into the ancient tunnels beneath the city without a very good reason. There were a thousand places to hide in Lume—more than a thousand. Anrel knew many of them already, where he knew nothing of Beynos except what he had seen riding through, and what he had observed since his arrival a few hours before.

Anrel also knew there were other places besides Beynos and Lume. Perhaps he should head for somewhere in Lithrayn, or even across the border into the Cousins—but he had never been there. He had never been anywhere except Aulix and Lume, and various points in between them.

He glanced at Tazia, who seemed happily oblivious of how much danger her sister was in.

"I'm supposed to meet Mistress li-Dargalleis tomorrow morning," Reva said. "We'll work out the details then of when I might best bewitch Lord Allutar."

"You'll need to have both of them present," Nivain said.

"Of *course*, Mother," Reva replied. "I *have* cast love spells before, you know!"

Perynis giggled at that. "Remember that one in Milinkor?" she said. "I thought he was going to pull up her skirt and tup her right there at the ball!"

"Perynis!" Nivain said, scandalized. She glanced around to make sure no one else had heard her daughter's remark.

"I'm not sure she would have minded," Garras said.

"That spell did affect both of them," Reva added. "It wasn't as one-sided as what Mistress li-Dargalleis seems to want."

"Well, let us hope that this Lord Allutar will be a little more restrained in his affections," Nivain replied.

"I'm sure he will," Anrel said. "He's a man of strong will."

Reva seemed irritated by this comment, and glared at Anrel. Tazia tugged gently at his hand, and he looked at her.

"Lord Allutar knows you, doesn't he?" she whispered.

"Yes, he does."

"He's the one who . . . he wants you dead?"

"I believe so, yes. Though I haven't asked him. It was Lord Neriam, the First Lord Magistrate, who recognized me and set Naith's city watch upon me, and Neriam is both Allutar's subordinate and his friend. I haven't had the opportunity to speak to Lord Allutar since I . . . since the incident in Naith, but I *assume* Lord Neriam informed the landgrave of the miscreant's identity."

He did not mention that once his identity was known his speech had also probably had some effect on Lord Allutar's courtship of Lady Saria, and that this might contribute to further ill will on Allutar's part.

Tazia nodded. "He must know, then, if he is Lord Neriam's superior. And he's here in Beynos?"

"So says Reva's client, and I have no reason to doubt it. Lord Allutar did name himself to the Grand Council, and it seems entirely reasonable that he would have a place in Beynos."

"Then you aren't safe here."

Anrel was startled that she had realized this; certainly, the rest of her family did not appear to have come to any such conclusion. He glanced at Tazia's parents, who were talking to Reva.

"I doubt Lord Allutar would ever set foot in a place like the Boar's Head," Anrel said.

"I suppose not—a great noble like him could surely do better. But he mustn't see you anywhere. You mustn't go out."

"That thought had occurred to me," Anrel conceded.

Tazia threw her father a glance, then returned her gaze to Anrel. "Perhaps you should go on, then," she said. "To Lume, or wherever you're going."

"I had been considering that possibility," Anrel admitted.

Tazia looked up at him, then at her father once more, then back at Anrel.

"If I were to go," Anrel whispered, slowly and deliberately, ready to stop at the first sign that he had misread Tazia's expression, "and I were to ask you to accompany me . . ."

"I would gladly do so," Tazia answered.

Anrel stared at her for a long moment, resisting the urge to pull her closer, perhaps to kiss her. Then the memory of Perynis's unfortunate remark came to him, and he smiled crookedly; he suddenly had a great deal of sympathy for that unknown victim of Reva's witchcraft in Milinkor, whoever he might have been.

And that reminded him that Reva was on the verge of committing unintentional suicide.

"We can't go yet, though," he told Tazia.

She once again looked at her father, more meaningfully this time.

"No, it's not that," Anrel said. "Though in truth I would prefer an honorable parting, with your parents' consent given and a wedding announced. I do not insist on it, however, and arranging such a thing here in Beynos might not be practical."

"I don't think Father would give his consent," Tazia whispered.

Anrel frowned at that; now it was his turn to glance at Garras.

"I don't think he'll ever willingly part with any of us, despite his complaints," Tazia said. "As long as we all bring in more than we cost, he'll want us to stay. That money Reva is collecting? It will *never* be enough to buy her freedom."

Anrel considered that for a moment, then decided it could wait. "We can discuss that further another time," he said. "Right now, there's something more urgent."

"What could be more urgent?"

"Your sister's life. I honestly do not believe she can safely enchant Lord Allutar, and if she is caught attempting it, she'll be hanged—or worse. Allutar sacrificed a young man's lifeblood to power one of his own spells at the autumnal equinox; I would rather not see him spend your sister's life in similar fashion at the vernal, or perhaps use her to enhance his sorcery in other ways."

Tazia glanced at Reva, who was huddled with their mother. "You're sure he is that dangerous? That he would do that, if he caught her?"

"How can I be sure?" Anrel asked. "But I have seen Lord Allutar kill a man with nothing but raw magic; he is the most powerful sorcerer I have ever met. I know that *I* can detect the wards your family casts, and I felt the binding Reva and your mother attempted on me the day we met—felt it, and resisted it. And I'm not a tenth the sorcerer Lord Allutar is."

"You think she should refuse the job?"

"I do."

Tazia frowned. "But *fifty guilders*! She'll never agree to forgo so much. She wants so badly to strike out on her own."

"Did you not just tell me that no amount of money would ever be enough for her father to release her?"

"*I* believe that, but *she* doesn't."

Anrel bit his lip. He knew Tazia was right.

Twice, though, he had failed to intervene when someone faced death at Lord Allutar's hands. He had done nothing at all to save Urunar Kazien, even when he had his hands on another criminal whose life might perhaps have been substituted for the baker's son. He had done nothing remotely effective for Lord Valin; his efforts to keep Valin and Allutar apart, or to talk sense into Valin, had been worse than useless. He had let an acquaintance and his best friend die, and he did not want to let yet a third life be needlessly snuffed out—particularly not the life of a sister of the woman he was coming to love. This time he would do *something*. He recalled the gold in his own coat again, and schemes began stirring in his brain.

"Let me see what I can do," he said at last. "There may be a way."

"How could there be?"

"I will concede that we may be unable to sway your sister, but there are other parties to this transaction," Anrel said. "If Mistress li-Dargalleis should change her mind, perhaps set her cap for someone other than Lord Allutar, then Reva will be safe enough."

"But why would she . . . ?"

"Let me see what I can do," he repeated.

Tazia looked unconvinced, but did not argue further. "And when this matter is resolved, and my sister has finished with Lord Allutar, in one way or another—then what do you intend?"

"Then I intend to travel," Anrel said lightly. "Eastward, I think—perhaps a stay in Lume, but then on to the eastern provinces, perhaps even a tour of the Cousins."

"Ah. Would you be traveling alone?"

"I sincerely hope not," Anrel said, looking her in the eye.

She smiled, threw her father a glance, then said, "I think I will have a few words with my parents while you see what you can do about Mistress li-Dargalleis."

"And just how direct will these words be?"

"Oh, I will be most circumspect initially, and judge the weather carefully before risking any blunt questions. There will be no demands or threats, I promise you—nothing that might provoke open antagonism."

"While you undoubtedly know your parents far better than I do, is anyone capable of such fine judgments?"

"Well—perhaps my promise is a trifle ambitious. Let us say rather that I will do my very best to avoid any unfortunate confrontations."

He smiled at her. "I can ask no more."

"What are you two whispering about?" Perynis demanded. She had been shut out of Reva's conversation with their parents, and had therefore turned her attention elsewhere.

"None of *your* concern, ninny!" Tazia replied.

"Plotting to assassinate the emperor and invade Ermetia, of course," Anrel told her.

"Ha! Telling each other romantic little lies, more likely."

"If you knew, then why did you ask?" Tazia retorted.

With that, the conversation became general once again, and a moment later Anrel made an excuse to slip away for a moment. He did not head for the privy, though; instead he made his way to the front room, where he found Dorrin Kabrig dozing by the door.

He started at the sound of Anrel's footsteps and sat up. "Master Adirane," he said. "Going out?"

"No," Anrel said. "But I would appreciate a word with you, Master Kabrig."

The doorkeeper looked puzzled. "Oh?"

"Yes."

"Then I am at your disposal, Master Adirane. How can I be of service?"

Anrel hesitated, trying to phrase his request well. "You are familiar with the town, I take it?"

"I have lived here all my life," Dorrin replied. "I think I know it tolerably well."

"I'm sure you do, then," Anrel said. "I have heard that several of the delegates to the Grand Council have made themselves at home here, when their presence is not required in Lume; is that true?"

"Oh, yes. There are several fine homes in Beynos, maintained by various great families for themselves and their friends, and I believe that virtually all of them are currently let to councillors. Why do you ask?"

"It is a delicate matter; bear with me."

"Of course."

"Is one of those councillors Lord Allutar, the landgrave of Aulix?"

"So I have heard," Dorrin answered, his eyes narrowing.

"Please, Master Kabrig, do not look so concerned! I assure you, I intend the landgrave no harm." That phrasing was deliberate; Anrel most certainly *wished* that harm might befall Lord Allutar, but he did not at present *intend* any. "As a citizen of Aulix, I merely want to know something of his present situation. I have heard some most peculiar rumors of late."

"Rumors?"

"Indeed."

"What sort of rumors?"

"Well—I told you it was a delicate matter."

"You did."

"I have heard rumors as to why Lord Allutar has not yet married and sired an heir. I would prefer to be no more specific."

A slow, crooked smile spread across Dorrin's face; apparently he found something very appealing in the rumors he now imagined. "I *see*," he said.

"Now, these may well be the most scurrilous sort of lies," Anrel said hastily. "I do not for a moment present them as fact. But I do admit that my curiosity has gotten the better of me—is there some foundation for these tales?"

"I wouldn't know," Dorrin said. "I hadn't heard anything of the sort."

"But you know, perhaps, which house Lord Allutar is residing in?"

"Oh, yes—it's his own, in fact, built by his grandfather, Faurien Hezir. It's up on Bridge Street Hill."

"Perhaps, when you have a moment, you might stop by, and have a word with a member or two of the landgrave's staff? I'm sure it would be a great relief to everyone if we could put these rumors to rest."

"I'm sure it would." He glanced at the front door, then back at Anrel. "You could go yourself, you know. I could give you directions; it's not hard to find."

"Thank you, but I'm afraid that won't be practical—Master Lir has hired me for certain duties that require me to remain close at hand at all times."

"Chaperoning his daughters, I suppose. That youngest one, Perynis, is a little heartbreaker, isn't she? But I believe you said you had your eye on the middle one."

"I'm afraid I couldn't say," Anrel said with a smile and a wink.

"Of course." Dorrin glanced at the door again. "I can't go just now, but I'm sure I'll find a chance to stroll up Bridge Street in the next day or two, and a word or two with a coachman or footman would be a pleasant diversion."

"That would please me very much," Anrel said. "I'm sure it's nothing, but I'm sure you know how troublesome a rumor can be, even if it's no more than a malicious lie. Best to put it to rest immediately."

"Indeed," Dorrin agreed. "Lord Allutar—who would have thought it?"

"Who, indeed?" He bowed to the doorkeeper. "Thank you, good sir; now, if you'll forgive me, duty calls."

"Of course."

As Anrel headed back toward the Lir family gathering in the back room, he allowed himself a smile.

He had no idea whether there were really any rumors circulating about Lord Allutar—but he was certain that now there *would* be, even if Master Kabrig was far more discreet than Anrel thought he would be. That would provide a petty irritant for the landgrave, and anything that discomfited Valin's killer would please Anrel.

More important, if there *was* any actual impediment to Lord Allutar marrying Mistress li-Dargalleis and siring children on her, the landgrave's staff would almost certainly know about it, and Master Kabrig would report it back to Anrel.

If there was no such impediment—well, that would be unfortunate, and Anrel would need to create one. He had not yet devised a means to do so, but he was sure something would occur to him in time.

25

In Which Anrel Discusses Lord Allutar's Marital Prospects

The following afternoon, while the Lir family was attending to the business of witchcraft, Anrel was in the Boar's Head's saloon, enjoying a fine and surprisingly inexpensive merlot. He looked up when the door opened; two men stepped in, and Anrel was startled to recognize both of them.

The presence of Dorrin Kabrig was hardly unexpected, but the man following him was someone Anrel had last seen in Alzur, a season ago—and someone who he did not want to see him. He started to turn away and look for somewhere to hide, but he did not have time.

"Master Adirane," Dorrin called. "A moment of your time, if you would."

Anrel sighed, and turned back to the new arrivals. He tried not to let his concern show, but he was well aware that at any moment he might need to run for his life.

"Master Kabrig," he said, lifting his glass. "A pleasure to see you again."

The other man's mouth twitched. "I thought it might be you, 'Master Adirane,'" he said.

"Hollem," Anrel said, acknowledging the man he had instantly recognized as Lord Allutar's footman. "I'm sorry, I'm afraid I don't know your full name."

"Hollem tel-Guriel," he said, holding out a hand.

Astonished by this friendly gesture, Anrel set down his wine and shook hands firmly. "Master tel-Guriel," he said. "I did not expect to see you here."

"And I never expected to see *you* again *anywhere*," Hollem said.

Anrel grimaced.

"How is it you two know each other?" Dorrin asked suspiciously.

"Oh, we grew up in the same village," Anrel said, before Hollem could speak. "I left under unfortunate circumstances, though."

"*Very* unfortunate," Hollem said.

"Indeed," Anrel agreed. "And what brings you to the Boar's Head, Master tel-Guriel?"

"Oh, that's simple enough," Hollem said. "When Master Kabrig came around asking questions about certain rumors, I demanded to know where he had heard these absurd allegations, and wouldn't tell him a thing until I had a name. When he told me 'Adirane' I thought it must be you, and I asked if he could arrange a meeting."

"Perhaps I should have used another name," Anrel said ruefully.

"Perhaps you should," Hollem said. "After all, you have in the past." He waved that aside. "Though I would have wanted to meet you, in any case."

"Of course." Anrel glanced around. The reference to a past alias seemed to imply that the footman knew him to be Alvos. "You know, given the circumstances, I confess to some surprise that you do not appear to be accompanied by members of the city watch."

"A pleasant surprise, I trust."

"Very much so."

"Why would the city watch be involved?" Dorrin asked, glancing from one man to the other.

"I told you the circumstances of my departure were unfortunate," Anrel said. "I assure you, I have committed no crime in Beynos, but there may be some question about my actions elsewhere. If our friend here has not brought me to their attention for past offenses, though, then the watchmen have no reason to be looking for me."

"I have my reasons for wanting to keep matters between ourselves," Hollem said. "In fact, is there somewhere more private we could speak?"

"I have a room upstairs," Anrel said. "I share it with certain others, but I don't believe any of them are there at the moment." He picked up his wine and finished it quickly.

"Wait a minute," Dorrin protested. "What's this about? I thought you just wanted to know who was spreading rumors about your master. And I thought *you* just wanted to know whether the rumors were true."

"I'm afraid it's more complicated than that," Anrel said, wondering whether it might be worth attempting to pay Dorrin for his silence.

Hollem's thoughts apparently ran along similar lines, as a coin appeared in his hand. "Master Kabrig," he said, "I thank you sincerely for bringing me here, but don't let me take up any more of your valuable time." He tucked the coin, a half-guilder by the look of it, into Dorrin's coat pocket.

Dorrin looked down, then thrust his hand into his pocket to feel the coin's size and weight. He blinked.

"Of course," he said. "In fact, I think Master Sharduil had a job for me that I really ought to be doing."

"Well, we shan't keep you," Anrel said. "Thank you."

With a final suspicious glance, Dorrin turned away.

When the door had closed behind him, Anrel set his empty glass on the bar with a threepenny coin beside it—the wine had been twopence, but the extra penny was to keep the barkeeper from feeling ill-used. That done, he led the way through the back parlor to the inn's central passage, then upstairs and through the maze of corridors that led to the big drafty room above the stable.

As he had thought, it was uninhabited; the witches were selling their witchcraft, and Garras was either helping them or amusing himself in some fashion. Anrel showed Hollem in, then closed the door behind them.

Hollem looked around the room, and shivered. Anrel crossed to the stove and slid open the dampers, then opened the stove door and shoveled in a scoop of fresh charcoal. It would not be enough to heat the room properly, but it would, he hoped, take off the worst of the chill.

"Now," Anrel said, as he latched the stove door and straightened up, "much as I appreciate it, suppose you tell me why I have not been dragged off to a dungeon somewhere. Is that Lord Allutar's doing, or your own?"

"Mine, so far," Hollem said. "I haven't spoken to Lord Allutar yet, not since your friend gave me your name. After all, I couldn't be *sure* this Dyssan Adirane was really Anrel Murau until I had seen you for myself."

"But you could have brought a brace of guards along, if you chose," Anrel said.

"Yes, I could," Hollem agreed. "And if I *wanted* to see you in a dungeon, I would have."

"I assume, from what you have said so far, that you *are* aware of my reasons for not returning to Alzur?"

Hollem nodded. "Oh, yes. Your actions in Naith are not a secret from my master or his household. We do know who the infamous Alvos was."

"Somehow," Anrel said, "I cannot bring myself to think you have become one of the radical populists, dedicated to the overthrow of the nobility, and therefore unwilling to aid Lord Allutar in the apprehension of a rabble-rouser like me. In fact, I find it very difficult to entertain any doubt at all about your loyalty to our overlord—I have certainly never seen the slightest sign that you are unhappy in your employment, and that half-guilder you gave Master Kabrig would seem to indicate that you are well paid in your present position. That would imply that you are acting in what you believe to be the landgrave's interest. Do you think, then, that Lord Allutar doesn't want me in a dungeon?"

Hollem smiled, which Anrel found curiously unsettling; he had never seen the footman smile before. It would not have been appropriate while he was performing his duties in his master's house, and the meeting downstairs had been a little too awkward for cheerful expressions.

"No one has ever said you're stupid, Master Murau," he said. "Indeed, I do believe that Lord Allutar would prefer you to stay free. However, it would be unwise of him to *say* so—as Alvos you are, after all, a notorious traitor and seditionist, responsible for a major riot. The Lords Magistrate in Naith circulated the knowledge of your true identity to their allies and confederates a day or so after your departure, but kept that information from the general population lest you gain further sympathy from the public at large. They very much want to see you hanged, or perhaps burned at the stake, for your actions."

Anrel grimaced. "And why do you believe that your employer does not share this desire?"

"Because I believe he would prefer to keep his future wife happy. Killing her favorite cousin would not contribute to his domestic tranquility."

Anrel stroked his beard thoughtfully. "His future wife?"

"Were you unaware of his intentions?"

"I was . . . uncertain," Anrel said. "As of the most recent news I had heard on the subject, which is none too recent, Lord Allutar and Lady Saria had given every sign of mutual interest, but nothing had yet been formalized. However, I had thought she had in the end refused his attentions."

"Why would she do that?" Hollem asked.

Anrel snorted. "It occurred to me that she might look askance at the killing of members of her household. While I yet live, her father's fosterling does not, having died horribly by your master's own hand."

"She appears to have accepted that Lord Valin brought his fate upon himself."

Anrel very much wished he was surprised by that; alas, he was not. "He is not the only inhabitant of the Adirane home to be threatened by Lord Allutar; as you have just said, I am under sentence of death."

"A sentence that was Lord Neriam's doing, not Lord Allutar's."

"Lord Allutar is Lord Neriam's superior."

"True, but it does not look well to undercut one's underlings in such matters without a very good reason indeed, and being betrothed to the traitor's cousin is not widely seen as a good reason."

Anrel lowered his hand from his beard. "Then they are indeed betrothed?"

"They are. It is to be a respectably long engagement, to allow for all the personal and financial arrangements and in hopes that the political situation will have resolved itself—and perhaps also to give the principals time to resolve any doubts they may have, since as you have pointed out,

Lord Allutar did kill your uncle's fosterling. The wedding is to be held on the autumnal equinox, if all goes well. In the interests of all going well, Lord Allutar would prefer not to execute or imprison any of Lady Saria's relatives."

The autumnal equinox—exactly a year after Urunar Kazien's execution. Anrel wondered whether that was deliberate, or mere coincidence. "Killing her father's fosterling was not sufficient to deter her?"

"Lord Valin was not her blood kin, and so far as Lady Saria knows, he died in a fair contest that he had provoked. I think we all know that Lord Valin was capable of reckless and foolish behavior, and that Lady Saria did not hold him in the highest regard. You, on the other hand, are considered a sensible fellow—though your actions in Naith would seem to contradict that widely held opinion—and Lady Saria is quite fond of you. The unexpressed consensus among the nobility of Alzur is that exile is an appropriate and sufficient penalty for your outburst, and death would be excessive."

Anrel stared at Hollem for a moment, and then said, "Forgive me for asking this, Master tel-Guriel, but why should I believe you? While your actions today would seem to imply that you do indeed believe what you have reported, how can I know that your beliefs are accurate? You are a well-spoken man, most particularly for one of your station, and I know that Lord Allutar trusts you in many things, but why should I believe he has confided in you just what he thinks of me, or how much weight he gives his fiancée's opinions, or even what her opinions *are*?"

"A very reasonable concern, Master Murau." Hollem grimaced. "You probably find it strange to be speaking to me as an equal—and I assure you, I find it strange myself. I am accustomed to seeing you as my social superior, though not, of course, a true aristocrat, yet here we are, in a situation where if anything, *I* am the superior. It does make it difficult to judge how reliable we are to each other."

"I think I would be just as doubting of anyone, regardless of their rank," Anrel said. "I have never found nobles to be any more truthful than commoners. I do not question your honor, Master tel-Guriel, so much as your ability to know what you claim to know."

"Ah," Hollem said. "Of course, I cannot truly know what lies in my master's heart, or in Lady Saria's. I can assure you, though, that Lord Allutar requires me to stay within earshot whenever he is entertaining guests in his home, so that I can be summoned instantly should he require my services, and I have therefore heard a great deal of conversation between the two, as well as many of Lord Allutar's conversations with others—Lord Dorias, Lord Neriam, and so on. I have also spoken with the other members of the household; as a member of the privileged classes, albeit not a sorcerer, you may not realize just how much we servants see and hear of what goes on in any nobleman's home. What's more, Lord Allutar has a habit, when a day has brought more inconveniences than the usual, of sitting up late, drinking heavily, and unburdening himself to his trusted chief footman—which is to say, to me. Perhaps one day in ten he will do this. I therefore feel that I am very much in his confidence, and can speak of his attitudes and opinions with some authority."

"I see," Anrel said.

"And I'm sure you also see that I could be lying about all of this—but why should I bother? If I wished you harm, it would have been very simple to arrange it."

"Obviously. Though you might have some subtler game in mind."

"I might, though I can't think what it would be. May we proceed, however, as if I am being truthful?"

"For the present, let us by all means assume we are both being frank and honest. And in that spirit, let me ask, why did you come to the Boar's Head today?"

Hollem spread his hands. "To meet this Dyssan Adirane who was spreading vile rumors about my employer, of course."

"Ah, but why did you want to meet him? Why not simply tell Master Kabrig that the rumors were nonsense?"

"A variety of reasons. First and foremost, simple curiosity—I recognized the name Adirane, of course, and immediately suspected your identity, so I was curious to see whether it was indeed you."

"I am indeed me—but you could have determined as much with a mere glance; you needn't have engaged me in conversation, or come up here with me."

"True. A second reason was to acquaint you with the circumstances of your exile. If you remain out of sight, I assure you Lord Allutar will make no effort to pursue and destroy you, but should you be seen in Naith or Alzur, he will have no choice but to see you captured and killed. I thought it would be best for all concerned if you knew this to be the case."

Anrel nodded thoughtfully. "And if I am seen in Lume?"

"Rumors about Alvos the orator haranguing the crowds in the Pensioners' Quarter are common, though nothing ever comes of them. As long as nothing *does* ever come of them, they are of no concern to Lord Allutar."

"I understand Alvos is seen as something of a hero in certain quarters."

"So I am told, yes. A hero whose open presence would be very inconvenient to many people. I think it would be best for all concerned if Alvos were to remain merely a legend. That brings me to another reason I came here—to ask you what your intentions are. Why are you *here*, in Beynos, rather than hiding in the hills of Pirienna, or fled to Quand? Where are you bound?"

Anrel smiled. "Oh, that's simple enough. I did not think that wandering aimlessly through the countryside would be either pleasant or safe; strangers who cannot account for themselves often attract unwelcome attention. I wanted to hide somewhere I knew my way around, somewhere I had friends and contacts. The entire province of Aulix would obviously be unsuitable, and the only place outside Aulix that fits that description is Lume, where I spent four years as a student. I have therefore been making my way to Lume, rather more slowly than I had intended, and Beynos is the last stop along my route."

"Well, I have just said that if you remain out of sight, your presence in Lume should not be a problem, but to be honest, I think Lord Allutar might prefer it if you were elsewhere. Lume is a big city, but the risk that you might accidentally encounter him, or perhaps Lady Saria, while very small, would still seem unnecessarily high."

"I have of late been considering the possibility of continuing eastward, to Lithrayn or the Cousins."

"I think that might be wise," Hollem said.

Anrel nodded. "Were there other reasons?"

"Oh, yes, at least two more," Hollem said. "Perhaps most important, I wanted to ensure that whoever this Dyssan Adirane proved to be, that he would stop spreading rumors about Lord Allutar. My master's relationship with Lady Saria is quite delicate enough, thanks to Lord Valin, without any questions arising about . . ." He hesitated, then concluded, "Well, without any unnecessary questions arising."

"Ah," Anrel said. "Well, I think I can offer you some assurance on that account; after speaking to you, I have no further use for such rumors. While it is tempting to continue them as a form of petty harassment, since I hardly feel that justice has been served in regard to Lord Allutar's murder of Lord Valin, I do not wish any harm to my cousin. If Saria really still wants to marry Lord Allutar, I have no desire to see her troubled by falsehoods." He sighed. "I could wish she were more troubled by the truth of Valin's death, but spreading lies is no way to encourage that."

"That brings me to my final reason for coming to see you, and asking to speak in private," Hollem said. "I wanted to know *why* you were spreading lies."

"You know, I really didn't spread any," Anrel said. "I gave Dorrin a few broad hints, but nothing more than that; if he cited any specifics when he spoke to you, I assure you, they were the product of his own imagination. If anyone else has spoken of these rumors, it was Dorrin's doing, not mine."

"That does not answer the question of why you gave Master Kabrig those hints."

"I would prefer not to answer it," Anrel said.

"I would prefer not to tell Lord Allutar you are here, in Beynos," Hollem replied. "Particularly when the roads out of town are still covered in snow, making it easy to track anyone who leaves the city."

"Oh," Anrel said. He frowned. "I hope you will forgive me if I name no names, and speak in generalities."

"I am not feeling unreasonably demanding today."

"There is a . . . person," he said. "A female, though I will not specify girl, woman, or lady. She has taken an interest in Lord Allutar, and a friend of hers was concerned about this, and asked my advice—specifically, she wanted to know whether I was aware of any impediment to her friend marrying Lord Allutar. I wasn't—I had thought that Lord Valin's death would most likely be sufficient to prevent the betrothal to Lady Saria, which I suppose was foolish of me. I thought that hinting at rumors, and making sure that reached the ears of a member or two of Lord Allutar's household, might provide me with useful information on that count, as in fact it has. There was a saying in the court schools that asking a question may not produce an answer, but giving a *wrong* answer will invariably provoke a dozen corrections, so I thought starting a false rumor or two might in time provide me with the truth I needed. As it has; if Lord Allutar is already engaged, then my friend's friend will need to look elsewhere."

"I see," Hollem said.

"Thus are we both satisfied," Anrel said. "I will trouble Lord Allutar no more, and his engagement assures me that my friend's friend will not trouble him, either."

"And that's all there was to it? There was no political significance, no attempt to interfere with the Grand Council's deliberations?"

"That's all," Anrel said. "It had not occurred to me to concern myself with the council's doings."

Hollem looked puzzled. "But you *are* Alvos, are you not? The man whose speech in Naith did so much to fill the council with firebrands and idealists?"

Anrel shrugged. "I spoke Valin's words," he said. "Lord Allutar had arranged his death so that those words might not be heard; in simple justice, I therefore felt it necessary that those words *would* be heard. I did not think it mattered whether *I* heard them, or remembered them, or believed them—as it happens, I don't remember just what I said, and I certainly didn't believe it. I wasn't speaking for myself, but for Valin, and solely to frustrate Lord Allutar, that he might not profit from his crime."

"I would say you accomplished that much," Hollem said, staring at

Anrel. "I would say those words were delivered far more effectively than if Lord Valin had lived to speak them himself."

"Then I am done with them, and with politics," Anrel said. "There was no political purpose to my rumormongering; I sought only to determine whether Lord Allutar was a suitable prospect for marriage. With that settled, I am done with rumors, as well, and will henceforth be happy to stay out of Lord Allutar's path as best I can."

"In that case, I, too, am done with the matter, and must be off."

"Let me escort you downstairs," Anrel offered. "Perhaps we could share a bottle of wine before you go."

Hollem shook his head. "No, I think not. I must be getting back to my duties at the House of Faurien Hezir."

Anrel shrugged. "As you please. I will still see you out, and ask that if you think it wise, and the appropriate circumstances present themselves, you will pass along my fond regards to my cousin, and my felicitations on her betrothal. I trust she will be understanding if I decline to attend the wedding."

"I'm sure she will," Hollem said. "I'm sure she will."

26

In Which Reva Proves Uncooperative

After seeing Hollem out, Anrel returned to the room above the stable and sat by the little stove, brooding silently as the skies outside the window darkened and the room grew dim.

He had not let it show when speaking to Hollem, had not even allowed himself to feel it, but he found the news that his cousin Saria still intended to marry Lord Allutar profoundly depressing. How could she want to share the bed of the man who had murdered Valin? He knew that she and Valin had bickered constantly, and that she had professed disdain for him, but Anrel had always assumed that to be a sort of sibling rivalry, disguising affection.

Apparently he had misjudged.

When he had first learned that Saria was interested in wedding Allutar he had been surprised, but he had not been greatly upset by the news. He had never liked Allutar, but he knew that did not make the landgrave a monster; good people could disagree, could even find each other intolerable, without either being significantly at fault. Allutar had never bothered to disguise his contempt for the common people of Aulix, but was that not simple honesty? Would it not have been hypocritical to pretend to a respect and compassion he did not feel? And the man had tried his best to keep the province happy and prosperous; no one could deny that. Yes, he practiced black magic, but despite the disapproval of Lord Blackfield and the Lantern Society, the Walasian

Empire had always allowed its sorcerous nobles to do so. It was not a crime; in fact, using his talents however might best benefit his subjects was his duty as their ruler, no matter how unpleasant Quandish sorcerers, or those unfortunates whose blood he used, might find it.

If Saria saw the landgrave's virtues more clearly than Anrel did, and was not troubled by his flaws, then why should she not marry him?

But then Lord Allutar had deliberately baited Valin, and killed him. Yes, it had been legal, but it was *wrong*, and for Saria to not see that troubled Anrel a great deal. Even if she did not know every detail of how the challenge had been made, and how the contest had played out, she certainly knew that Valin, the young man who had shared her father's roof for almost a dozen years, was dead at Lord Allutar's hand.

Had she so little respect for Valin's memory? Not half a year after his death, she was betrothed to his killer.

For that matter, Anrel realized that he, too, seemed willing to let Valin's slayer carry on undisturbed by the memory of his crime. It was not Allutar who was a hunted exile, condemned by the Lords Magistrate for Valin's death; it was Anrel, for daring to speak Valin's words to the ordinary folk of Naith. He had delivered the speech he thought Valin would have wanted to give, but since then he had done nothing more than survive and tend to his own affairs. He had made no further effort to avenge Valin, or to punish Lord Allutar or Lord Neriam or Lord Lindred for their various roles in his death.

He did not really know what he might have done, but he could not help thinking he should have done *something*.

And now he learned that Lord Allutar did not particularly care whether he lived or died. His only concern was not for Anrel at all, but for whether his actions might displease Lady Saria. Anrel, as a commoner, was almost beneath his notice.

Not that being a sorcerer would necessarily have helped. After all, Lord Valin had died when he got in Lord Allutar's way. The Lord Anrel who might have been, had Anrel not failed his trials, would probably have fared no better.

Perhaps Valin had been right in arguing that the system that gave Lord Allutar such authority ought to be changed.

Perhaps the Grand Council would change it.

Anrel, though, did not see any way he could do anything about it. The system was in place, he had lived under it all his life, and he was just one man. The empire was not his concern. His family, his friends—*those* were his concerns.

Valin was dead, and while revenge would be pleasant, if he could find a way to arrange it, it would do nothing to restore Valin to life. Lord Dorias and Lady Saria did not need Anrel's help—but Reva did, whether she knew it or not, and he could provide it, not by brooding here in the dark, but by telling Mimmin li-Dargalleis that Lord Allutar was engaged to marry Lady Saria, and therefore unavailable, love spell or no.

He shook his head, then got to his feet, his joints stiff with cold. He closed the dampers on the stove, then marched out of the room.

He found Garras and Tazia in the dining hall, talking quietly; the other three witches were not present.

"Ah, Anrel!" Garras said.

Anrel glanced around hurriedly, and saw no one else paying any attention; he stepped close and said, "Remember, I go by Dyssan Adirane here."

"Yes, of course," Garras said. "A man of many names, our Anrel. Dyssan or Alvos or Anrel—are there others? Are you Prince Sharal in disguise, perhaps?"

"No," Anrel said sharply, not finding this sally even remotely amusing. He could smell wine on Garras's breath. He seated himself across the table from Garras, around a corner from Tazia, then leaned forward and said, "I have learned something I think Reva should know."

"Oh?" Garras asked, regarding him owlishly.

"What is it?" Tazia asked.

"It would seem that Lord Allutar is betrothed; he's to marry Lady Saria Adirane at the end of this coming summer."

"Adirane?" Tazia asked.

"My cousin," Anrel said. "But the point is, he's engaged. A love spell would be most unwise, under the circumstances—Lady Saria is a moderately talented sorceress herself, and would certainly detect such a binding upon her beloved when next she saw him."

Even as he said this, Anrel wondered whether it was true—*would* Saria notice an enchantment on Lord Allutar? Would it occur to her to look for one, when her intended husband suddenly developed an infatuation for some stranger?

For that matter, was Lord Allutar truly her beloved, or merely her best prospect for marrying well?

It didn't matter. What mattered was that Reva must be convinced not to attempt her love spell.

"Marry your cousin?" Garras said. "Did you arrange this, then, to keep my daughter from earning her fifty guilders?"

"What?" The accusation caught Anrel completely off guard. "No, of course not! Why would I do that?"

Garras drew himself up and looked down his rather thick nose at Anrel. "I don't pretend to know, Master Murau."

"I wouldn't!" Anrel exclaimed. "They were engaged . . . I don't know precisely when they were engaged, but they have been for some time, and I only learned of it today. I had nothing to do with arranging it. Really, Master Lir, why would I want my cousin to marry my worst enemy?"

"To frustrate Mimmin li-Dargalleis, perhaps. To frustrate my daughter. To place a spy in your foe's household. I can think of any number of reasons."

"But I desire none of these! Sir, I have only your family's best interests at heart, I assure you."

"Really? Because you seem to be costing us fifty guilders."

"That is not my intent! Perhaps Mistress li-Dargalleis can be persuaded to redirect her interests—surely, there are other worthy bachelors to be found in Beynos?"

"Ah, but would any of these others be worth fifty guilders?"

Anrel's mouth worked. "Perhaps not, but surely, it cannot help a witch's reputation to be unaware of something vital to the success of her spell! Your wife and daughters pretend to know the future; what, then, will your customers think of Reva if she proceeds with a love spell that cannot help but produce scandal and unhappiness?"

Garras frowned.

"He has a point, Father," Tazia said.

"No one expects you girls to know *everything*," Garras protested.

"But something like this—it will certainly look better if we *do* know it, and act accordingly!"

"But we'll lose the fifty guilders!"

"And perhaps earn it back with fortune-telling."

"*Fifty* guilders? I think not."

Tazia surrendered. "No, not all of it, you're right. But if we can direct her to another target, we can perhaps make up the difference."

"Confound it." Garras glared down at the table for a moment, as if smothering a belch, then at Anrel. "Can't you talk your cousin into breaking her engagement?"

Anrel sighed. "Sir, I do not dare speak to my cousin at all."

"Write her a letter!"

"It would avail you nothing, I assure you," Anrel replied. "Lady Saria has always been headstrong, and accustomed to having her own way."

"Yet she wants to marry Lord Allutar?" Tazia said.

Anrel's mouth quirked upward. "Indeed she does," he said. "I do not think their marriage will be a calm one."

"May they make each other endlessly miserable, then, for costing us fifty guilders," Garras said.

"I would not wish that on my cousin," Anrel said, "but if she contrives to make Lord Allutar suffer, I will not be dismayed." He looked around. "Where is Reva? I want to warn her about the betrothal."

"She's out earning her keep," Garras snapped. "As Tazia here ought to be."

"I told you, Father, I just needed a little rest."

"No one pays you to rest."

"Master Lir," Anrel interrupted, before Tazia could respond. "Where can I find Reva?"

"You probably can't. But if you wait here, she'll be back for supper."

"Ah," Anrel said. He glanced at Tazia. "I hope I didn't interrupt anything important just now, when I came in here."

"No," Tazia said. "We weren't discussing anything important."

Anrel wanted to ask, "Why not?" but he restrained himself. Tazia knew her father far better than he did, so if she thought this was not the time to initiate a discussion of her future, Anrel had to respect that decision. Perhaps Garras's prodigious consumption of wine had something to do with it.

He thought he could use something to ease his own mind a little; he turned in his chair and raised a hand to signal a servant. When a plump serving wench hurried over, he ordered another bottle of the merlot he had enjoyed so much earlier.

Half the bottle was gone when Nivain and Perynis entered the room, and the last of it had just been poured when Reva finally appeared.

"Ah, there you are!" Garras called. He had consumed another bottle himself. "Come here, girl—Master Adirane has some news for you."

Reva came, and took a seat next to Anrel, looking at him curiously.

"I thought it might be wise to find out more about Lord Allutar before attempting to enchant him," Anrel said. "Alas, what I found out is that he is engaged to be wed—he will be marrying Lady Saria Adirane in the fall."

"Adirane?" Reva asked, in precisely the same tone her sister had used.

"My cousin."

Reva looked at him for a moment, then said, "You mean he would marry her if I did not intervene."

Flustered, Anrel said, "Well, I . . . maybe."

Reva shook her head, tossing back her long hair. "I think I can cast a love spell strong enough to make him break his engagement to this Lady Saria, and wed my client instead," she said.

"On a sorcerer of his stature?" Anrel protested. "You don't think he'll notice something amiss when he abandons a betrothal?"

"I think so," Reva insisted defiantly.

"I think you should discuss it with your client," Tazia said.

Reva glared at her, then shrugged. "Fine. I'll discuss it with her."

"Had you made any plans as to when you would be enchanting him?" Anrel asked.

"Tomorrow night," Reva said. "There's to be a reception at his house."

"A good choice," Anrel said.

"I'm so *thrilled* that you approve!" Reva said icily.

"Please, Mistress Lir, there is no need for sarcasm."

Now it was Anrel's turn to be a recipient of Reva's glare. "It worked, didn't it?" she demanded.

"That depends on how you define 'work.'"

"It let you know that I've had my fill of your condescending aid."

"Well, yes," Anrel conceded.

"He's just trying to help," Tazia said.

"I didn't ask for his help!"

"Reva, we're just worried about you. Lord Allutar is a dangerous man!"

"And one Anrel might have in his own family soon, if I don't meddle," Reva retorted. "Do you think a pardon might be available then? Oh, but if he marries someone who *isn't* Anrel's cousin, then by the Father and the Mother, why would he lift that death sentence? Really, Tazia, how stupid do you think I am, not to see what you two are up to?"

Tazia blinked, astonished, then said, "Apparently not as stupid as *I* am, since *I* hadn't seen what we were up to."

"Oh, really? Well, ask your lover, then!" She turned to Anrel.

"There will be no pardon," Anrel said coldly, "but it's true that if my cousin marries Lord Allutar, he won't press for my apprehension and execution."

"You admit it?"

"Of course I do, since it's true. But that did not prompt me to speak to you. I don't expect to be captured in any case, and really, I would almost prefer my family not be allied to the likes of Allutar Hezir. No, I was merely providing a bit of information I thought you should know. I had assumed that you would not continue with your spell, knowing that Lord Allutar was betrothed, but if you are so certain of yourself, and of your client's determination, then so be it. I will make no attempt to dissuade you." He tried not to let his voice reveal the bitterness he felt at her assumptions about his motives.

"But, Anrel!" Tazia said.

"Hush," he replied, raising a hand. "She has made her decision."

"Anrel!" She leaned over and whispered, "What are you saying? She'll be killed!"

"One cannot save a fool from his folly."

"One can *try*, when the fool is my sister! I know she offended you, I know she's been rude, but I don't want her dead, and neither do you!"

Anrel met Tazia's eyes, and after a moment he relented. "What would you have me do, then?"

"Just . . . be quiet, all right?"

"As you please." He settled back in his chair, arms folded across his chest.

He had more reason than ever to offer to give her fifty guilders *not* to attempt her spell, since now not only would she be risking death if she failed, but if she succeeded it might involve Lady Saria in a scandal, and might well result in an end to Lord Allutar's tolerance of Anrel's survival.

But he also had more reason than ever to *not* make the offer, given her behavior. He was beginning to think she *wanted* to cast her spell, no matter how dangerous it might be, regardless of the money, to prove her skill to herself, to Anrel, and to her family.

And he certainly wasn't going to reveal in front of the entire family that he had been hiding a significant sum of money from them.

Tazia turned back to her sister. "Reva, please, talk it over with your client before you do anything dangerous."

"I have said that I will."

"And give her a fair chance to change her mind. I know you feel as if your pride demands you try to make Lord Allutar break off his engagement, but really, it doesn't. See what *she* wants to do."

Reva glared for a moment, then yielded. "I will."

"Good," their father remarked. "The customer knows his own mind better than anyone, as the saying has it."

"*Her* mind, in this case," Reva said.

"And Reva, take Anrel with you," Tazia said.

"What?" Both Reva and Anrel turned to stare at Tazia.

"Take him with you when you talk to your client," Tazia insisted. "He knows Lady Saria. He can answer any questions you might have about her."

Reva looked distastefully at Anrel. "I don't want any interruptions."

Anrel did not reply immediately. He had not yet agreed to accompany her at all—but then he saw the pleading expression on Tazia's face, and gave in. "I won't make any," he said. "I will be quiet, and speak only when spoken to."

"You won't contradict me?"

"No." He had no intention of doing anything to further anger Reva; he knew now that the more he argued, the more stubborn she would become.

But this might give him a chance to speak to her in private, and perhaps then he could offer to pay her *not* to risk the spell. He thought she might be more willing to listen when her parents were not present.

In particular, he thought she might be more willing to take his money and keep quiet regarding the arrangement if her father knew nothing about it. If she accepted the commission, and earned the fifty guilders that way, her father would undoubtedly demand a share; if she declined the commission and was paid secretly by Anrel instead, then Garras need never know, and she would be that much closer to striking out on her own.

Reva considered him thoughtfully, then shrugged. "Very well," she said. "Come on, we might as well do it right now."

"Now?" Anrel glanced at Tazia.

"She's in the front room, talking to Master Kabrig."

"Oh." Anrel had not expected that, but he pushed back his chair and got to his feet. "Then, now it is."

27

In Which Mistress li-Dargalleis Proves Uncooperative, as Well

Mimmin li-Dargalleis cast a quick glance at Anrel, then dismissed him as unimportant. "Is something wrong?" she asked, in response to the somber expression on Reva's face.

The three of them were in the room above the stable, for the sake of privacy, and Mimmin clearly assumed that if Reva didn't mind Anrel's presence, neither should she. She focused her attention entirely on the dark-haired witch.

"I have been scrying, Mistress li-Dargalleis," Reva said. "I have been learning the secrets of Lord Allutar's heart, in preparation for the spell."

"Yes?"

Reva folded her hands in front of her. "Lord Allutar is betrothed to another," she said.

"Oh, I know that!" Mimmin said, dismissing the matter with a wave. "That backcountry sorceress, Lady Saria. Everyone knows that. They announced it half a season ago. But she's home in Aulix, and I'm here."

Reva pursed her lips. "You had not mentioned this," she chided gently.

Mimmin shrugged. "I didn't think it mattered."

"You hired me to cast a love spell on Lord Allutar that would put him in your power, did you not?"

"Yes, of course!"

"I had assumed that you intended to marry him yourself."

"Oh, no," Mimmin said, almost blushing. "No, no. I knew that wasn't possible. He is a sorcerer, a landgrave, and I am a commoner. Sorcerers marry their own kind, to breed the next generation of magicians, but they take mistresses for love, and *that* was what I sought—what I seek."

Reva was silent for a moment, considering this.

"I see," she said at last. "You do know that there is no written law forbidding sorcerers from marrying commoners, don't you?"

"But that's the custom, all the same."

"Yes, of course, but customs can be broken, and that was what I had understood you to intend."

"No, no. Let him marry Lady Saria, as long as he otherwise does what I want."

"You understand that a sorcerer's betrothal is an actual binding? A spell?"

"It is?"

Anrel bit his lip, struggling to stay silent. *Some* betrothals were bindings; most weren't.

"It does make casting my own spell more complicated."

Anrel held his breath; was Reva preparing to refuse the commission? Was she using this as an excuse to back out gracefully?

"Oh," Mimmin said. There was a pregnant silence; then she said, "*Sixty* guilders, perhaps? It's all I have. I'll need to sell my mother's rings to find *that* much."

Reva blinked. This was clearly not the reaction she had expected. It was also clearly not an offer she could resist. "I think sixty would be fair," she acknowledged.

Anrel suppressed a frown. He was not sure he could spare *sixty* guilders. The idea of bribing Reva was suddenly less appealing.

He could not say anything about it while Mimmin was listening, in any case; he still had time to decide.

"Good, good!" Mimmin said, visibly relieved. "Then we're all set for tomorrow night?"

"One more thing," Reva said, turning to stare at Anrel. "It would be convenient if you could arrange an invitation for my brother Dyssan, as well."

Anrel did his best to conceal his surprise, but almost spoke up at that.

He did not want to attend Lord Allutar's reception. There would be people there who knew him, Lord Allutar himself among them.

But he had promised to remain quiet, so he remained quiet.

Mimmin glanced at him, then said, "I'll try. I can't promise. Dyssan Lir?"

"That would be the name, yes," Reva said.

"I'll try."

"Thank you. You understand, payment must be made in advance."

"Of course."

"Then we'll see you tomorrow?"

"Yes, indeed."

With that, Mimmin rose. Anrel followed suit, and escorted her to the door. There he paused and glanced back at Reva, wondering whether he should escort her customer down to the front door.

"I can find my own way, Master Lir," Mimmin said.

"Of course, Mistress li-Dargalleis," Anrel said with a bow. He held the door for her and watched her until she had rounded the first turn in the corridor. Then he stepped back into the room, closed the door, and turned to face Reva.

He had still not decided what to do about the money. Sixty guilders—he could live on sixty guilders for a season, and he had no prospects of earning more.

But surely, saving the life of Tazia's sister was worth it.

Still, it might not be necessary. She seemed to have some scheme of her own. "What do you want me at Allutar's reception for?" he demanded.

Startled, she said, "I thought you might want to attend, for your cousin's sake."

"Not particularly, thank you," Anrel answered. "Not when any of a dozen people might be there who could recognize me and send me to the gallows."

"It's a shame you don't know more witchcraft," Reva said with a sigh. "You might be able to cast a glamour on yourself, so that they *wouldn't* recognize you."

"Can *you* do that? Perhaps *you* could cast a glamour on me."

Reva shook her head. "No," she said.

"Your mother, perhaps?"

"I don't *think* so, but maybe."

Anrel gazed thoughtfully at the witch.

She was quite right that a glamour could change one's appearance, or at least make everyone *think* it had changed—it worked more on people's perceptions than on the subject's own physical self. That could be a very useful spell, and Anrel wondered why he had never heard of criminals using glamours to escape justice.

But then, most magicians were sorcerers, who were automatically members of the nobility; why would they need to commit any crimes? And most of them couldn't cast glamours, in any case; it was, as Anrel understood it, a difficult and specialized skill that most magicians did not bother to learn, since its uses were limited.

If someone *did* use glamours to commit crimes, would anyone else know it?

There were other spells that would also be of great use to criminals—memory-altering spells, for example. If a thief could make his victim forget the stolen goods had ever existed . . .

This was part of *why* sorcerers were made nobles. Put them in charge, and they had no reason to steal, or to go meddling with anyone's thoughts.

Or at any rate, *less* reason.

Witches, on the other hand, were outlaws by definition. Why didn't witches ever tamper with memories, or use glamours to hide from the authorities?

Perhaps they did, and were so successful at it that no one knew it happened. Anrel had been traveling with four witches for almost a season and hadn't seen them do anything of the sort, but maybe other witches were more gifted.

Or maybe he simply didn't *remember* seeing them cast glamours or bind memories. Did he still have the money he thought he did? Perhaps the witches had already taken it, and had altered his memories.

But no, he could feel the weight of it in his coat, and had they taken it and tampered with his memory, why would they allow him to remember it had ever existed at all?

He shook his head. Such treachery, such complex magic, was far beyond these people. Indeed, it was likely that *no* witch ever managed to learn such advanced magical techniques. If they could perform such feats, why would they bother with false luck spells and fortune-telling?

No, the witches were probably no more than they seemed—but then why did Reva want him to accompany her? "I think it would be unwise for me to attend the reception," he said.

Reva looked annoyed by this—and something more, Anrel thought. He studied her face, and tried to sense her emotions.

Then suddenly he understood. "You're afraid," he said.

"No!"

"Yes, you are," Anrel insisted. "You want me there—why? In case the spell goes wrong? But what do you expect me to do, in such a case? I'm no great hero from the old folktales, to carry you off on a winged horse before the guards can seize you."

"But you're a witch," Reva said. "Not a very good one yet, but a witch, and you know Lord Allutar. If something goes wrong, you can . . . I don't know. Hold him back, perhaps, or distract him somehow."

"I doubt it," Anrel said dryly. "I'm less a witch than either of your sisters, let alone your mother."

"Tazia thinks you can do anything," Reva retorted bitterly.

Anrel grimaced. "Tazia is a wonderful girl, but no great judge of my abilities."

"What am I supposed to do, then? My father has no magic at all!"

"Your mother is a more talented witch than either of us."

"Yes, but . . ." Reva hesitated, unable to find the words she wanted.

Anrel thought he understood. "You don't want your mother to see you fail."

"I don't want to put my mother at risk!"

"But you have no qualms about endangering *me*," Anrel said.

Reva had no reply to that; she simply stared at him.

Anrel sighed. "I've said all along you shouldn't attempt this spell."

"But *sixty guilders*!"

"Is that money worth your life?"

She glared angrily at him. "It's worth taking a risk, yes," she said.

Anrel shook his head again. "I think you're acting like a fool," he said. His hand rose to his lapel, where he could feel the weight of a golden five-guilder piece. Sixty guilders, along with the other expenses he had incurred since fleeing Naith, would leave him with no more than twenty—he was not sure of the exact amount. Still, he was about to say something, to suggest an alternative to attempting to enchant the landgrave.

"I think you're acting like an arrogant ass!" Reva snapped back before he could continue, and Anrel's hand fell from his coat.

"Then why would you trust me to help you? Why not bring someone you trust—Nivain or Tazia or Perynis? Why me?" Even as he asked, he dreaded the thought that she might drag Tazia along into such dangerous circumstances.

"Because I don't want my mother or my sisters to know how frightened I am!"

For a moment after she said that, the two of them stared silently at each other. The fire in the little stove crackled, but there was no other sound. Reva's gaze was defiant, unwavering—but Anrel could see her underlying terror.

"I may have a way out of this," Anrel said at last, stroking his coat.

Reva shook her head. "I said I would do it."

"What if I knew another way you could earn sixty guilders? A far less dangerous way?"

"I *said* I would *do* it," Reva repeated. "I told Mistress li-Dargalleis I would. I can't back out now."

"But if it's just for the money . . ."

"It's not," Reva said. "I said I would do it."

"You could tell Mistress li-Dargalleis that Lord Allutar's wards are too strong."

"I will tell her that if they *are* too strong. I won't lie about it."

"Why *not*?" Anrel demanded. "You lie often enough when you tell fortunes!"

"That's not the same thing!"

"*How* does it differ?"

"My father would know I was lying about the wards. He knows me too well, and *he* wants that fifty guilders!"

"I thought the money was for *you*," Anrel said.

"It *is*, but . . . you don't understand."

"No, I don't," Anrel agreed. "Explain it to me."

Reva looked around the room as if seeking assistance, then turned back to Anrel. "We owe him a debt," she said. "My mother and my sisters and I, we all owe him a debt, and I need to pay my share of it before I can go."

"What sort of debt?" Anrel asked, genuinely puzzled. "How much?"

"I don't . . . I can't say. I can't tell you exactly."

"Would fifty guilders be enough to pay your share?"

"I'm not sure. I think . . . I'm not sure."

Anrel stared at her.

Hesitantly, Reva said, "You said . . . you said you might have another way to earn sixty guilders?"

"I might," Anrel said.

"But then if I did that, as well, I would have more than a hundred! Father would surely release me for *that* much!"

Anrel remembered what Tazia had said, that no matter how much money they earned, their father would never release any of them. If Tazia understood that, why didn't Reva?

He shook his head. "No. You cannot do both."

"Why not?"

He could not think of any palatable way to present the truth, to admit that he had been hiding money from them all, to say that he wanted to pay her to save her own life, but would not give her the money if she continued with her spell. He was more certain than ever that if he gave her the money, she would still take Mimmin's fee, as well, and attempt the spell.

But a lie occurred to him.

"I have reason to believe," he said, "that Lady Saria would pay you sixty guilders *not* to enchant her betrothed."

Reva stared at him, then shook her head. "No," she said. "I can't do that."

Astonished, he asked, "Why *not*?"

"Because it's a trap."

"What?" Anrel blinked. "Why do you think that?"

"I grew up a witch's daughter, Anrel. While it may be *possible* that a sorceress would hire a witch honestly, I know better than to trust one in a situation like this. No, she would pay me the money, then claim I had stolen it and send me to the gallows. Or if she did not, then when I told Mistress li-Dargalleis that I was refusing her request, *she* might summon the watchmen, and neither of them would feel the slightest guilt about sending a criminal to her death. Don't you see? As a witch, I never dare betray a customer. If a spell goes wrong or a fortune fails to come true I can always say the spirits were uncooperative, or another witch interfered, but if I were to betray a trust as you propose—no. I can't do that."

Anrel stood silently for a moment, absorbing that, and then nodded reluctantly. He thought he understood. As a witch and the daughter of a witch, Reva's life had *always* been in danger, and always would be. Casting a spell on Lord Allutar would increase the danger briefly, yes, but *any* course of action—or inaction—might get her killed. Anything that antagonized a customer could put her head in a noose. She had lived her entire life in the shadow of the gallows.

Perhaps if he had spoken sooner, before she had agreed to cast the love spell, he might have been able to persuade her, but now it was too late. He simply couldn't see any way to convince her to abandon the job she had accepted.

He felt he had failed her by allowing the situation to reach this state, and that being the case, he could not refuse to do whatever he could to help her survive. "I'll want your help disguising myself for the reception," he said. "My hair hasn't been cut since I fled Naith, and surely we can do something with that."

"Agreed," she replied.

Anrel knew he was making a mistake, and that Reva was probably making an even worse one, but she was so determined that he saw no alternative. He tried to make the best of it.

"Even if you can't cast a proper glamour, could you perhaps change my skin color, or reshape my features a little?" he asked.

"I can try. I might not be able to change it back."

"I'll live with it.

"One more thing," he said.

"What?" Reva asked warily.

"When this is over, you'll help me talk to your father. About Tazia."

"Oh." She relaxed slightly. "Oh, yes. Of course." She smiled. "I'm happy for you two, you know. I hope it will work out."

"Thank you," Anrel said. "I hope so, too."

28

In Which Anrel Prepares for Lord Allutar's Reception

When the two of them returned to the dining hall they found Garras asleep in the corner, his head flung back against the wall. He was snoring softly.

The other Lir women, though, were still gathered around a table. Anrel and Reva joined them, and found themselves facing three questioning faces.

"Well?" Perynis demanded.

"We saw Mistress li-Dargalleis leave," Tazia said. "She seemed nervous." Her own expression was hopeful as she looked at Anrel.

"She has to sell her jewelry," Reva said. "We agreed on sixty guilders."

Tazia's head snapped around to look at her sister, then swung back to Anrel. "She agreed? Even though he's betrothed?"

"She knew about the betrothal," Anrel said. "She will be satisfied to be the landgrave's mistress, rather than his wife."

"I think she *prefers* to be his mistress," Reva said.

"Then why did she agree to a higher price?" Nivain asked.

"I said there might be a binding between Allutar and Saria," Reva explained. "That it was more dangerous than I had realized."

"It *is* too dangerous!" Tazia said. "How could you agree?"

"*Sixty guilders*, Tazia. Sixty guilders, and a good reputation here in Beynos."

"How could you *let* her agree?" Tazia demanded, turning to Anrel once more.

"How could I stop her? She's a free woman, or so I assume."

"Of course she is, but . . ." Tazia frowned.

"Anrel has agreed to accompany me to Lord Allutar's reception, to aid me should anything go wrong," Reva said. "And he did *try* to sway me." She threw him a glance. "I don't think he entirely understood what a witch's life is like—neither the risks we take nor how much sixty guilders will mean to us."

Anrel bowed in acknowledgment. "But I fear, mistress, that *you* may not understand how very dangerous Lord Allutar is. I have seen him kill a man in cold blood, and I do not think he would scruple to hang a witch."

"Nor would any landgrave," Reva retorted. "And I will have you there to protect me."

"But—doesn't Lord Allutar know Anrel?" Perynis asked.

"He does," Anrel admitted. "I will be attending as one Dyssan Lir, Reva's brother, and it is my hope that you might all assist in disguising me, so that Master Lir will not be recognized as either the fugitive Murau or the notorious Alvos."

"Disguise how?" Nivain asked.

Anrel glanced at Reva. "I thought perhaps a spell to change my features, or my skin—a glamour, if any of you know how."

The four witches looked at one another, then all leaned forward across the table, shutting Anrel out, as they began discussing the possibilities.

None of them knew how to cast a proper glamour; the three daughters all looked expectantly at their mother, but she shook her head. "No," Nivain said. "I tried it once. It's beyond me."

"Then we might lengthen his nose," Perynis suggested.

"I was thinking about his ears," Reva replied.

In the end they decided not to alter Anrel's features—for one thing, Tazia vigorously objected to the idea. "I like his face the way it is," she insisted.

While Anrel was flattered by that, he found Nivain's argument for avoiding any magical changes much more convincing. She was unsure how stable any such magic would be, in particular in a house as heavily warded as Lord Allutar's surely was, and if the spell were disrupted the result would almost certainly draw more attention than Anrel's own face.

"I'll just stay out of sight as much as I can," he agreed.

Later, after supper, when Tazia was able to get Anrel alone in a quiet passageway, she tried to convince him not to go at all. "Lord Allutar knows you!" she said. "Even if he doesn't particularly want you dead, do you think he'll just let you go if he sees you there in his own house?"

"I don't intend to let him see me," Anrel said. "I'll stay in the shadows, in the corners. If I see anyone looking at me, I'll slip away."

"If you *can*," Tazia retorted.

"Yes, if I can."

"It's dangerous!"

"Of course it is, but I told Reva I would go."

Tazia frowned. She did not bother to argue further, but she did say emphatically, "I don't like it."

"Neither do I," Anrel said. "But if there's a chance I might save your sister by being there, then I must be there."

"Why should *you* go, and not my mother? She's a much better witch, and Lord Allutar doesn't know her!"

Anrel smiled. "I asked Reva the same thing, and I respect her answer."

Tazia stared at him for a moment, then said, "But you aren't going to tell me what she said."

"No, I am not."

"Anrel, this is madness. You're risking your life."

"I am, yes. I'm risking it in hopes of preserving your sister's life."

Tazia's eyes were suddenly wet. "I don't want to lose *both* of you!"

"And I don't want to lose *you*," Anrel said gently. "If I let Reva go to her death without at least *trying* to help her, I wouldn't be worthy of you—and you would know it, in your heart. You wouldn't want me if I did that."

Tazia hesitated. "I think you overestimate me," she said.

"I know I do not," Anrel said. "If I will not face danger for those I love, then what is my love worth? How can I call it love at all? Would you have a man who knows nothing of love?"

"But you don't love Reva!" Tazia protested.

"No," Anrel agreed, "but I love *you,* and you love her."

At that Tazia broke down in tears, and Anrel took her in his arms, offering reassurances that needed no words.

Anrel spent much of the following day in the room above the stable, preparing his attire. He needed to dress in a way that he would not be obviously out of place at a landgrave's reception, but that would allow him to at least partially conceal his identity. Fortunately the weather was still cold, so at least at first he could wrap a scarf around the lower half of his face and pull a hat down on his forehead without attracting suspicion. If he stayed near the door, that might be enough.

He brushed out his brown velvet coat, and with Tazia's assistance made some alterations—it seemed unlikely that anyone would recognize it after so long, in any case, and he had been wearing it openly, but there was no point in taking any unnecessary risk. New trim on the lapels and white lace at the collar transformed it sufficiently to satisfy him. His hidden money remained in the lining; if Tazia had noticed the extra weight she did not mention it.

Anrel's hat had been utterly nondescript to begin with, and had become rather more battered since his speech in Naith, so that it was even less noticeable. It only needed a little cleaning.

His beard, which he had customarily kept trimmed evenly, he carefully reshaped to a point below his chin. He decided he rather liked the effect, and might want to keep it permanently.

He had thought that would probably be sufficient disguise, but shortly after lunch Tazia dragged him aside and proceeded to bleach his hair and beard—not with magic, but with some foul-smelling liquid she had spent much of the morning in obtaining. When she was done he looked in a glass, and marveled at the result—the blond hair and pointed beard made him look somehow foreign, more like a Quandishman or a Cousiner than a Walasian. He hardly recognized himself.

He could certainly *smell* himself, though; he needed to wash thoroughly several times to remove the stink of the bleach. That was what he was doing, using water heated on the little stove, when Dorrin Kabrig knocked on the open door of the room over the stable and told Reva she had a visitor waiting downstairs.

"Mistress li-Dargalleis?" she asked.

Master Kabrig nodded.

"I will come at once."

Anrel started to say something, but Reva was out the door before he could offer to accompany her. He shrugged, and went back to his washing.

Anrel therefore did not see Mimmin li-Dargalleis deliver the promised payment, but he saw the smile on Reva's face when she returned to the room clutching a little leather purse. "Fifty guilders!" she said.

"I thought you had agreed on sixty," Anrel said, as he poured yet another dipper of lukewarm water on his head.

"I'll have the rest when the spell is cast," Reva said.

"You hope," Garras said.

Tazia snorted, and passed Anrel another bucket of water.

When his hair was finally done, the smell dissipated, and his altered clothing in place, Anrel thought his appearance was sufficiently altered to minimize the risk of recognition. Now he needed only wait until the appointed hour.

29

In Which Anrel Attends Lord Allutar's Reception

Lord Allutar's town house was impressive—smaller than his estate in Alzur, but newer and more luxuriously appointed, with high white ceilings and gleaming brass chandeliers.

The house stood at the top of Bridge Street Hill, where Bridge Street ended in a cobblestone plaza. Reva and Anrel had walked up through town, but when they arrived the street was crowded with carriages, and they had to wind their way through a maze of horses and coach wheels to reach the grand curving stair that led up to the entryway. They joined the flow of guests up that stair, across a brick terrace, and in through the town house door.

Anrel noticed that most of the other guests seemed to be better dressed than he and Reva were; many wore the stark black and white modern fashions that had just been coming into style when Anrel completed his education and departed the capital. Even those in more traditional and colorful garb seemed to be adorned with far more velvet and fur than Anrel would have expected in a town like Beynos.

His own coat was velvet, of course, with lace at the collar and cuffs, but showed visible wear despite his best efforts, and his black hat was a simple, practical affair that bore little resemblance to some of the fanciful headgear he saw on the other guests.

Reva's cloak was heavy black wool but very plain, and the dark blue dress beneath was trimmed with silk, rather than being entirely composed of that fabric. Her sisters had gone to some lengths to arrange her hair elegantly, and she wore an absurd little feathered concoction as a hat, but compared to most of the women she appeared somewhat shabby.

When at last they reached the grand front door Anrel was displeased to feel the odd, skin-tugging sensation of passing strong wards as he stepped across the threshold—but really, he could hardly expect that a sorcerer's home would *not* be warded in such troubled times. At least the wards did not seem to have reacted to his own presence; he had no idea just what they were designed to detect or prevent, but whatever it was, his presence did not seem to be included.

Once inside they found themselves in an anteroom where guests were doffing their outer garments and either making their way through the left-hand door into the salon or waiting at the much larger right-hand door to be announced before entering the ballroom. The discarded coats were being stowed in a cloakroom by the entrance; Anrel was slightly startled to see that it was staffed by a homunculus, rather than a human being, and not the same homunculus he had seen in Lord Allutar's hall back in Alzur. Anrel had not known the landgrave had made more than one.

Perhaps he hadn't; perhaps his grandfather had made this one, and Allutar had inherited it with the house. In any case, the homunculus stood silently by the entrance, calmly accepting and stowing whatever outerwear guests might give it.

It made no attempt to take coats or hats from those who did not offer them, and it did not make any comments or suggestions. In fact, it was utterly silent, and Anrel suspected it had no voice. Sorcerers often did not bother to give their animate creations unnecessary features; most were hairless and sexless. Certainly this one, while it was dressed in a man's jacket, showed no trace of hair or beard and appeared quite epicene.

Homunculi did not have free will, of course; they would only do as they were told, and this cloakroom attendant had obviously not been ordered to make any demands. The automaton was perfectly willing to let Anrel keep his hat and scarf. At least that much of Anrel's planning had worked out—he was able to keep his features largely hidden. A human servant might have been more insistent upon helping.

Reva did hand the homunculus her woolen cloak; she had no need to conceal her identity. It seemed unlikely that anyone in this gathering would recognize her as a witch, or make anything of it if they did.

They joined the line to enter the ballroom, Reva standing straight, Anrel crouching in his scarf and hat. When at last the herald announced "Reva Lir and Dyssan Lir!" and let Anrel and Reva pass, no one paid much attention; there was no title to draw interest, no famous name. What was more, back at the inn Anrel had done his best to place a ward of his own—nothing serious, just something that would make the casual passerby uninterested in him. Whether it was working or was unnecessary he wasn't entirely sure, but no one bothered to look at him very closely.

The ballroom glittered, the brilliant glow of the chandeliers sparkling from jewelry and silk. Anrel wished the chandeliers had not been there; they provided all too much light. He was accustomed to darker rooms, where one could easily stay half hidden in the shadows; had he known just how bright the landgrave's salon and ballroom were, he might have been even more reluctant to accompany Reva.

Still, the only one who appeared to notice their arrival or pay them any attention was Mimmin li-Dargalleis. She was already in the ballroom, and looked up when the names were announced; she hurried over to greet Reva, then cast a puzzled look at Anrel, his broad-brimmed hat, and the white scarf wrapped around his neck.

"He's prone to chills," Reva explained.

"This is your brother? He looks different, somehow."

Reva glanced at Anrel, then shrugged. "It's just Dyssan," she said.

Anrel admired her calm. "Off with you two," he said. "I can see to myself." Then he turned and moved to one side, slipping past a knot of people.

Mimmin promptly seemed to forget his existence; the ward might be working, he thought, or she might just be oblivious.

He found a place by the wall, and looked out at the room. He estimated there were at least forty people there—enough to make even a room as large as this one seem a trifle crowded. Lord Allutar had not yet made his entrance, but a harpist was playing in one corner, and servants were carrying wine and trays of tidbits around to the guests.

Anrel was relieved to see no familiar faces—at first. Then he noticed Hollem tel-Guriel on the far side of the room, where he appeared to be directing the servants. At the sight of him, Anrel slid farther back toward the corner.

Reva and Mimmin were working their way across the room, talking quietly as they went. Anrel watched them closely.

Then a stir ran through the room, and Anrel saw heads turn. He turned himself, to see a herald in the far doorway straighten and announce, "In the name of the emperor, may the Father and the Mother bless him, I present Lord Allutar Hezir, landgrave of Aulix!"

The herald stepped aside, then two footmen marched in and took up positions on either side of the doorway. A heartbeat later their master appeared, and Anrel watched as Lord Allutar walked in.

He had to admit that the landgrave looked good. He was wearing court finery, rather than the more ordinary attire Anrel had usually seen him wear back in Alzur or the landgrave's regalia he had worn when he killed Valin. These garments were in traditional style, not at all like the modern monochrome fashion. His cuffs dripped with lace, his hair gleamed with pomade, and his frock coat was fine purple silk. He wore an expression of dignified amusement, quite unlike the slightly annoyed frown that Anrel was accustomed to seeing.

The host stood just inside the doorway for a moment, surveying his guests, then bowed to the company. Most of the people near him bowed in reply; those farther away did not bother, but for a moment Anrel had a clearer view of Lord Allutar—clearer than he was entirely comfortable with. He stepped back, farther into the inadequate shadows.

Then heads bobbed back up, and people began clustering around Lord Allutar—mostly, Anrel noticed, women.

He had not given that a great deal of thought, despite what he knew of Lady Saria and Mimmin, but obviously Lord Allutar was considered more than a little attractive. This was hardly surprising. Allutar was wealthy, powerful, handsome, a man in the prime of life—of course women would take an interest in him. Anrel's own cousin certainly had.

One of the women crowding around the landgrave was Mimmin; Anrel recognized her elaborately styled hair. She was trying to speak to him, but at least for the moment he seemed more interested in a small man in a silver-gray frock coat.

Anrel looked around for Reva and spotted her a few feet to one side, not part of the group surrounding Lord Allutar. She was watching her client and their host intently.

The little man in the gray coat nodded, then turned and hurried away; whatever business he had had with Lord Allutar was obviously concluded. Allutar smiled at the company as a whole, then turned his attention to the closest, most persistent of the women around him.

Mimmin li-Dargalleis.

Anrel could not hear what was being said over the babble in the room, but he saw Lord Allutar smile broadly at Mimmin, and say something to her. She tilted her head coquettishly, one hand to her mouth.

Anrel turned his attention to Reva, and as he had expected she had raised her hands to chest height, preparing to channel the magic of her binding spell. She was trying to make the gesture look innocent, perhaps like an attempt to fend off someone backing into her, but Anrel could see it for what it was.

He did not feel the spell itself at all—but Lord Allutar obviously did. His smile vanished and his head whipped around to stare directly at Reva.

"Seize her!" he shouted, pointing. "Bring her to me!"

For a moment a stunned silence descended over the room as all conversation died, and the astonished harpist stopped playing, her fingers striking a final cascade of false notes from the strings. Most of the guests turned to stare at Lord Allutar, clearly astonished. Almost no one moved; they seemed rooted in place.

Almost no one; Reva herself had turned the instant the words left Lord Allutar's lips, and was now trying to push her way through the crowd.

Anrel raised his own hands, trying to think what he could do to help

Reva. He was no sorcerer, though; he was barely even a witch. Still, this situation was exactly what he had feared, and exactly why Reva had brought him; surely he could do *something*. He tried to draw magic into himself, to be ready, but could not feel any flow, whether because of wards or some other impediment he could not be sure. Only tiny wisps of power came to him.

The two footmen who had been standing beside the door were the first others to move; they charged forward into the crowd in pursuit of the fleeing witch. Anrel knew his magic was not strong enough to stop and hold them—certainly not without giving away his presence to Lord Allutar! But even with just the feeble trace he held, there were obstacles he could put in their path . . .

A young woman, turning to watch Reva run, suddenly felt something pull at her ankle; she stumbled directly into the path of one of the footmen, and she and the footman both toppled to the floor, sending three or four other people tumbling, as well.

The second footman avoided this collision, and was almost out of the main body of people; Anrel raised his hands again as Reva reached the door to the foyer.

But then Lord Allutar spread his own hands and said something that might or might not have been words in a strange language. The power seemed to vanish completely from Anrel's body; he slumped and almost fell himself. The wards that had been in place all along had closed down completely, blocking all other magic.

Reva stumbled, but kept moving; no one else in the room seemed to notice anything. She made it out the door into the foyer, and Anrel relaxed—too soon. She screamed, and Anrel pushed past the nearest guests, trying to reach the door himself.

Then he stopped, as the homunculus from the cloakroom marched stolidly into the room, Reva slung over its shoulder, pinned in place by the creature's arm. Anrel could do nothing but watch helplessly as it carried her across the ballroom to Lord Allutar, the crowd parting before it—no one wanted to be in the thing's way. When it reached its master it stopped and set Reva back on her feet, but it kept one hand around her neck.

She squirmed briefly, but then Lord Allutar reached out and grabbed her chin, turning her face toward his own. The room seemed to freeze anew; no one moved, and a silence so complete that Anrel thought he could hear his own heart beating fell.

"Who are you?" Allutar demanded, shattering the momentary stillness. "Who sent you?"

Anrel glanced at Mimmin li-Dargalleis, but she was standing silently at Lord Allutar's side, showing no sign she knew anything more about the situation that anyone else.

Reva, he noticed, did *not* glance at her. The fifty guilders Mimmin had paid had bought Reva's loyalty.

The footman who had fallen was once again on his feet; he and his compatriot were moving back toward their master.

"Were you trying to kill me?" the landgrave asked, still holding Reva's chin.

"*No*, my lord!" Reva said, speaking for the first time. "No, no! Nothing like that."

"Then what *were* you doing?"

"A harmless spell, my lord, to influence your vote when the Grand Council reconvenes."

Lord Allutar did not look convinced. "Influence my vote in what manner?"

"I don't know, my lord. My employer was to speak a certain phrase, and you would then be inclined to vote as he suggested, nothing more than that, I swear by the Mother of Us All!"

"*What* phrase?"

"It . . . the phrase is, 'With weather like this we might as well be in Quand,' my lord."

Anrel admired Reva's quick invention; it sounded believable to him, and he hoped that Lord Allutar would find it equally convincing—but he doubted they would be that fortunate. Sorcerers of Lord Allutar's abilities could probably force people to tell the truth. Anrel hadn't happened to hear any lessons from his uncle that addressed that subject directly, but it certainly seemed likely.

"And is your employer here tonight, woman?" He released her chin and instead grabbed her shoulder, turning her in the homunculus's grip. The two footmen, now standing one on either side, grabbed her arms to help.

"I don't know, my lord!" Reva cried. "I don't see him!"

"What's your name?"

"Arissa Palineir, my lord!"

"That name was not on my guest list; how did you get in here?"

"I . . . I was invited," Reva said.

"Not under *that* name. Do you think I don't know who I invited into my home? Do you think I don't know how to set a ward against intruders?" He turned her around to face him again.

"I don't—" Reva didn't finish the sentence; her invention, or perhaps her nerve, had finally failed her.

"You aren't a sorceress, are you? You're a witch."

Reva just stared blankly at him.

Anrel thought desperately, trying to come up with something he could do to help Reva, but every idea he came up with would simply get them both killed. He couldn't attempt any magic while the wards were in place, and any more direct action would be stopped by those footmen, or by the homunculus, or perhaps by the other guests at the reception—he was hopelessly outnumbered. Perhaps if he had brought his sword—but of course, he couldn't have brought such a weapon to an event like this, even if it were not still being held as collateral by Dorrin Kabrig, the doorkeeper at the Boar's Head Inn.

Then Lord Allutar released his captive's shoulder, and instead pressed his hand to her forehead. She slumped in the homunculus's arms, and Anrel knew there was nothing he could do. Any chance he might have had of rescuing her would have depended on her being conscious and able to help.

"Take her to my study and bind her securely," Lord Allutar ordered.

His *study*? That caught Anrel by surprise. But then, this was Lord Allutar's home, not a courthouse; there would be no prison cells here, no dungeons.

On the other hand, Lord Allutar was a sorcerer familiar with black magic; his study was probably equipped with a variety of restraints. It would be even more heavily warded than the rest of the house, as well.

The homunculus hoisted Reva's limp form back onto its shoulder and trudged out of the room, the two footmen following close behind. For a moment there was a shocked silence, broken only by the receding footsteps; then a murmur of voices began and built quickly to a resounding hubbub.

"My lord!" someone called—a woman. "Who was that? What's to become of her?"

"That, my dear, is a witch," Allutar replied, "and a very foolish one. She attempted to place a spell on me—whether the sort she claimed or something else entirely, I cannot say, but I sensed it immediately."

"What will you do with her?"

"Imperial law is very clear," the landgrave replied solemnly. "Any attempt to perform magic by any citizen of the empire whose name is not on the Great List is witchcraft, and witchcraft is to be considered treason. The witch will hang."

"How do you know she's a citizen?" a man asked. "She might be an Ermetian spy."

Lord Allutar paused; clearly, he had not thought of that. The solution was obvious, though.

"The penalty for espionage is also death by hanging," he pointed out. "If she has diplomatic letters from the Ermetian king, or from one of their councils, then I will turn her over to the emperor's court and let them deal with her, but I doubt that will be the case." He looked out at his guests, standing motionless on all sides, staring at him. "Come now, friends—I know this incident has been upsetting, but please, it's done now, and the evening is still young. I welcome you all to my home, and I ask you all to enjoy yourselves." He spread his arms to gesture expansively, and the harpist took that as her cue to play a quick arpeggio and begin a new tune.

His guests were not ready to consider the matter closed, though; several pressed toward him with more questions about the captured witch.

"What if she escapes?"

"Who is she? I didn't hear the name she gave."

"Do you know her *real* name, my lord?"

"Will you check the guest list to see who she really is?"

"When will she hang?"

"Wouldn't it be better to use her as a blood sacrifice?"

Anrel saw that Mimmin was among those making these inquiries. In her case it was not mere curiosity that motivated her, but that would hardly be obvious to anyone else. She must, Anrel thought, be greatly relieved that Reva had not given her employer's name, but she was probably on the verge of panic over what the witch might say when she regained consciousness in Lord Allutar's study.

Lord Allutar ignored most of these questions, but when the barrage continued he finally deigned to reply to some recurring points.

"She won't escape; I am not so careless as that. If Lord Diosin has no objection she will hang the morning after next, I expect—I will allow her a day's time to make her peace with whatever spirits she may revere, and that same time for any appeals to be considered. That should suffice, but of course, bad weather or other such inconveniences might delay the execution. I have no particular need of any magic requiring blood or life at present, and holding her until the equinox would be awkward, to say the least—this house is not a prison—so I won't delay the business any longer than necessary."

"You could send her to the courthouse to be held," someone suggested.

"To what end?" Lord Allutar asked. "I have said I have no use for her." He took a wineglass a servant handed him, and lifted it. "Please, eat, drink!"

Anrel suppressed a shudder.

The morning after next.

Anrel could not think of any way to get Reva free now, but he had a day and a night to devise some method of saving her from the noose.

He could do nothing here, so he began moving quietly toward the door, planning to slip away and return to the inn, to tell Reva's family what had befallen her. Perhaps one of them could suggest a means of rescue.

As he reached the door he took a final look at the crowd. None of them seemed dismayed by the prospect of seeing a woman hanged two mornings hence. In fact, some gave every impression of looking forward to the event.

He fervently hoped they would be disappointed.

He turned and slipped unnoticed out into the foyer, and then out across the terrace, down the steps, and into the street beyond.

30

In Which Garras Lir Devises a Scheme

Nivain turned pale but said nothing when Anrel delivered the news; Perynis stared and kept trying to phrase a protest, but could never get out more than a word or two.

Tazia and Garras were not so reticent.

"You couldn't do *anything*?" Tazia asked.

"Nothing," Anrel said. "I was on the far side of the room, the entire house was warded, and she was being held by a sorcerer, two footmen, and a homunculus bigger than I am."

"Wouldn't Mimmin have helped you?"

"Probably not," Anrel said. "She seemed much more interested in her own situation than in Reva's."

"You should have killed them all," Garras growled. "Brought the ceiling down on their heads!"

"And how might I have accomplished this, sir?"

"You're a magician, aren't you?"

"A very poor one, as I have frequently reminded you, and the house was *warded*, warded heavily."

"What does *that* matter?"

"A ward is a protective spell, Master Lir."

"I know what a ward is! My wife sets them to warn us of intruders."

"That's hardly the same, sir. Wards come in a thousand varieties. The simple little warnings that your family uses are like mice beside a lion when compared to the wards Lord Allutar had set on his house."

"Well, blast it, if you were so outmatched, then why did Reva go in there?"

"For fifty guilders," Anrel replied.

"Humph. Well, what are you going to do about it?"

"I'm not aware that there is anything I *can* do, sir."

Garras glared at him. "Well, *someone* needs to get my daughter out of there!"

"I don't think it's possible, sir. The morning after next she'll hang."

Nivain let out a muffled sob.

"She will *not*!" Garras bellowed. "I won't allow it!"

"How will you stop it?" Perynis asked quietly.

Garras turned to stare at his youngest daughter, and his rage faltered. His gaze fled from her to her mother, to Tazia, and finally back to Anrel.

"There must be some way," he said. He turned to Nivain again. "You're witches, the three of you—aren't you a match for a single sorcerer?"

"A sorcerer who has the weight of the empire itself behind him," Anrel said.

"Shut up!" Garras snapped. "Go away, and leave us to work this out."

Anrel started a harsh retort, then bit it off short. He had just told this man that his eldest daughter was about to die; he could hardly expect gratitude. "As you wish, sir," he said. "I will be downstairs, should you need me for anything."

"Just go," Garras said.

Anrel glanced at Tazia. She met his eyes, and nodded ever so slightly. He nodded back, then turned and headed for the door.

He half expected someone to call him back, but none of them did. He left the room, closing the door carefully behind him, then made his way through the corridors and down the stairs.

He sat in the saloon, sipping a glass of good red wine, for what seemed like hours, thinking about his unhappy situation.

He was a fugitive, under sentence of death, unable to speak safely to any member of his family. His best friend had been murdered and remained unavenged, and his own cousin was soon to marry that friend's murderer. He had found a place of sorts with a new family, and had fallen in love with a charming young woman, and now all that was jeopardized by the impending death of his beloved's sister.

There was no doubt in his mind that Reva was going to die. Lord Allutar had put Urunar Kazien to death without hesitation; he had murdered Valin; why, then, would he spare a witch who had attempted to bespell him in his own house? Nor could Anrel see any way to rescue her; Lord Allutar was a landgrave, with all Walasia's resources at his command, not the least of those resources being his own sorcery. It was entirely possible, perhaps even likely, that he had enchanted Reva so that she no longer *wanted* to escape or be rescued—certainly, that had been done before when one magician held another prisoner. If Reva were to sabotage any attempt to free her, Anrel could not imagine how he and the family Lir could save her.

As for a legal solution, no magistrate would overrule a landgrave; it would take a decree from the emperor himself, or from the Grand Council, to obtain her release . . .

Anrel hesitated at that thought.

Was it not true that many of the delegates to the Grand Council had been elected at the urging of the legendary Alvos of Naith? Might they feel some debt to the mysterious orator?

And wasn't he himself that same Alvos? Perhaps he could somehow use that to obtain a pardon for Reva. He frowned.

Perhaps he could use that to obtain a pardon for *himself*, he realized.

Reva's situation was much more immediate, of course. He pushed aside any consideration of his own problems to concentrate on hers. If there were some way he could get word to the radicals on the Grand Council—but he didn't even know any names!

Or did he? Back in Naith he had named Derhin li-Parsil and Amanir tel-Kabanim in his speech from the First Emperor's statue; had the townsfolk elected them?

What's more, those two had met him, and could attest that he was indeed the mysterious orator. If he simply presented himself to the

Grand Council claiming to be Alvos, why would they believe a word he said? But if Derhin and Amanir acknowledged him, that should settle the matter in his favor.

He began to regret bleaching and reshaping his hair and beard; after all, Valin's friends had only spent that one afternoon with him. If he wanted them to recognize him—but he had wanted Lord Allutar to *not* recognize him, and he could hardly hope to have it both ways.

He only had a single day to get to Lume, get a hearing before the Grand Council, and bring the pardon back to Beynos—was that possible?

The Grand Council was not even in session; if it were, Lord Allutar would not have been in Beynos holding his reception in honor of the new prince.

This was going to be a challenge, certainly. He would need to get to Lume, find Amanir and Derhin, convince them of his identity and the urgency of his request, gather the Grand Council, sway enough delegates to decree a pardon . . .

"Anrel?"

He turned to see Tazia standing in the saloon door.

"Anrel, I think . . . I thought you should know . . ."

She spoke hesitantly, and Anrel thought she was on the verge of tears. That was hardly remarkable, given her sister's situation. Anrel crossed the room in three quick strides and held out his arms. She flung herself into them and pressed her head to his breast.

For a moment they simply stood, taking comfort in each other; then Tazia looked up at Anrel.

"My father didn't want any of us to tell you; he ordered us not to, but I . . . I don't trust Lord Allutar," she said.

Anrel blinked. What did trusting Lord Allutar have to do with anything? "Tell me what?" he said.

"He has this idea," she replied, then stopped, apparently unable to continue.

"What idea is that?" Anrel said soothingly, looking her in the eye.

"He's going to see Lord Allutar," she said.

"Who is, your father?"

She nodded.

"To beg for mercy?" Anrel shook his head. "He can try, but I don't think—"

"Not to beg," Tazia interrupted. "To bargain."

Anrel felt a chill. "Bargain?"

"Yes. He intends to trade your life for Reva's."

Anrel stood as if frozen. He could think of nothing to say in response; indeed, he could hardly think at all. For some reason he found himself remembering the stranger in his uncle's grove, and how he had not seriously considered trying to trade his life for Urunar Kazien's.

That was a very different situation; the stakes were far higher for Anrel in this new bargain.

"But I don't want you to hang!" Tazia said in a rush. "Even for my sister, I couldn't . . . and I don't trust Lord Allutar; I don't trust him at all. I think he'll hang you both!"

Anrel still could not speak, but his mind was starting to work again.

On the surface, such a bargain would certainly seem likely to appeal to Lord Allutar—give up an unremarkable witch for a notorious traitor? Of course he would agree!

So Garras had undoubtedly reasoned, but Anrel was far less certain. Hollem had said that for the sake of his betrothal, Allutar did not really want to capture Anrel at all. He could not admit as much openly, of course.

Anrel thought Hollem was probably right, which would make the exchange Garras was offering much less appealing.

But given that, how would the landgrave respond? Would he refuse the deal outright? He could easily accuse Garras of trickery, demand proof that he could deliver what he promised. He could say that the law's majesty did not allow for such tawdry transactions.

Or he could accept, and either keep his side of the agreement and release Reva, or as Tazia feared, announce that he was not bound by bargains with criminals, and hang them both—he might prefer to let Anrel live, but that did not mean he would do so if he thought it would harm his reputation.

"Lord Allutar thinks himself a man of honor," Anrel said, thinking aloud. "If he swears an oath, he will keep it. If he makes an agreement but will not swear to it, then he cannot be trusted to keep it."

"But I don't want you to die in her place!" Tazia said. "I don't want *either* of you hanged!"

"I assure you, the prospect does not appeal to me in the slightest," Anrel said. "Nonetheless, it seems likely that at least one of us *will* hang. Your father clearly prefers it to be me, rather than his daughter, and I can scarcely fault him for that."

"He has no right, no claim on you! You must flee!"

"If I do, your sister will hang."

Tazia looked wordlessly up at him.

"No one will ask you to choose between us," Anrel told her gently. "Certainly, I could not be so cruel. This is my choice to make, not yours."

"You cannot be considering it?"

"I am considering several possibilities," he replied. "I may have resources in Lume that can be applied to your sister's case, if only I have the time to marshal them." He frowned. "If you might persuade your father to say he needs more time to deliver the infamous Alvos, that a single day is not sufficient, perhaps a stay of execution could be had."

"But he's on his way to Lord Allutar right now! I followed him down the stairs, trying to dissuade him, and only turned back at the front door."

That put a different face on matters. "Then I must make use of what time I have. I assume the landgrave's men, or the burgrave's, will be here within the hour, and I would prefer not to be here when they arrive." He released Tazia, then leaned over and kissed her on the forehead. "Tell your father not to despair. Don't say you told me anything; say merely that I was gone, but left you a message saying that I will return."

Then he strode quickly out of the room.

He hesitated in the passage—his meager belongings were mostly in the room above the stable; did he dare retrieve them? Nivain and Pernis would be there, and might try to hold him until Garras's return. Dorrin Kabrig still had the stolen sword—or perhaps Mistress Sharduil did, but at any rate Anrel did not. Should he ask for its return?

No, he would be better off not drawing any attention from the inn's staff, and without any added burden. That sword had been of very little use to him, and he did not see that as likely to change in the immediate future. He still had the dagger in his boot, but his best weapons were his words, his ability to sway others; he had been trained in rhetoric, history, and oratory, not in swordsmanship. Most of his money was still in the lining of his coat, and he could replace anything he left with the Lirs. He turned to the left and hurried out the inn's front door. On the way he passed a drowsing Dorrin and did not disturb him.

The cold outside was almost like a physical blow; Anrel had not realized just how pleasantly warm the saloon was. He was not wearing his jacket, only his velvet coat, though fortunately, in his haste to inform the family of Reva's misfortune, he had never taken off his hat or scarf.

He hurried across the forecourt and out through the iron arch, then along the brief length of Cobbler Street and onto the high street. Between the cold and the lateness of the hour the streets appeared entirely deserted, save for himself. Clouds hid the stars, and there were no streetlamps, so the only light came from shop lanterns and lit windows, and there were not many of either; he was alone in shadowy gloom.

Now he had to decide where to go. He could head directly for Lume—but leaving Beynos at this hour would be suspicious, and the gates were manned. For that matter, the city gates of Lume might well be closed; these were troubled times. And while the distance between the two cities was not great, still, the night was overcast, and he might lose his way in the darkness—he had no lantern.

No, best to stay in Beynos for tonight, and make for Lume in the morning. Obviously, he could not stay at the Boar's Head; he would need to find other lodging. He had a guilder or two in his pocket, which should serve to pay for a room without requiring him to disturb his coat's lining; all he had to do was find a suitable establishment.

The two customary locations for an inn were by the gate and in the center of town; he had not noticed any other lodgings near the gate where he had entered Beynos, so he turned his steps toward the town square, just a few dozen yards away.

The Sunrise House was closed and dark, its lantern extinguished.

The Flying Duck, if that was indeed what the signboard indicated, was no better; he tried the door there, and knocked, but received no answer. Anrel was beginning to shiver with cold, and to worry that he might run afoul of a night watchman if he wandered the streets much longer.

Then he heard something worse than a watchman—a party of men was marching down a street, and some of them wore gear that creaked and jingled, indicating that they were armed. He ducked into the mouth of an alley, listening intently.

They were west of the square. Anrel listened for any exchange of words that might help identify them, but no one spoke; he heard only the tramp of boots, and the rattle of armor and weapons.

They turned onto the high street, Anrel judged, and turned *away* from the square—but then turned again. Into Cobbler Street, he was fairly sure.

Those were obviously the men Lord Allutar had sent to apprehend him. If not for Tazia's warning he would be waiting for them in calm ignorance, rather than listening to their passage from the temporary refuge of the alley.

He wondered whether the landgrave himself was accompanying them, and whether Garras was with them, but he was not curious enough to take a look. Certainly he could not hope to stage an ambush, alone against a company and armed only with a dagger.

Then the sound was gone, out of earshot, and he emerged from the alley. Finding shelter was now more urgent than ever—when they found he was not at the Boar's Head they might well come seeking him elsewhere.

They might check the other inns, Anrel realized, feeling foolish for not having thought of that sooner. Perhaps it was just as well he had not yet found lodging.

If the inns were all closed to him, he would need to find some other shelter; even if Lord Allutar's men were not looking for him, he could not sleep in the street in this weather. He looked around the square, hoping for inspiration.

One side, the south, was open to the river, and the magnificent bridge across the Galdin, with its elaborate railings and grand lampposts, served as a centerpiece. To east and west stood inns, taverns, and shops. To the north, grand houses lined the side, not unlike Lord Allutar's house on Bridge Street Hill, though these were all smaller and less ostentatious. Anrel looked at them, and a crooked smile spread across his face despite his shivering.

There was one place in Beynos that no one would ever look for Alvos of Naith, one place besides the Boar's Head where he had already been made welcome. He turned and trotted northward out of the square, up Bridge Street.

31

In Which Anrel Finds Shelter in an Unlikely Place

Naturally, there were lights still blazing in Lord Allutar's house; there were probably still dozens of guests enjoying the landgrave's hospitality. A few carriages stood in the drive below the steps; Anrel could see their drivers huddled in a little group in a corner out of the wind, chatting amongst themselves as they awaited their employers.

One driver was seated upright upon his bench, ignoring the others and seemingly oblivious to the cold; Anrel took a closer look at this individual and realized it was a homunculus, rather than a human being. He had never heard of anyone but the margrave of Kallai using homunculi as drivers—horses were said to dislike them; the margrave of Kallai was said to enchant all his horses to tolerate them—and wondered whether this might mean the margrave was attending the reception.

It hardly mattered, though. He hurried past the line of vehicles and up the steps to the grand entrance.

A footman was tending the door; Anrel said, "I'm Dyssan Lir. I was here earlier, and I believe I've left my walking stick."

"Yes, sir, just a moment," the footman said, consulting the guest list. "Dyssan Lir—yes, I see. Shall I send someone to fetch your stick?"

"I'm not sure just where it is—might I just come in and see if I can't retrace my steps and find it?"

"Of course, sir." The footman stepped aside and admitted him. "I believe the festivities have largely moved upstairs to the drawing rooms."

"Thank you." He hurried in, not giving the homunculus tending the cloakroom more than a brief glance. He found it reassuring that the creature was back at its post, though, and not standing guard over Reva somewhere.

The foyer was empty of guests; the grand ballroom beyond was almost deserted as well, though the chandeliers still blazed, and an elderly fellow in a wine-stained jacket was asleep on a chair against the wall. Empty plates and other such detritus were the only other evidence of the gathering that had filled the room a few hours earlier. The corner where the harpist had played now held a semicircle of four chairs, but no musicians occupied them, and no instruments remained visible.

Anrel crossed the empty dance floor, glancing into the brightly lit salon where half a dozen guests were scattered on the chairs and couches, talking quietly; he considered joining that party, but decided against it. He had no reason to make idle conversation with these people, and while it was unlikely any of them would recognize him, there was no reason to take even such a small risk. Instead he crossed to the door where Lord Allutar had made his grand entrance, and where Reva had been taken away.

He had no real hope of finding and rescuing the witch, but if an opportunity presented itself, neither would he ignore it. He had come here not to set Reva free, but only to keep *himself* free—he was fairly certain this was the one place in Beynos where no one would look for him once he was found to have departed the Boar's Head. He intended to blend in with the remaining guests, and settle in a quiet corner for the night as if overcome by an excess of wine. In the morning he would leave as early as he could, and see about petitioning the Grand Council for a pardon for Reva.

He was not optimistic about such a petition—if only he had more time! But he saw no better alternative. He had done nothing to help Urunar Kazien, and very little to aid Lord Valin li-Tarbek, but he would not stand by this time and let Reva Lir die without making *some* attempt to prevent it. He just could not think of anything that would be effective in saving her.

Beyond the door, as he had expected, he found a dining hall, where an elaborate candlelit buffet had been thoroughly picked over. A young couple was whispering to each other in one corner, but the room was otherwise abandoned by the revelers. Anrel found an apple that had somehow been overlooked and took a healthy bite as he looked around.

Double doors stood open at one side, revealing a well-lit marble-floored hallway and a broad white marble staircase. That was obviously the next stage of the public rooms; the other doors were small and closed, clearly intended for servants. Anrel judged that the hallway would also connect to the salon, which made sense. He ambled in that direction, his boots loud on the marble.

He could hear voices from upstairs, men speaking and women laughing. The only open doors off the hallway on this floor led to the dining hall and the salon; the rest of the party was clearly on the next level up, as the footman at the door had suggested. He started up the wide steps, in no particular hurry.

If he was going to play drunk, he thought, it would add verisimilitude if he could find a bottle of wine, or perhaps some stronger spirit. He had downed three or four glasses at the Boar's Head before Tazia had sought him out, but the walk in the cold had cleared that from his head quite thoroughly, and he feared it had removed the odor from his breath, as well. He had not seen any displayed on the buffet, not even empty bottles; presumably the staff had already cleared away whatever little had been left.

The stairway emerged into a spacious gallery with several doors opening off it; three men were standing near the head of the stair arguing politics, while a courting couple was discussing far more personal matters in the shadows beyond. Anrel nodded at the debaters as he passed; he did not take a very close look at them, lest one look too closely at him in response, but he did not think he knew any of them.

The first door he came to opened into a large drawing room where perhaps a score of people were still celebrating; one wit had gathered an audience of half a dozen women who were laughing vigorously as he held forth, but most of the conversations were being carried on in groups of three or four.

Lord Allutar was in one such group, talking to Mimmin li-Dargalleis and a man and woman Anrel did not recognize. Anrel was mildly startled that the landgrave had not accompanied his men to the Boar's Head—but then, on second thought, why should he? He had guests to attend to, and apprehending a traitor was the job of the town's watchmen, not a landgrave's responsibility at all.

Besides, he probably did not want to be in a position to tell his fiancée that, yes, he had personally overseen the capture of her favorite cousin. If the burgrave of Beynos happened to take Anrel and execute him, that was unfortunate, but there was no need for Allutar to emphasize his own role to Lady Saria.

The presence of Mimmin li-Dargalleis was another small surprise. Apparently no one had made any connection between Reva and Mistress li-Dargalleis; it was obvious from their expressions that she and Lord Allutar were anything but hostile toward each other.

At least Garras was nowhere to be seen; his presence would have been disastrous. Presumably he *had* gone with the men sent to fetch Anrel; after all, they would need to have *someone* who could point out their target. Lord Allutar had presumably felt it would be inappropriate to leave his own reception on such business, but Garras could identify Anrel as well as anyone.

Even without Garras, though, Anrel dared not set foot in that drawing room; either Allutar or Mimmin might spot him. He walked on.

The next open door revealed a library—easily a hundred fine volumes stood on well-made shelves. Unlike most of the rooms Anrel had seen up to this point, the room was fairly dim; a single lamp burned on a desk.

Its light sparkled from a cut-glass decanter half full of golden liquid; that was exactly what Anrel had hoped to see somewhere. He turned his steps into the library.

A white-haired man was asleep in one of the red leather chairs, making it even more perfect. Anrel helped himself to a glass of brandy, deliberately not swallowing it quickly, then settled in another chair. He leaned his head back against the upholstery, and pulled his hat forward to cover his face.

He hoped that Lord Allutar would not disturb sleeping guests, leaving them to wake and depart in their own time. Anrel intended to spend the night here, in this very chair, and in the morning he would make his way to Lume as quickly as he could, and seek out allies on the Grand Council. If he found them, and could arrange a pardon or at least a stay of execution, he would return posthaste to Beynos; if he could not, then he would do his best to vanish into the streets of Lume.

That would mean giving up Tazia, and the thought pained him, but how could he possibly return to her if he allowed her sister to die? He was sure that in that event Tazia would not forgive him for refusing to die in Reva's place.

He could not leave the city until the gates opened at dawn, though, and he would need to be as rested as he could contrive to be.

Staying in his enemy's own home was audacious, but he honestly believed it his best course of action. Watchmen were probably scouring the inns and taverns at this very moment, perhaps even rousing innocent citizens who might be suspected of harboring outlaws, but no one would look for him here. If his suspicion that Lord Allutar would prefer not to find him at all was correct, then even if he *was* found, it might not prove fatal. He could think of nowhere safer in all Beynos.

He tried to sleep, but the chair was designed for reading, not sleeping, and he could not find a truly comfortable position. The light of the lamp was mildly distracting, but far more so was the knowledge of where he was, and at what risk. He was also eager to get on with the business at hand, of finding some way to save Reva. The taste of brandy lingered on his tongue, but the alcohol did little to ease his mind. He considered drinking more.

He wanted to be alert in the morning, but which would be worse for that, a sleepless night, or the lingering effects of an excess of brandy? He had never been a heavy drinker; it would probably not take much to send him to sleep. He pushed his hat back and reached for the decanter.

Just as he did, he heard a woman's quiet laugh. He looked up.

Mimmin li-Dargalleis and Lord Allutar were standing in the gallery, just outside the library door; Mimmin's head was resting on the landgrave's shoulder. It was she who had laughed, presumably at some witticism Allutar had whispered in her ear.

"My lord," another voice said—Hollem's voice. Anrel froze for an instant, then slowly sat back in his chair, praying that none of them would glance in and recognize him. He tugged his hat back down over his face.

"I'm going to bed," Lord Allutar said. "See to our remaining guests, would you?"

"Of course, my lord," Hollem said. Anrel could not see him, but he imagined the servant bowing politely. "To what limits shall I extend your hospitality?"

"I would prefer to have them all safely in their own beds by dawn, and I certainly don't want to find any carriages still waiting out front when I arise, but if anyone doesn't look fit to go home, offer a bed here. There's no need to move anyone who's already asleep, either—let them stay until morning." Anrel thought he could feel the landgrave glance into the library as he said that. "Don't feed them, though, or we'll never get rid of them."

"Very good. And the witch?"

"She should be fine where she is, but see she has water, and food if she asks for it."

"Yes, my lord."

"Good night, Hollem."

"Good night, my lord, Mistress li-Dargalleis."

Then there were footsteps, and blessed silence descended. Anrel waited several long minutes, staring at the dark inside of his own hat and becoming far better acquainted with the smell of his own sweat than he liked, before he dared move.

When at last he dared lift his hat, his hand trembled. He looked quickly out the door.

The gallery was silent and dim; obviously, several lights had been extinguished. There were no signs of life; the voices from the salon had ceased.

Anrel decided he really needed that drink. He poured himself another brandy.

That was followed by a second, and a third, and by then his hands were steady again. He set the decanter back in its place, took a final look around, sighed, then sank back and pulled the hat down once more.

32

In Which Anrel Attempts a Rescue

At first, upon awakening, Anrel did not remember where he was. His back was stiff, and his side was sore where he had been slumped against the arm of the chair. He brushed his hat off his face before he was entirely awake, thinking it was some random bit of material that had fallen onto him as he slept.

Then he blinked at the white plaster ceiling and realized he was neither at the Boar's Head, nor back in Alzur, nor in his rented rooms in Lume. He sat up, and the previous evening's events came back to him. He snatched up his hat and clapped it back in place.

The white-haired man was still snoring gently in the other chair; the lamp on the desk had long since gone out, but more than enough sunlight was leaking in through the shutters to let Anrel see his surroundings—and to tell him that it was well past dawn, and well past when he should have headed for Lume. He got to his feet and straightened his coat.

As he did, he began reconsidering his intentions. He remembered that his plan the previous night had been to rush to Lume to see if he could use his reputation as Alvos to coax a pardon for Reva from the Grand Council, but now that he had slept on the idea, it seemed even more hopeless than he had thought it last night. The Grand Council was not in session, after all—that was why Lord Allutar was in Beynos in the first place. Yes, the three-day recess in honor of the emperor's new heir would be ending soon, but Reva was to hang tomorrow morning, and the Grand Council would not reconvene so quickly as that. Could enough of them somehow be convinced to issue the pardon in time anyway? Not all of the delegates considered Alvos a hero, after all—roughly half of them were sorcerers or their supporters.

Even getting to Lume quickly would not be very easy; the road was probably a mix of mud and snow, and the morning coach on this route ran westward, from Lume to Beynos, rather than the reverse. He would have to walk, and that would mean arriving in Lume muddy and tired, not in the ideal condition to impress delegates.

What's more, he was right here in Lord Allutar's home, where Reva was being held. Was there no way he could free her himself? It seemed cowardly not to try. He had followed the rules and obeyed the law when Urunar Kazien had been sentenced to die, and again when Lord Valin had inadvertently challenged Lord Allutar, and they were both dead, while he had saved himself in Naith by taking direct action, heedless of laws and limits. If he was to save Reva, perhaps he should once again discard rules and propriety.

She was in Lord Allutar's study, which would ordinarily be where Anrel would expect to find the landgrave himself, but last night Allutar had apparently taken Mimmin li-Dargalleis to bed with him, and surely he would be gracious enough to entertain her for a time this morning before sending her about her business. Furthermore, he might involve himself in the search for Alvos, if that was ongoing. He had charged Hollem with seeing that Reva had the essentials, so Hollem would presumably be checking in on her every so often, but Lord Allutar himself would quite likely be kept busy elsewhere.

Anrel thought he could handle Hollem, should the need arise, though he now rather regretted leaving his sword at the inn.

This was certainly as good an opportunity for rescue as Anrel could reasonably hope to have; at the very least, he thought he should investigate further. Where, then, would the landgrave's study be?

There were, Anrel knew from growing up among sorcerers, two schools of thought as to the best location for a magician's workroom. One was to put it as high as possible, as close to the sky as it could be, so as to draw upon the power of the heavens. The other was to put it as deep in the ground as possible, so as to draw upon the power of the earth. The other, lesser power sources—chiefly blood, death, and sex—were not limited to a specific location.

Any competent sorcerer would draw on both sources, of course, as well as the lesser forces, depending on just what he wished to accomplish with a given spell, but a central location, where they might be in balance, was never considered; apparently centuries of experience had demonstrated this to be less effective than choosing one or the other. Since magic often consisted of disturbing the natural balance, this was perhaps not surprising. No magician would set his place of power in the center of a structure; it would always, always, be at the top or bottom. Some would even maintain two workshops, one in a tower or attic and the other in a cellar or earthen-floored room. Anrel's uncle Dorias had his primary workroom under the drawing room at the rear of the house, but kept a small area in the attic clear, as well.

From all Anrel had heard, despite his drawing on the sky to strike down Valin, Lord Allutar was generally given to the magic of blood and earth. That would imply that his study was in the cellars.

Then Anrel looked around at his surroundings, and frowned. He was in a library; wouldn't Lord Allutar want his library convenient to his study? Uncle Dorias did not keep many books in his study because the dampness was bad for them, but he did keep them shelved near the stairs. Anrel crossed to one of the nearby shelves and pulled out a volume in a fine leather binding, and opened it.

"Ah," he said, as he read the title—*The Wantons of Quand.* The next volume revealed itself to be *Nocturnal Customs of the Old Empire. Mistress of the Harem* was after that.

These were not the sort of books a sorcerer would need close at hand. Anrel closed *Mistress of the Harem* and returned it to its place, then moved on to another shelf.

This second collection was somewhat more mundane—*Ten Years in the Cousins, Swordsmen of the Fallen Empire,* and other alleged histories. Anrel was familiar with some of these from his studies at the court schools. Again, these were not anything a magician would refer to.

That made sense, though—this library was open to guests. Presumably

Allutar had a more private one somewhere else. Probably, Anrel thought, in the cellars, near his study.

He put the books back where he had found them, gave the gently snoring white-haired guest a final glance, then slipped quietly out into the gallery and looked around.

There were no signs of life; the gallery was bright with sunlight from the windows at either end and a skylight above, but empty of people. Anrel hurried to the stairs and down, finding himself once again in the marble-floored hallway. The door to the salon was open, and that room was silent and still; the double door to the dining room was now closed.

Those did not lead anywhere he wanted to go; he turned and looked the other way. There were several closed doors; he chose one at random, and began exploring.

It took about three attempts before he found a passage leading to a stair going down, and each new exploration stretched his nerves tighter. He was, after all, in his enemy's home, and even if Lord Allutar was asleep or elsewhere—which was by no means certain—there were servants up and about, and if any one of them stumbled upon him in any of these places, there would be questions. Guests would not ordinarily go wandering about like this uninvited.

With his nerves so tense, he did not immediately recognize the wards. It was only when he found himself turning away from the head of the staircase without having made any conscious decision to turn back that he caught himself and forced himself to think about what he was doing and what he was feeling.

He stopped. He knew perfectly well that he wanted to go down a flight of stairs, and here was a flight of stairs leading down, but the thought of walking down it somehow filled him with loathing. He could feel his gorge rise at the very idea.

He smiled bitterly. He had felt this sort of ward before; when he was very young his parents had used them to keep him from going anywhere he shouldn't. Uncle Dorias had used them occasionally, as well. More than one of his professors had invoked them to keep the students from intruding where they were unwelcome. His own magical attempt to avoid notice the night before had been similar in concept, though far less effective.

None of those other wards had ever been quite so strong as this, but Lord Allutar was a very powerful sorcerer.

Students being what they were, ways of defeating such protections had been discussed frequently in the taverns and residential courts, and various theories advanced. Certain of Anrel's classmates had even claimed to have succeeded in defying such wards, though they were not universally believed. Anrel tried to remember exactly what methods they had advocated. He closed his eyes in an attempt to recall Dariel vo-Basig's boasts; Dariel had been the most convincing of those who said they had gotten through serious warding spells unharmed.

Closing his eyes had been the right thing to do, Anrel immediately realized; once he could not *see* the stairs the incipient nausea vanished.

"It's all in your mind," Dariel had said. "Oh, there are spells that set physical wards, but the ones that make you not *want* to go there, they work entirely on your mind—and not the surface, where you think about what you're doing, but down deep in your soul, where you *know* what you want, without thinking about it. So you have to fool that part of yourself. You have to *know* that you're doing something else entirely, not doing the thing the wards are preventing."

That had a logic to it that had seemed very reasonable at the time, but at the time he heard Dariel's explanation Anrel had been slightly drunk and not personally involved. Now, as he stood in a corridor in Lord Allutar's town house, Anrel was not fully convinced. Dariel had not been a sorcerer, after all, merely a clever young man from a wealthy family of merchants. Anrel had grown up among sorcerers, as Dariel had not, and had heard his parents and his uncle discuss the nature of magic, and he could not quite see how Dariel's theory fit. Sorcery drew power from earth, or from sky, or from living things, or things that had once lived, and used that energy to manipulate the natural forces that kept the world in order. Bindings, the most common and useful spells, forced mind and matter into a particular shape, or tied a spirit to a specific course of action. Unbinding spells broke down the natural forces that maintained forms, as Lord Allutar's unbinding had destroyed the integrity of Valin's flesh. Wards put forces in a particular place so that they would react when mind or matter of the right sort impinged upon them. How could you *fool* the forces of nature?

But then Anrel stopped, and smiled bitterly. He opened his eyes.

He had unconsciously been moving away from the stairs. The warding was still working on him, even if he did not feel ill. It was working on him in several ways. It was even, Anrel was sure, making him reject Dariel's ideas. Fooling natural forces happened all the time in sorcery. After all, how did a sorcerer draw power from the earth or the sky, other than by *convincing* it to flow through him?

And it wasn't the ward he had to fool, in any case; it was *himself.*

Anrel reached out and pressed his left hand against the wall. *That's my right,* he told himself. *If I keep that hand on the wall as I walk, I'll be moving away from the stairs.*

Then he closed his eyes and forced himself to start walking.

My right hand is on the wall, he reminded himself. *My right hand.*

He repeated it, and kept forcing his feet forward, one step at a time, until he brought one foot down and found no floor; he tumbled forward, and rather than try to catch himself he curled into a ball and allowed himself to fall down the stairs. As he thumped and banged his way down, he hoped that none of Lord Allutar's servants heard the regrettable clatter he was making.

But then, a sorcerer's servants were likely to be accustomed to strange noises.

He landed at the foot of the stairs with a bump to the back of his head, and lay dazed for a moment, staring up at the shadowy ceiling. It had rather fine plasterwork—elaborate moldings at the edges, and an ornate medallion in the center.

But he shouldn't be down here; he knew that; he felt it in his bones. He felt a strong urge to jump up and scramble back up the stairs . . .

No. He forced himself to lie still while he gathered his wits. He must not be hasty, he told himself. He could not go back up those stairs—he would be seen.

Not those stairs, he told himself. The ward wanted to send him back up, and he would go back upstairs soon, but not up *those* stairs. They weren't safe. He would be hurt, perhaps killed, if he went back up those stairs.

With just a very little practice, he discovered, it was really startlingly easy to lie to himself.

He rolled over and rose to hands and knees, then looked around.

He was in a small, windowless, unlit hall at the foot of the stair, illuminated only by the daylight that spilled down the stairwell from above. Four doors opened off the room; all were closed.

One of them, to his left, was difficult to look at; he seemed to be unable to focus on it. Another ward, he thought. That was surely the landgrave's study, and Reva was presumably inside.

He had come to rescue her, but now that he had come this far, he didn't want to go in there. He really, *really* didn't want to go in there. Even though he knew that was just the ward, and not his own heart, he still could not bring himself to move toward it, or even look directly at the door. He swallowed bile at the very thought, and looked down.

And inspiration struck him. He was in a cellar, kneeling on stone flags that were presumably laid directly on the earth; all the Mother's power was here at his fingertips. He was not a true sorcerer, since he was untrained, but he was a witch, was he not? Though he had long denied it, he had inherited his parents' talents, and he had taken lessons from Nivain and Tazia while they traveled. He had worked a few spells successfully, including that ward the night before.

He spread his hands on the stone and felt the cool strength beneath, and drew it upward through his arms and into his body.

It was as if sunlight had burst through clouds; the warding burned away, and the door that had been a terrifying threat to his sanity a moment before was suddenly just painted wood. He lifted his head to stare at it, then slowly got to his feet, brushing off his knees as he rose.

He gazed at the door for a moment, feeling the earth's power through the soles of his boots.

It was just a door. If not for the spell guarding it, he would not have known it was any different from the other three. He stepped forward and grasped the handle, half expecting to find some other magical defense.

He did not. Indeed, the door was not even locked. Presumably Lord Allutar had thought the repulsion ward to be sufficient protection. The knob turned easily, and Anrel swung the door open.

The good-sized room beyond was lit by a single thick candle upon a battered table in the center of the floor; the walls were rough white-washed stone, rather than the fine plaster or finished masonry Anrel had seen everywhere else in this house. A few chairs and a pair of benches were shoved back against the walls, leaving most of the stone floor around the central table bare and empty. Shelves on one wall held an assortment of tools and books, and these were not the elegant leather-bound editions intended for lending or for show that Anrel had seen in the library, but the battered and dog-eared volumes of a working professional. The tools included not just the usual mallets, blades, and ironmongery that one might find in any workroom, but assorted jars, skulls, bones, and twigs, as well as a dozen carefully draped snakeskins and some dried flowers. Lord Allutar clearly used a varied assortment of the arcane arts.

That much was unremarkable, and similar to every sorcerer's study Anrel had ever seen. Less common, though still far from unique, were the several pairs of chains and manacles bolted to one wall, starkly black against the whitewash. Two pairs of these manacles were in use, securing Reva Lir's wrists and ankles as she sat dozing on a simple wooden chair; she was slumped forward, her dark hair hiding her face, and the dim candlelight washed her in shadow, but there could be no doubt of her identity—she was still clad in the dark blue dress she had worn to the reception, and who else could be there?

She did not stir as Anrel stepped into the room. With a glance back at the stairs, he quietly called her name.

She still did not respond. Worried, Anrel crossed the room and put a gentle hand on her shoulder.

She started, and looked up. "Anrel?" she said. She quickly peered past him, as if she expected to see other people there with him.

"Yes. I was—"

"I can't hear you," she interrupted, speaking far too loudly for Anrel's liking. "I can see your lips move, so I know you're speaking, but I can't hear you. Lord Allutar put a spell on me—the only human voices I can hear are his and that man Hollem's." Her voice rose. "I can't even hear my own." She stared at him desperately.

Anrel blinked and fell silent. This was a complication he had not anticipated. He frowned, then held a finger to his lips.

She nodded. Then she, too, frowned. "I need to tell you something first," she said in a loud whisper. "Lord Allutar was in here last night, asking about you. He said my father claimed to be holding you captive. He said Father had offered an exchange of prisoners."

Anrel nodded. "I know," he said.

"Are you here to take my place?"

Anrel shook his head.

"You're trying to rescue me, then?"

A nod.

"How?"

"I don't know," Anrel said, but of course Reva couldn't hear him. He gave an exaggerated shrug.

Then he looked at the manacles, which were very solid iron, and which he was fairly certain were warded. He considered the hearing spell—he had never heard of such an enchantment before. It was obviously a binding, probably nothing terribly difficult, but rather clever in concept, Anrel had to admit. She might have other spells on her, as well, and for that matter, simply by setting foot in this room he might have triggered any number of wardings that would alert Lord Allutar to his presence.

This entire enterprise was beginning to look foolish in the extreme—but he was here, this was his beloved's sister, and she needed his help. At least she seemed to want to escape; he had feared she might have been enchanted to *want* to hang. He reached for the shackles on her wrists.

She snatched her hands away, as far as the chains would allow.

"It hurts if anyone touches them," she said. "Anyone but Hollem or Lord Allutar."

Anrel grimaced.

It was plain to him now why Allutar had rejected any idea of turning Reva over to the city's watchmen to be held at the courthouse; he could clearly hold her far more effectively here by means of his magic. Anrel had thought he might have ensorceled Reva so that she would refuse to leave, but he had never considered enchanted shackles, or hearing spells; he had assumed he could simply carry her out if he had to.

And perhaps he still could, if he could get her out of those manacles.

"Try not to scream," he said, knowing she couldn't hear him. Then he grabbed her arms, pulled them to one side, and reached for the lock on her right wrist to see whether there was some obvious way to open it.

Reva took a deep breath, but Anrel never found out whether she was preparing to scream or merely tensing against the anticipated pain, because he heard a sound that made him release his hold on her and whirl toward the door.

There were footsteps on the stairs.

33

In Which Anrel Confronts His Foe

The sorcerer's study offered little obvious cover, but there was one place to hide in any room, as Anrel had learned in his years at the court schools. Moving as quickly and quietly as he could, he ducked behind the door and snatched the dagger from his boot.

The approaching footsteps came to the end of the staircase, and the sound changed as they moved from the wooden treads to the stone floor. They came closer, closer—and stopped.

"I did not leave this door open," Lord Allutar's voice announced. "Nor do I believe that Hollem would make such an error; he knows better. It has been not long at all since the wards were disturbed, and I encountered no one upon the stairs or in the hallway above. Further, I see the witch is still chained, so any attempt at rescue has not gotten far. I therefore think it likely that you are still here, whoever you are, lurking somewhere out of sight—behind the door, perhaps? Armed, I assume, and hoping to catch me unprepared? A vain hope, I assure you."

Anrel held his breath.

Allutar sighed. "At times like these, I wish the tales of second sight had more of a basis in fact," he said. "You, witch—who is here? Your brother? Your lover? After meeting him last night, I cannot believe your father would have the courage. Perhaps another witch, come to aid her fellow outlaw?"

Reva lifted her head, but said nothing.

"You do know I can compel you to speak," the landgrave said warningly. "I demonstrated that last night."

"Then do it," Reva said. "I will not willingly aid you. Why should I, when you intend to hang me?"

"To save yourself the discomfort, perhaps? But please yourself."

Anrel could not see Lord Allutar from where he stood, but he could see Reva's face, and saw her tense; clearly, whatever magic the landgrave used to force her to speak was not pleasant. There was no need for Reva to suffer further; no escape was possible.

He slid his dagger back in its sheath. "Do not trouble yourself, my lord," he said, stepping out from behind the door and tipping back his hat. "Here I am."

"Indeed you are," Lord Allutar said. He stood in the little lounge, clad in a fine silk dressing gown, one hand on his hip and his hair in disarray. He frowned at the sight of Anrel. "Do I know—"

Then he stopped in midsentence, and an expression of wonderment spread over his features. "Father and Mother—Master Murau! Is that you? Whatever have you done to your hair?"

Anrel sighed. "A misguided attempt at disguise, my lord."

"But this is marvelous! How did you get in there? How did you get past the wards? I set those myself, and I *know* them to be effective, yet here you are, apparently untroubled—how? I had assumed the intruder must be a magician, either sorcerer or witch, but you are neither. Did you have help?"

"No, my lord." He would not have admitted it if he had, of course.

"Then how . . . ?"

"I learned certain things from my uncle, my lord, and received four years of the best education money could buy."

"Oh, but without magic! I am *very* impressed, sir! I knew you to be a clever and resolute fellow, but to make your way past my wards is truly an accomplishment. I admire your determination, however misguided it may be." He sounded quite sincere, Anrel thought.

Anrel bowed mockingly in acknowledgment, but said nothing.

"And you are here in Beynos—astonishing! Then the witch's father was not lying when he claimed to have seen you? Were you in truth lodging at the Boar's Head? Perhaps I misjudged the old scoundrel."

"I did stay at that establishment, yes."

"Remarkable! I thought he had fabricated the entire tale in hopes of delaying his daughter's death."

"I am afraid not."

Allutar's expression turned somber. "How very unfortunate for us both."

"Is it, my lord?"

"It may be." He cocked his head to the side. "Or perhaps not. Whatever are you doing here?"

"I would think it obvious." He gestured toward the chained woman.

"I meant, sir, what are you doing in Beynos?"

"Only passing through, my lord; it is mere unhappy chance that we should both be within these city walls at the same time."

"You are not pursuing me in some mad hope of further vengeance for Lord Valin's death?"

"I regret to say I was not."

"And I should not expect you to turn up on my doorstep in Lume or Alzur?"

"Unless I should somehow be pardoned of all my supposed crimes I have no intention of ever setting foot in Alzur again, and I would think Lume quite large enough for us both. I certainly have no plans for troubling you there."

Allutar considered that for a moment, then nodded. "Step back, lad, and if you would be so kind as to keep your hands in sight—I think we need to talk at some length, and I would prefer to do it behind a closed door." He gestured.

Anrel hesitated, then stepped back, away from the door.

Lord Allutar advanced into the study, and closed the door behind him. "Pray be seated, Master Murau," he said.

A moment later both men had pulled chairs out from the wall and sat facing each other across the central table, eyeing each other warily.

"Now," Lord Allutar said, "let us begin at the beginning. I killed your friend, Lord Valin, because I considered him to be a rabble-rousing fool who might well incite riot and insurrection with his populist rhetoric. You were understandably upset by his death. After failing to obtain any satisfaction by legal means you resolved to retaliate by carrying out the very acts I had killed him to prevent. You prepared a pretty speech espousing his idiotic politics, which you, calling yourself Alvos, delivered from the statue of the First Emperor in Aulix Square. Do we understand these events similarly?"

"I believe you have stated them accurately enough, my lord," Anrel answered.

"You do not argue with my description of your motives?"

"I could quibble, I suppose, but all in all, I think you have described my actions fairly."

"Lord Neriam did not take your posturing well, and sent the city watch to silence you, whereupon you quite sensibly fled."

"Yes."

"I am given to understand that you then disguised yourself as a guardsman and commandeered a canal boat in order to escape from Naith, and were last seen fleeing on foot northward along the bank of the Raish."

"Yes."

"That was roughly a season ago, and in that time sightings of the mysterious Alvos have been reported in any number of places, scattered across the empire from Kallai to Swoi. None of these reports held up to scrutiny."

"I would not know about that, my lord. I made no more speeches."

"You did not."

"No."

"So these reports are all fiction, then?"

"Not necessarily, my lord. They may be fiction, or they may be cases of mistaken identity, or of impersonation. I only know that *I* did not play the role of Alvos again after leaving Naith."

Allutar nodded. "You had accomplished what you set out to do."

"More or less. Ideally, I would have seen you dead, or ruined, to avenge Valin's memory, but I could see no way to encompass that. I had made sure, though, that the voice you attempted to silence was heard in Naith."

"And those words were seeds on fertile ground, exactly as I feared they might be. Half the Grand Council is made up of idealistic fools thinking they can somehow overthrow the natural order."

Anrel smiled grimly. "I am pleased to hear that, my lord."

Lord Allutar smiled back. "Fortunately, I had overestimated how much damage this might do. This popular uprising you helped bring about, this great groundswell that peopled the Grand Council with dreamers and idiots, frightened the emperor—did you know that, Master Murau? You gave our dear overlord a mighty scare, because he knows what I feared he did not—that without sorcerers, the empire is ungovernable."

"Oh?"

"Oh, yes. He had summoned the Grand Council as a club to use against the nobility, to force us to straighten out his finances. He had required it to be largely elected by the common people because he thought that the commoners would love and obey him, that these delegates would be overawed by his magnificence in a way that we sorcerers are not. He thought he was filling the council with loyal sheep. *You*, dear fellow, ensured that he was wrong, by seeing to it that hundreds of radicals and malcontents were sent to Lume instead."

"Did I?" Anrel asked uneasily; his smile vanished.

"Oh, indeed you did," Allutar replied with a grin. "And your acolytes so terrified the emperor that he would not permit them in the courts, instead sending them, and the rest of us with them, to that drafty ruin, the Aldian Baths, to hold our meetings in an ancient bathing pool. And while it is still much too early to be certain, it appeared to me from our first gathering that the Grand Council is now so divided, so disunited in purpose, that it cannot possibly accomplish anything, for either good or ill. We will sit and discuss and argue, and in the end we will all shrug our shoulders, pay off the most pressing of the emperor's debts and repudiate the others, and then put everything back just as it was, before we all go home to our own affairs."

Anrel blinked at him. "It had never occurred to me, my lord, that the Grand Council might do anything other than what you describe."

"Alvos claimed that the Grand Council could be the agent of sweeping change."

"Alvos spoke the beliefs of Lord Valin, and much as I loved my friend, I never took his politics seriously. I like to think myself more realistic than that."

"If the Grand Council had indeed become the emperor's tool, it might have been dangerous," Allutar said. "It would give what would otherwise be seen as acts of open tyranny a veneer of legitimacy."

"Was that what you feared, then?"

"Let us say I was . . . concerned," Lord Allutar said. He glanced at the closed door. "We are not here to debate politics, though."

"Indeed. I came here to save a young woman from the noose." He nodded toward Reva, who was listening to Allutar's side of the conversation with interest.

"I do not think that will be possible," the landgrave said.

"Then what are we discussing?" Anrel demanded angrily.

"We are discussing whether you will hang *with* her, of course."

Anrel heard Reva suck in her breath. He frowned. "I am afraid I do not see how the Grand Council's composition is relevant to that issue. Though I confess, I am not sure what *would* be relevant."

"Ah, Master Murau, you are such an innocent! I have been explaining the political situation because it has a very direct influence indeed on your own fate. As Alvos, you created a new faction in the empire's governance. Previously there was the emperor, and there was the nobility, and each held the other in check. The emperor was the highest authority, but could scarcely enforce his will without the cooperation of the sorcerers. The sorcerers held all the real power, but could not exercise it freely because the emperor has the Great List, and can render any rebellious sorcerer powerless by invoking the miscreant's true name. It was a fine balance, and worked for centuries, until the present occupant of the imperial throne decided to tip it in his favor by summoning the council. He had intended the council to be his tool, but you saw to it that the council is instead a third force, compelling the emperor to make common cause with his nobles in order to restrain it. A new balance has been created, and with luck we can maintain it until the council is once again disbanded and the old order restored."

"This is all very interesting, but I—"

"Do not see how it matters to *you*?" Allutar finished for him. "That's very simple. I do not want you meddling with these matters any further. As Alvos, you have acquired a great deal of influence and could cause a great deal of trouble. One way to ensure you do not do so would be to kill you. *Now* do you see?"

"Oh," Anrel said.

"That would really be the simplest solution, and the Lords Magistrate have indeed sentenced you to death, so that no one could possibly question it."

"But Lady Saria would not be pleased," Anrel said. "My death would impede your expectations of marital tranquility."

"Exactly. Your cousin holds you in high esteem—as do I, for that matter, though I do not share her affection for you. My wife will be required to tolerate a great deal, simply because of who and what I am, and I would prefer not to burden our relationship with any unnecessary additional strain. I do not want to kill you. If you were to be captured and killed elsewhere, I confess I would not be displeased, but *I* do not want to be involved. I did not send the guards to arrest you, nor did I pass sentence upon you for treason, so my betrothed cannot hold your present situation against me—"

"You killed Valin," Anrel interrupted.

"Well, yes, I did precipitate your actions by killing Lord Valin, but really, how could I have known it would come to this? I believe Saria can accept that much, as she has so far." He shook his head. "But if you are captured in *my* house, or by my orders—that would be a very unfortunate circumstance."

"For both of us."

"Yes. Which brings us to a possible bargain."

"What would this bargain be?"

"You would give me your word, as a Murau and an Adirane, that you will not interfere further in political matters—no more speeches, no grand gestures, no further attempts to assert the unfortunate Lord Valin's beliefs—and that you will do your best to stay away from me and mine, and cause me no embarrassment. In exchange, I would let you live, and depart freely from this house. I would further undertake to say nothing of this meeting to anyone."

Anrel stared at him for a moment. "So all I would get from this bargain is my life."

"And your freedom. Surely, that is enough, under the circumstances? You are here, in my study, under sentence of death, with no weapons or allies in evidence. I am a sorcerer of some note, and you are a commoner. You have nothing I want save your silence. What more could you expect from me?"

Anrel turned and looked at Reva. "The witch, for one."

Lord Allutar frowned. "Why *do* you want her? In fact, why are you here at all? Why risk your own neck in a hopeless attempt at rescue?"

Anrel saw no point in avoiding the truth. "For reasons not unlike your own for letting me live," he said. "I am courting her sister."

"Ah. How very awkward." Allutar glanced at Reva, then back at Anrel. "If her sister is as beautiful, I can understand how that might be a powerful motivation indeed. Alas, I do not believe I can let her live, not even if it means I must kill you, as well."

"You told her father you would trade her life for mine."

"I lied, of course. I had assumed *he* was lying, and why should I not be equally false in return? The possibility that he might actually deliver you simply did not occur to me. I confess to some dismay upon your admission that his tale was not entirely a fabrication—I do not enjoy learning that I have misjudged a man, or that I may have inadvertently compromised my honor as a result."

Anrel felt a grim satisfaction in this vindication of Tazia's mistrust. "She is just an ordinary witch," he said. "A poor unfortunate never given an opportunity to become the sorceress she was born to be, and relegated instead to roaming from town to town treating the diseases of cattle and telling impressionable girls pleasant lies about their marital prospects. Why does she need to hang?"

"Do you not know? I had assumed that whoever sent you here would have told you what she did." Allutar sounded genuinely surprised.

"Her sister said nothing of the nature of her offense," Anrel said. He knew, of course, exactly what had happened, but he wanted to hear Lord Allutar's reasoning.

"She tried to enchant *me*, sir. That cannot be tolerated. Had she confined her activities to what you describe she would be free today, but casting spells on sorcerers is simply unacceptable."

"But you, more than anyone else, are proof against such magic!"

"That is not the *point*," Allutar said, tapping the table with a fingertip. "The point is that the person of a sorcerer is due respect, and is not to be defiled by commoners, not even those commoners who through some mischance are capable of magic. No such defiance of the natural order can be permitted; the authority of sorcerers cannot be compromised. That was the same crime that cost your friend Lord Valin his life; I would think you would understand my position by now."

"Do I understand that you are construing her attempt to bewitch you as *treason*?"

Lord Allutar leaned back in his chair, lips pursed, and considered for a moment before replying. "That does not overstate my position. And of course, a traitor cannot be permitted to live."

Anrel stared silently for a moment, carefully not commenting on the contradiction between this statement and the bargain Lord Allutar had offered a moment before. Then he asked, "And what of the person who hired her? Has that individual not suborned treason, then?"

"To my mind, she has indeed, but the law as written does not agree, just as it did not agree that Lord Valin's importunities constituted a real crime."

"And have you—" Anrel began.

Allutar interrupted, "Do you know who hired her, Master Murau? I had assumed you were ignorant of the specifics, but perhaps not."

"I—"

Allutar did not give Anrel time to respond. "She was hired by a woman named Mimmin li-Dargalleis," he said, "who is asleep in my bed upstairs even now. Mistress li-Dargalleis sought to become my mistress in hopes of capturing a portion of my wealth and power, and to that end she hired Mistress Lir to cast a love spell upon me."

"You know that?"

"You heard me say that Mistress Lir knows I can compel her to speak, whether she will or no. She has had this demonstrated."

"Yet you say Mistress li-Dargalleis is in your bed?"

"Yes—but she is there on *my* terms, rather than hers. The law perversely does not deem her to have committed a serious crime by hiring the witch, but *I* do, and I intend to make her pay an appropriate penalty for her offense. Yes, I could send her to prison or even kill her, but she has powerful friends, an influential family, and a good bit of money, so that to do so would be troublesome."

"Her father is not just a village baker, then?" Anrel asked bitterly.

"No, he is not. He is, in fact, a banker, and one of the emperor's creditors. I prefer not to affront him. He can hardly object, though, if I take his daughter into my bed when she offers herself—and I cannot believe she will tell him what I do to her there, what degrading acts I have forced upon her, or how little profit this role will gain her. Believe me, I do *not* love her, and she can have no doubt of that, but I have use for her—are you aware that there are certain spells that draw their energy not from earth or sky, nor from blood, but from sexual acts? I have never before pursued these, and would never inflict them upon your cousin, but Mistress li-Dargalleis has made herself available for extensive experimentation in this field. It amuses me to punish her thus, rather than in some more open fashion; it seems very fitting, given the nature of her indiscretion."

"You think she will tolerate this?"

"I think she has no choice. I am a sorcerer, Master Murau. Witches are not the only ones who can cast love spells and other compulsive bindings."

"You have enchanted her?"

"I have enslaved her."

Anrel shuddered. "But she is a free woman, not a bond servant," he said.

"She is a woman who attempted to place me under her control. Whatever the law may say, I make no apology for imposing upon her much the same fate she intended for me."

Anrel glanced at Reva. "Then you have dealt with the true villain; can you not show mercy to the witch? Flog her, perhaps, but allow her to live?"

"The law specifies that witches are to hang."

"But you are the landgrave of Aulix! Can you not set aside the statute?"

"We are not *in* Aulix. What's more, she has seen and heard things that I cannot allow her to describe."

"Are there no spells that would suppress her memories of those secrets?"

"There are, but really, sir, why should I trouble myself with them? She will hang, and that will be the end of it."

Reva whimpered; Anrel glanced at her again, then turned back to Lord Allutar. "You asked what more I wanted, in addition to my freedom, and I am telling you, I want the witch's life."

"You can't have it. I said before a houseful of guests that she would hang, so she must hang."

That was the true reason for the landgrave's intransigence, Anrel realized. He was not willing to lose face.

But he did not want to antagonize Lady Saria, either. Which did he want less?

"And if I refuse to accept a bargain that does not include her?" Anrel asked.

"Why, then you shall hang with her. Master Murau, forgive my bluntness, but you are at my mercy here; we bargain on my terms or not at all."

That did not sound like a bluff. Anrel did not look at Reva again; he did not want to see her face when he gave in. "Very well, then. If I cannot have the witch, then I want three things from you in exchange for forswearing all further involvement in politics and doing my best to stay out of your way."

"Three?" Allutar frowned. "Name them."

"My life."

"Done."

"My freedom."

"Of course. And the third?"

"An apology for the murder of Lord Valin, who had committed no crime deserving death."

"An apology? An *apology*?"

"Yes."

Lord Allutar leaned back in his chair. "You amaze me. You are bargaining for your *life*, yet you still concern yourself with an apology that will change nothing?"

"Yes." Anrel made no attempt to explain. He was not sure he *could* explain why an apology was important; he merely knew that it was.

"And if I refuse to apologize, what will you do? You would not die for the sake of this woman; will you die for an apology?"

"Will it harm you to make one, my lord?"

"Harm is not the issue. Do you think you can make demands of me because I intend to wed your cousin? I have offered you your life after you threw it away for the sake of your friend's memory, and you are not satisfied? I have offered you your freedom after you invaded my private study to rescue a condemned felon, and you want more? Do you feel no gratitude at all that I am allowing you to go unharmed? Father and Mother, man, but your insolence astonishes me!"

"And your arrogance appalls me, my lord. You have taken an innocent man's life, you have by your own admission enslaved a woman the law does not consider deserving of such treatment, yet you cannot bring yourself to make a simple expression of regret?"

"Oh, I have my regrets, sir!" Allutar exclaimed. "I regret I did not kill *both* of you!"

"You can, of course, remedy that omission, if you are willing to forgo my cousin's embrace."

"You forget yourself, sir! And you forget who and what I am. I could enchant Lady Saria, as this witch would have enchanted me, and wipe all memory of your existence from her mind—have you forgotten that? I do not do so because I am an honorable man and would prefer my marriage to be built upon genuine affection, but you provoke me—do not think it beyond me."

"Oh, I am sure it is not, my lord. A man who would rather hang a helpless young woman than be seen to change his mind, a man who would rather commit a second murder than apologize for his first—what could be beyond you? But you know as well as I do that memory spells are difficult and unreliable, and that Lady Saria is an accomplished sorceress herself. Ensorceling her effectively would not be an easy task. Better to tolerate my insolence, and allow yourself a pretense of benevolence."

Lord Allutar stuttered with rage, and leapt to his feet, knocking his chair over backward. "You *dare*? You, a mere commoner, speak to *me* like that?"

Anrel rose, as well. "I speak as I choose, my lord. I am a free man, commoner or not. Your wards could not keep me out, and your words cannot intimidate me."

"Get out!" Allutar bellowed, pointing at the door. "Get out, before I forget my own best intentions and rip your heart out!"

Anrel hesitated for a fraction of a second, tempted to stay and argue—but Lord Allutar could indeed rip his heart out with a spell, and was even now raising his hands as if preparing to cast one. If Anrel fled now he might still find a way to free Reva; if he died, or stayed under Lord Allutar's eye, the witch was doomed.

And he had not yet sworn to any part of Lord Allutar's bargain, a fact that the landgrave might recall at any instant. Nor had he revealed how he passed the wards, a bit of information that might well alter Lord Allutar's attitude toward him.

Anrel turned and ran.

34

In Which Anrel Marshals His Resources

Anrel made no attempt at stealth or discretion as he fled; he ran up the stairs at full tilt, and charged through the house and out the front door, past a footman and the homunculus, without pausing.

His first impulse was to direct his path toward the city gate and head for Lume, but what could he possibly hope to accomplish there? Half the morning was gone, and he had only the vaguest notion of how he might locate members of the Grand Council in the capital's sprawling labyrinth of streets, courts, and alleys. There simply wasn't *time* to arrange a pardon, and after what he had just heard he was not at all certain Lord Allutar would respect one if by some miracle it were issued. Wasting the one day Reva had on such a hopeless effort would be foolish. He needed to find some other way to rescue her.

A pardon was not to be had, nor would Lord Allutar show mercy. A direct attempt to free her had failed, and Anrel could see no way another attempt would fare better—she was held fast by chains and spells, and Lord Allutar was aware that efforts were under way to save her, so she would almost certainly be guarded even more thoroughly now.

If he could not convince Lord Allutar to free her, and could not free her himself, what other possibilities remained?

He could not immediately think of any, but nonetheless, he no longer saw any point in going to Lume. Instead, once he had stumbled down the sweeping stair from Lord Allutar's front door to the street, he turned his steps toward the bridge, not because he had any great need to cross the Galdin, but simply because it gave him a direction.

The sun was bright, and overnight the air had turned unseasonably warm; the snow underfoot was melting, turning to slush and puddles as he hurried down the slope. Several townspeople were taking advantage of this thaw to go about business they had put off over the past few days, and the streets were busy.

The sight of all those other people finally brought the obvious answer to his question to Anrel's mind. If he could not free her, and Allutar would not free her, then he must find someone else who could and would—or several someones.

None of Reva's family could do anything. The best any of them could devise was Garras's plan to trade Anrel's life for Reva's.

Lady Saria—Anrel did not know for certain where she was, whether she was in Beynos or Alzur or somewhere else entirely, and he not only doubted that she could persuade Lord Allutar; he doubted that *he* could persuade *her* to intervene. Her affection for Anrel would probably not extend to making demands on her own future husband on behalf of Anrel's possible future sister-in-law.

The person Lord Allutar seemed to most trust in all the world was that servant of his, Hollem tel-Guriel, but Anrel could think of no way to sway Hollem to aid Reva, and trusted or not, Hollem was still Lord Allutar's servant, not his master.

There was, in fact, no one Anrel could see how to usefully recruit—as Anrel Murau.

But Alvos of Naith, on the other hand . . .

He paused at the foot of the bridge and looked at the dozens of townspeople around him, wrapped in coats of fur and wool and leather, going about their business. These were the ordinary people of the empire, not sorcerers and witches, but workmen and merchants and housewives. These were the common people that Valin had spoken about, the people he had said should be running the empire, should be in charge of their own destinies.

These same workmen and merchants and housewives hired witches to treat their ills and tell their fortunes, to place their wells and bless their livestock—and a good many of them would probably come tomorrow morning to watch one of those witches hang.

Perhaps these ordinary people should be given a chance to assert the authority Valin had claimed for them. Perhaps Alvos could advise them to do so, if he had the opportunity to speak at the hanging.

Anrel frowned. Where was the hanging to be? Hangings were traditionally public spectacles, allowing everyone to see justice being done. In Lume there was a permanent gallows in a place called Executioner's Court, perhaps a hundred yards downwind from the emperor's palace in the direction of the Pensioners' Quarter, near the headquarters of the Emperor's Watch; it was surrounded on all sides by arcades surmounted by watchmen's walks, to allow for control of unruly crowds. Anrel had seen no evidence of such a place in Beynos.

Alzur did not hold hangings; had any criminal ever been captured there he would have been sent to face the magistrates in Naith. Anrel had never seen a hanging in Naith, but they did occur, and he had the impression that they took place in a yard behind the courthouse.

Did Beynos operate on the same model as Alzur? Would Reva be sent to the Executioner's Court in Lume? That seemed unlikely—but if it *was* the case it opened new possibilities, as her escort to the capital might be waylaid on the road.

But it really *did* seem unlikely; Anrel could not imagine the bureaucrats of Lume allowing outsiders to hang someone in the Executioner's Court without days of negotiation and paperwork. No, Beynos presumably had a gallows somewhere, or a place where one could be improvised. He would need to learn more.

He also needed to plan out exactly what he intended to say and do.

The inns—the Sunrise House and the Flying Duck and whatever others there might be—were presumably open for business now, as they had not been late last night; he could get something to eat and drink and talk to a few people, find out where Reva was to die, and perhaps get a feel for the mood of the populace, and an idea what words might best sway them. He turned back toward the square.

He did not think Lord Allutar intended to pursue him; the landgrave wanted Anrel to live, or at least he did not want to be responsible for Anrel's death. Anrel did not think Allutar would send either his own men or the burgrave's watchmen to canvass the inns and taverns, looking for the fugitive. He should be safe enough.

Anrel took a final glance upstream toward Lume. Was he doing the right thing? Was his trust in his own ability in oratory misplaced? Might it be better to rush to Lume and try to find Derhin, to try to arrange a stay of execution, pending a pardon?

But he doubted he could find and sway Derhin in time. A fiery speech asking the townspeople to intervene might not save Reva, but it seemed to Anrel the best of the available options.

Now he had to devise one.

The Sunrise House was open for business, and his presence in the saloon there was accepted without question. A few pence got him a breakfast of bland hash and scrambled eggs that were not as fresh as one might have hoped, washed down with a mug of small beer. A smile and a few wry remarks got him the ear of two of the locals, who filled his appetite for information as well as the hash and eggs had filled his belly.

Hangings, he learned, were conducted on the famous bridge itself. A structure that Anrel had taken for mere decorative elaboration that extended out over the water on the downstream side was, he was informed, a hoist that also served as a gallows. The remains of the condemned would dangle over open water, simplifying the eventual cleanup. If no friends or relatives claimed the body and paid the appropriate fees within the customary three days the rope would be cut, dropping the corpse into the river to be carried away by the current; there would be no need to put any effort into disposal of the remains.

This did not strike Anrel as a particularly healthy idea for anyone downstream, as everyone knew the dead carried harmful influences if not properly placated and buried, but he did not suppose the people of Beynos greatly concerned themselves with such details.

Word that a witch was to be hanged on the morrow had indeed spread through town. Not everyone at the inn had been aware of it, but one of Anrel's breakfast companions knew the entire tale of how some poor foolish woman had been caught trying to enchant Lord Allutar at the landgrave's own reception, and had been flung into a dungeon, where she was now awaiting her doom.

Some details in his version were not quite what Anrel knew to be the truth; they had altered in the telling, as such things are wont to do. The witch was now reported to have been in the pay of Quandish agents who had hoped to force Lord Allutar to spy for them. Anrel supposed this theory came from Reva's improvised code phrase.

"I had heard it was a love spell," he said. He hoped this might displace the story of Quandish duplicity. It would be far easier to defend a woman hoping to capture a man's heart than a witch attempting to subvert a government official, and this story had the advantage of being the truth. "I had heard she made up some foolish tale about Quandish spies to protect the identity of the girl who had hired her, some poor young thing with more money than sense who had fallen madly in love with the landgrave."

"Well, if she didn't admit it, how do you know?" the man who had brought up the espionage theory demanded.

"From Lord Allutar's servants, of course. The witch revealed the truth later, when Lord Allutar questioned her. I suppose he ensorceled her. Anyway, that man Hollem heard the whole thing, and told my cousin Nilue, and she told me."

"My brother's mistress was at the reception, and *she* said it was Quandish spies."

"That's what the witch claimed, yes, but Nilue swears that the truth came out under later questioning. Just a girl smitten with the landgrave, no Quandish agents. After all, friend, have you seen any Quandishmen in town? I haven't."

"Well, they wouldn't *admit* they were Quandish!"

"Could any foreigner pass for Walasian? You don't think his speech and appearance would give him away?"

"Speaking of appearance," another man remarked, "*you* look Quandish."

Anrel suddenly found himself the focus of attention for everyone else in the room.

"I won't deny some Quandish blood," he said, in the most casual tone he could manage, "but I was born and raised in Aulix."

"How do we know that? Maybe *you* hired the witch!"

"Friends, I can barely afford this beer—how would I pay a witch enough to enchant Lord Allutar? It would take far more money than *I* have to pay for such folly! I'd say overcoming a witch's common sense that way must have cost at least a dozen guilders, and if I had a dozen guilders, do you think I'd be wearing this hand-me-down ruin instead of a good warm coat?"

That seemed to mollify most of the drinkers' suspicions, but one man was not so easily deterred. "It could be a disguise," he said. "How do we know you don't have half the Quandish treasury to draw on?"

Anrel shook his head. "You poor, poor man. Do you think the Quandish government would be stupid enough to send a spy dressed like *this*?" He tugged at his coat. "Do you think they can't afford walnut juice to dye their man's hair? That's the *easy* part of disguising a man! It's getting the language, the accent, and the manner right that's difficult, but here I am, blond as any Ondiner, dressed in castoffs and speaking Walasian as well as any of you."

"You could be a Quandish sorcerer, casting a glamour on your speech!"

Anrel laughed outright. "Oh, certainly, they would send a sorcerer who can cast a glamour to hire a Walasian witch, rather than having him ensorcel Lord Allutar himself. And of course, such a master magician would enchant his speech, but not his appearance! Tell me, friend, do you see a great many Quandish spies around here? Perhaps hiding in your woodpile, or sweeping the streets?"

That got a laugh from the crowd. Anrel's questioner looked angry for a moment, but then glanced around at the smiles on his neighbors' faces, and his expression turned sheepish. "You're right," he admitted. "A sorcerer wouldn't need to hire a witch, and a Quandish spy wouldn't dress like you." His features hardened. "But there *could* be a Quandish spy involved, all the same!"

"That girl who wanted the love spell," someone suggested. "Perhaps *she's* the Quandish spy, and *both* stories are true! She planned to control Lord Allutar with her charms."

"That could be," Anrel said. He shrugged. "Who knows?" He drank, then asked, "What does your burgrave think of all this? It sounds to me as if Lord Allutar seized this witch and plans to hang her without so much as asking the burgrave's blessing."

"Lord Diosin?" Someone laughed. "Lord Diosin isn't going to argue with the landgrave of Aulix. If Lord Allutar wants to hang someone, Lord Diosin will gladly hand him the rope."

"Not jealous of his prerogatives, then?"

"Not if it would get in the way of toadying to his betters."

"Ah," Anrel said. He beckoned to the innkeeper. "Another beer, if you please?"

As he waited for his mug to be filled, Anrel looked over the crowd and listened to their chatter. They were now making crude jokes about the burgrave of Beynos; clearly, Lord Diosin was not greatly beloved by his people.

The jokes were good-humored, though; they did not seem to feel any real rancor against the burgrave.

Mentions of the promised hanging were surprisingly few, really. These people did not seem particularly upset about the coming execution, nor particularly pleased by the prospect.

Anrel thought it would be easier to sway them if there were more obvious resentment of Lord Allutar's high-handed actions, but at least they were not applauding the witch's capture. They were more concerned with Lord Diosin's sexual habits and imaginary Quandish spies than with Reva's impending death.

Bringing these people to acts of open defiance would be difficult, very difficult—but Anrel had no other choice. He would, he decided, spend the rest of the day trying to lay the groundwork.

And tomorrow, he would gamble Reva's life, and quite possibly his own, on the legend and oratorical skills of the infamous Alvos.

35

In Which Anrel Attempts the Impossible

Anrel was on the bridge across the Galdin bright and early the next morning, taking a place by the upstream railing and settling in for a wait. He had blackened his coat with char from the inn's fireplace, and stuffed rushes into his shirt to pad it out and make himself appear a much larger man. He kept his hat pulled down to hide his face as much as he could without drawing suspicion, and spent much of his time looking out over the water.

The river had never entirely frozen over, so far as Anrel had seen, and right now it was mostly open water, flowing sluggishly between ice-covered banks. He could see no boats moving—hardly surprising, this time of year. Several were tied up along either side, most of them at least partially icebound.

There were a good many pedestrians around, though, encouraged by the milder weather to get out into the fresh air and go about their business. No one paid any attention to Anrel, so far as he could tell. He had feared that someone might notice him there, recognize him, and call the watchmen, but the townsfolk seemed happy to attend to their own concerns and leave him undisturbed.

After a time, though, a crowd began to gather in the square and on the bridge. Where people had been crossing the bridge briskly before, now they were beginning to linger, leaning on the rails as he was himself, or sitting on the steepest part of the bridge, or standing about in twos and threes, chatting quietly.

It was not long after he first observed this accumulation of townspeople that three uniformed officials appeared, marching across the square in a line. The man in the center carried a banner in one hand and a scroll in the other, while the individuals flanking him bore raised spears—not the simple everyday weapons that watchmen or guards might carry on patrol, but polished wooden shafts with elaborately barbed heads that gleamed silver in the sun. One of the spearmen had a large pack slung on his shoulder; Anrel found that curious for such a ceremony.

The banner hung from a crosspiece near the top of a pole at least eight feet in height; it was a long rectangle of pale gold cloth bearing a device Anrel did not recognize, but which looked suspiciously like a man juggling fish.

The three men stopped at the foot of the bridge, and most of the people on the bridge and in the square stopped whatever they were doing, fell silent, and turned to watch and listen. A few who had been sitting on the slope moved aside, but then waited expectantly.

As everyone watched, the man in the middle unrolled his scroll, a bit awkwardly—one hand had to keep hold of the pole bearing the banner, and was limited thereby. He held up the document, as if to read from it.

"Hear, citizens of Beynos!" he proclaimed, in a slightly hoarse voice.

"Louder!" someone shouted from the east end of the square.

"Hear, citizens of Beynos!" the herald shouted back. Then he cleared his throat and read, "Whereas, by the ancient law of the Walasians, it is forbidden for any subject of the emperor to perform feats of magic, unless that person's true name shall be duly inscribed upon the roll of recognized sorcerers, and patent of nobility granted in recognition thereof; and whereas a woman of unknown origin calling herself Reva Lir did two nights ago attempt to perform magic upon the body of Lord Allutar Hezir, who is landgrave of Aulix in the service of the emperor, against his will and without his consent, and whereas this woman can present no evidence nor witness that she is a recognized sorceress or the holder of any patent of nobility, therefore has Lord Diosin Folivie, burgrave of

Beynos, as representative of the emperor's peace within these walls, when informed of these facts, declared her outlaw and traitor."

He paused for a breath, and Anrel looked out over the crowd. They were watching and listening silently. There was no sign yet of Lord Allutar or Reva, though; had there been a change in plans?

"Accordingly, Lord Diosin has decreed that justice shall be done upon her, and be seen to be done upon her, on this day and in this place," the herald continued. "For that purpose, I, Illis tel-Parniar, am sent by Lord Diosin to ready this place, and to prepare the mechanisms of justice. Let none obstruct me. If any shall have reason to question what Lord Diosin has decreed, let him marshal his words, and an opportunity to speak shall be provided, but let none interfere with the rightful preparations I am commanded to make."

Now Anrel was confused; what preparations? He watched as the herald rolled up the scroll, straightened the banner, and marched forward again, up the arch of the bridge—but not up the center; instead he headed to the western rail. At the peak of the bridge he stopped, slid the scroll into his belt, and handed the banner to the spearman on his left. Then he turned to the spearman on his right, who was taking his pack off his shoulder, and reached out to open the pack.

Understanding dawned as the herald reached into the pack and began pulling out heavy tarred rope. This Illis tel-Parniar was not a herald, Anrel realized. This was the hangman, come to ready the gallows.

Anrel swallowed bile as he watched the three men go about their duties no more than twenty feet away from where he leaned against the eastern rail. The hangman climbed up on the railing, rope draped over his shoulder, while the two spearmen stood by, each with one hand raised, ready to grab him should he lose his footing. He clambered up onto a graceful iron arch that Anrel had once thought a mere decorative frippery, and laid himself out onto a diagonal shaft that jutted out over the river. Then he signaled to one of the spearmen and began hauling at the rope.

The noose, already tied, slid out of the pack and up the iron arch. The hangman maneuvered a loop of rope through an iron flower—Anrel could not see, from his vantage point, exactly what went where, but in only a moment the noose was dangling from the very end of the iron strut, and the rope had been run along a path through the ironwork, the free end flung down to one of the spearmen.

Then the hangman was sliding back down, to be caught by his assistants. He thumped onto the stone arch of the bridge, then took the end of the rope from his helper and secured it to the railing with a complicated knot.

The entire job was done with astonishing speed.

The three men turned and looked it over, tugging at the rope and watching the noose dance. A thin white cord hung from the noose, looping back to the railing; when the hangman was satisfied with the rope he grabbed this cord and used it to pull the noose back to the bridge, He secured it to an iron finial where it could easily be reached when the time came to place it around Reva's throat.

Then he turned and murmured something to one of the spearmen, who nodded, turned, and trotted back down the bridge and across the square in the direction of the burgrave's mansion.

Anrel waited. The hangman had said there would be an opportunity to speak; this was clearly not yet the time.

The hangman and his remaining assistant waited, as well, as did the crowd that had gathered on the bridge and in the square. Anrel noticed that people were now lining the waterfront downstream from the bridge—not upstream, though, as the hanged woman would be invisible from that side, hidden by the bridge's arch.

Anrel wondered angrily why these people were so eager to see a woman die. What satisfaction would they get from the sight? There was no pleasure to be had in a needless death, was there?

His own place on the railing had a fairly good view; he was able to see over most of the heads, and the ironwork was not in a direct line with the noose. He hoped, though, that there would be nothing to see—or rather, that there would be no hanging.

A riot, on the other hand, would suit him very nicely.

Other people were climbing up on the railing beside him now, on both sides. He frowned. That would make him less visible when he spoke, but he could not see any way to prevent it.

A murmur in the crowd made him turn his head in time to see a procession approaching. He craned his neck for a better view.

A dozen people were moving across the square toward the bridge. Reva was at the center of the group, head down, surrounded by watchmen; she wore no coat, despite the cold, but only the dress she had been wearing when she was captured. Her woolen cloak was presumably still in the coatroom at the Hezir family's town house on Bridge Street Hill, and Anrel guessed it might well stay there unclaimed for some time.

Anrel could not tell at this distance whether Reva was shivering, but he thought she must be—and he could imagine what the response would be if someone suggested she be kept warm.

She won't be feeling the cold—or anything else—for very much longer, will she? That was what someone always said on such occasions. Anrel clenched his teeth to keep from shuddering himself.

At the head of the procession were two heralds, bearing banners similar to the one the hangman had carried, which his assistant now held loosely, more or less upright. Immediately behind them Anrel thought he recognized Lord Allutar. Another man, white-haired and presumably much older, walked beside the landgrave; he had the look of an official, and might well be Lord Diosin, burgrave of Beynos.

The party came steadily nearer, the crowd making way for them as they approached the bridge.

This presented Anrel with an interesting decision. If he remained where he was, Lord Allutar would soon be close enough to recognize him. If that happened, what would Allutar do?

And what should Anrel do in response?

Then another movement caught his eye. A second party was pushing toward the bridge from the west, a man and three women.

"Father and Mother," Anrel murmured to himself. "This could be complicated." Now he had to worry not only about whether Lord Allutar would see him and demand his capture, but whether Garras Lir would denounce him and try to exchange Anrel's life for Reva's. Offering such an exchange would be useless at this point, but Garras was not a man to let logic or reason hinder him when his emotions were roused.

Nor was it clear what Nivain, Tazia, and Perynis would do. They were all witches, and while the three of them together probably did not have the sheer magical power or skill that Lord Allutar possessed, let alone the equal of both Allutar and Diosin, they did have surprise on their side.

Anrel told himself he should have anticipated this; naturally, the Lir family would want to make their farewells. That he had not taken this into account dismayed him; once again, he seemed to have made his plans without thinking them through. He had no trouble coming up with things he wanted to do, but anticipating what others might do in response—well, his failings in that regard were why he had done so poorly at certain games in his student days, and had abandoned gambling in consequence.

Any of five people could ruin his plans. He had intended to wait until the promised moment when an opportunity would be provided to protest the hanging, but now he wondered if he could afford to delay that long.

He pulled his hat down and stooped, ducking down behind some of the gawkers. Now no one who might know his face could see him—but on the other hand, he couldn't see them, either, nor could he judge the burgrave's approach accurately, to choose the optimum moment to show himself.

The sound of the crowd did provide *some* information, but the temptation to thrust his head up was strong. He resisted.

Then relative silence fell; the gathered mob seemed to hush.

"People of Beynos!" a stentorian voice bellowed. "By order of Lord Diosin Folivie, sorcerer of the empire and burgrave of this city, the woman Reva Lir is brought before you today that justice may be done upon her for her crimes! She stands accused of witchcraft and treason, by testimony of Lord Allutar Hezir, landgrave of Aulix, and has offered no credible defense, wherefore Lord Diosin has ordered her death by hanging. If there is any present who can give reason this hanging should not proceed, let him speak now!"

That was obviously his cue; Anrel straightened up, and shouted, "*I* have a reason!"

The crowd stirred, and a hundred faces turned to stare at him.

The two heralds were no more than thirty feet away, near the center of the bridge, staring at him in openmouthed surprise. Lord Allutar was beside them, glaring at Anrel—but at least so far, he did not interrupt.

The white-haired man, undoubtedly Lord Diosin, was behind the heralds, and clearly flabbergasted by this interruption. The group of watchmen, with Reva in their midst, was on the western edge of the bridge, almost against the railing, not far from the gallows.

Reva's parents and sisters were on the west side of the bridge as well, a few feet down the slope from the watchmen. All four of them were staring at Anrel, but he thought he read confusion on the faces of Nivain and Perynis, delight on Tazia's features, and fury in Garras's eyes.

"Why should this woman die?" Anrel demanded. "What harm has she done? What offense has she committed that merits her death? Yes, I know she is a witch, we all know that—she does not deny that, I do not deny that, it would be pointless to deny it. She is a witch—but I ask you all, what does that *mean*?"

Lord Allutar stirred, and looked as if he was about to respond to that question, so Anrel decided to forgo the dramatic pause he had originally planned for this point in his speech, and hastily answered himself.

"It means that for a modest fee, she will perform the little magics that our sorcerous overlords can't be bothered with, all the little things that make our lives that much more manageable. She heals the sick and comforts the dying; she delivers your children and guides your steps. She tells well-diggers where to drill, finds treasures carelessly lost, counsels the troubled, does every little task we set her, for just a few pence. She *serves* us all! She helps all those who ask in whatever way she can—and for this, for *this*, our masters demand that she must die hideously, and they have the effrontery, the sheer *arrogance*, to call this abomination *justice*! Justice! By the Father and the Mother, I ask you all, where is the justice in killing a young woman who has never harmed a soul, whose only failing was that she was a dutiful daughter, and did not protest when her father forbade her to attempt the trials that would have made her a sorceress and noblewoman? What sort of justice is that? Justice? *Justice?* This is not justice, this is *murder*!"

A murmur ran through the crowd.

"Who are you, sir?" the burgrave demanded, his voice unsteady.

Anrel had not planned for that question at this point in the speech, but he knew better than to pass up the opportunity it presented. "I?" he said. "Oh, I am no one very special. You wouldn't have heard of me. My name is Alvos, and I hail from Naith."

It seemed to Anrel as if the entire crowd in all its hundreds drew in breath simultaneously at that, in one great communal gasp.

"How do we know you're the real Alvos?" someone called—not an official, merely someone in the crowd.

"It doesn't matter who *I* am," Anrel said, refusing to let himself be distracted. "What matters is who *she* is—an innocent, a friend to all, a kind and generous person—"

"I know who you are," Lord Allutar interrupted, taking a step toward him. "I was in Naith when you spoke there. This *is* the true Alvos, people of Beynos—the lying traitor who plunged Naith into riots and chaos, the loudmouthed fool who fled from the scene the moment the city watch appeared. He is an enemy of order, a destroyer of the peace—"

"An enemy of *your* order, landgrave!" Anrel shouted back, pointing at Allutar. "An enemy of the sort of order that requires the death of anyone who displeases you. I know you, Lord Allutar Hezir. You intend to hang this woman not because she cast spells, but because she tried to cast a spell on *you*, on one of our sorcerous rulers. You murdered Lord Valin li-Tarbek because he dared argue politics with you. You cut out Urunar Kazien's heart because he took a few of your herbs. Three needless deaths in half a year, Landgrave, to appease your vanity—have you no shame, no shred of decency or mercy remaining?"

Lord Allutar took a step forward—only a single step, as the press of the crowd allowed no more unless he intended to push commoners aside. "I am the landgrave of Aulix, wretch," he said. "It is my duty to protect my people from those who would rob them, who would deceive them, who would mislead them or cheat them or endanger them—people like *you*, you who call yourself Alvos!"

"Rob them? Deceive them?" Anrel spread his hands to the crowd. "What has Reva Lir stolen, then? Who has she deceived? What has she done that harms the people of Aulix in any way, Landgrave? What has she done that harms anyone in Beynos, Lord Diosin? Why do you want her dead? You people, people of Beynos—when your child has a fever and lies in bed crying, her skin so hot to the touch you fear she'll scorch the sheets, her belly unable to keep down the thinnest gruel, who do you call upon? Do you take her to Lord Diosin? Do you take her to Lord Allutar? Do you go to the Lords Magistrate in Lume? You *know* you don't. You look for a witch, and you pray to the Mother that you'll find one in time!" He pointed at the gallows. "And is *this* how you repay that witch for saving your children? Is this the gratitude she deserves?"

"She is a *traitor*," Allutar roared back. "Every Walasian magician must have his true name inscribed upon the Great List! Is *her* name there?"

"So she must die for not giving her true name?" Anrel demanded. "Failing to give her *name* is punishable by death? Tell me, Lord Allutar, your Quandish friend, Lord Blackfield—is *his* name written upon this list? The magicians from the Cousins whom the empress has brought to our court—are *their* names duly inscribed? No? *No*, they aren't! It seems that the high-and-mighty magicians from Quand and Ermetia and the Cousins can roam freely throughout the empire without being included in the Great List, but this woman, who has never been *asked* for her true name, who was born in our own land and has been all her life a true and loyal Walasian, who has done nothing but serve the empire, *this* woman must have her neck stretched for our masters' amusement. Why is that? People of Beynos, *why is that*?"

"Other nations regulate their magicians in their own manner," the burgrave said. His voice was barely audible over the intervening distance.

"And does that involve killing their healers?" Anrel turned his attention from the two sorcerers to the surrounding crowd. "Listen to me, people! These nobles, these sorcerers—they are not concerned with the good of the empire. They are not concerned with the good of the people. They are not concerned with the welfare of Walasia, or of the emperor, or of you, or of you, or of *you*! They are concerned with no one's welfare but their own. They do not allow witches simply because they want no competition! They want no one who is not one of their cabal to wield even the feeblest magic. We have stood for their arrogance, their tyranny, for centuries, because we feared our neighbors and ourselves, but why? We are strong! We are a mighty people, the favored descendants of the Mother and the Father; we do not *need* these sorcerers anymore! Let us take charge of our own affairs! Let us show mercy to those who deserve it. This woman, Reva Lir, does not need to die. Is there anyone here other than the sorcerers who wishes her ill? Has she harmed a single soul in all Beynos, all the empire? Set her free, good people! There are hundreds of you, and only a handful of guards. There are hundreds of you, and only two sorcerers. There are hundreds of you, and it was you who chose half the Grand Council, the highest authority in this land—who can tell you no, if you demand this woman be set free? Cast her out of your walls, if you like; if you think it necessary to punish her somehow and placate your burgrave, send her into exile, but do not *kill* her! There is no return from death, no second chance, no way to reconsider—and no way to wash her blood from your hands, if you allow her to die. If you allow her to hang here today, it is not just the sorcerers and their watchmen who have slain her; you are all complicit in her death."

He gazed out over the crowd. His listeners seemed stirred by his words, but not yet ready to take any action. He turned his attention back to Diosin and Allutar, a little surprised that neither of them had interrupted so long a speech, and he saw that Lord Allutar was not even looking at him. Instead, the landgrave was watching Reva.

Reva, who had moved away from her captors and was climbing up on the railing opposite Anrel. She was moving slowly, deliberately, toward the gallows and the waiting noose, paying no attention to anyone or anything else.

Anrel blinked. What was she doing? Was she going to make a speech of her own?

No, that hardly seemed likely. She was no orator. In fact, did she even know what was happening? After all, if Lord Allutar's spells on her were still working, she had not heard anything Anrel had said.

Her guards were making no move to stop her; they were simply standing there, keeping anyone else from getting close to her.

A murmur ran through the crowd; now dozens of eyes, perhaps hundreds, had turned from Alvos, the famous orator, to Reva, the poor doomed witch.

Anrel looked for the other Lirs, thinking perhaps they knew what was going on, but they looked as surprised as anyone.

Then Tazia screamed, "Reva, no!"

Anrel turned quickly, and saw Reva take the noose from where the hangman had secured it and lift it over her head.

"No!" Anrel shouted. He saw Lord Allutar smile a bitter little smile, and he understood it all. Why should the guards be required to deal with a reluctant prisoner, when a fairly simple binding would make her all too cooperative? Allutar had not bothered to enchant her into obedience when he first captured her, but this morning, when she was fetched from his study to be hanged, Allutar had known that Anrel was still alive and free somewhere in Beynos, and likely to make one final attempt to free her. Of *course* the landgrave had put a spell on her before she was brought out to the bridge.

But perhaps she could fight it off. Perhaps she could still free herself. Perhaps the spell could be broken in time.

Anrel tried to draw magic up from the Mother's earth, but he was standing on the railing of a bridge, over the middle of a river—the earth was too far away, and he had never learned to draw the Father's magic from the sky. There was no power to be had, not with his feeble skills.

His nerve broke, and even though he knew it could not help, knew that his words would not reach her, he cried, "No, Reva! Stop!"

But she couldn't hear him. She couldn't hear anyone but Lord Allutar, who was staring back at Anrel, his crooked little smile turning into a victorious grin as Reva pulled the noose snug around her throat, the knot behind her right ear.

"Stop her! She's ensorceled, not acting of her own will!" Anrel called, pointing. "Stop her!"

Some of the observers on the bridge moved forward uncertainly, to be met by the watchmen—but then Reva stepped off the railing, and it didn't matter anymore.

Anrel could hear the sickening crack clearly. He saw her twitch once, and go limp.

"Seize him!" Lord Allutar called, pointing at Anrel.

Anrel swallowed bile, staring at the landgrave.

Allutar had won again. He had killed his third victim, despite anything Anrel could do. Anrel had thrown away his old life to make Allutar pay for Valin's death, and now Allutar had destroyed Anrel's hopes of a new life with Tazia. Reva was dead, and with her, any prospect of marrying Tazia.

There was nothing left. The crowd had not rebelled, had not saved Reva. The burgrave's guardsmen were starting to push through the crowd, and there was no way Anrel could escape them on the crowded bridge.

Anrel turned away, away from the crowd, away from the guards, away from Reva's corpse, and looked down at the icy waters of the Galdin.

He had never been a strong swimmer, and he knew nothing about diving, but none of that mattered. He jumped from the railing of the bridge out into space, and with arms outstretched he plummeted toward the dark water below.

36

In Which Anrel Returns at Last to Lume

The water was bitterly cold. Even if the river had not frozen solid, this was still midwinter, and a mere day or two of relatively mild weather had done little to warm the chilly currents; hitting the water was a shock. The instant Anrel burst through the surface into the frigid darkness below, the river seemed to suck all the heat and life from his flesh. He struggled to force himself up toward light and air and warmth, but the water closed over his head and he could feel himself being dragged down.

His coat and boots were weighing him down. He pulled at the coat, freeing the rushes he had used for padding, and the stalks spun away through the water, but the garment was still heavy, still dragging, and he realized it was the weight of the coins sewn into the lining. As he fought to hold his breath and push upward he clawed at the fabric, and felt something tear.

Then at last he was able to thrust himself back toward the surface.

His head emerged from the black water and his teeth began chattering, but even so he could hear angry shouting from above, the shouting of many, many voices. He pulled an arm up and out and swung it forward, scooping at the water, driving himself forward. He did not know who was shouting or why; he could not distinguish words in the roar of noise, but he did not think he should stay to find out what was happening. He needed to get away before the burgrave's guards came after him—not that he thought they would dive in after him, but they might well line the banks, ready to capture or kill him.

And he needed to get out of the water. He could feel the cold draining his strength; he knew that if he stayed in the water he would die, he would freeze, he would lose consciousness and sink down into the airless dark and never emerge.

He struck out for the south bank.

It was no more than thirty yards away, he knew that, but he was not at all sure he would make it. The cold was soaking into him, his wet clothes were dragging him down, his strength was fading.

"Mother of Us All, please . . ." he murmured to himself as he took another breath. He did not have time or energy to complete the prayer, or even the thought that had prompted it. The world seemed to be going dark around him, and he was unable to keep moving. His soaked clothing, his coat in particular, felt like iron armor weighing him down.

He reached out for energy.

A sudden rush of power surged through him, and he was alert once more. He swam desperately, and then his hand slapped onto ice, which shattered, but he pulled himself forward, onto thicker ice, and pulled himself up out of the river, his drenched attire pouring dirty water onto the ice and stone as he stood on hands and knees, shivering on the frozen bank.

He had lost his hat, of course; he turned to see it floating away, vanishing into the shadowy darkness beneath the bridge.

But then noise drew his gaze upward.

The crowd on the bridge was shouting, screaming, fighting; he could see raised fists, hands clutching throats, improvised weapons. Someone was weeping loudly. Several people were leaning over the rail, watching him crawl out of the water. They did not look happy.

"Alvos!" someone bellowed. "Come back! We'll defend you!"

Anrel hesitated, allowing himself to think for a moment.

When Reva's neck had snapped, and Lord Allutar had ordered his apprehension, he had reacted without thinking. He had failed in his attempt to save Reva, there was nothing more to be done for her, everything was lost, and he was standing there exposed before his enemies, so he had fled before any move could be made to capture him—but perhaps he had acted hastily. He had given no thought to what the crowd would think, how they would react. He had not thought about what might become of Tazia. She and her family were still somewhere in that seething mob, in the midst of what appeared to be another riot. The crowd that had stood listening and done nothing while Reva climbed up the gallows and hanged herself had finally come to life, too late to do her any good.

He felt nothing for those people, not even contempt. They simply did not matter to him at the moment. Certainly, he felt no need to return to them. What would he do back there?

He got to his feet, peering at the opposite shore, hoping for some glimpse of Tazia or Nivain or Perynis, but he could make out no familiar faces; he recognized no clothing. From his present vantage point he could not see most of the people on the bridge, only those against or on the eastern railing, and none of the Lirs were there.

He rose to his feet and clambered up the stony bank onto the street that edged the river, where he paused anew. He could hear raised voices and clashing metal in the square and on the bridge, but he did not bother to look back.

If he turned left the road led to Beynos's eastern gate, and he could be out of the city and on the road to Lume in a matter of moments.

If he turned right, a few paces would bring him to the south end of the bridge, and he could try to make his way through the riot to find Tazia and make sure she was safe. He might even, he supposed, try to take command of the rioters, and lead them—but lead them where, and for what? All he had wanted was Reva's freedom, and it was too late for that. Any victory he might gain against the sorcerers would be short-lived and futile; this place was mere hours from Lume, whence the emperor's army could be sent to put down any rebellion. Any attempt to overthrow the empire's present system by violence must surely be doomed; the sorcerers controlled all the magic . . .

Well, not *all* the magic. There were witches. There were people like himself, who did not work as witches but could draw power—he was fairly sure he had used magic to warm himself in the river just now. But the sorcerers certainly controlled *most* of the magic, and the emperor controlled the army, and what rabble could stand against those?

And if by some miracle they did overthrow the empire, what could they possibly put in its place that would be any better? Without the sorcerers, they might all starve; the landgraves did their best to keep the fields fertile, and even with that, the country was on the edge of famine. Remove the sorcerers and people would be starving in the streets.

No, there was no point in trying to lead the rioters. They could not hope to accomplish anything constructive. If he turned right, it would be to make his way through the mob and see that Tazia was safe, to be with her.

But if he did that, what could he offer her? He was a fugitive, now more than ever—he did not think his cousin's affections would be enough to restrain Lord Allutar after *this*. What kind of life could he possibly hope to give Tazia? What could he do to protect her against the rioters?

And he had failed her. He had tried to save Reva, and he had failed. He had let Tazia's sister die because he had never thought about the possibility that Lord Allutar might have enchanted her after Anrel's precipitous flight from the house where she was held.

He had failed Reva as he had failed Valin, as he had failed himself, as he had failed everyone he had tried to help. If he had been a sorcerer he might have made something of himself, he might have had something to offer Tazia, but as a child he had chosen to reject his magical heritage, to live without magic.

He had nothing now, nothing but however much of his hidden money might still remain in the torn lining of his coat, nothing to make himself worthy of Tazia.

She was probably already fleeing back to the Boar's Head with her family; Anrel could not see any of them wanting to stay around for the riot. She was probably cursing his name for giving her false hopes and then allowing Reva to die. She probably wished she had never warned him about her father's scheme; who knows, perhaps it would have worked after all.

He could not hope that she would still want him to court her. Certainly, her father would not permit it. He had lost her. All he could be to her now was a reminder of her sister's death, and he could not ask her to live with that.

There was nothing for him in Beynos, nothing but heartbreak and disaster.

Perhaps it would be better to turn back, to plunge back into the river and let himself freeze or drown, but no, he was not ready for that, not yet. He did not want to face his ancestors' spirits with his soul in its present sad state. He had no prospects, no family, nothing, but he was still alive, and that was a gift not lightly to be discarded. He might yet atone somehow for his failings.

He turned left, and trotted up the muddy street toward the town's eastern gate.

Perhaps he could send Tazia a message from Lume, once he had found himself a place—a letter, an apology. He would not beg her forgiveness; he did not deserve it. He would certainly not ask her to join him. It would be unkind, though, not to let her know he was alive and well; while he could not imagine she would ever want to see him again, he did not want her to feel guilty about his circumstances.

Behind him the roar of the mob grew louder and fiercer, and he thought he heard voices calling for Alvos, but he ignored them. Indeed, he quickened his pace.

When Anrel arrived at the city wall, dripping and shivering, the gate stood open, and the guard standing beside it was staring past him. He turned and looked back.

A thick plume of black smoke was rising from the center of Beynos. Distant shouting could be heard, as well. Too late, the crowd had turned on the sorcerers and their servants.

But that no longer concerned him.

"What happened?" the guard asked. "What's going on?" He held a spear, but seemed uncertain what he should do with it.

"I don't know," Anrel lied, with a final glance back. "I heard the noise, but I did not trouble myself to investigate. I have urgent business in Lume."

The guard lowered his gaze and looked at Anrel, as if noticing him for the first time. His eyes narrowed. "How did you get wet?" he asked.

"I fell in the river," Anrel replied, in a tone of utter disgust. "Just back there." He pointed. "The wind blew my hat off, and it landed on the ice, and when I tried to recover it the ice broke and I fell in." He shivered. "It's too cold for a swim! Better to lose my hat than to freeze to death."

The guard grimaced sympathetically. "You should get inside, then—somewhere warm!"

Anrel shook his head. "I need to get to Lume. Quickly."

The guard frowned at that, then shrugged. "Go on, then," he said. "Please yourself." He motioned toward the gate and the road beyond.

Anrel hurried through the gate, past the pale, onto the high road.

He had been afraid that the guard would detain him on some pretext, and it was a relief that had not happened. The man's job was to keep trouble *out* of the city, not in, so it wasn't too great a surprise, but it *was* a relief.

Anrel was not sorry to be out of Beynos; his stay there had been a disaster almost from start to finish. He had let Reva die. He had left Tazia behind. He had been betrayed by Garras. He had let Lord Allutar know he was alive and near. He had lost his hat, and now he was on his way to Lume, tired and wet and thoroughly chilled, still condemned to death, still a fugitive, and once again alone.

And it was cold, the temperature dropping—the brief thaw seemed to be ending. He quickened his pace once he was clear of the gate, breaking into a brisk trot, as much to keep warm as to avoid pursuit or get to Lume more quickly.

The road was largely clear of snow, at any rate; traffic between Lume and Beynos had been sufficient to clear it away, or trample it into the half-frozen mud. Nor was there any risk of losing his way; he needed merely follow the ruts left by the regular coaches that followed this route. The footing was occasionally slippery or uneven, but he was able to keep up a good pace nonetheless.

He shivered constantly, alternately clutching his coat about him and flapping it in the breeze to dry it, but he kept moving. His fingers and toes went numb, and his jaw began to ache from his efforts to keep his teeth from chattering.

He knew he did not have far to go, and in fact he was scarcely out of sight of Beynos, and *not* out of sight of the ominous columns of smoke rising from the town, when he first glimpsed the towers of Lume in the distance. Still shivering, he pressed on.

At least, he told himself, his clothes dried quickly in the cold wind. He felt his coat as he hurried eastward, and determined that he had ripped a seam in the lining while he was struggling under the river. He had lost several of his concealed coins, but by no means all of them. He would not know exactly how much remained until he was somewhere warm and safe, where he could take off the coat, remove the lining, and count his treasure.

That would wait until he was inside the walls of Lume, where he could lose himself in the familiar streets and avoid any pursuers who might follow him from Beynos.

And it would wait until he was *warm*.

He stumbled on as the huge gray barrier of the capital city's massive walls gradually rose up before him.

The sun was directly overhead, but the wind had risen and was blowing fiercely cold from the northwest, when he came stumbling up to one of the gates of the capital. Two guards in the red and gold colors of the burgrave of Lume watched his approach with interest.

"You look miserable," one of them remarked, as Anrel came to a stop a few feet away from the guard's lowered pikes.

"I am," Anrel said, clapping his gloveless hands against his sides and trying once again to keep his teeth from chattering. "My hat blew into the river, and the weather was considerably warmer when I left the inn in Beynos."

"And what brings you to Lume?" the other guard demanded.

"I'm coming home after visiting my uncle in Aulix," Anrel said, pretending to be startled by the question.

"Where is home, then?"

"The Court of the Red Serpent, number four, third floor, at the rear," Anrel said. That had been his address for almost four years, and came readily to his tongue. He was fairly certain he could not actually return to live there, as an eager young student had already claimed the space, but he hoped he could find a place to stay somewhere else in the courts. His remaining funds would not last him very long at an inn or hotel.

"Student or clerk?" the guard asked.

The man was obviously familiar with Red Serpent Court, to ask such a question. "Clerk now," Anrel replied.

The soldier nodded and raised his pike. "If you've been gone for a while, you should know—there's a curfew in effect now. No one is to be on the streets between midnight and dawn."

"Thank you for the warning," Anrel said sincerely. He hesitated. "Is there anything else I should know? Did I hear something about a prince?"

"Prince Lurias," the guard said with a smile. "Born three nights ago. Mother and child reported to be doing well, thank the Father and the Mother!"

Anrel managed to stop shivering enough to smile. "Wonderful! And . . . there were rumors at the last inn that demons had been seen in the streets. Is that why the curfew was set?"

The smile vanished. "No," the guard said. "There are no demons. Just rumors."

"There are foreign magicians at the palace," the other guard said. "Who knows what they might be doing?"

"It's just rumors," the first guard insisted, annoyed. He waved for Anrel to pass. "Go on, then, get on to the Court of the Red Serpent!"

"Thank you," Anrel repeated, ducking his head and hurrying forward.

Then he was past the two guards, plunging into the shadowy passage through the ancient city walls, bound for a new life with nothing but the clothes on his back and a few hidden guilders.

He had lost everything else. He had lost his parents to sorcery long ago. Lord Allutar had taken his best friend from him, and his own folly in response had lost him his home, his uncle, and everything else he had. He had found his love, the woman he had wanted to spend his life with, and now he had lost her, as well.

But he still lived. He had his life, his fragmentary and untrained magic, and enough coins to see him through perhaps half a season.

And that was enough that, even now, he still had, not the actuality, but the possibility of hope.